Well written, u [illegible]

CW01159647

Let superb storyt[illegible] *take you on a captivating trip to* [illegible]*, as she weaves an engrossing tale of suspense and romance.*

Amazon.com

The people in this story talk to you from her pages in a way not often found in thriller writing and she makes the reader feel very much part of the scene and the action as her story unfolds.

Goodreads.com

I felt as if I were right there with him. I felt the heat, saw the bright sun, smelled the smells, tasted the tastes. And I felt the suspense.

Diane Stephenson

The essence of "Death in Malta" is really contained in the character of Dr Phineas Micallef. A great read, with a realistic ending.

Amazon.co.uk

Death in Malta

Rosanne Dingli

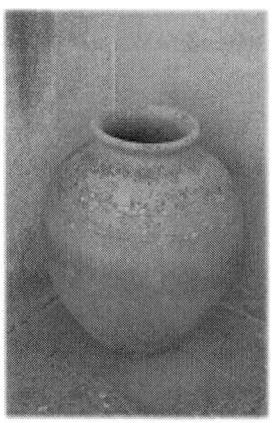

© Rosanne Dingli

The right of Rosanne Dingli to be identified as the author has been asserted in accordance with sections and of the Copyright, Designs and Patents Act.

All rights reserved.

Yellow Teapot Books

ISBN-13: 978-1479159574

ISBN-10: 1479159573

First published in Australia by Jacobyte Books 2001
Published internationally by BeWrite Books 2003

This book is sold subject to the condition that it shall not, by way of trade or otherwise, be lent, resold, hired out or otherwise circulated without the publisher's consent in any form other than this current form and without a similar condition being imposed upon a subsequent purchaser. This book is a work of fiction. Any similarity between the characters and situations within its pages and places or persons, living or dead, is unintentional and co-incidental.

This edition typeset in Gentium Book Basic

Author portrait © Jill Beaver

Also by Rosanne Dingli

According to Luke
Camera Obscura
The Day of the Bird
The Astronomer's Pig
Making a Name
Counting Churches – The Malta Stories
Encore
All the Wrong Places (Poetry)

Rosanne Dingli, award-winning Western Australian author of *Death in Malta, According to Luke,* and *Camera Obscura,* was born and educated in Malta. Her work has appeared in print and on the Internet since 1985. She has worked in various publishing roles, and has lectured in writing.

For more information, please visit
rosannedingli.com

for Hugo

They say that when Censinu Mifsud died, his small body was pushed into a bomblu: a clay jar, one of a dozen or so standing outside the cellar door of a stone farmhouse. This is how the story goes. It is the summer of little Censinu's death.

A hot summer, full of sunshine. But for the little boy, it is also full of dread and darkness. He is wiry and energetic, but he is scared. Of the dark, of the mouldy cellar where his father is preparing for this year's vintage. Of his own mother. It is the summer his vague but honest father gathers an unusually large number of empty jars in the sunken courtyard outside the cellar door. The little boy runs away into the fields when his father is filling them with wine. Fear cuts into his days in spite of the fact his mother's eyes rarely meet his. He fears her hands. He fears the sharp lashes from her unpredictable tongue. He is terrified when she takes up the broom, or the long knife with the wooden handle. The sharp curved knife is safe in his father's hands, Censinu knows.

But it is a dangerous one, a threatening knife, stropped often and fiercely by his mother, and waved at him as she speaks in the middle of her chores. The curve of the knife sends him scuttling away to the fields. The squeaking noise the blade makes slitting through the cork sets his teeth on edge.

This bright and otherwise calm day, Censinu can stand neither the curve and shimmer of the blade nor the screech of its passage through tough layers of cork. He bears the bawled invective of his mother for an hour until the softly spoken urges of his father to her: 'Leave him. Leave the boy alone,' allow him a quick exit and a trot out into the hot vineyard.

❏

Part One

1

Gregory Worthington stopped as he was about to enter the house. A bloodcurdling scream rent the hot afternoon air. His sudden pause made the house agent hard at his heels walk onto the backs of his shoes.

'I'm so sorry.'

The writer looked back. 'I'm sorry,' he repeated foolishly. 'What was that?'

'What?'

'That scream. Did you hear a scream?'

'It's children playing in the fields.' She made a gesture to hurry him on.

Worthington stopped abruptly again, grazing his knuckles on the flaking limestone wall. A streak of blood stayed on the stone. 'Ah! Oh dear, I'm afraid I'm making a mess, Mrs Fri... uh, Mrs Ferg–'

'Friggieri,' she said. 'Look, Mr Worthington. This is a bad omen. Perhaps you'd rather have the house we saw this morning.' She frowned, muttering under her breath about the man's bleeding hand. '*Sinjal hazin,*' she said. 'It's a bad sign,' and looked at spattered blood on the threshold.

The writer tried to stem the quick red flow from his hand. Clumsily, he took a handkerchief from a pocket and wrapped it around three fingers. 'No, no,' he insisted, a touch too loudly. 'I want to see this one. I like the uh ... the atmosphere.' What he liked was the solitude.

Set away from others in the alley, the house stood alone, bounded on one side by a prickly pear hedge and on the other by a rubble wall from where came the sounds of scrabbling and cackling.

'Perhaps you would rather live in a seaside town. Not many tourists come here.'

'I am not a tourist, Mrs Friggy,' he said. 'I am a writer, and I need the peace, the solitude.' His last two words were muffled by a motor scooter whizzing up the lane. He thought he heard another scream in the distance. It was a shrill scream, a shriek, nothing like children playing at all.

'Did you hear that?' he asked.

'What?' The house agent was unwilling to even listen. The writer looked at her strangely. She had irritated him all day, but intimidated him at the same time.

He wanted nothing more than to get rid of her, but not at the cost of renting something he would not be able to work in. 'Never mind. Let's look inside, shall we? My hand is all right now.'

It was not quite all right. It smarted sharply and he knew it would begin to throb unless he dressed it rather soon. The heat, sweat and dust would not help to keep it clean.

'That's not a good omen,' said the plump woman ominously. 'Spilling blood on the doorstep like that. Are you sure you want to see this house?'

Gregory Worthington was seized by an immediate desire to take the house unseen, just to be awkward, just to prove to this annoying little woman he cared nothing for her omens. 'I like the outside. Show me the rest.'

Mrs Friggieri strode inside, and he followed. It was cool and dark, quiet, smelling slightly of mildew. Without preamble, the agent walked into a large kitchen, hurried to the sink and turned on the tap. A clanking of pipes announced the arrival of a fierce shot of water. The tap spluttered.

'There! Isn't that something? Just a few years ago, you didn't take water for granted in Malta. Look at this – fresh water, just like that!'

The writer had not spent the entire day with this woman without learning that everything she said was a political statement. 'Indeed,' he said, trying not to encourage her.

He walked about, taking in what he saw.

'A large kitchen, as you can see. Plenty of room for a good fridge.' The agent walked on. 'And two bedrooms of good size. Shutters on all the windows.'

'What's out there?'

'A garden – nothing much.'

They went through glass doors into a courtyard tiled in red and white, and came to a gated archway. A new length of chain with a stout padlock held the gate together.

'Do you have a key?' asked the writer. The more he saw, the more he knew this was the house he would rent for the time he was on the island.

The woman dangled a key she separated from the rest on the tag she held. Her eyes never left his. 'Later, later,' she promised, teasing. 'I know you like the house already. I saw you looking at the straight walls and the nice shutters on the windows. Good shutters are important, sir.' Again she smiled, the beginning of a small laugh making her round shape wobble slightly. 'This heat, this bright sunlight. It's crazy to be out at this time. We should be lying down, having a rest.' Then she blushed brightly, like a teenager.

'It's mad dogs and Englishmen weather, I suppose.' Gregory Worthington said chivalrously, reduced to platitudes to save her from embarrassment. He was becoming curious about the garden gate. Why was it padlocked?

'And which part of England exactly ...?'

'Not England at all, I'm afraid. I'm from Perth. Australia. I – uh.' He fumbled with the straw hat.

The afternoon sun slanted in yellow streaks at their feet as they walked. Gregory Worthington wiped his forehead. His hand came away damp and salty. He wiped it quickly on the handkerchief twisted around his bloody knuckles and looked down at his creased dusty trousers. It was entirely silly to wear a suit. It had become grubby, and a dark spot of blood now stained the jacket. Short-sleeved shirt and slacks would have been more sensible.

As if reading his mind, the woman said, 'You will soon get used to the heat. After all, it is only the beginning of July!' She stopped suddenly, causing the tall man to run into her heels again.

His irritation rose afresh, but decided this time to be more assertive and decisive. After all, he was going to be there for some time. On his comfort and satisfaction depended the outcome of his next release.

It was months, too many months, since he had appeased his publishing house in Melbourne. This project was a desperate one, an urgent one, necessary to prove that Gregory Worthington was still writing, still writing well and making money for Cross & Ormondsey, publishers, Melbourne, Australia. And for himself of course, but it seemed not to matter as much at the moment.

The woman was rambling on again, 'This house has not been lived in for some time. Still, it has good shutters, some furniture – remember, you must always get your own fridge and cooker – and excellent plumbing.'

He smiled, a bit indulgently. 'Ah!' the woman snapped, taking advantage of the small smile and turning it into her selling ploy. 'You really like this place, I can see. Come, we will look into all the rooms and you can decide on one to write in. You said you were a writer. Which paper?'

Gregory found he had to apologise once more, damning his inability to take the upper hand with this woman. 'Um – I am not a journalist. I –'

He did not know what to say without seeming pompous. He had never encountered such difficulty before. 'I write books, Mrs Frigg–'

'How nice. How interesting. You must have quite an income, like Francis Ebejer.'

Gregory knew of the island's English language novelist. He even had a glimpse of the tall eccentric in Valletta, pointed out by a taxi driver.

'That is Francis Ebejer,' the driver said. 'Like you, sir. He writes books. It makes him money. He doesn't have to work!'

Gregory Worthington smiled wryly, thinking of the hour upon hour he spent agonising over a particular tract. Or rewriting what appeared to be perfectly acceptable prose for a publisher who always knew better.

Now, he wished he had never told the taxi driver or Mrs Friggieri why he was on the island and why he needed peace and quiet and a secluded place to work. But these people had a way of prising words out of him.

Back in the kitchen, he was shown a vast deal table and four unmatched chairs, but he was more interested in the small tiled courtyard. The open space was crowded with clay pots of philodendrons, some choked with weeds. He looked again at the wrought iron gate locked with its length of chain, and a low wall that emitted the twitterings and scrapings of fowl.

'There are chickens,' said the woman, eagerly turning the sound into a selling point. 'And turkeys, I think. Someone from the village has been feeding them over the wall.'

Gregory Worthington had a vision of a young countrywoman throwing kitchen scraps over a rubble wall into a chicken run full of brown scrabbling hens. He had no idea how accurate his mind picture was.

'Never mind the outside – it is too hot and dusty.' The agent waved a dismissive hand.

But the writer was intrigued by the wrought iron gate, the new length of chain and brass padlock. 'Is there more garden?' he asked.

'Oh, look, here's that key.' Mrs Friggieri humoured him like a petulant child. 'Perhaps we'd better have a peep, since you are so interested. Your nearest neighbour, by the way, is the president of the local band club.' She said the sentence with pecuniary intention, rather than pride, but it was as if to acknowledge the status he would have in the village. 'There is also a young village doctor and his family. The chemist, who is a woman –' This she said with a smile and a raised eyebrow, as if she expected him to take up a feminist debate, or as if to state implicitly that the island was by no means backward in that regard. '– And of course Doctor Phineas Micallef, who is retired.'

Her quick dramatis personae ended with a sniff that seemed to indicate disapproval of the last character mentioned, but Gregory could not be sure what he found in the plump agent's voice, and he was certainly in no state to ask questions of an inquisitive nature. Besides, he was half listening for another scream. It never came. Perhaps it was his imagination. Or cats. That was what he knew the wily agent would say if he mentioned it again.

The woman seemed anxious to finalise the rental. She spoke about the village again, and its people. Leading the writer out into the bright sunlight, she waddled towards the padlocked gate. The thin disapproving line her mouth made at the mention of the retired doctor widened suddenly when the key worked immediately and they were let out into a small weed-grown field. Immediately to the right was a sunken area, flag-stoned and crowded with more weedy terracotta pots, reached by a set of concave steps. The steps were in a slant of shadow, and all but hid a small green door whose paint was faded and peeling away.

'That door has no key.' The woman, anticipated his question. 'And no one has ever shown interest in opening it, but inside is probably a small cellar. You have plenty of storage space in the house – a man on your own. I wouldn't bother with the cellar. Dark and damp ...' She turned lightly on her heel and led the way back to the house, reeling off a list of figures and prices and times.

The tall man had a hard time trying to listen and remember. It turned out the rent for the small farmhouse, as the woman kept calling it, was quite affordable.

'These are the bedrooms.' She opened narrow doors in a corridor into two cool darkened rooms. In one of them, Gregory saw the white wraith of an iron double bed. All the back and side rooms except one were paved in large limestone flagstones, scrubbed concave and porous, with remnants of shiny oiling in the corners. The larger bedroom was tiled in yellow ceramic squares, some of which were loose and uneven. The room seemed cooler than the others.

'I can give you a cheque immediately,' he found himself saying.

'So you want it!' she exclaimed.

Gregory raised his eyebrows at her feigned surprise. Perhaps she was prepared to trail all over the small villages in the south west of the island all afternoon.

'Like I said, it's been deserted for some time, I don't really know why.' The way her mouth twisted said a very different story. This woman knew very well why the property was vacant. She was just not telling.

He had no doubt what attracted him to the place: it was that no one else seemed to want it. The automatic selling words from the woman continued to come in spite of the fact the man remained silent. He wanted her to stop. To go away. After all, she had convinced him. What else did she want?

But the woman continued. 'So perhaps someone should come in and do some thorough cleaning for you. It will be some time before you can have a telephone connected, but there is always the café in the village, and the police station. There is no mailbox. I think a person of your profession –' She raised an eyebrow and smiled conspiratorially, as if it were an occupation of doubtful moral worth, '– must receive many letters and things. Perhaps we can have a flap cut in the front door.' She trailed off, mumbling she would try to make arrangements.

Moving in was uneventful and easy. Gregory, although he would never have mentioned it to Mrs Friggieri, intended to do all the cleaning himself, despite the throbbing from his cut knuckles. It might have been a silly decision at his age, he found himself thinking, as he splashed buckets of water onto the courtyard tiles, sweeping with long strokes until the water took most of the dust away with it. But he needed the exercise and the distraction, the work he accepted as penance for his present inertia.

Evaporation was almost immediate in the afternoon sun, and he resolved to find an earlier time during the day for his chores. Gardening would be a pleasant diversion from writing: if indeed he ever did start to write. His cases were half unpacked in the larger bedroom. He found a good mosquito net in a wardrobe behind the door. The windows had no insect screens, something he wondered about after a lifetime in Australia.

The climate, things Maggie had said: they all somehow indicated a range of similarities between the country of his birth and this strange Mediterranean island where the only thing he found to be predictable so far was the weather. The computer arrived by van from Valletta and was installed in the second bedroom, which only served partly well as a writing room. Its window faced the narrow lane.

To look across the back, to have a flat view over the weed-grown field and own all the sunsets: that was what he would have liked. It took him an entire afternoon to shift rooms. The double bed gave him a lot of trouble, so he eventually collapsed and took it apart, and re-erected it in the smaller bedroom, where he had to push it up in the far corner under the street window. His writing room was now the larger room with its massive oiled beams, recessed shelves in thick walls, and uneven yellow-tiled floor. He did not realise he would miss a telephone so badly, but supposed it would save him a lot of money having to think and decide and time his calls, after a walk up the long lane, which turned into a steep street at the top.

It took him one simple walk to discover the lay of the small village. There were two cafés, one of which was called *Il-Hanut* and also sold wine. The police station still sported a blue lamp over its threshold from colonial days. The constable was affable but quiet and allowed him use of the single black telephone with no remonstrance, telling him that when the station was closed, he could always try the booth at the crossroads, but he did not know how often it was in working order.

The resigned smile and friendly open-handed gesture was what Gregory had come to expect of Maltese people. He knew it hid a shrewd and calculating character that analysed and dissected strangers and fellow citizens alike, but friendly form and congeniality preceded and replaced all other demonstration.

'And remember, you have to book calls to Australia!'

It was a while after the policeman's parting shot before Gregory realised he had not told the man where he was from. Perhaps it was his accent? Or had word already got around that a strange writer from down under had come to this small Maltese village to try and write something to rescue his reputation and career?

'Something like the second book. Something dark and foreboding and full of suspense like The Altruist. Something to chill readers back into a following.' That was what Paul De Souza said at their last meeting. Cross & Ormondsey needed more suspense and mystery from Gregory Worthington, more crime and horror, if he *could*.

The last was said sarcastically, the stress on the hypothetical turned into a virtual insult by the publisher. So Paul thought he had lost it. So Paul thought Gregory no longer had the staying power or the imagination to turn out another Altruist, which won the Premier's award two years ago.

So Paul thought it was all finished for a writer who, at forty-five, had found himself in the grip of doubt and inertia. Gregory was fully installed in a few days. The heat and dust continued unchanged. Someone said he should not expect change until September, when the moist winds would blow; the humid winds laden with rain that would fall in torrents, hopefully where it could be caught and stored. But the writer was from Australia – was it not just as hot there?

Gregory smiled at repeated interrogation from inquisitive

strangers. They were friendly, peaceful and polite, but they asked a thousand questions each.

He found himself repeating the story of his travels and of his 'life' – whether he was married, whether his children had grown up – to a dozen different strangers. The shopkeeper who sold him groceries. The haberdasher, who happened to be the only newsagent in the village. The butcher, who told him not to eat pork in summer. And of course the man behind the bar of *Il-Hanut*.

He had spoken, on his third or fourth visit to the wine shop, of the delivery of his appliances; a small gas cooker, a large fridge, and a motley collection of small things such as a kettle, a toaster, and a small coffee percolator. He found that whatever he said, conversation in the shop would halt, and all present would listen to his words, interjecting politely in English when he was finished.

'I hope you did not give them a big tip!'

'Remember not to trust your gas pipes.'

'Keep candles for blackouts!'

The last came from a wizened old man who turned out to be the bass drum player in the village band. He was also the village drainage plumber, much in demand because of the decrepit state of the prehistoric maze of clay pipes lying beneath the dusty streets. After someone pointed him out and described the way he earned his livelihood, Gregory would often see the plumber weaving about the village streets, carrying a bunch of long canes and attachments with which he would unblock underground pipes after lifting the limestone lid of the '*spuk-shin*'.

Gregory smiled at the abbreviated English terms turned vernacular. This one, for inspection cavity, was to become one he himself would use. The men spoke among themselves in Maltese, a jolly guttural language with loud stressing and embroidered with much head moving and gesticulation. They drank sweetened tea and coffee laced with orange blossom water with as much fervour as they knocked back tumblers of beer and thick red wine. Its scent was heavy in the close space of the shop, and Gregory soon became familiar with their way of paying for rounds. Because he was still a stranger and 'English', he was not allowed the honour of paying for one himself for some days.

They spoke to him in friendly snatches of conversation, composed mainly of curious questions about his solitude, his writing, and whether he went to church. They held a strange monopoly on Catholicism, Gregory found, and were surprised and full of disbelief to hear of the existence of Australian Catholics with similar habits to theirs.

'Is this some invented tale you tell us, Mister Writer?' asked a member of the group, a particularly vociferous debater when it came to politics.

'No, no,' protested Gregory.

And he was saved from having to debate on Irish, Australian and Maltese religious observances by another loud conversation taking place just outside the café.

He escaped unnoticed in the hiatus, finding the street cooled, the sun gone away, and a bevy of small children playing with a ball outside his front door.

Morning noises were country noises, interspersed with the buzz of motor scooters in the lane, the drone of aeroplanes from the nearby international airport, and a high hum someone told him came from the limestone quarries outside the Southern villages.

So now he knew the provenance of all that dust. Gregory looked at the scab on his hand. It was the only reminder now of his first days on the island. He was used to the dust now, and the noise. It was a background din, punctuated frequently by shrill yells from nearby streets. Alarmed at first, thinking it was a repetition of the screams he had heard that first day, Gregory would look out of his front windows and find the conversation, shrill as it was, to be a friendly exchange between women shouting from one end of the lane, or from one corner of a street, to another.

One afternoon, a sawing sound came from his own front door. A lad of about fourteen was hacking a hole in the thick wood.

'Letterbox, sir!' The smile was wide and infectious.

'A slit, you mean. The mail will fall on the floor on the inside.'

'Oh no! I have this for you.' Out of a plastic bag the lad produced a metal box, which he soon fixed onto the inside of the front door to catch letters.

Gregory was informed deliveries would occur every day, including Saturday mornings. 'But you must fix that,' said the boy, pointing to the faint barely legible number six painted above the fanlight of the front door. It would be a while before Gregory obeyed the boy's instructions and found a brush suitable for the small job.

The chicken run provided a background of noises and scrapings. There were nine brown hens and three larger fowl Gregory took to be turkeys, never having seen one that had not been denuded of its feathers, stuffed and roasted. They were largely silent, uttering a low gobbling only when they were angered or chased into a corner while Gregory placed a dish of kitchen scraps or bran mash in the middle of the run. He topped up a wide tin pan of water from the kitchen tap.

Another tap he found on a pipe in the yard, just above the hollowed steps to the sunken yard, turned but produced nothing.

Occasionally, Gregory found a scattering of someone else's scraps littering the run when he looked in. Obviously the habit of feeding the abandoned fowl was established, and some well-meaning neighbour was still fulfilling the task.

'You fat birds!' Gregory found himself mumbling. 'Perhaps someone should thank your benefactor.'

He had still not sat at the table in the back room that held the new computer. He attended to a multitude of domestic chores and tasks, which included finally the touching up of the number six over his front door. He moved all the plant pots in the courtyard and space in front of the cellar door out the back, and swept around them.

He cleaned the windows with balled up damp newspaper, as he saw village women do, and polished the brass knocker with liquid he found under the sink, much to the hilarity of a passing woman.

'You do your wife's work, eh?' She laughed as she went by, expecting no answer.

Gregory found himself thinking cynically about Maggie. Polishing brass doorknockers was never her work. He replaced the bottle of polish under the sink and, still squatting, thought of his estranged wife in Australia.

Maggie. Loud and bright and full of laughter and song, she was. Her quick passion was startling, and the easiest emotion with her was anger.

Fights. He needed little imagination to conjure what she would be doing in Australia now. He looked at his watch automatically, thinking at the same time he made the quick calculation of time difference, about how long it had been since he last thought of her in that way. In any way.

'Sick! Terrible, Greg. All you can think about blood and gore. Yuk. I couldn't finish your books if I tried. Whatever possesses you to write like that? Yuk,' she repeated, screwing her face and banging the paperback edition of his second book down.

It had not always been like that. Once she liked everything about him, including his writing. Perhaps she came to use insults and disparagement as weapons. Weapons that worked.

Her attacks on his writing continued until he could do either of two things. Stop work or go away and do it somewhere else.

Paul De Souza had shown him there was really only one alternative. 'Come on, Greg, face it. What can you do besides write? Teach? Mate, be realistic. You have a readership. People have come to expect this stuff from you.'

Maggie called it stuff too. They were probably right: Gregory would be totally misled to entertain thoughts that his works approached literary achievements. They were popular novels; they were commercial horror stories. They were sensationalist trash. He stood in the semi-darkened kitchen and drank a glass of tepid tap water with an automatic gesture. It tasted heavy and metallic, but he remembered the words of the agent who let him the house. It was nothing short of a miracle he should have running water at any time of day. Or perhaps it was not. Perhaps it was not sensationalist trash. He thought of the many arguments and debates he had with Maggie about his writing; how she grudgingly supported him at first, even when she expressed distaste.

'Is it your aim to send shivers down the spine of every reader?' she asked once, her sarcastic question reaching him from across their Perth apartment, where she was riffling through a draft copy of The Altruist. It was a difficult afternoon; a hot and humiliating one when he threw open all the windows to catch a breeze, to cool his brow that had started to bead from the humidity, or from something inside him. Her high voice was filled with criticism, then anger, then accusation. She did not stop when he fell into silence himself. She shouted flippant but sharp abuse, hurling sentences at him in a loud voice until they heard 'Ssh!' coming from one of the other apartments. Gregory knew neighbours had heard every word.

They also heard Maggie's subsequent loud exclamations when they made up, the shrill laughter and delight in her own attempts at reconciliation. Only the eventual success of the novel took some of the remnant embarrassment away.

Did he remember her properly? Gregory stood at his own kitchen window, staring at the neat courtyard he had swept the day before. Did he picture Maggie as she really was? Small head. Red hair cut in a very short urchin style that accentuated wide eyes and small pixie ears, from where large colourful earrings swung. The swinging of red, yellow or gilt earrings always managed to stress the gravity or levity of what she said. Her anger was always pulsed by the swaying of rainbow earrings. Was she still like that? Although they spoke on the telephone as recently as a week before he left for Malta, he had not seen Maggie for almost seven years. After the separation, she had taken her 'things', as she called most of the contents of the flat, which included their daughter, and returned to Melbourne. 'I am not going to let her grow up reading that lurid stuff!' was one of the last things he watched her say.

Gregory drank another small glass of metallic water and walked to the back room clutching the empty tumbler. The computer on the small table, the blue pack of paper near the printer, the mug full of yellow pencils – they all stood in a neat assemblage that attested to the absence of work. Gregory was not a neat worker. He would screw paper up and break pencils. His desk would quickly become a massed heap of letters and books and papers once he decided to work. He would riffle through reference works, scribble in the margins of newspaper articles, and rip notebooks to shreds when in the height of composition. He thought of his noticeboard in the Perth flat after Maggie left. It was full of pinned notices and messages, torn newspaper and cards long out of date. He remembered letting his gaze sift through the collection of words there for a start – a trigger – the suggestion of an idea.

❑

2

'So tell me, Mr Worthington – am I supposed to have heard of you? I am not familiar with your name or work.'

The face was earnest, the eyes eager. Gregory looked at the short-sleeved shirt so similar to the one he now wore himself. The words were not slurred yet, but Gregory had heard this man's speech before, had seen him hold audience with bright lines containing garbled jokes and surprisingly well-turned phrases in English. The face turned toward him now had not yet taken on the low flush of drunkenness, but he had seen the man stagger in the steep street.

He had seen him avoid, but not adroitly enough, cats and dogs on his way past the church and the closed shops when the bar closed at night. Doctor Phineas Micallef was a well-known figure in the village, presenting himself a touch pompously to little groups debating politics at the wine bar, offering opinionated lines and being greeted with correctness and prescribed respect.

The man was prone to change, gradual change that turned him, in the space of one evening, from an eloquent village elder into a bent and babbling fool. Gregory had seen the change and was intrigued by it, watching the man from his own seat at the wine bar during gaps in the lively conversations he held with some of the men.

'You see,' the doctor continued, 'I am retired now, and I don't often go into Belt is-Sebh to see what is new at the library. Sometimes, though, I do go down to Sliema to the bookshops on Tower Road. I used to live in Sliema, you know.' He said this with a wave of his hand as if to say that anyone who was anybody at all must one day have lived in Sliema.

Gregory nodded, knowing the man would continue.

'But,' he said after a pause. 'But –' The older man held a

finger up as if to make an important point.

Gregory realised the man had totally lost his train of thought. He found the doctor's mannerisms fascinating, partly because of their correctness early in the evening and their degeneration into muddled confusion at night. Partly because of the man's accent and sample gems of what must have been a formal and comprehensive education that glimmered through the daily fog of alcohol.

'Ah!' exclaimed the doctor loudly. 'As I was saying, I have been to the bookshops in Sliema and I'm afraid I have not seen your name among the authors there.' The chin jutted out belligerently, as if demanding from Gregory an explanation of the absence.

'My genre,' started Gregory, looking down at the doctor's glass and wondering whether he should offer him more wine, 'is suspense. Or horror.' He did not say the word mainstream. And he hated the word pulp, but he suspected this man had already thought of it.

There was no reply from the doctor. He looked into his glass himself and then at Gregory, who quickly signalled to the barman. When both glasses were full and the man in the apron drew away, the doctor started nodding his head slowly, gradually speeding the motion until a small smile of comprehension sat on his puckered lips.

'Then you are living in the right place.'

'Here? Malta is hardly –'

'Not the whole island, Mr Worthington. Your house. Do you know it has been vacant for – what is it now? Twenty years?'

'The agent said something.' She did not say twenty years. It did not appear so abandoned. There was evidence of cleaning. Gregory had found old newspapers. Not recent ones, but certainly not from the 1960s.

'I arrived in this village soon after that *razzett* – that farmhouse – was ah ... vacated. Any attempts at renting it out have proved futile. Most leave after a week. In a hurry. Not a happy house, I take it.' The doctor made a mock facial leer, winking at Gregory conspiratorially. 'But you must know all about these things.'

'Things?'

'Mysteries, perhaps ... hauntings.' The doctor sounded cynical.

But the writer felt there was more than met the eye in his suggestions. There was a hint of something sinister in his eyes, if not in his actual words. Gregory thought of his first viewing. The house agent, who seemed to know more than she was willing to impart. The screams. He smiled and shook his head, bidding himself mentally to be realistic.

The doctor gave a little laugh, then drained his glass. The conversation seemed to be over. Gregory watched the older man struggle out of the chair.

'Er – Dr Micallef. I would like ...'

'Of course. Of course. But it is very late today. I am expected somewhere. I have many acquaintances, you know. Many friends.' This last was accompanied by an expansive gesture, perhaps to impress Gregory with his popularity, his broad circle of social interaction.

The Australian made a face to suggest he was suitably persuaded, pursing his lips in a way he had seen the doctor do himself. Both men smiled.

'If you want to find a good story, you may have some research to do, Mr Worthington.'

The writer cocked his head.

'At the Times, in Valletta. Their records might not be complete but they still may have something interesting.' And with those words, Dr Micallef stepped lightly out of the wine bar, barely unsettling the bead curtain, which tinkled only slightly with his passage.

So he was not so drunk after all, mused Gregory. Was this the kind of man one could befriend, one whose information and knowledge could become valuable? Or was the old fellow merely trying to scare him away from the house?

Gregory looked around the bar at the small congregation of village men. They were mainly tradesmen, shopkeepers and market gardeners, who talked in Maltese in rapid flows and swift articulations. It was mainly politics, he had come to know. Politics and gossip.

In spite of his inebriated ways, Dr Phineas Micallef was the only likely one who may yet prove to be a source of inspiration. It was not the thought of the computer, standing in the dark in the back room with its supply of paper and clutch of yellow pencils in the old enamel mug he unearthed in a cupboard. It was not the thought of Paul De Souza, waiting in Australia for some indication of work being done, words being written. It was the thought of a young girl who awaited letters from the Mediterranean that finally pushed Gregory to turn the light switch in the backroom and finger a sheet of paper.

She was seventeen now, and his last couple of brief scribblings to her home in Melbourne had prompted letters. Letters from Emma, his daughter, who was only a little voice on the phone after the separation, and who became the writer of such long complicated voluble affectionate sentences for the last couple of years.

It was the thought of changes, and having a lot to describe to Emma, that sent Gregory back to the room where the dark window would have to be closed before he settled there too long with the light on.

'Why don't these windows have insect screens?' he grumbled.

Seventeen. What did seventeen year-olds want to read about? What did they know?

Maggie's rare statements swung between describing their daughter, depending on the argument of the time, from a little girl requiring careful attention to a grown up young woman with expensive tastes. The reflection of Gregory's face in the windowpane directly opposite the old table he used as a desk seemed unusually round. Outside, it was as extremely black as it had been bright and blue all day.

The doctor remarked it was only early summer, and Gregory would soon get used to the heat. How many times had he been reassured of that? How many times had he been advised to take a rest in the height of the afternoon, instead of trailing around the dusty deserted village on foot? All the shops closed between one and four, when a silence descended on the whole place. White reflected on white, and dust and heat shimmered mirages over the narrow streets. Light green buses stopped arriving at the square. If one of the lumbering vehicles happened to be caught there over the afternoon rest, the driver would go off to some spot of shade, drape a newspaper over the top half of his body and sleep.

Dogs would throw themselves down in the comparative coolness of church entrances, whose large wooden doors were also closed until evening. The hum from the quarries would stop and the only sound, the interminable one of crickets scraping their perpetual exclamation, droned and whirred until it filled the suffocating air. Was that what Emma would want to hear? Was it what he wanted Malta to sound like to her when she read his letters?

Gregory thought of his arrival, his stay at the crowded noisy Sliema hotel and the first explorations of the island that taught him much more than any book or brochure he read. It all showed him it was a good destination to choose. Strangely enough, it was Maggie who prompted his choice. 'Go to Malta,' her tinny voice had said on the phone from Melbourne, when he was gripped by immobility, and what he hated to term writer's block, in Perth.

'You remember. Mum's people are from Malta. You'll probably find someone to put you up. You're sure to come up with some new form of abhorrence and terror there. They say it's an island of history and drama. Who knows what sordid legends and nasty little woes you can turn into another best seller?' Her sarcasm even seemed friendly at the time. Gregory wrote down Maggie's mother's maiden name in the hope of tracking down some relative.

His hopes were dashed immediately he opened the telephone directory at the airport on arrival. There were four pages of Spiteris. He thought again of Maggie's dark red hair and what he thought to be Mediterranean passion in the tilt of her head and her loud voice when she sang or fought, attributing it to her Maltese ancestry. He had known little then about the people, and felt he knew not much more now, although Dr Micallef seemed a realistic source to tap. Tap for what? Although Gregory could not disagree he had found an ideal place to write, inspiration was not immediately forthcoming. Of course not. It rarely presented itself to him as conveniently as Paul De Souza at Cross & Ormondsey always thought it should. Tap for what? The doctor's leer and the mention of a haunting? Precious little to show for a fortnight on the island, a fortnight during which he found the inexpensiveness, the relative comfort and convenience of the small village, and the friendliness and tact of its people to make it an optimal place to work.

But there had to be something to work on. And something to write to Emma about. His hand was turning the light switch off even before he consciously made the decision to quit the room and try to sleep in the smaller one where the high bed and its white linen, its mosquito net and widely flung-open shutters were vastly more attractive.

❏

3

'What do you mean you saw me? How do you know it was me?' *Il-Hanut* was crowded with the usual assortment of wine and coffee drinkers. A young man hurried in bearing a large tin tray of golden warm *pastizzi*, which, like the proverb they were surely the instigator of, were sold in an instant in paper-bagged dozens to a small crowd which appeared as if by magic. The rest of the savoury and crisp pastries, stuffed with ricotta and parsley or mushy peas and garlic, were quickly placed in twos on glass saucers, to be consumed by the wine shop patrons.

Gregory spoke his second question through a hot mouthful of ricotta and flaky pastry, saucer held under his chin to catch crumbs.

'It was you. It could only have been you,' replied Dr Phineas Micallef, sitting at Gregory's table uninvited and peering at the remaining pastry on the plate. 'After all, how many tall hatted fair foreigners do I know?'

The barman brought a bottle of wine and another saucer of *pastizzi* to the table.

Gregory, while musing whether the doctor had been following him, was astonished at his own relief at not having to relinquish his second pastry. It was bad enough having to eat it in company. His eyebrows were still raised in interrogation when he reached for it.

The doctor was busily pouring wine into two glasses, ignoring Gregory's steaming cup of tea on the table.

'I'm not sure I want that,' the writer said, as politely as he could.

'Of course you are not! It is only after the first few sips that we become enamoured once more of the glorious taste of the red grape ... that we fall through the delicious tunnel of its russet beckoning.'

Gregory could not help smiling. 'I have often wondered about your English, your accent –'

'A Sliema accent. You have heard it before.'

'Mm.' Crumbs descended into the saucer. 'But your intonation sometimes is so –'

'British. Of course. Five years in the British Army. I had an English colonel, an English RSM. Now you know.'

'During the war?'

'Exactly! They interrupted my university studies to put me behind a gun. In return for saving the islands – not to mention the whole Allies' involvement in the Med – I was allowed to wear a colourful braid on my uniformed shoulder!'

In spite of the actual meaning, the doctor's tone showed no remorse or blame. Like many Maltese men of his age, resignation and pride took place of resentment, even during discussions on past colonialism and future economic dependence on European trade.

Gregory could not help comparing the attitude with that of Australians of similar vintage. 'You know, I think Malta and Australia have a lot in common.'

'Is that so, Mr Worthington?' The doctor seemed amused. 'Two islands so far apart? So diverse in size, population, culture?'

'Mm – islands nevertheless.'

The two men laughed.

'But now, where did you say you saw me?'

The older man seemed unwilling to return to the subject. He looked at his shoes, the ceiling and to the left and right of him. Then he spoke. 'I saw you in Valletta, in St Paul Street. You could only have been going to one place.'

'Oh yes?' Gregory's amusement was clear.

'I stood in Britannia Street – I still call it Britannia Street in spite of *certain changes*.' He stressed the last two words, but Gregory refused to be drawn into debates about political street name changes.

'And I saw you striding quite purposefully, in your conspicuous hat, down St Paul Street, in the direction of the Times office. No doubt you have done a bit of research.'

'Yes.'

'And was it fruitful? And are you intrigued? And has the midnight oil been burnt?'

'How do you know I write at night?'

'You seem the nocturnal type to me. That is why, Mr Worthington, that is why –' the doctor raised his finger as was his habit when trying to stress an important point. It usually happened at a stage in the evening when his state of inebriation was reaching a slight change of pace. His papery eyelids closed momentarily, his solid frame creaked.

There was a lull in the conversation elsewhere in the wine bar and the doctor waited, his face clearing somewhat, until there was enough noise to cover what he was about to say to the writer.

'You are a very pleasant person to talk to, Mr Worthington.'

The writer nodded and the doctor continued.

'A delight to know and to converse with.'

Gregory nodded again, but he failed to connect the flattery with what the doctor was about to say before. How were his nocturnal habits linked to his conversation?

'We have had many a delightful chat, you and I,' the doctor continued.

Obviously, it was going to be quite a monologue, so Gregory looked into his plate of crumbs and waited.

'Because we share a colonial past, and because we share a language –' the older man paused for effect. He had told Gregory during a previous conversation, one during which he had become increasingly loquacious and glib as the evening wore on and the wine flowed, that English was his tongue. That he tolerated no other, if the truth were to be known. And he only spoke Maltese and Italian under sufferance and out of patience with those who insisted or knew no better.

'English, you see, is the language of the Empire, Mr Worthington. And it is those persons like yourself and I –' Here the doctor suffered another of the lapses of memory that prevented him from continuing.

Gregory was not disappointed. He was becoming used to the doctor's diatribes, and would with time come to predict, he supposed, at which stage of the old man's drinking he could safely sidestep his arguments.

'As I say, because we share something, both in history and in habit, I am going to invite you to one of my soirées. I have many acquaintances, you see. Many friends.'

This to Gregory was becoming comical rather than boring. The old man had a sweet pathetic nature, which he found, in spite of himself, endearing.

'So, you will please to grace us – myself and my friends – with your presence.' And the doctor proceeded to give Gregory some very exact details about time and place.

Gregory often wondered whether his thoughts went back to the cocktail party at Dr Micallef's so often because of his fascination with the old man, or because it was where he met Patricia. The doctor introduced them formally, saying she was the daughter of an old colleague. He remembered her dark eyes, their solid gaze. But most of all he remembered the way she spoke. She talked incessantly, in a voice that sometimes fell into a husky whisper. Dark curly hair was a thick unruly bush caught into the semblance of a chignon at the nape of her neck, perhaps just missing the elegance she intended.

'We don't often get to meet Dr Micallef's foreign friends,' she said as an introduction.

Gregory found he was grateful for her light conversation. Introductions to others in the room led inevitably to philosophical debates on politics and religion. In spite of the difference in treatment, the subject of conversations seemed identical to those carried on at the humble village wine shop. The venue, of course, was very different.

Dr Phineas Micallef owned an old house with walls as thick as those of Gregory's farmhouse. It had been restored and decorated, though, rather recently. The furniture and fittings were fine, falling just short of opulence. Shiny granite lined all the floors, grey speckles picked up in curtains and upholstery. China cabinets displayed antique artefacts and porcelain, and the crystal glasses in which they drank were either Irish or Polish, Gregory thought. He expected nothing less, thinking of the doctor's bearing and the way he spoke.

The man's loneliness, though, and his easy degeneration into a grotesque lumbering figure at night after a session at the wine bar, made him wonder about his life.

'He is a childless widower,' Patricia stated simply, after an oblique question from the writer whose meaning she immediately picked up.

'Yes,' said Gregory, watching the doctor smile and converse with some friends. 'But there's something about him. I can't quite figure whether he's encouraging me or trying to get me to leave the village.'

Patricia smiled. 'I suppose that, like psychologists, you are rather interested in people's motives. Writers seem to be obliged to compose a clear analysis of all their characters, aren't they? You must find it tiresome.'

'No – but it's certainly *tiring*, when I am really writing. Which is something I have not been able to apply myself to since arriving,' he confessed.

'Malta is too distracting?'

'Chores at the farmhouse, really. I have tidied up quite nicely. Discovered some vines.'

'Really?' Patricia seemed only politely interested in his gardening efforts. Her dark eyes were roaming the room, examining what the women were wearing, perhaps, or looking for the maid who was serving drinks. But she swivelled back to Gregory gracefully, launching into a series of questions about himself, which he fully expected. Instead of letting him carry on as he did to the men in the bar, she interrupted often with long bursts of her own, telling him about herself. Her voice fascinated him because of its hoarse breaks, its husky interludes during which she descended almost to a whisper.

'When I left school, I really wanted to travel the world. The only way I could do it without spending my father's fortune against his will was to join Air Malta as a stewardess. I was always too tired after flights to explore any of the cities we flew to. And I always seemed to draw Rome and Amsterdam!'

'It must have been a good way to leave home and find your wings.' Gregory regretted the clumsy pun the minute it left his lips, then wondered why on earth he would want to impress this young woman favourably, after all.

'Oh – I am still at home with my parents. That's one thing you'll learn about Malta. It's very difficult for young people to branch out and live on their own. Mainly it is social and religious restraints. And there used to be a housing shortage, until recently. I wonder what would happen if half the population demanded new flats. I wonder how my mother would react if I told her I'd found one!' She turned it into a joke, but Gregory was startled at his disappointment.

He tried a mental distraction, looking away at a close group in the middle of some strenuous discussion, but would not willingly detach himself from the woman, who occasionally leaned forward and looked past him. She did this, he saw, not to approach him physically, but to check her appearance in the reflective glass of a double door, thrown open to allow flow between a formal dining room and the lounge where they stood.

It was an action that belied her outward confidence, making her seem insecure about the way she looked, as if desiring to please him above anything else. It was unusually endearing.

'Are they here tonight?' Gregory had only a vague mental

image of her parents, which he tried to dispel. It was impossible to conjure an accurate picture of the parents of this slim dark creature whose quick gestures and soft voice coupled with continually roaming inquisitive eyes compelled him to study her. She looked at him closely herself, then at her reflection again.

'Oh, no. They're shopping in Sicily at the moment. I am quite a free spirit in spite of what you think. But you must tell me more about this fascinating farmhouse.'

'I thought you'd be bored by talk of gardening and housekeeping.'

'I like old buildings. Have you got an animal trough, a well ... and little steps let into a wall to take you to the roof? Have you got little metal rings fixed to your yard walls and big wooden beams? And there must be a loggia.' Her words sank to a whisper, as if to have a loggia would be the height of indiscretion.

Although he knew it was the flaw in her voice, it made Gregory smile. He did not know what she was referring to.

'A loggia,' she explained, 'is a large window, almost semicircular. The top part is a huge fanlight, and the bottom opens outward to let in light and air. They are usually built into the sides of corridors – tiled corridors on the top floor of a house.'

'My house has only one storey. Don't you know it? It is at the bottom of Spring Lane.'

'I don't know this village at all. I really don't know why Dr Micallef insists on burying himself out here. The really lovely places to live are Santa Marija, Madliena and of course St Andrews.'

'It's perfect here for what I want to do.'

'Far from the sea. Far from Sliema.' She looked at her reflection again and then straight into Gregory's eyes.

'Spring Lane will do me fine,' he insisted. 'And I think I do have one of those windows – the corridor outside the bedrooms is lit by one. But I have not found a well anywhere, although everyone says I should have one. Perhaps it is in the cellar. I have not been down there yet. But yes, it's a nice enough place.'

'Oh, I must see it. One afternoon I'll drive here and come and pay you a surprise visit. Oh – no. Perhaps I shouldn't. I'd hate to interrupt you in the middle of your important writing!'

Gregory was not expecting such forthrightness, especially after hearing the woman's description of her parents' life and strict religious observances. He was held momentarily by a quick confusion, the kind he scarcely thought he would re-experience in his mid-forties, or after the break-up of his marriage.

He could not sort out whether he would have liked a visit from this young unusual woman or if he should disconnect himself and start another conversation somewhere else in the room, which was buzzing with vital discussion.

'Oh – you must excuse me for a minute,' he said formally, and retreated quickly to look for the bathroom. In the mirror, he saw his face was oval and pale, unlike what he saw in dark windowpanes at the farmhouse. He gave the pale face a mental rebuke, telling himself he had no business getting confused about young women, and no time to spend wondering about dark eyes and thick hair and husky voices: he had a book to write. Simultaneously to the scolding, he found himself checking his face for signs of ageing. What was he looking for?

Gregory stood up straight and attributed his confusion to the fact he had not recently met any attractive single women. This one was probably the first among many Maltese women he would find himself thinking about. It was neither unusual nor unlikely. What would they see in him? His spare frame was neither muscular nor strong in appearance, although Gregory knew he had resilience. A great advantage was his height, which put him in a position of authority even when he did not feel assertive enough.

The hat he wore out of doors was seen as unusual, even on this hot sunny island whose climate certainly warranted it. Without it, as he was tonight, he felt almost naked and defenceless. He was grateful for thick hair that still retained most of its dark brown. Almost reflexively, his hand shot to the crown of his head. He dreaded the thought of baldness, even partial receding, which had fortunately not happened, in spite of his own father's shiny high forehead.

It was a flattering mirror, giving his skin a more golden glow than was really his, in spite of the hours of sunshine he enjoyed, or endured, while digging up weeds in his field. Gregory wrinkled his forehead, then his nose, turning with a hand on his abdomen to check his profile, making himself laugh in the process. It did not really matter, after all, what these people thought of him.

When he re-entered the lounge, it was with a complacent smile. He took a fresh glass of white wine from a tray. It was crisp and cool.

'Do you like my choice in wines?' The voice over his shoulder was blurred, but cordial and pleasant.

'Excellent. Local?'

The doctor laughed. 'I have friends in Valletta who import the finest European vintages. I leave the local wine for more ... informal occasions.'

Gregory looked into his glass. 'You have some very pleasant friends.'

'There are some wonderful people in Sliema – as a writer, you would find it fascinating.'

Gregory hazarded a friendly nudge. 'Are you trying to send me away from this village, Doctor?' He laughed, but it came out awkwardly, a nervous snigger.

The doctor made a swift friendly rebuttal. 'Whatever made you think that?' He laughed too, but it was not convincing.

'Nothing – like I said, your friends are nice people.'

'Yes. You must have noticed that some of them call me Fin – a remnant of army times. You may do so too, here, and in other private places.'

This seemed a bit precious. So was he still expected to address the older man formally when they met in the wine bar?

It was another of the many cultural quirks he would have to get used to, he decided. But he was still nagged by something in the doctor's eyes. It made him pursue his intrigue.

'Some of your friends too, Fin, seem to think I should be living in a more fashionable area.'

'Hah!' The doctor seemed to explode. 'Hah! Let them think. Fashionable. Acceptable. What's the difference? I live in this village from choice. A fine choice, may I add.' But there was something in his voice that belied his words, a kind of wistfulness Gregory often heard in migrants' voices back in Australia.

It was the voice of the exile, the voice that said one thing when the eyes said another. An outcast, that was what the doctor was, the writer noted. He would have to look for a reason for it, a cause that urged the doctor to leave a fashionable district and fashionable friends to bury himself in a village where his drinking mates were farmers and ordinary workmen. Where adulatory remarks took the place of equality and social acceptance of another class.

'So you wouldn't return to Sliema to stay for good?' Gregory wondered if he were pushing the subject too far.

'The advantage of living out here is that you only see the people you want to see, and only when you invite them!' And with those words of poor victory, the doctor turned lightly on his heels. His poise was still unmarred, his demeanour still impeccable except for a slight slur. Could it be that Dr Micallef, the village fool, stayed sober and upright when he was Fin, the lovable host of his few remaining Sliema friends?

Around him, conversation gathered momentum, and Gregory Worthington found himself explaining his provenance and presence once more to a clutch of elegant guests who appraised his words as carefully as they judged his clothing and bearing.

'I'd love to know what you are writing,' a woman in diamond earrings and heavily painted lips said, in tones modulated to affect an accent, changeable on demand. 'I am fascinated by writers.' Her eyes twinkled, and a hand crept out automatically and blindly to rest on her husband's forearm, which was exactly where she knew it would be.

The writer found her flustering, impossible to adjust to with any comfort, just as he had felt with the estate agent, Mrs Friggieri. Perhaps it was a certain kind of woman that made him feel this discomfort.

'And I am fascinated by ...' but Gregory's polite rebuttal was interrupted by Patricia. She joined the circle with the obvious intention of catching his eye.

'I know you have no telephone,' she said.

'But I am sure you will give me yours. Your number, I mean.' Gregory replied. The minute he said them, he could not believe he let her wrest these words from him. He looked down at his own shoes, chastising himself for acting so predictably.

The woman with the red lips was smiling brightly and knowingly at him, obviously delighted by his discomfort. What gossip was going to circulate in Sliema about him the following day?

Patricia said the name of the office where she worked, clearly, so he could not possibly mistake it. It was the name of a firm of insurance brokers. She knew he would have no trouble looking it up. He gazed at her departing back, noting loose wisps of hair that escaped her chignon curling childishly on her shoulders.

In his vineyard, with the soft cackling of hens from the run and the swish of wind through some canes near his rubble wall, Gregory let thoughts of the party filter through his mind until he had done with them. He had left the smart house with an informal invitation to Dr Micallef, to visit him at the farmhouse whenever he felt like it. A mere ten-minute walk separated their houses; a mere ten minutes that spanned the entire village and the lives of a small community in between.

He had not questioned Dr Micallef about Patricia. It would be precipitous to register interest so soon. But the young woman was on his mind as he dragged half an oil drum, found submerged in the red soil of his garden, away to be discarded. The pile of rubbish accumulated from his morning's labour was considerable. Apart from the usual mess of bottle glass, remnants of plastic and old spark plugs, he unearthed many pieces of broken earthenware and two almost whole amphorae.

Gregory rather fancied he could clean up one of them, which was only missing an ear, to place in one of his many stone alcoves and niches inside. There was also an old metal throat-lozenge box, still with working hinges, which contained a rusty conglomeration of safety pins, old screws and nails.

'If only I could find the key to that old cellar door,' he said, as if to some invisible companion. It would have been good indeed, to have a helper that afternoon. Lunch gave him a few more hours' worth of energy, but the sun in the west was so hot now he continually wiped his brow. He poured with sweat from every inch of him.

The rubbish yielded no key. It would have to be quite a large key, to fit the hole in the ornate escutcheon. Gregory knew it would be a comparatively simple job to find one that fitted, seeing it pre-dated Yale style or tumbler locks by some decades. Was it worth the bother?

'If only it revealed the mouth of the well,' he said, once more aloud. He thought of the taste of rainwater stored in cool stone: infinitely better than the metallic tepid stuff that spat noisily into his kitchen sink.

There was gobbling from the run, and Gregory noticed the turkeys had grown considerably since his arrival. 'Christmas is coming!' he shouted at the birds, and broke into a laugh. Then he shook his head. Would he have achieved anything real by December? Anything substantial to send to Paul De Souza?

It was a sobering thought that hurried him in the packing of rubbish into cardboard boxes and back into the cool kitchen, where a drink of beer from his cavern of a fridge provided all the relief and comfort he needed.

A slight rustle from one of the cupboards revealed the fact he had not got rid of all the cockroaches disturbed the first week. There were cupboards and recesses, and a number of open alcoves, all over the house. And yes, a small set of carved stone steps set into the outside wall of the house, just like Patricia said there would be, which led to the roof. Gregory was reluctant until that day to trust the steps – or his sense of balance – to reach that height. With beer in hand, he stood out in the tiled courtyard and looked at them. Providing no handrail or risers, they presented a daunting climb to one not entirely at ease with heights.

He suddenly shook his head, put his beer glass to one side and stepped the sixteen steps quickly until he reached the flat roof. From where he stood transfixed after the breathless climb, he could see for some distance: he saw his lane, which turned into a steep street of terraced houses and entered the village square, where a light green bus was waiting.

The double line of rubble walls on the other side reached a narrow bituminised country road between fields. And the vaguest suggestion in the distance of a quarry bounded by stone walls. The only green there was appeared in small patches. Fields, tiny clumps of trees, mainly what he supposed were olives, carobs and umbrella pines. With the sun in his eyes, Gregory looked west to a view partially obstructed by a small water tank, fed from the mains supply and obviously the source of water for his kitchen and bathroom taps and flushing. It had been recently painted – in the last few years or so at any rate – in rust-proofing pink paint, and the pipes leading to and from it appeared in good condition. Gregory walked gingerly to the tank, wondering how much use he would make of the flat roof.

The surface was grey, cemented, painted with a whiter substance in places where it was cracked. The entire roof was bounded by a limestone block wall, slightly lower than Gregory's waist. And crisscrossing in front of him, and behind, from wooden posts placed at intervals, was a series of loose wire washing lines. Gregory knew then that his roof, like others he saw from buses and when he had crested a hill, was used as a utility area.

Some people had potted plants, seats and small sheds up there, and in villages, many a dog barked from the elevation of two storeys at anyone approaching their house. Partially visible behind the water tank, Gregory glimpsed the blue painted facade and wooden balcony of the Victory Band Club, whose president he was told was his immediate neighbour. The club was festooned with coloured lights. Perhaps a celebration or festival was on the calendar.

The sun sank behind the water tank before Gregory decided to quit the roof and the view it provided over his village, to brave the climb down the narrow stone steps. His village. Perhaps he would come to think of it as his, if he stayed there for some time. He received nothing but warm hospitality since his arrival. Still, he sometimes felt as if he were a guest, tolerated amiably as long as his behaviour remained acceptable.

Gregory reached the wrought iron gate and lingered underneath its arched opening, thinking of his solitude and calm. There was so much less despondency in solitude these days, since he arrived in Malta. The kitchen doors stood open, glass panes reflecting the last of the afternoon's hot glow. So much less despondency, within these thick walls, where he ate his solitary meals at the large deal table, looking for radio stations on the stereo set, one of his impulse purchases. Soft music would accompany his cooking and his meal. Music and the guttural garbling in Maltese, the smooth ease of Italian when he twiddled the knob, and of course the inevitable accented English on two or three island stations offering entertainment to locals and tourists alike. News services were frequent and good, but Gregory found himself avoiding them, turning the knob forward to more music or switching the set off altogether after his first week.

He juggled with spoons and utensils, trying to imitate meals he enjoyed at a small restaurant on the road between this and the next village to the south. This evening, he was intent on his small pot of spaghetti sauce, lowering his tall frame over the stove often to catch its scent and compare it to what he smelled in the restaurant. He was startled by sharp knocking at his front door. The bright brass dolphin he polished had not sounded before.

'This is my daughter, Katie,' announced a thin woman loudly, as he opened the thick wooden door. It was almost dark outside, the street lamp from which a yellow glow emitted too far up the lane for him to see with any clarity either the older woman or the daughter she introduced. And why was this introduction taking place?

Gregory felt foolish, wooden spoon in hand and eyes squinting in order to adjust his vision in the gathering gloom. He took one step backward and hit a light switch, flooding his hallway with bright light and blinding them all momentarily.

'Please, come in.'

The women stood in his hallway, both circumspect and well in control of the situation. He noted to his discomfort the stunning beauty of Katie, the daughter. But he had to listen carefully to her mother, who was proceeding in correct but heavily accented English.

Gregory was used to polite questions about himself from the village people, but this was different.

'You live on your own,' the mother said steadily. It was a statement on which he knew she would elaborate, by the way she stood. The daughter's eyes were down cast, intently examining the flag-stoned floor. There would be no conversation from her.

'You are a man on your own.' The woman said nothing he could contradict so far, but he wondered where it would all lead.

She went on. 'Katie has two hours free on Fridays. She come to do your washing and housework.'

'But I wasn't ...'

'Of course not. Men do not think about these things.' Her bright smile displayed an obvious pink denture. But her eyebrow was raised, as if to exclaim that who knew how much dust and what collar stains were left unattended in that house?

'So I don't know ...'

'So you don't know what reasonable money Katie will charge for two hours on Friday and how much more comfortable you will be. Is next week good? If you are out she will find the key you will leave under a stone near the step.'

Gregory had no doubt that she would. Contained amusement at the exchange erased his initial discomfort and confusion. He had a host of questions, which he supposed would be answered by and by.

The women disappeared into the ghostly lane before he could to stop them or restart the dialogue. In the kitchen, the sauce had boiled over, marking the new stove surface with bright red splotches that reminded him of blood. His own blood, the blood he had shed when he took the house.

Sitting over what he salvaged of the sauce and some spaghetti, which somehow tasted nothing like the meal he had eaten at the small restaurant, Gregory mused over the exchange. It was not worry about the expense that was first on his mind, but proximity to such a beautiful young woman. Were these villagers not cautious of strangers at all? Were they so accepting of foreigners who came from who knew where, with who knew what in their past? They knew nothing of his habits or practices.

He could be a chainsaw murderer, a serial rapist, a pathological criminal. He thought of the words he wrote, the crimes he created for his books, and smiled wryly. But perhaps Maltese maids were used to working for foreigners. Perhaps, in spite of the ardent Catholicism evident all over the island, it was not perceived as potential danger for young women to be employed as maids for single men. Perhaps they had no idea, and cared little, for what happened in big cities all over the world, where to venture into the territory of a stranger was foolish, if not actually hazardous.

Gregory shook his head to clear it. He was bringing his old paranoid urban thoughts to a small quiet village, where nothing ever happened. He decided to put it out of his mind until Friday. After all, the girl may very well prove to be hopeless, or *reasonable money Katie charges* turn out to be too exorbitant for work he could do himself, or simply ignore. But he could not put it out of his mind, and Gregory did his dishes desultorily, thinking of the slight girl with the beautiful eyes he only saw once, just after she was blinded by his hall light. After that, he only saw the top of her smooth head with its severe centre parting, the short flowered dress and tiny feet in white sandals. He could not with any accuracy tell her age.

'We'll see!' he exclaimed aloud to himself. He was putting down the tea towel and looked around his large kitchen thinking it was becoming ridiculous. He was talking to himself. He should get himself a dog, at least. The knocker rapped again. Half expecting the two women once more on his threshold, Gregory was surprised to find Dr Micallef.

'Have you eaten yet, my friend?' The old man wore a long-sleeved shirt. A tie bisected its luminosity in the gloom of the lane.

Gregory hit the light switch quickly.

'Ha!' the doctor exclaimed. 'You do not stint on electricity, I see!' He smiled widely, but shyly, as if he did not make it a habit to drop in on people, and this was a challenge he had set himself.

'Come in. Please come in, Fin.' This was a private enough location to use the doctor's nickname, Gregory supposed. 'Yes, I have eaten. I made myself some spaghetti, trying to imitate one of Zija Roza's sauces, but somehow it did not come off.'

The doctor moved slowly into the hallway and walked ahead of Gregory, looking to his right and left curiously. He stopped at the door to the lounge. There was something about the way he stood that made Gregory uncomfortable. He was being formal. Or perhaps he was simply a bit nervous.

'Come into the kitchen, Fin. I was just going to make myself some coffee.'

'I was actually on my way to have dinner in Rabat and thought you might join me. But another evening, perhaps. So – Zija Roza's restaurant is one of your haunts? She makes excellent *ross il-forn*.'

'Yes, I've had her baked rice. I have been there a few times. Tonight's sauce was a kind of compromise.'

'Did you remember bay leaves, garlic – sliced, not chopped! – and plenty of red wine?' The doctor raised his finger and smiled, his eyebrows arching comically.

'None of those, I'm afraid!'

'No wonder. Stock up, and you will never have a disappointing sauce again.'

The two men laughed.

'Please stay a while. I can give you an aperitif before you head off for your dinner, and I'll have a brandy with my coffee. It is a real pleasure to see you.'

'For the space of one cigar, then ...' the older man said grandly, placing his neat form on one of the unmatched kitchen chairs and lighting up.

Gregory looked in his cupboard for something to serve as an ashtray and brought out a saucer.

'And brandy sounds fine,' finished the doctor. The two glasses and Gregory's cup reflected the bright unshaded overhead light globe. Inexplicably, Gregory found himself at a loss for words. To repeat what he told the doctor before about enjoying his cocktail party seemed repetitive, but he had not long to wait for Dr Micallef to speak.

'Have you met your ghost yet?'

Gregory laughed. 'No! But I've not sat up writing until the small hours yet. I've tapped a few words into the computer, but the latest I've stayed up is about midnight. My garden needs a lot of work and it's extremely demanding physically.'

'So you sleep well, you lucky man.'

'And long, I'm afraid.'

The doctor's cigar fumes made a spectral cloud around the light globe.

Gregory observed the way he puffed the smoke gently, enjoying every inhalation, squinting his eyes slightly as he exhaled. He was not an unattractive man in spite of his thick figure and facial lines. The way he sleeked his hair back from his forehead, the way he shot his cuffs, picked the creases of his trousers before sitting, showed a kind of attention to grooming and appearance that belied the man's late night drunkenness. Now, he was nursing his small glass of brandy, looking around him and nodding.

'A woman, they say – or rather, a woman's screams, at dead of night,' he said, matter-of-factly.

Gregory looked up suddenly, understanding the doctor's unconnected remark after a small pause. 'Screams! When? When were they heard?'

He still nursed perfect recall of the shrieks he heard himself, a woman's screams, perhaps.

'I can only tell you what I heard from villagers after some people who so very briefly lived in this house, four or five years ago now, departed as suddenly as they came. Some said they heard screams at night. Other said they saw a spectre ... a small luminous vision.'

Smoke rose to the ceiling, and the doctor's satisfied smile was partially hidden as he leaned forward, rose, and stubbed the cigar out.

But Gregory had seen through the doctor's words. He was trying to fill him with uneasiness about the house. Rather than scare him away with talk of ghosts, he had stimulated Gregory's interest.

'Please come again,' said the writer lamely, disappointed

there was to be no more talk of screams or ghosts or visions.

'I most certainly shall,' replied the doctor amicably. 'Perhaps you can provide a Zija Roza equivalent and I can bring a bottle of Lachryma Vitis!' His laugh was bold, loud and totally sober.

Gregory watched him walk steadily and climb the beginning of the steep street at the end of the lane, in the darkness punctuated by three or four weak yellow street lamps. There was a satisfying feeling to this unannounced visit, the writer felt.

Whatever the doctor's motives, his interest was stimulating. He was starting to think in whole sentences again, in the rhythm of his written prose. He was starting to get inspired, and it felt like a kind of restoration, a kind of resumption of a familiar mind-set.

❏

4

Monsinjur Dimech marched at such a pace Gregory could hardly keep up with him.

'This is a quiet parish, Mr Worthington,' he was saying. 'Nothing much has happened here in the fifteen years I have been minding this flock.'

'But there was a disappearance. A little boy –'

The priest in the black ample robe stopped in his tracks. All previous urgency to get to the church seemed to have suddenly evaporated. The two men stood in the village square. Gregory's white hat glimmered in the bright sunlight. The priest had shown flattery and pride in being asked to conduct the newcomer around the parish church after their meeting at the newsagent's.

'It is not unusual for tourists and other visitors to show an interest in our church,' the robed man said. 'After all, it is one of the oldest in this district. It is almost impossible to tell how old, because many of the records disappeared a long time ago. Anyway, there were days when people were more concerned with eternity than with temporal and earthly record keeping.'

Gregory smiled at the priest's remarks. He looked at his paunch, the wrinkles on either side of his downturned mouth. There was a small crease between the priest's eyebrows that contradicted his calm and placid bearing. He was practised in his ways, and had streams of words to say. Gregory let him say them.

'So you have chosen our little place to do your writing. I see you have taken the *razzett*.'

'It's quiet and comfortable. I have tidied the garden. There are a lot of vines.'

'It has been standing empty for years,' said the priest pointedly.

'Do you know who the owners are?'

At this question, the priest shook his head.

It was impossible for Gregory to decipher whether the nod was negative or affirmative. When they stopped in the middle of the square, the writer could see the Monsinjur was quickly trying to make a mental decision whether to answer his questions or to merely deflect them. The priest started walking towards the church with a sudden lurch, taking quick measured paces that made his soutane swing. It had gathered dust in its creases, especially around the buttonholes.

Nothing is spared from dust here, the writer thought.

'You can see the church's foundations are in a perfect circle. That is of course in contrast with the church in Mqabba, which is an oval church, built from the sale of eggs and lemons by the parishioners. Our church, in fact, was financed by one single contribution – a princely sum – from a Count related in some way to the sovereign line of Sicily. Tradition says it was in reparation of some wrong he committed.' The priest looked sideways to note Gregory's expression. Perhaps he thought the information would find its way into the writer's books.

'As there are no records, we can only ...' he spread his hands apart in an expressive, eloquent gesture.

'Do you know all your parishioners personally?' Gregory supposed this man would be another source of information for the story that had started to germinate in his head. He had imagined, as he lay in bed, that his hands travelled over the keyboard, writing passages that were still a figment, still a ghostly possibility.

He would not start to write solidly until he was sure there was a plot, a line of inquiry on which he could take his readers.

'Between us, we Dimechs know everyone in the district. Before I became the Monsinjur, I was a young priest fulfilling all the day-to-day functions here. Before that, I was a deacon. Before that still, I was an altar boy, serving at the very same altar where I say Mass now and which you shall presently see.' With this, the robed man took out a large key from his soutane pocket.

It was the largest one Gregory had ever seen. 'What a key!'

'This is a *muftieh*. It has been opening this side church door for centuries. Look. It is blackened with use, oiled by the very hands that open this door to the servants of the Lord. Why knows how many?' The priest was waxing rhetorical.

The questions that were raised in the writer's head were more practical, relating to one of his own needs. 'How could it be replaced if it were lost?'

'Oh! Mr Worthington. What a thought. We would have to rely on the Lord, or Saint Anthony – patron saint of lost items. Or we would go to the ironmonger, Franz. You know, the shop right at the top of your lane.'

Gregory smiled and made the mental note. Franz, the ironmonger, was the place to go for a key. The church was a cool cavern resplendent in gilt and red damask. Gregory found himself gasping at the wealth of precious metals adorning altars and candelabras, not to mention the central hanging in the shape of a large tulip, made he was told of solid silver, from which the glimmer of an oil flame sent an eerie glow to the central aisle of the church.

They spoke in hushed tones, amid a sea of shiny wooden pews. 'We have only had the benches for two years,' the priest declared proudly. 'Before that, we had traditional Maltese church chairs with woven rush seats. They could be stacked away to display the inlaid marble floor, which is not possible now.'

Gregory looked down. His feet rested on a script of Latin words inlaid underneath some red and blue shapes he made out to be a coat of arms, partially hidden by the base of a long pew. He knew enough Latin to see it was something about time and death.

The smell of lilies and incense accompanied them into the sacristy, a long room whose walls were wholly taken up by mahogany cupboards carved finely with cherubs, engraved scrolls and biblical symbols. The priest spoke now in a normal voice, describing certain observances and seasonal rites. He pointed to the large parish registers.

'How far do the records go back?'

'Generations. Well before both the wars. It's all there. Births, marriages, deaths of villagers. And we know most of them well. We know them by their family names, their Christian names and their nicknames. Nicknames are very common – and infinitely useful – in a place like a small village, where you have as few as ten surnames for the entire population. Yes, we know all our parishioners. It's a pity we know so little about the church building itself.'

'We?' Gregory could not help questioning the priest's choice of pronoun.

'My sister is Miss Dimech!' He said it as if she were a celebrity, a household name acknowledged by even the most recent newcomer. 'For most of her life, she practically ran the primary school in this village, giving pragmatic instruction, while I give spiritual guidance and teach the doctrine. Most of the families in the village, if not all, have passed under our hands. My sister remained unmarried, as female schoolteachers would in the past. If they married, you see, they would have had to retire immediately. My sister retired at sixty, a few years ago. She is still instrumental in providing private instruction to young people.' The pride in his voice was typical.

Gregory had felt it before in others describing their family members. 'And she lives close by?' he asked quickly.

The address rolled off the priest's tongue.

Gregory noted it mentally. She was sure to have some memory of Censinu Mifsud, the boy who disappeared the year Malta achieved republic status, the boy whose loss was not important enough to displace news of a more political nature in the national paper.

'She would know more than, say, Dr Micallef, who's only been here a few years, wouldn't she?'

At the mention of Phineas Micallef's name, a sudden change

came over the priest. His eyes narrowed into slits, and a breath seemed caught in his chest, unable to be expelled. It escaped slowly, and his face relaxed, but not soon enough to avoid telegraphing to Gregory the unmistakeable dislike the priest had for the doctor. The eyes had held real hostility, but the words that came belied everything. 'Dr Micallef is a comparatively recent arrival. We Dimechs know this village intimately. The old doctor is from Sliema, you see.' There seemed to be more, but the priest held his peace.

Gregory stood outside the church, mentally riffling through words he imagined coursing through his keyboard. He had never worked this way before. Was this work? Had he consciously made the decision to start a novel about the boy? He shook his shoulders in order to physically bring himself to heel and made his way slowly to the address he memorised.

'Of course I remember. Please come in. I have the memory of an elephant, as you English say.' The large woman laughed; a sweet self-deprecating laugh with which the reference to her enormous size became a kind of permission for Gregory to laugh at her as well.

His small smile was looked at sideways. 'Please come into the cool sitting room. I will offer you a whisky.' She stooped to open a cabinet full of shimmering glasses.

Gregory protested. He met the custom of offering a visitor spirits before and knew now to counter it swiftly.

'Or a nice glass of Kinnie with plenty of ice,' she continued. Her wide smile was the kind of welcome Gregory was expecting.

Perhaps his detective work would not be so difficult. Miss Dimech presided over large glasses of the soft drink she poured over ice blocks and wedges of lemon. They moved to a well-lit dining room furnished with a massive mahogany suite and bedecked with all manner of lace doilies, tablecloths and curtains.

Framed photographs and ornaments crowded the tops of both dresser and sideboard. A mottled mirror graced the back of a chiffonier. It too was crammed with photographs stuck under the frame.

'I've had many pupils. Generations of them,' she said, twittering, 'I've taught three generations of the one family.' Her thick arm reached out to a photograph.

Gregory observed the deep dimpling of flesh at her elbow, where the short sleeve fabric dug into her upper arm. Her small wristwatch on its silver band was all but buried in the folds of her wrist. The nails were short but painted a bright pink. Careful grooming was evident in tightly permed grey hair, arranged in shingles over the wide forehead. Laugh lines creased into her small double chin, which wobbled when she spoke. The heat obviously made her breathless because she panted as she spoke her accented words, making Gregory consciously resist the reflexive reaction of panting with her, or holding his breath until she caught hers.

'Look at these, for example – three generations of Attards, and me in the middle of them!' The colour photo showed Miss Dimech in a tent of a blue dress, holding in the embrace of thick outstretched arms a large family of adults and children of all ages. 'And yes, I remember the Mifsuds who had the *razzett*. Sad lives. Tragic –'

'Was there ever a body?'

The fat woman wheezed, looked earnestly at Gregory, then made some sort of mental decision.

'No. It remained a disappearance. You may find, if you inquire with the police, that the case was kept open for seven years, and then abandoned on the presumption of death.' She seemed conversant with legal terminology.

Gregory silently blessed his meeting with her brother the parish priest that morning.

Miss Dimech sipped daintily, eagerly willing to continue the story. 'Censinu was a good little boy. He learnt quickly. Sums, reading, and careful writing. Of course I don't remember all the detail, but he is marked in my mind because of what happened, you understand?'

Gregory nodded.

'He suffered from swings in temperament. One day he would be as bright as a button, as you English say –'

'I'm actually from Australia, but it doesn't matter.'

'Really? How interesting.' She raised an eyebrow, but was so engrossed in her story she proceeded with a dismissive pant. 'Anyway, as I was saying – one day he would be bright and cheerful, playing with the other little boys and responding to the lessons. The next he would be silent and withdrawn, as if full of some morbid fear. Of course, with all those children, it was impossible to be attentive to each individual, but I asked him many times, you know, if he was all right. If everything at home ... I had started to hear gossip. Not that I really listen to hearsay, but the village was buzzing at one point with talk about his mother. She was not a village girl, originally, you see. But that's immaterial. She had a terrible temper. She would terrify Mananni at the shop. Mananni died a few years ago, so she can't confirm ... But there were terrible stories of tantrums and rages, of fights with other village women, of screams coming from the farmhouse. That poor man, he tried everything. Those poor children.'

'And when the boy disappeared?'

'Oh – is all this for a book perhaps?' Miss Dimech's podgy hands flew to her sides to straighten her dress. As if for a photographer, she tried to arrange herself, wishing she would present a leaner figure, a figure less prone to jokes and prods from the community that she knew went on behind her back.

Trying not to smile, Gregory reassured her with a tilt of his head. 'I really don't know yet what will be included,' he said carefully.

The woman hid a disappointed look quickly, visibly reassembling her thoughts and returning to her account of what she recalled about Censinu's family. 'It was grape harvest time. Was it? Let me try and remember. Yes, it was harvest time. The boy was known for his truancy. He would run to the fields and play for hours on his own. Perhaps he even ventured over the quarry walls. I don't know. After a particularly disturbing scene with his mother ... well, I don't really know, but it must have been – as I say – a particularly disturbing scene, the boy was seen running through the village. His arm was still bandaged from some scrape he was in earlier in the week. I remember hearing the ironmonger say his eyes were wide. Wide with terror. He ran with all his might through the square, into the path of a departing bus, whose driver howled in alarm.'

Miss Dimech wobbled a bit as she laughed at what she saw as the antics of a young boy. 'You know how children are! Nothing is more urgent than their games and fantasies!'

'But this particular game never ended, did it?' Gregory leaned forward, wanting details.

The smile faded. She nodded, penitent of her humour. 'He was never seen again. Never. The alarm was raised the following morning. He had not returned home in the night. No one remembered seeing him cross the square back to *Sqaq Ghajn il-Bettieh*. That is, Spring Lane, as you know it. Its real name is Melon Spring Lane, you know. He might have gone that way again, you see. Or he might not. That night, I remember, the whole village was frantic. Many people do not like talking about it, you may have found that out already. You see, this is a quiet place and nothing very much ever happens. When something like that hits a quiet place, people react very differently.' She wheezed. 'The best and the worst of behaviours, you know. Some feel sorry they did not help more. Some may be ashamed of the panic and anxiety they displayed when he was not found – all that.' Her hands waved about to stress the explanation.

Gregory saw there was a trace of regret in her own eyes, but admired her analytic capacity. Perhaps it stemmed from self-examination. Perhaps she was one of those who wished they had done more.

'There was a tremendous search,' she continued. 'The whole village was turned upside down. Do you Australians have that expression too?'

He nodded.

'I see. Extra constables were brought in from Floriana. You have no idea what movement and what activity took place. They looked in the quarries – sometimes after rain, you see, water gathers at the bottoms of quarries, but they were all dry that season. They looked through the fields. The grass was high on the verges under rubble walls. They looked underneath all the fig and carob trees in the district. They went even as far as dragging Chadwick Lakes, and they are miles away from here.'

Gregory smiled at her concept of distance. The whole island was only nineteen miles long.

'They considered kidnapping,' she continued, 'or a hit and run, but no children's bodies were ever found.'

'Did they look closer to home?'

Miss Dimech looked at him pointedly, pursing her lips. 'Exactly what do you mean, Mr Worthington?'

He could not read her expression, so he persisted. 'Was the garden dug up? Were there any traces of anything ... suspicious? What about the well?'

'Maltese children do not fall into wells, Mr Worthington. They keep away from the rim for fear of the *belliha*, the monster that lives in wells and swallows humans. It is a myth, of course, but it serves to save lives!' Her smile was there again, glimmering as she sipped her drink. 'As for anything suspicious – the Mifsuds were a nice family. Law abiding, pious. I don't know what you mean.' The ice cubes were now smooth pebbles jingling at the surface. Gregory sipped, resisting the temptation to crunch the ice in his teeth.

'But yes,' she continued, 'I think some effort was made to check wells. I don't know how they did it though.' A little shudder wobbled through her shoulders. Perhaps she did not think the *belliha* was such a myth, after all.

'What happened after that?'

'Nothing. After a month or so life returned to normal, more or less.'

❏

5

The constable looked down at some register he was checking, then through the station window, which was barred with wrought iron. Then he looked outward, through the open door at the street, where a small group of urchins was chasing a dusty dog. He looked at the ceiling, dotted and specked by the landing and alighting of a decade of flies. He looked anywhere except at Gregory, who leaned on the chest-high counter, riffling through the slim telephone directory. He found Patricia's office number with no difficulty. It was a harder matter trying to get through. He caught the constable's eye.

'You are trying to get through to Valletta in the middle of the day,' the policeman said, as if the writer were attempting something ridiculous. 'Of course it takes a long time.'

Gregory said he would return later. Perhaps a visit to *Il-Hanut* would ease the wait.

'No, no. Don't give up. It will be exactly the same later. You have to keep trying. You must keep trying to get in.' The constable held out both palms as if displaying a self-evident truth. How was it that seemingly intelligent people had no idea even of how to make a telephone call?

'I see.' Gregory tried the number a few more times.

'The problem is, you are keeping the station phone engaged.'

Gregory looked at the man. What did he want? He arched an eyebrow, searching for words.

'But you cannot give up,' insisted the constable. 'That way you might never get through. Your call must be urgent. Is it?'

'Well ...'

'I thought so. Continue then. Have a few more tries.'

When he heard a female voice on the other end, rattling off the firm's name and a cheery *Good morning!* Gregory suddenly remembered he did not know Patricia's surname.

'Um. Hallo ... Patricia –'

'Hold on, please.' There were a few loud pips and Patricia's voice was on the line.

Gregory felt like a fool.

The constable's gaze once more travelled the length and breadth of the station without resting on him.

'This is Gregory Worthington,' he said.

Her voice was warm, slipping from a businesslike tone into a casual one. He felt relaxed, able to converse with her no matter who was listening.

'I thought tonight, or tomorrow, if you cared to take the drive out here. I might either make something or we might go ... but we can always decide when you get here.'

'I'll come tonight, and I'll come at seven-thirty,' she said huskily but clearly.

Gregory could hear the smile in her voice and unconsciously smiled himself, finding himself looking straight into the eyes of the constable, who was winking widely, acting the full conspirator in the conquering of a lady.

'Have a nice evening, sir!' he called from behind the counter at Gregory's retreating back.

He found himself fidgeting in his own kitchen, looking at his watch. It was only five. Should he attempt another Zija Roza counterfeit and impress Patricia with lasagne or rice? The kitchen looked too neat and tidy to fill with pots and wooden spoons, splashes of tomato sauce and tea towels knotted in frustration or panic as something boiled over or burned. Why did he not stick to some old favourite he could turn out in half an hour?

Gregory thought suddenly of the tuna casserole and boiled potato he made years ago, in anticipation of Maggie's first visit to his bachelor flat. The image of himself then, the awkwardness and ineptitude worsened by a bottle of cheap red wine, made him retreat from the wide tiled room, telling himself he ought to have grown up in the intervening years.

Taking Maggie off his mind was not altogether simple. She accompanied him out of the kitchen and into the yard, where the shadows seemed hardly lengthened at all. Soon though, twilight would bring relief from the blistering heat. The short red hair and dangling earrings – would they ever totally leave his mind? They went with him through the arched gateway to the vineyard, whose gnarled grapevines in their eminent age sobered him for a minute.

But Maggie was still there. He remembered her just before Emma was born, wearing a striped robe and Persian slippers, curled up in their old sofa. It was not long after the surprising success of his first novel.

'My God, they actually like it,' Maggie had said in disbelief. She was buried underneath held-up pages of a section of *The Australian*.

'What's that?'

'There's another review of your book here.'

Gregory was excited. 'Who wrote it?'

'Some academic. Listen to this: Exciting the reader more by intricate form than by alarming content, Worthington weaves a story worthy of note. Rather than create disgust or fear, he promotes respect in a reader who, with a vast basis of comparison in today's market, can believe the narrative, believe the characters, and be chilled by the reality, the feasibility, of his tale.'

'Fantastic!'

'You used to say you couldn't understand critics and reviewers.'

'Now I do. Now that it's about my work!' He would not allow her cynicism to dampen his elation. 'See that? Aha! Great!' Gregory poured them both a celebratory glass of wine.

'I can't drink this, Greg.' She said coldly. 'I'm carrying a baby, remember?'

'Yes I remember. Maggie, don't be so disapproving. Have one sip and I'll get you an apple juice.'

But she had dampened his verve, crippled his sense of success, and he was once more reduced to despondency and insecurity.

'Sometimes I think you are jealous when things go well for me.' He was surprised at his own bravery. He rarely tried lines like that with her.

'What? What do you think I am, Greg? What do you reckon I feel about myself?' She held herself upright, furious and gasping with affront. 'It's you who is the competitive one in this family!' Her ironic tone was driven home when she pointed at her swollen abdomen.

'Don't shout,' he begged, annoyed with her outburst.

'I'll do exactly as I please – just as you do. I don't like what you write. I don't like it that you write at all. You still do it. So I can jolly well scream!' And she uttered a loud wail, banshee-like, falling into a huddle of sudden laughter on the sofa as she did.

Gregory looked into his long vineyard, still hearing her wail, her laughter, and remembering the birth of Emma only a few days after that.

Patricia's knock almost went unnoticed, after he had listened out for it for a whole hour. Gregory placed the new radio on the floor behind a chair in the lounge, plugging into the only electric socket in the room. Bent and kneeling as he was, he heard a tap. Her hand was still up to try again when he opened the front door quickly.

'Have you been knocking long? I'm sorry. I was bent over on the sitting room floor,' he said apologetically.

'Oh,' she laughed. 'Do you do that often?'

His nervousness was dispelled immediately and he followed her through the hallway and into the lounge. He had not turned the radio on in his hurry to get the door.

'It's just as I imagined,' she was saying hoarsely. 'These country houses are so wonderful. Look – you can see the thickness of the walls at the windows, the recess is so deep.' There was a step cut into the stone recess she was looking at, so one could stand on it and look out of the window.

Gregory had drawn the louvred shutters to, as he found it was useful in keeping mosquitoes at bay. There were no curtains hanging from the simple wooden rod.

'The house is very cool – coming in from an afternoon of working in the garden is bliss,' he said. 'I sometimes lie on the floor in the hall and soak up the coolness of the stone.'

'They used to do that in the olden days,' she said approvingly, 'before fans and air conditioning! They would pull their bedclothes into halls or loggias and spend the night there. Where's your loggia, by the way?'

He led her to the corridor outside the two bedrooms, where the large window, whose lower panels were open to the gathering dusk, still lit the way.

'This one is rather special. The fanlight has some blue glass in it. I hear it used to be very expensive.'

They looked up at the pointed segments of blue glass.

'Is this where you write?' Patricia glimpsed the glimmer of a computer monitor through the open door of the back room.

'We'll have a drink first,' he said quickly, 'and then I'll show you the rest and a bit of the garden before it gets completely dark. I thought we might go out to Zija Roza's. I don't want to scare you off forever with one of my brave sauces.' Gregory realised the implication of what he said the minute it left his lips. Forever, he said.

Patricia smiled, a quizzical smile.

He saw she had let her hair loose, its chestnut thickness crowding her shoulders, tendrils kept away from her face by two large tortoiseshell combs. She was dressed casually, in navy slacks and a white top that caught the late light and luminesced in the dim corridor.

Gregory hurried away ahead of her towards the kitchen and looked back, to see the glimmer of white shoes, and white bag clutched in both hands in what he thought was a nervous clasp.

'White wine?' He attempted to keep his voice casual.

'Have you started writing yet?' Her words followed him into the bright kitchen. 'My goodness. It is certainly bright in here!'

'Everybody says that.'

He saw a raised eyebrow when he said everybody. 'Dr Micallef thinks I do not stint on electricity,' he went on.

'Maltese people, especially in the country, are very thrifty, Gregory. Positively frugal.' It was the first time she said his name. Or was it?

It sounded like the first time, in his kitchen, where the newness of his fridge and gas cooker seemed out of chronology with the thick uneven walls and their alcoves.

'Oh look, a *bomblu*. Was that here when you came?' Her question lifted at the end as she looked up.

'A what?' He followed her gaze.

'That amphora, that clay jar. It's called a *bomblu* in Maltese,' she said. 'Yours has an ear missing. They come in all sizes. They were used for keeping water cool. You probably have a huge one on the roof in the place of a gravity tank. Have you looked?'

'Yes, I have. No clay jar. There is a galvanised drum, rust-proofed and all. I found this little one buried in the garden. And lots and lots of broken pottery.'

'When we lived in Sliema, there was a huge clay jar on the roof of the washing room, attached by a broad metal band round its widest part to the wall of the house.'

'Was there a well?' Gregory listened intently to the details of what she said.

'Of course. Its cone, its mouth, was built into the side of our yard, with a small iron pulley hanging over it, which soon became hidden and overgrown by honeysuckle. A huge honeysuckle creeper grew with its roots in the well, over one corner of the yard. The shutters of one of the bedrooms upstairs were choked with it.'

'Tell me about the well.' They sat on kitchen chairs,

forgetting about looking at the garden before it got dark.

'Do you know about Maltese wells?' she asked. 'They are really below-ground storage reservoirs for rainwater. They're not bores or artesian wells let into the water table, or anything. Ours had a corniced rim, and a lid made of stone, heavy and almost immovable. I only remember it being opened once, and that noise of stone grinding against stone is something I'll never forget. All children are afraid of wells.'

'I've heard.'

'But of course it must have been used from time to time. We also had a *bomblu* exactly like yours, perhaps a bit smaller, in a kind of niche over the kitchen door.'

Bomblu. He must remember that word. A clay jar. He had a feeling about a clay jar. A large one. But he asked more about architecture, thinking it would be a good place to start some research. 'Was there a cellar?'

'Not one we could use. We were told the cellar of our house and the one next door were turned into an air-raid shelter during the war. Later, it was walled up and forgotten about, but there was certainly a cavity under the house because footsteps sounded hollow in places, especially in the hall. Like they do in your loggia.'

Gregory had not noticed. 'My loggia?'

'Mm – come and listen,' she said in amusement. They took their glasses and walked through the small corridor several times, comparing the sound their steps made there and in the outer hallway, laughing and drinking their wine as they went. Patricia was having fun, talking incessantly, telling what she knew about old houses and enjoying the fascination she created in the writer. He could see from her expression and casualness that she trusted him and felt at ease.

'So the cellar goes most of the way under the house, up to the loggia at least,' he said.

'I thought you'd have found your way down there by now.'

He held up a finger, in parody of what he saw Dr Micallef do when he wanted to make a point.

The young woman laughed.

'Franz is making me a key,' he said in a mock devious voice.

'Franz?'

'The ironmonger. He is also the local locksmith, among other things. He is finding me a moof...'

'A *muftieh*!'

'Yes, to fit the cellar door. Soon, I'll be under the house. There is probably a well mouth down there.' He craved delicious well water, but was intrigued by more than that.

'Oh please, Gregory! Let me be here when you open it. I'd love to be in on the exploration.'

'What?' he exclaimed jestingly. 'All those spiders and cobwebs and cockroaches and horrible poisonous snakes?'

She laughed like a child, enjoying his pantomime. He wriggled his fingers and made faces while taking their glasses to the kitchen. 'Let's go to Zija Roza's before it's too late,' he said.

On the way, she went into an explanation brought on by Gregory's exclamation about her car.

'Yes, I know. It is rather flashy, isn't it? But Papa insisted. If I was going to race around the island like the devil was behind me – no, those were not his exact words! – I would have to do it in a safe car. I was not going to complain since he put up more than half the money. So a small Volvo it was!' She smiled and wriggled proudly in her seat. 'Now, about snakes! Malta has no poisonous snakes. No poisonous creatures at all, as a matter of fact.'

'Really?' So the boy was not poisoned as he hid somewhere, dying in a crouched position where he was never found. The boy? Was this what he was doing – researching the boy's story? Looking for possibilities?

But Patricia was going on about snakes. 'St Paul was shipwrecked here ... you know how a snake leapt from the fire and wound itself round his arm, don't you?' Her husky voice broke and fell to a whisper.

'Vaguely.' Gregory couldn't help laughing. The way she

drove, too, filled him with a kind of dread coupled with amused admiration. They sped through the narrow country roads with abandon. Her father was right.

'Well, from that moment,' she continued breathlessly, 'the venom was removed, by miracle, from all the island's creatures. Mind you, they say there still is a scorpion on Gozo that is poisonous. But it is as much part of the legend as –'

'So! You say it's a legend. I thought you believed the whole thing!'

'Of course I do!' she laughed. 'Although I've never actually seen a snake. Or a scorpion.'

'The time is yet to come,' Gregory said, in a mock ominous tone. 'Next week, in my cellar.'

'I can't wait.'

The meal at Zija Roza's proved light and entertaining. They ate and drank without much attention to what was placed before them, and when Gregory suggested coffee at the farmhouse, Patricia was quick to rise from her chair.

Gregory noticed she allowed him to pay the bill without much fuss, adopting an old-fashioned gesture of discretion, looking away while he did it. He smiled at what he took to be the island's custom, thinking of the many debates he entertained on dates in Australia.

'So you are not a feminist?' he joked in the car.

'I really don't know.' Her face was serious and her whispered reply gave it added gravity that made Gregory laugh. He guessed she was in her late twenties, and not as inexperienced as he had imagined at Dr Micallef's party, where she tried almost childishly to appear elegant and reserved. He viewed her in profile as she drove.

'I'll have to leave soon after having coffee,' she said in a careful way, the voice remaining steady until the last word, when it broke, making coffee sound deliciously illicit. 'Although my parents know it is silly to impose a curfew on someone my age in this day and age, I don't like to worry them. They're just back from Sicily and rather tired. They say they won't stay up for me, but I often hear them mumbling in the dark if it's after one.'

'Fine. Do you have a long drive home?' Gregory meant it as a joke on the smallness of the island.

'Oh yes. I have to go through Pawla, Msida – all that. Of course there is the bypass now.'

'Of course.' Gregory suppressed his mirth.

'I asked you if you had started writing and you didn't really answer,' she said later, sitting on his sofa.

Gregory was bent over, trying to switch on the radio on the floor. 'As a matter of fact, I have been writing like mad. But only in my head. Tonight, something you said gave me a jumping-off point. I may put down a few words tomorrow. I have made notes – of words and things. Descriptions of characters I will use.'

'People you have met here?' Her tone was curious.

'They will not be recognisable when I'm finished. I use a bit of this one, a characteristic of that one.' He did not want to talk about his methods.

'Will I ever be able to read –?'

'If you ever read anything I write, it will have to be in print, I'm afraid,' he said. 'But ...' He dashed away on his last word, leaving her to sip coffee on her own, and returned with a paperback. 'This is one of my most successful releases. I think you do have to know what to expect.'

'Strange title.' She ran a finger across the red letters. 'The Altruist. Is it autobiographical?' Her smile was sweet.

'No. But read it.'

When she stood in his hallway, under the bright light, clutching his book and her white bag, Gregory wondered whether to kiss her. Her pause seemed to invite it, her chatter stopped. She had both book and bag clasped in one arm against her chest as he drew her towards him.

She returned his kiss eagerly, with warmth contained by the occasion. At another time, in another place, he knew she would be capable of a more passionate embrace.

'I'll call you when I get the key to the cellar,' he said.

Patricia nodded and skipped out to her car. The gloom in the lane swallowed her, and Gregory saw only the white splash of her top disappearing into the small car.

❑

6

They say that when Censinu Mifsud died, his small body was pushed into a bomblu. A clay jar, one of a dozen or so standing outside the cellar door of a stone farmhouse. This is how the story goes. It is the summer of little Censinu's death. A hot summer, full of sunshine. But for the little boy, it is also full of dread and darkness. He is wiry and energetic, but he is scared. Of the dark, of the mouldy cellar where his father is preparing for this year's vintage. Of his own mother. It is the summer his vague but honest father gathers an unusually large number of empty jars in the sunken courtyard outside the cellar door.

The little boy runs away into the fields when his father is filling them with wine. Fear cuts into his days in spite of the fact his mother's eyes rarely meet his. He fears her hands. He fears the sharp lashes from her vindictive tongue. He is terrified when she takes up the broom, or the long knife with the wooden handle.

Gregory looked at the words on the screen. Outside, the world was quiet. He threw open the shutters of the writing room and looked across a dark space where he knew his vines were. The first hum of a mosquito made him close them again quickly, sit at the keyboard and tap out the words at once. Exactly like they used to before, words came to him with slick ease, tumbling into his animated fingers as if they alone knew the story he wanted to relate.

Patricia had given him the word, the key word he was waiting for. Not consciously, of course. Gregory did not wait consciously. He procrastinated consciously. But when he was given the word, his mind would leap, bringing together all the mental 'writing' he did before. He was surprised that he could still summon, in more or less the same order, words he conjured while lying awake at night, waiting to drop off, listening to the barking of dogs or the solitary buzz of a motor scooter up the lane. He stopped only once that night, to percolate a jug of coffee, which he poured quickly into a thermal flask. He held a yellow pencil between his teeth as he screwed the cap on, walking back to the writing room with the next words on the tips of his fingers. He scribbled words in the spring-bound notebook on the table, making a list he would have to check for spelling.

Maltese was a complicated language, so he used the words sparingly, his list only a few words long. BOMBLU, he wrote. And again, *bomblu.* A clay jar, a large one, large enough to accommodate the small crumpled corpse of a boy who met his end ... How did he meet his end? The dawn chorus hardly noticed, Gregory pounded the keys well into the morning, not even pausing to re-read the passages he wrote, stopping only when insistent knocking came from his front door.

❑

7

It is the second day of the grape harvest, and Censinu disappears again. His parents are too busy to notice the exact time he left the house, but it is soon plain there is one person less at the receiving end of the line of hands lifting the baskets. They pile up, several of them waiting to be emptied.

'Where is that boy?' Terezina his mother straightens her back, which is giving her much more trouble this year than last. She hopes against hope she is not pregnant again. If she is pregnant again... But there is no time for self-pity or for anger. She tightens the loose knot of hair at the back of her neck and goes on sorting through the grapes.

Some are good enough for the table. Dessert grapes always fetch good prices. But the wine grapes – these form the bulk of the harvest and will be crushed soon. As soon as... But where is that boy? Rage threatens to engulf her, to spill over and rush in. A red wave, a current of overpowering yet mortifying rage and fear. Some day, if she does not control herself, she will hurt someone badly. Maybe herself. Or her babies. Her unborn baby, if there is another on the way. Or Nikol, who is such a patient and undemanding man, such a quiet husband. Or that boy. That Censinu, whose presence is becoming increasingly confusing. It is impossible, isn't it? Or is it possible that you could dislike one of your own children? Your own son?

From the minute he turned eight something happened. Censinu changed. Or perhaps she is changing. She has an almost grown up son now. A son who can help in the vineyard, who is strong and intelligent, who does well at school. Perhaps Censinu will make a successful career one day, Nikol says. Perhaps he will not have to work in a vineyard like us until he grows old and bent and tired.

'Leave him, let him go,' Nikol says when Terezina complains of the boy's truancy, his waywardness around the house. 'Leave the boy alone. You disagree too much, you two!' He says it jokingly, sweetly, but they both know it to be the truth.

The sad truth; that Terezina and her son Censinu can hardly occupy the same space without some altercation, some scolding, some violence in the eyes of the mother reflected quickly with fear in those of the boy. Fear. What is he afraid of? That she would hit him like she often does, with the broomstick? With whatever she happens to have in hand at the time? That she would threaten him with a hiding with the stropping leather? That she would lock him in the cellar?

No. No. Not the dark cellar. Not the cellar where there are cockroaches and spiders. Censinu's eyes fill with apprehension when his mother's voice whines and teases him about his fear. He knows she is capable of cruelty, that she is capable of dragging him down there against his will.

'*No, not the cellar. Not the dark,*' *she sings out in a taunting tease.* '*Censinu is afraid of the dark. Aren't you, eh?*'

'*Leave the boy alone.*'

'*We'll leave you alone, then, to read and become educated. Don't come here or I'll cut off your writing fingers with this knife!*' *And she breaks into a high laugh as the boy runs out of the front door into the lane, past the rubble walls and up the steep street into the village where friends playing with a small puppy and a piece of string shout and laugh and urge him to join them.*

Censinu looks at that knife when he returns, hanging by its leather thong from a nail above the breadboard. He slinks in and takes his plate, eating quietly at the kitchen table where his father is still nursing his last tumbler of red wine. But some afternoons, after a threat or a scolding, Censinu disappears completely. No one in the village knows where he goes and his parents resign themselves to knowing he turns up eventually.

Later and later, usually at night, the boy climbs into the high iron bed he shares with his toddler brother and sleeps away breathlessness and fear. Fear that his mother will lean over him in bed as she often does, look into his face, on which he tries to place the feigned calm of sleep, and covers him tightly. This time, she grabs his arms, attempting to move him, to make more space for the younger child.

Censinu stiffens, resisting his mother's grip.

'*Don't resist me! Even in your sleep you fight me, you stubborn* boy!'

Censinu feigns sleep, mumbles under his breath and exhales with relief, throwing off the covers when she moves away to the other room.

'I am afraid of my mother,' he says at the confessional, not looking into the priest's eyes. As is the custom, he kneels like other boys at the front of the confessional box, every Saturday, facing the priest. He crosses himself and hopes he can remember the words of the Act of Contrition. He breathes his fear, his grave sin, his anguish, to the monk; holds his breath to hear his penance.

'So you should be, my boy! Hold your father and your mother in fear and respect, as you do God the Father.' The insensitive blessing sends him reeling into the bright street, thinking of the sharp bent knife, the broom handle and the threat of the darkened cellar.

❑

8

The writer reached the pottery by a longer route, having confused directions given to him at the tearooms where he had a snack. To his disappointment, the shop was merely a showroom of the potter's, and he could not watch the process of clay being worked or artefacts being fired.

The shop was at the edge of Mdina, reached from the street by a short flight of steps, making it feel cellar-like and enclosed. It was more a lane than a street, bounded on one side by the fortification of the bastion; thick grey stone fused together by time, weathered into iron-like consistency and appearance. Shelves lined all the walls; glass shelves arranged to show off the wares.

The shape of the earless amphora he had cleaned and placed in his kitchen alcove was repeated throughout the shop. It appeared to be a popular shape, modified only slightly by size. Some of the ones on the glass shelves were glazed and coloured in bright hues, mainly blue and yellow, popular colours of the Mediterranean. He had a fleeting memory of touring the west coast of Italy as a child, his parents avidly enthusiastic about showing him Europe to spice up a childhood spent almost entirely in the quiet suburbs of Perth. What stuck in his mind, to resurface in this pottery, where the glint of glazes and the rounded shapes of urns and jars surrounded him, were the colours.

'I thought I would be able to see someone making a *bomblu*,' he said to the young man behind the counter. He could have been speaking to someone in Fremantle, he thought, looking at the small earring in one ear and the sleek ponytail, the T-shirt proclaiming some perspicacious pearl of ingenuity.

'You will have to go to the craft village at Ta' Qali for that,' the young man said, 'it's not far from here. The bus will take you from Saqqajja,' he directed, not in the least curious at Gregory's request. He must have had stranger inquiries from tourists clamouring for souvenirs.

Many of them crowded in and out even during Gregory's brief visit, and the young man was kept constantly busy, wrapping the awkward shape of miniature jars, *bomblu* after *bomblu*, in tissue paper in a quick practised way.

Gregory remembered he laughed when someone told him it would be hard for him to get around Malta without a car. On an island so small, what could possibly prevent him from getting around on foot, or even on a pushbike? The latter was mostly conspicuous by its absence; a surprise to Gregory at first, but infinitely understandable after some weeks. To ride about on a bike in that scorching sun, up so many steep hills, would be far from enjoyable. Besides, the streets were crammed with all manner of vehicle; from humble tiny Fiat to serious prime movers towing containers. From ancient English models he thought extinct, to sleek German saloons of the latest design.

Public transport proved rather good and inexpensive, after he got used to the light green buses. They were often overcrowded and erratic in timing, but they kept more or less to a schedule that coincided with shop and pub opening hours. He rode in converted coaches and derelict vintage buses, paying a few cents for a small paper ticket he screwed up and pushed through the slot of the *Box for Used Tickets* as he alighted.

The smiles and mirth he felt when seeing notices in careful English were unshared. He moved about alone, noting the curious and the comical, the familiarity or utter strangeness of some things on his own, feeling his solitude at times and wishing for a companion with whom to share an observation or a joke.

The shrine in each bus, for example, was certainly worthy of note. A representation of Christ or Mary, framed in a prominent position on the driver's cabin, was usually lit with tiny lights or artificial candles, and superscribed by some Latin, English or Maltese exhortation. *Verbum Dei Caro Factum Est* was a popular one. *In God We Trust* another one that probably dated to the sixties. He saw one dedicated to John Kennedy, with a stereotypical photograph of the dead president taking the place of the saint.

At Ta' Qali, the bus joined the tail of several others standing in the wide clearing in the sun. He got off and followed signs until he found a Nissen hut in which potters were working. The back was sectioned off and he could see a group of tourists watching two men working at wheels. The clay they used was beige, very nearly a dark pink. They worked with heads bent over the slowly forming bodies of two identical jars, almost in unison, the growth occurring at once, as if it were planned that way. Seemingly unconscious of the crowd gathered there to watch them, the men pedalled their wheels and gently worked the clay until they completed two identical jars. The wheels stopped and they looked up as one.

There was jabbering from the crowd in a host of languages. 'That's a nice *bomblu*,' he said to one of the men, who broke into a wide smile at the familiar word.

'We have many on the shelves. They are down there, on the way in. Have a look, have a look.'

The sales pitch did not deter Gregory. The massed crowd had moved to the display shelves and hands were moving, picking first one artefact and then another. The colours, the smell of raw clay, and the buzz of talk in many languages, were what these men were used to.

'Do you make really large ones?' Large enough for a body, he could not say.

'Oh yes, very big. Over there.'

Gregory followed the pointing finger and spied a cluster of large pots placed on the floor behind a stand of shelves. They were much larger than his earless one, or the ones still standing on the turntables, but nothing as large as he hoped. He guessed the capacity of the largest one to be not more than about ten litres.

'Much larger.' He held a hand up to his waist, thinking he might be asking for the impossible. Perhaps what had flown out of his hands at the keyboard was not in fact possible.

'Oh, sir, not these days. The kind of clay jar you are talking about is not in use any more. Perhaps you will find one or two in antique shops.'

'But they used to exist?' he insisted, suddenly wanting his writing to have foundation, solidity.

'Water jars, yes. In Gozo, you can still see them sometimes on roof tops. But we don't make them anymore.'

What Patricia described was certainly possible, then. A large clay bomblu, standing as high as a man's waist.

'How wide would you say the mouth would be?' He had to be sure it was possible to cram what he wrote had been crammed into one of those jars.

The potter put the cigarette he was smoking on his lower lip and squinted, making a gurgling sound in his throat as if he were calculating something complicated. 'About this, sir,' he said, holding his hands out, thumbs and forefingers describing a circle about thirty centimetres in diameter. 'Sometimes a bit more.'

'Perfect!' Gregory paused. Why did he feel like a criminal?

'But I don't know if you will find one.' How was the man to know that the writer did not really need the actual jar itself, but just its possibility, its potential?

'Thank you,' said the Australian. He had what he wanted at last. 'As long as I know they existed – that's all.'

The man shrugged, smiling and returning to his wheel with a bemused expression. If he knew the sinister reason behind Gregory's questions, he would have turned away sooner, the smile on his face turning into distrust or even disgust.

Back at the farmhouse, Katie the maid had already finished her tasks and left. He stopped writing that morning at her arrival, stopping her insistent knocking by opening the thick door and letting her in.

'You left no key,' she said quietly.

Startled by the difference in physique between this country girl and Patricia, whose image was still vivid in his mind's eye because he had not yet slept, Gregory allowed her entrance. He was tongue-tied and myopic from having sat at his computer all night, annoyed at being interrupted. 'I have been up all night,' he said needlessly.

She did not seem to listen. 'I will wash all the floors, sir. If you have any clothes that need washing I'll take them away with me and bring them back tomorrow. Ironed, too.'

'There is no need ... I have looked after myself a long ...' Gregory's impatience had more to do with written words than housework.

But she looked at him strangely and walked ahead of him, starting a search for cleaning materials in the kitchen before he had time to think of what next to say.

'If you have not slept, perhaps you better sleep now,' she said without turning her head to look at him.

'No, no.'

'I'll be very quiet.'

'Oh, no. It's not that. I think I'll go out and look for a potter.' The man had given up. He needed to think now, rather than write.

'*X'inhu?*'

He looked blank.

'A what?'

'A potter. One who makes pots and jars and things out of clay. Like this –' he reached and grabbed hold of the jar in the alcove, holding it up for her to see. 'I want to see the maker of a *bomblu*.'

She looked at him strangely but continued what she was doing. She amassed all Gregory's cleaning implements in the middle of the kitchen. Mop, broom, brushes, basins and bucket, sponges and cloths. There was also a clutch of cleaning liquids and powders. 'Now I will start. The two hours are from now,' she said in a businesslike voice.

Gregory nodded. 'I'll leave you to it, then. Look – I'd better pay you now. How much do you –'

'How can you pay me before you see my work?' She seemed puzzled.

Gregory felt once more as if he had transgressed some custom or other. He was suddenly glad he was dealing with the girl rather than her mother or the estate agent. Somehow, the assertive ways of the women put him at a kind of disadvantage. They always seemed to know exactly what to do.

'How then?'

'Tonight my mother comes to ask you if it is okay.' So he would have to face her mother again. Some things were inevitable. With that thought, Gregory donned his hat and left the house, pacing the lane and the steep street to the waiting bus in the square.

❑

9

'Wine is not made like that anymore,' the man behind the bar at *Il-Hanut* said with a smile that would have appeared condescending if Gregory did not know better. 'These days they make wine according to European norms. You should see the wineries of Delicata and Marsovin! They have laboratories on the premises, large stainless steel vats – you should see them!' The barman was as proud as if they belonged to him.

Gregory persisted. His research so far resulted in much of what he needed being illustrated to him by locals. 'But surely small winemakers exist. Surely in the villages ... they must do something with all the grapevines I have seen.'

'Malta grows good grapes, sir. Our soil is the best. Have you seen the colour of our soil?' Once more, the man sounded as if he was the owner of all he spoke about. His pride was amusing, but very real. 'Red. Red like blood. It contains iron and everything. Grapes that grow here are small but sweet. Good. Of course, the harvest is small. So each year we import some to add to what we already have. But the main taste, sir, the main flavour, is Maltese. From the Maltese grape. *L- ghenba maltija.*' He pulled a bottle from underneath the counter, showing its label, by now totally familiar to Gregory, and poured a small tumbler with a flourish.

'But you are right, of course,' the man continued. 'In the villages, they make their own wine. Take Toni, my brother-in-law. He makes such wine! All a secret recipe. A secret, ah – what do you call it? Formula! A formula not even his own wife – my sister! – he does not trust to tell. He always omits to tell her the vital ingredient, or the correct order! So I will never know. My nephews will one day have the secret of this wonderful wine.'

'And what about the Mifsud wine?'

The barman was silent for a while. He appeared to be

making up his mind about something. 'That too was wine.' But he lost his enthusiasm. Words stopped pouring from him, and he stopped pouring wine into the two tumblers he was refilling with such fervour. He took a sip from his own glass, appearing to be experiencing some sort of mental struggle.

There was only the Australian in the shop. It was a hot and sultry afternoon. What was the harm in indulging in a little gossip, after all? Who would know? His thin face seemed to telegraph his feelings as they surfaced, and Gregory knew he would learn more the instant the man made the decision.

'Nikol Mifsud was as old as my father, but he made better wine than anyone here. Better than anyone in Rabat, too. *Isma* – listen, better than Toni my brother-in-law. But he had an impossible wife. How can you do anything with a woman like that? She wasn't like other village women. She heard voices, you know.' These last words were said softly, the man leaning closely over the breadth of the counter to half-whisper them to Gregory, while he waggled a finger at his temple.

He looked apologetic, but continued. 'I was a child at the time. Just a dumb kid, as you say.' The colloquialism left his lips in a smile. 'I was a few classes behind Censinu. You know which Censinu I mean. He was a clever boy, that one. And his father made the best wine around. Still, they lived in an impossible situation. That woman ...'

Gregory pulled his wallet out as the man spoke, placing a note on the counter. Automatically, while still speaking, the barman took it and counted out the exact change for the bottle of wine they were swiftly emptying between them.

'She screamed like a *mignuna*.' He nodded repentantly at the harsh word. 'Like a madwoman. But really, it seemed as if she was really demented. She quarrelled with all the women, and ran after her children with a broom. That Nikol, he was frightened of his own shadow. With a wife like that, what chance did he have at trying to eke out a living? People avoided them. I remember running an errand to their farmhouse once. In those days we called it *Tad-dielja*, which means of the grapevine. The house of the grapevines, you know.' He looked around him. 'Everyone seems to have forgotten that name. These days, we call it – *heq*, well, we call it the writer's house,' he invented quickly. 'Yes, we call it the writer's house! Anyway. I knocked on the door and hoped to see Censinu, to play in the lane for a while after I gave his father the empty jar someone sent.'

'A *bomblu*.'

The man smiled. 'You will soon learn Maltese at this rate, sir! Well, Censinu came out of the house, his eyes wide as if he had seen a ghost. He pushed me into the lane and I almost smashed the jar. From inside the house came a woman's screams and shouts and a lower voice, a male voice, telling her to be quiet, to leave the boy alone. I tell you, it still makes me shiver to remember those screams.'

Gregory nodded. He knew how unsettling it could be to hear wailing you could not identify. He reached for the bottle and poured the last of the wine into one of the tumblers.

The barman looked at the empty bottle. 'Now we open one on the house, sir. I am drinking more than you.'

The honesty made Gregory smile.

'But let me tell you ...' The barman now seemed taken with the story. His eyes were bright with wine and recollection. 'The stories that were heard outside that house, outside the church after early Mass in the morning ... they were something. I think people made a lot of it up, but they said that she heard voices, that the farmhouse was haunted and she used to have discourses with the spectre! I think word went round in that fashion because, if you were brave enough to walk down the lane at dead of night, when the street lamp was out – in those days there was only one – you could hear horrific screams coming from the house.'

'Was this ghost ever heard by anyone else?' Gregory was slowly putting the story together.

'Censinu would terrify all the kids at school with stories of a ghoul who walked in the loggia of his house, groaning and moaning and wringing the hem of a long dress. Sometimes a nun, sometimes a bride. Because his story changed we did not always believe him. But now I think they were just a boy's story. You know, fantasy.' The man laughed. 'Can I offer you a cigar, sir?'

'Thank you, but I don't smoke.'

'Not like Dr Micallef, eh? He smokes all right. Here we call him the brewery chimney! Oh – he doesn't know, of course.'

Just as I do not know the house I live in is called the house of the murdered boy, thought Gregory.

'Of course not. He is a pleasant man.' He did not want to enter into any gossip about the man who befriended him and entertained him in his own house.

'Poor Dr Micallef. He is a learned man.' The barman's expression was almost comical. He was relishing the gossip. 'He was a successful doctor in Sliema, you know. Then, something terrible happened – still, retirement has brought back his health.' Suddenly, the barman seemed to be spent on the subject.

Gregory felt a bit lightheaded. Was it lack of sleep or a surfeit of information? It was more probably the red wine, copious amounts of which he found himself drinking in the company of the loquacious barkeeper.

'He is not very welcome in Sliema now, you see,' the man finished.

The cryptic words sent Gregory into the hot street with more questions in his mind. What had Phineas Micallef done in Sliema to cause this unlikely exile? The blinding sunlight made his head pound, his eyes protesting by squeezing almost shut. He made his way to the steep street and the connecting lane, trying not to reel with the effects of talk and wine. After the visit to Rabat, Mdina and Ta' Qali, he had only meant to pay a very brief visit to the bar, perhaps to pick up a few bottles of beer to chill in his cavernous fridge, which always seemed half empty.

The barman's intriguing conversation kept him there over

an hour. It was only five or so, but his head swam and his legs seemed to hurry on, out of control. Before he knew how he had done it, Gregory was lying in his big iron bed, falling into a whirling deep sleep.

❑

Part Two

1

'If you tease your little brother again, I will lock you in the cellar!' Her voice is sharp, strident against the background hum of afternoon crickets. It is hot and humid. Censinu moves away from his toddler brother who is towing a small tin truck on a long piece of twine. The truck overturns but the toddler seems not to care.

'I was only going to turn his tru-'

'Leave him alone!' The scream rents the still air once more and Nikol Mifsud comes out into the sun. He is wearing an expression of patience, head tilted to one side as he regards his wife. She is becoming more and more edgy in her pregnancy, more and more prone to violent verbal attacks on him and the children, but especially on Censinu. The boy loses no opportunity to leave the house, so he runs all the errands, taking messages and running off on little escapades from which he returns later and later each time.

Nikol wonders whether he should scold the boy for his truancy, and berate him for his absence at such crucial busy times. There are moments when the child is sorely needed, especially now that the grapes have been crushed and fermentation is taking place.

School is on its yearly three-month summer recess. It is much too hot for anything, and a long time since Nikol has bundled his family into the battered van and driven down to Birzebbuga for a dip in the cool bay. It is ages since they did anything happy together.

'Shall we go to the sea?' The father is still wondering whether ignoring his young son's escapades encourages his naughtiness or allows him the breathing space and the respite he certainly needs from the wrath of his mother.

'The sea! Oh, yes. When shall we go?' The boy's bright eyes and enthusiasm are infectious.

Even Terezina looks up from the tomatoes she is laying out to dry in the sun. She picks up the toddler and bounces him on her hip. 'Let's *go tomorrow,'* she says. *'We'll get everything ready early and go to the bay in the van for the whole day.'*

Then her eyes cloud, her head spins. 'Keep away from the front rooms!' she yells suddenly at Censinu. 'I've just washed the floors!' Putting the baby down angrily, she follows her son into the kitchen and through to the hallway, where the flagstones are still damp from her washing. She grabs something from the kitchen table on the way.

Nikol thinks it is an enamel ladle. 'Let the boy go. He's done no harm.'

'Let the boy go! Leave him alone!' she mimics like one demented. 'That's all you ever say. I'll show him. After all my work. Down on my knees, washing floors!' She throws what is in her clenched fist at Censinu, who starts to edge his way back into the kitchen, picking his way from dry patch to dry patch on the floor.

His yell as the object hits him is dark and low, unlike his mother's shrill scream. 'Ajma! Ajma! You hit me!' His voice breaks into a cry.

With his left hand over his right elbow, from where a thin bright stream of blood already starts to trickle, Censinu runs past his mother and out into the yard. Somehow, he manages to scramble over the low rubble wall, leaving bright red blotches and smudged stains behind him.

Nikol's mouth hangs open in disbelief. He wants to grab his wife, shake her. What have you done? he wants to shout. But he is immobile with shock. He sees the sharp curved knife where it fell. But words cannot leave his mouth. His chest pounds, and he knows in his anger to leave Terezina alone and try to pursue his son.

Still, he can hardly move. He looks at the limestone boulder that makes up part of the wall over which his son scrambled like a maddened frightened animal. Already drying, already darkening, splatters of blood leave a trail that seem worse at the top of the wall. He should be able to follow Censinu with no difficulty at all.

◼

2

The letter from Emma made a clattering noise as it fell into the letterbox on Gregory's front door. It was a welcome respite from the eternal writing that seemed to have him in its thrall.

Since he started a week ago after Patricia's visit, he spent almost every available minute fixed to the chair in front of the computer. A decidedly uncomfortable wooden chair it was, with an unrelenting seat. A pillow taken from his bed did little to improve his comfort, so Gregory riffled through the section at the back of the telephone directory one afternoon at the police station, looking for a place that supplied office furniture.

The calls and arrangements that finally led to a decision about delivery of a padded swivel chair took a long time and turned out to be more complicated than the transaction warranted, but he knew he could look forward to days and nights – especially nights – of writing in comparative comfort. He would have plenty to tell his daughter when he wrote a reply to the yet unopened letter on his kitchen table.

He made a pot of tea, something he had promised himself all day. The letter was just the occasion to enjoy a pot of tea. He read the letter slowly, savouring the phrasing, the way his daughter turned sentences. Ways with words he had not forgotten, but which seemed almost foreign after these weeks of listening to heavily accented English.

She wrote of Melbourne in the depths of winter. Gregory almost longed to be there, but caught himself in the thought. He never really liked Melbourne, nor the episodes he had there with Maggie. What was this feeling that rose so unexpectedly about a city he always compared unfavourably with Perth? He was homesick. But it was Perth he really missed. The smooth manageable traffic, the slow pace. Even compared to Malta, an island he thought would be laid-back and slow compared to a big city, Perth now seemed infinitely lethargic and yielding. It was easy in Perth to feel in charge, to feel as if one's days were entirely under control.

There were times he had sat on the beach in winter, watching the surf, trying to glimpse Rottnest on the horizon, thinking of the past. Thinking of when he used to watch his little daughter play in the sand, dressed against sharp winds off the ocean in a red plastic raincoat and tiny boots. He took her to little parks where a black sling swing made from a car tyre would keep her happily swaying to and fro until she fell asleep. This same daughter who now, almost a stranger, wrote to him in complicated sentences of Melbourne, a city he no longer remembered properly.

She wrote of being in Brighton with her mother, at a little restaurant in Bay Street 'where Mum persistently confuses the waiter about the menu,' she wrote. Yes, Maggie had always been good at confusing young men.

He read of his daughter's studies, her sport activities and her writing, which Maggie did not altogether encourage. He grinned at Maggie's annoyance about their daughter's love of writing. How dare Emma take after him?

He read the letter twice, stopping often to compare his daughter's descriptions of places in Melbourne with comparable ones in Perth. He thought of Perth, how it changed in his absence and still more while he lived there, the reflection of city buildings in the stretch of water before it, changing from month to month. He thought of sailing boats inching white sails across that very stretch of water, Melville Water, the spread in the Swan River whose bridges and shores were so familiar he could name them to visitors from a perch at King's Park that overlooked the whole scene.

If only his daughter were writing from Perth instead of Melbourne, he thought. Then she would be mentioning the same places he left only a few weeks ago, when rain poured over the city and its sprawling suburbs, diluting the colours, streaking with rain and wind all scenes and places through which he drove daily in his battered old Ford. If only she would write to him of City Beach, of Fremantle Harbour.

Fremantle – he had thought of the port town frequently since he had been in Malta. Come to think of it, there were a couple of small similarities to Fremantle he found here. In Birzebbuga, perhaps, or some of the interiors of the old office buildings in Valletta.

If only she wrote of the national parks he loved to walk in – the dense bush with its scent of eucalyptus, its towering trees, its birdcalls and distinct seasonal changes. If only she wrote of the endless stretch of beach, the thundering surf, the packed wet sand and flights of seagulls, the solitary flight of a cormorant skimming the waves.

Gregory reined himself in, feeling he had been in Malta for too short a time to start getting homesick for Western Australia. He thought of his words, imprisoned as they were inside his computer. It would be a while before he had enough words down to warrant printing a first draft. It would be ages still before he could even consider leaving.

The kitchen was darkening. The black letters of Emma's crowded letter on acid green paper were disappearing in the twilight. Soon he would have to send a reply. She seemed voraciously curious, eager to receive words from him, sending quick replies on pages and pages of cheap repro paper, printed in such haste. Her omission of Perth was of course total – it simply was not where she was living – and that was what he mainly wanted to hear, apart from his natural interest in her activities and personal expressions.

Strangely, this last letter lacked what some others made him feel. It lacked any disclosure about her private feelings. Sometimes she would put in hopes and dissatisfactions, or put in a diatribe of emotion about some transpiring in her life. This one felt less private, less intimate, than her other letters. He had a sudden feeling of dismay as an image he conjured mentally took form. Maggie, her earrings swinging dramatically, leaning over Emma's shoulder as she wrote, breathing close to their daughter's ear.

'Writing to him, are you? I'm surprised he answers. I'm surprised he stops from whatever horror he is writing at the moment to send sickly sweet regards and salutations!' But of course it was only his imagination.

He should not continue to cast Maggie in the role of the domineering mother. He knew his wife and daughter got on well enough. The girl was doing well in Melbourne, enjoying life at high school and writing of her achievements with more than a modicum of pleasure. Of course she was happy. She sent photographs – which was all he had seen of her for some time. How long was it now?

He remembered a slight freckled child waving vaguely at a rainy airport. He hated to think how long ago it was. It had been easy to comply with Maggie's wishes. 'Stay away, Greg. Don't bother. All we will do is fight anyway. Save your money.'

So he stayed away. There was not much money to start with, the bulk of which he would send to her for Emma's sake and welfare. When his royalties began approaching the reasonable sums Cross & Ormondsey promised all those years ago, his cheques to Maggie grew accordingly. Still, he would get the occasional telephone call demanding more.

'Don't think that just because I'm interstate I don't know how much your books sell,' she said once. 'I speak to Paul De Souza too, you know.'

Whether it was true or not, he never bothered to find out. Although she had no business talking to his publishers, there was really nothing to hide.

Gregory looked at his watch in the gathering gloom. He would not turn on any lights for now, to avoid attracting mosquitoes. He walked in the dark to the archway, whose gates now always hung open. He had removed the length of chain and brass padlock. To his right, the steps to the cellar were invisible, failing light making the whole area, including the sunken yard outside the cellar door, appear as one pool of darkness.

The writer slapped his forehead. 'Damn! I totally forgot to pick up that key! Whatever must Franz think? After all my urgency. Oh – for heaven's sake! And I've waited so long for that key.' He scolded himself soundly in a loud voice, noticing he was talking to himself again. Now he would have to wait until the morning.

In the morning, he would phone Patricia at her office, pick the key up at Franz's, buy some bay leaves and a bottle of cheap red wine, and make a spaghetti sauce, to surprise the young woman who had occupied his mind whenever he thought back to the evening they spent together. But first, he had his daughter's letter to answer. The morning dawned grey and overcast, twittering of small birds accompanying Gregory's shamble to the kitchen in search of coffee.

He looked through the loggia window at the sky, not fooled for a minute by what looked like rain. The day would prove to be just as hot and dusty as preceding ones. Why had he stayed up writing so late? The letter to Emma had taken an hour or so, but his scribbling and casting of drafts took much longer. His head was filled now with clay jars, the sharp reflected sunlight on the blade of a knife. And some other flash.

Oh, yes. He waited for the kettle to boil while he remembered a flash at his bedroom window in the night. As he prepared for bed, he heard the low hum of a powerful car and saw the retreating glow of its red taillights soften and disappear on the window frame. Who was up so late in the village? He remembered shaking his head and thinking it had nothing to do with him, and the feeling someone was watching the house was simply a late-night figment of his imagination.

He took his mug of hot coffee out through the double glass doors into the yard and drank it quickly, listening to water running in the bathroom, a few metres behind his back. He found the small gas instantaneous water heater in there familiar, almost identical to one in a flat he had in Perth. It looked threatening, as if it would blow up any minute, but he knew heaters of that nature. They may leak gas a little, may resist tampering and tinkering, but worked forever. The thought of a warm bath before a gruelling hot day, the thought of collecting the key, and calling Patricia on the police station telephone filled him with anticipation – it was going to be quite a day.

After the bath, another slow cup of coffee took him out into his garden under the arched gateway. There, a long-forgotten reek hit his nostrils. Sewage. Gregory looked around him, hoping wildly that the smell blew over the rubble wall from some distant house, that it would dissipate by the time Patricia came to the house. But no – looking down into the sunken area outside the cellar door, he saw a dismaying grey pool of water, scummy and smelly; obviously the contents of his own bath, the kitchen sink – and more. It was still rising, the cellar door submerged for over half a metre in the scungy liquid.

'Oh *no*! What is going on? Not today!' He yelled at the water, as if it could hear, panicking about how he could possibly solve this problem.

In minutes, he was at Franz the ironmonger's. The small shop, crammed as it was with spools of wire, boxes of nails and sacks of lime and cement, was deserted but for Monsinjur Dimech. Was he always at the ironmonger's?

Gregory must have uttered the question aloud, because the priest beamed and answered it. 'I am always here, especially when it is nearing festa time, Mr Worthington, especially when we are rigging up for celebrations!' He gurgled with enthusiasm. 'This is the essence of the Mediterranean – we are southern people, Europeans, passionate and full of fire. We ...' But the priest was interrupted.

Franz, a burly old retainer with a totally bald head and muscled shoulders, tattoos exposed by a brilliant white singlet, smiled a welcome. 'I 'ave that key all ready f'yew.' His English was redolent of days in the Royal Navy. It bristled with nautical jargon and broken phrasing of comical remnants from wartime days. 'In't that wha' yew after, mate?'

'No,' muttered Gregory. How was he going to define his needs delicately? 'I mean *yes*! Thank you! But I have a more urgent chore to attend to. I ... um – my yard is full of foul water. I think I need ...'

The priest and the ironmonger sang out together. 'A drainage plumber! Blockage! Sewage!' Both of them beamed smiles at Gregory, as if at last he had entered some fraternity of which he was hitherto utterly ignorant.

'Hey, Boy!' the priest and the ironmonger shouted past him almost simultaneously, using the same phrases and the same words, sometimes in different order. 'Where's the little Camilleri boy? Hey! You!'

A tiny head rounded the entrance to the shop and listened. 'Hey! Boy! Fetch Rigoletto, you hear? Go get the man for the Australian. Now! Go!'

'Rigoletto? Like in the opera?' The writer could not believe his ears.

'You are a cultured man, Mr Worthington,' the parish priest said, hands deep in soutane pockets. 'Yes. Rigoletto is the traditional nickname for drainage plumbers everywhere.' He seemed to include the whole world.

Gregory was too full of trepidation to laugh. While they waited for the plumber's appearance, talk turned to the key.

'Here it is.' Franz was weighing a huge key in one palm. 'When yew gave me de drawin', I knew the kind you wann'ed. Dead cert, mate. Full steam ahead.' He handed over the black iron key, about twenty centimetres in length.

'You *drew* what you wanted?' The priest was intrigued.

'I traced the escutcheon on the door, and the shape of the keyhole.'

'Y'see,' the ironmonger explained in English for Gregory's sake, lifting his eyebrows often at the priest as if to say, you see,

I too can converse with ease with foreigners in the language acquired on my travels. 'That ruddy 'ole, the shape an' all. Only two maybe three types of dat kind of openin' anyways. I figured on S-shape, y'see. Prob'ly right, too. S-shape. All engines full!'

Gregory found it hard now to keep a straight face, so dug a hand in his pocket for his wallet.

'First try it, matey. Test the water, so to speak! *Then* y'settle, okay?' Franz's grip of vernacular seemed to give him a level of familiarity with the Australian, as if he felt they were more able to communicate because of the term *mate*, excluding the priest.

There was a bustle at the shop entrance and there appeared Rigoletto, complete with his bundle of canes and attachments.

'You must attend to your problem, I suppose,' the parish priest said benignly, his smile seeming to confer a blessing on what was going to be an education for the foreigner.

Together, the plumber and his bundle and the writer in his white hat descended the steep street and into the lane. If he could only have seen himself as half of that unlikely pair, Gregory would have laughed, but he was not in a humorous mood.

At his front door, the little man spoke for the first time. 'You know where the *spuk-shin*?'

For a minute Gregory looked blankly at him. Then he remembered encountering the word before. 'The inspection cavity! Of course. I think we are standing on it.' Looking at their feet, the men regarded the large limestone rectangle, which looked like it had not been raised for decades.

'Dis not so good,' Rigoletto said ominously. But he put his weight on one knee and used a long metal spike to lever the slab.

Gregory thought he might leave him to it.

'Wait please!' the plumber said smartly. 'Must be another *spuk-shin* inside.' The slab slid to one side, the grating noise of stone upon stone filling the lane. A small crowd of fascinated boys gathered, looking down with Gregory onto a complicated junction of brown glazed clay pipes covered in dust and other debris.

Leaving the exposed pipes behind them, the Australian, with Rigoletto at his heels, walked through the house and emerged in the garden.

'Ohhh. Oohhh. *Il-lahwa!*' The old man's voice was full of dread. The wrinkled face was impassive. He was looking at the pool of stinking water in the sunken yard. 'Oh, *brother*.'

'Bad?'

'Not good.' He smiled at Gregory's wrinkled nose. 'But not a disaster. All over by lunch.'

'I hope so.'

'Not to worry. I work. I work fast. My time start now.' His finger pointing upward in exclamation, the little plumber sped away to his sticks and plungers.

It was a good time for Gregory to disappear. His final look at the semi-submerged door gave him little hope of a pleasant afternoon exploring the cellar. No wonder the door was wedged closed. This episode must have happened before, expanding the bottom of the wooden door until it could no longer be opened. He hated to think what he would find inside.

At the police station, the constable beamed a welcome. 'So you have trouble with the pipes.' He said it victoriously, as if the writer had now joined the village population, as if some kind of rite of passage was achieved.

Patricia's voice on the other end was warm. Gregory felt a kind of relief he had not felt in years.

'Everything is upside down here today,' he said to warn her. 'I've had a plumbing problem. And it's not over yet.'

'Oh dear,' she laughed.

'I don't know whether to postpone the whole thing. I have no idea how long it will all take.' He found himself making desperate hand gestures although she could not see him.

The policeman watched him, amused.

'It sounds like you need company and reassurance more than ever,' she said, to his surprise. 'Don't postpone a thing. I'll be there after work in the late afternoon and we can see how it all goes.'

Gregory could hardly believe she would be willing to confront the scene happening at his house at that moment.

'What's happened has stopped everything else, I'm afraid.'

'We may still have some fun at the end of it all,' she said.

Gregory laid his ten-cent coin on the counter and smiled at the policeman.

'You look like a happy man, sir,' he said, not attempting to disguise his amusement.

'Mixed blessings, today,' muttered Gregory.

'That's life, sir.'

The writer almost ran down the sloping street into his lane. The knot of little boys had disappeared and the slab was replaced. On top of it, to his exasperation, stood the thin woman he recognised as Lieni, Katie's mother. How was he to deal with her on top of it all?

'I sent the nosy boys off,' she announced, in charge already. 'They went in a hurry!'

'I'm sure they did. How are you?' The salutation left Gregory's mouth awkwardly.

But the woman smiled wryly, taking the solicitation literally. 'I am always in pain, but I am used to it. The villagers will tell you, Lieni is always in pain with the sciatica but she puts on a brave face.'

Gregory did not know how to deal with the revelation.

Lieni stood her ground with a stoic smile, so he imitated it.

'Katie did a good job?' asked the woman.

He could hardly remember what his impression of the young girl's cleaning had been. He only recalled her fine eyes and tiny figure.

'She could not find your dirty washing to take away,' accused Lieni.

'I – um. There was none. It – yes, the housework was fine.'

'So you owe her two pounds.'

The small amount was more than reasonable. Gregory dipped his hand for the wallet.

'Not to me,' muttered the woman, getting impatient with his lack of common sense. 'To her. She will come again Friday. Please leave the key. And put the washing where she can find it.' Her precise instructions and language left him standing on his own threshold, dumbfounded.

At the back, he was assaulted by the fierce smell of potent disinfectant. The small plumber was sweeping water vigorously down a drainage grid in the sunken area. His little arms pumped as he swept.

'Orright now! *Ghall-erwieh!* For the souls in purgatory!'

'What was wrong?' asked the writer, deciding not to question the connection between sewage and the hereafter.

'Everything!' The small man blinked up from the yard, broom in hand and feet in water clouded and milky with the addition of disinfectant. Its pine aroma was so strong Gregory had to gasp and exhale quickly.

'Cage was blocked.' He pointed at the little grid, which the writer had never seen before. It must have been totally choked with dust and debris and he had walked right over it.

'Main sewage pipe blocked. Connection junction blocked. Terrible!'

'It didn't take you long.'

He looked at Gregory with a mild smile. '*Mela!* Of course! Because I know what to do. All clear now, orright?' His cheerful question was a rhetorical blessing. He flooded the whole area with litres and litres of fresh water. A small hose was connected to the yard tap: it flowed slowly. The man swept again, in vigorous motions that showed a kind of latent aggression.

'How did you fix that?' Gregory asked, pointing to the tap. 'It wouldn't work at all.'

'I tell you my secrets, you take my job!' the plumber joked.

He laughed at the comic expression on Gregory's face, who could not in a hundred years imagine himself even thinking of taking on such a demanding messy occupation.

The plumber climbed the steps, turned off the tap and started rolling down trouser-legs, which were hitched to the knees. 'Four pounds, please. My time stop now.'

It was the happiest payment Gregory had made for some time. There was no trace of the disaster except a strong clean pine smell. 'You certainly cleaned up well.'

The man's eyes twinkled. What did the Australian expect? The sky cleared and strong sunlight bathed the area they stood in. There was a sudden loud explosion overhead.

'My God! What was that?' Gregory fully expected another disaster. His gas line?

'Hah! *Luqa. Sant' Andrija.*'

'Who?'

'The festa at Luqa. Two parishes that way. Fireworks, sir. Very loud, very long.'

As if to confirm what he said, the air was rent by a series of loud bangs. Several puffs of smoke appeared in the sky, high over the vineyard, drifting slowly over them.

'They sound like bombs!' The writer was thinking aloud again.

'Exactly. Petards. Loud bombs. They think they the best. Huh!'

'How long does this go on?'

'All the festa. You wait.' With that, Rigoletto turned on his heels and with bundle on back, walked through the house and away.

'And I thought I was going to have a peaceful drink after all that.' Talking to himself, Gregory poured a cold beer and sat in his kitchen, listening to the explosions going on at what seemed like a few metres over the top of his house. It was a frightful racket. He could hardly hear the words he said to himself.

'If there were anybody else here,' he yelled, 'we couldn't

hear each other!' And then, in a normal voice, 'My god, I'm going mad.' He burst into a small laugh and finished his beer in one draught.

'Well,' said Patricia later, 'he was right. This is the sound of Malta in summer, Gregory. You'll get used to it very quickly.'

The writer looked at her and smiled sorrowfully, comically.

She looked fresh in her jeans and T-shirt, small white sandals on brown feet. He did not think he would get used to the noise at all. Their conversation was punctuated with loud bangs since she arrived, herself almost unaware of the explosions going on all around them.

'Luqa is one of the most competitive parishes, it seems. It's their village feast this weekend. There are several parish festas every weekend, all through summer. Wait until your village has its own. I can see the decorations are already going up.'

'Yes. Monsinjur Dimech is at the hardware store almost every day. He buys wire, screws and nails, light globes ...'

'It will look very nice. You should take photos. A village festa is quite something. You'll be impressed.'

'I'm sure I will. The noise alone is terrific!'

Patricia laughed. She drew close to Gregory and he slipped his arms around her. Quick to respond, he found her warm and genuinely affectionate. The kitchen was cool, and so was the lounge. They sat and talked for a while, mainly about Patricia's life and work, her family and friends. It was not long before he found her slipping into an explanation of her situation.

'I was dating the second son of one of my father's colleagues,' she said, looking up and into Gregory's eyes candidly, 'and it lasted for quite some time. Then it was expected we would get engaged. But I was afraid it wouldn't have worked at all. That's how I felt. So I broke it off ... a few months ago.'

'It explains why someone so beautiful was unattached when I happened on the scene.'

She laughed. 'Beautiful! I have no illusions about the way I look. What about this nose? My father calls it a patrician nose. Maybe that's how I got my name!'

The writer was taken by her ways, but the intermittent explosions made it impossible for him to have an intimate conversation.

'Look, let's get out of here,' she said suddenly, sensing his discomfort. 'You jump every time a petard goes. Let's drive to the coast and get you some sightseeing.'

'But what about the cellar?' Gregory wanted to explore.

'The cellar.' She grimaced, as if thinking hard. She had seen the key, which was now on the kitchen table. Its weight and potential almost made her change her mind. 'In the morning. Definitely in the morning.' She picked up her bag and led the way to her car.

In the morning? Gregory was mentally, and not without a little prickle of excitement, trying to figure out what she meant. Would she drive back in the morning, or was she intending to spend the night? But no – he had already been made clear about her parents' expectations and she could hardly explain away a whole night.

In the car, they spoke about differences and similarities between Malta and Australia, joking most of the time. She seemed to have a comprehensive knowledge of a scattered collection of subjects, ranging from the comparison of languages and customs to difficulties experienced by emigrants and entry laws of a number of countries.

'It's what we get in the papers, so I suppose it's mostly common knowledge.' She told him of the island's colleges and university, how she had spent two years in junior college. She spoke in a voice that weakened often, falling into husky tones as she prattled on.

'But flying was much more fun,' she concluded.

As they drew away from the noise, their conversation became calmer and more intimate.

'There are so many things I'd like to explain about myself it's hard to know where to start,' she said, to Gregory's surprise. 'For example, in spite of rites and rituals and all the evident Catholicism around us, this is quite an open, earnest place.' She spread her hands in explanation, apparently lost for words. 'Take my sister –'

'I didn't know you had a sister,' he joked, trying to keep the conversation light.

'Mm. There are a lot of things about *you* I don't know, either.'

Gregory smiled. This invitation to disclose personal details was less threatening than it could have been. 'I'm a pretty secretive man,' he joked.

Patricia smiled and looked away. 'Take my sister, for example.' she continued. 'She married quite late. They've only just had their first baby, and she will definitely go back to work next year. She's just over a couple of years older than I am and will be thirty-three soon. Life is pretty similar all over the world, I suppose, but don't let the village give you the impression that the whole island is the same.'

She went on to outline, in her breaking voice, what life was like for those who lived in the more crowded, more cosmopolitan parts of Malta, where tourists flocked, exerting their influences of change and tolerance on the population.

Sometimes, she took one hand from the wheel to settle her hair, which streamed and ruffled in the breeze from her open window.

He watched her animated talking which, linked to the way she drove, was infinitely amusing. Alarm was always at the back of his mind though, when she turned blind corners suddenly, hardly decreasing speed at all.

'Whew!' he breathed, after she turned at a hairpin bend onto a sudden steep ascent.

'I know that corner.'

'A lot of other drivers probably think the same, coming the

other way!'

'What is this, a driving lesson?' She was laughing.

Gregory submitted to being driven, relaxing into his seat. After all, he had never driven on the island and wondered whether he could cope with such erratic casual observance of road rules. They reached a solitary spot in a region whose altitude he felt was greater than that of the village. He was right. Soon, he glimpsed the silver sheen of the sea over the top of a rise and the sudden falling away of land. They were on top of some cliffs, heading on a winding narrow road bounded by rubble walls almost exactly like those that flanked his house.

Clumps of cactus similar to what grew at the end of his lane formed hedges in places.

'Prickly pears!' Patricia extended a hand from the window.

'I know, we have them in Australia. Nearly took over entire states. But they got rid of it. With a moth. You still see the odd clump in gardens around Fremantle.'

'A moth?' She thought he was joking.

'Yes. The grubs of a certain moth that eats only cactus, apparently. Did the job.'

'It's not a problem here – we love the fruit.'

Their way led mainly downhill, but an occasional rise took them to a wide clearing where Patricia parked outside a lone shop.

'Here we are! Hagar Qim and Mnajdra temples,' she said.

Gregory was not prepared for the fascinating tour she had planned for him. They walked hand in hand to a fenced area, which contained a host of monolithic temples. The great stones, called dolmens, seemed to have been erected by giants.

Clearings contained by the massive erect boulders were paved in gigantic slabs. Sunlight slanted across the monoliths, throwing dramatic shadows across the ground. They saw oracle holes and altars, low doorways and threshold slabs speckled and pocked with designs made of tiny indentures and holes.

'This is fantastic!' Gregory roamed around, taking mental

notes. There had to be a good travel article in this.

'I knew you'd like it here,' Patricia said calmly.

They walked downhill for about a kilometre, the cliffs falling away to their left. The sea glimmered, deceptively still from this distance.

'What's that?' Gregory pointed. 'I can't see for the glare.'

What looked like a sleek black car was nestled behind some prickly pear bushes, but he could not be sure.

But Patricia thought he was pointing out to sea. 'That's Filfla, an uninhabited island. It looks like a hat, doesn't it?'

Sheer cliffs rose from the sea, he could now make out. It would be impossible to land there from a boat.

'It's not only impossible, but illegal, to land there,' said Patricia. 'It's a bird sanctuary now. It used to be a practice target for training ships and the Fleet Air Arm when the British navy was stationed here. It's been bombarded and torpedoed and heaven knows what else.'

Gregory shaded his eyes. He looked at the spot where he thought he had seen a car. It was empty now. He wondered if his eyes had tricked him. Had he seen someone there? Someone watching him? He dismissed the thought and tried to get a better view of what seemed like a minuscule island. He thought of Rottnest Island, off Perth.

'It is larger than it looks. And very far out.'

At the lower temples, which were unfenced, his fascination for the huge monolithic structures returned. The layout of this set of buildings was very unusual.

'Each opening or room is in the shape of a gigantic footprint, can you see?' she shouted from one end of an opening. The writer had not noticed the fact, and only after careful examination did he appreciate the ground plan. Curved wall after curved wall, they made a complete tour of the temples, marvelling again at the size of the slabs and boulders.

'How did they bring these massive stones here?'

'Who knows? There are a few theories as to who built the

temples, when and for what reason. They are so old – they predate the pyramids in Egypt by some centuries – no one can be absolutely sure.'

They bought a booklet at the shop and Gregory pored over it on the way back.

'I must warn you the noise will be much worse tonight,' said Patricia, her voice weakening on the last word, making it sound deliciously promising. 'The fireworks will go on until about eleven. But that won't be so bad, will it?'

'We'll go to Zija Roza's again. Or to some restaurant further away.'

'Fine,' she accepted. 'But we'll still have to return to the house at some point.'

Gregory regarded her closely. He reached across from the passenger seat and kissed her softly on the cheek. 'We shall certainly return to the house at some point,' he repeated meaningfully.

They laughed together.

Much later, at the farmhouse, it was cool and quiet except for the occasional loud bang overhead. A strong smell of pine disinfectant still permeated the house. Gregory made a pot of tea. 'We'll go out and eat after I've changed. I've heard from my daughter this week,' he said, making the words sound casual, as if he had not been organising them in his head all afternoon. 'I must tell you what she said about Melbourne.'

'I didn't know you had a daughter,' she said, in a tone that mimicked the one he used when she mentioned her sister. They sat in the lounge and he told her about Emma, about Maggie and his failed marriage.

Patricia listened, nodding when he paused, but said little. 'So technically, I suppose, although we have been separated for over seven years, I am still a married man.' He waited to see how this affected her, wondering, not for the first time, why he had never bothered to formalise his separation with a divorce.

Her face was impassive. 'Does it all still hurt?'

'Oh no –' He shook his head emphatically. 'I've passed the stage where I'd become emotional or angry at every second step. It's been years since the separation. Emma was a little girl. She is now seventeen. We just have not got down to the paperwork, that's all.'

She stood and walked to the window recess, her back to him. 'Under normal circumstances ...' she started, paused, and then continued, '... it would be foolish to get involved with a married man.' She turned and looked at him. 'Oh yes, it happens quite often in Malta, too, you know.'

Gregory felt it was necessary for her to say certain things, so kept silent. He sensed she was not about to launch into any sort of involvement with him without making both their positions clear. It was at once exciting and threatening. Not for her a light-hearted fling. Looking at her in this way, Gregory felt the initial stirring of an emotion he had not felt for some time. What it was he would not admit. That it scared him was not what he wanted to concede, not at that moment.

'But these are unusual circumstances,' she continued. She did not say why. Her smile was all he needed. In two quick but slightly hesitant paces he was at her side and she was engulfed in his embrace. The kiss was reminiscent of their first one in the hallway, days ago. But it was at the same time new. There was nothing virginal or restrained about her response. They kissed and embraced with all the passion that had been latent between them all afternoon.

She whispered small things hoarsely, things he could not altogether make out, but she seemed lost in their caresses, in the urgency they aroused in each other. He started to talk too, unsure about how to pause without signifying displeasure in the intimate interlude. What he did not want to do was scare her off by being too ardent.

'Let's go out and eat. We can come back later.' Then he stopped. 'Will you have time to come back later?'

As she raised her arms to tidy her tousled hair she smiled. 'I have made arrangements. My parents will not worry about me tonight. I'm free as a bird!'

Gregory raised an eyebrow. His broad smile required no more explanation from her. She was sure to tell him all later.

'Really?'

'Really. Let's go.'

They drove to Rabat, where they ate a meal of rabbit marinated in wine. It was probably the most delicious way Gregory ever had rabbit, but he was not concentrating on cuisine that night. They talked animatedly, tumbling over the ends of each other's sentences. The excitement was electric and neither of them finished their meal.

On the winding drive back to the farmhouse they fell into a companionable silence. Some kilometres away on the approach to the village, they heard the full impact of the Luqa celebratory fireworks.

'Good heavens, is this how it will be all night?' The writer popped his head out of the car window. The sky some distance away was full of coloured sparks and smoke.

'No, this is one of the long volleys. It means the statue is re-entering the church.'

'There was a procession?'

'Look – you'll soon have your own village festa. And in August, if you like, we'll go to the *Santa Marija* festa in Gozo. Then you'll see a large scale Maltese festa in full swing. It's quite something.'

The bangs accompanied them to the door, then lessened to an occasional loud salvo. He was becoming partly accustomed to being startled to a jump every few minutes. Hours later, Gregory could not remember how they got to the big iron bed in the front room. Pushed as it was underneath the window, it exposed them to the full brunt of the fireworks' noise, but by that stage he was totally oblivious to the bangs. Or was he? Forever after, Gregory thought, as he stood at the door in the corridor, the festive explosion of fireworks would arouse in him the quick erotic sensation he felt that evening.

They had tumbled fully clothed onto the made bed, kissing deeply. By the same lapse of time and memory, how they got out of their clothes and under the sheets was lost now to Gregory. He may remember one day, after this first rush of excitement cooled. He remembered only the sensation of her warm tense body against his and the way her hands fluttered over his skin. She was at once compliant and explorative, bringing new feelings to his body. It was not surprising, as it was some time since he had been with a woman. What was revelatory to him that night, even before their lovemaking ended and Patricia drifted off to sleep, was the awareness of involvement, the tender certainty of relating to her in more than just a superficial or physical way.

In spite of efforts to chase the thought away, Gregory remained entranced. 'Come on, man – this is not the first and only casual encounter you've had.' He mumbled to himself as he dusted a hand past his face, as if to dispel any entrapping tendrils she may have woven around him. But he knew it was not a casual feeling.

He watched her sleeping form from where he stood at the door and felt again the passion, the wild desire he experienced and satisfied so completely. He felt again her breasts, the soft skin stretched over her hip bones under his hands, the straight series of knobs her spine made down her back. He re-experienced the flush of excitement as he recalled the quick movement of her body against his, the urgency she neither imitated nor faked. And her soft hoarse voice.

He longed to wake her, to lie again beside her and hold her as before in his arms, but he slid softly under the sheets on the side of the bed furthest from the window and lay on his back, staring at the ceiling, which was becoming gradually lighter. He realised he had not noticed when the fireworks stopped.

Crickets were already humming when Patricia walked into the

kitchen in the morning. She wore a large T-shirt that fell to mid-thigh, and her feet were bare.

'What time is it? Have you been awake long?'

Gregory smiled and turned from what he was doing at the sound of her voice, which was much more hoarse in the morning. She looked lovely half asleep, thick hair tousled and eyes half-shut against the bright light falling across the table.

'Well, I never thought I'd be doing this,' he said in a teasing tone. 'But I got up with the lark and ran up to the bakery for some fresh rolls for breakfast.'

'How sweet. How wonderful – I'm ravenous. But I don't think we have any larks in Malta!'

He turned away, mumbling words over his shoulder. 'Neither of us had much to eat last night.'

'Last night ...' she repeated.

A thrill of pleasure held him, making him look at her again. She sat and was pouring coffee slowly. A soft smile lit up her face. She was fully awake now.

Breakfast was full of the euphoria of the night and the promise of the day's exploration of the cellar. The key lay between them on the table, where crumbs from the small crusty loaves had fallen.

'I wonder where your ironmonger got this key. They are pretty rare these days. He must have asked scrap merchants. Perhaps in Marsa.'

'I really don't know. But if it works –' Leaving the table uncleared, Gregory and Patricia emerged from the kitchen into the bright yard. The day was already hot. She clutched the key, stepping gingerly in bare feet.

'Hop inside quickly for your sandals,' he told her. 'We have to walk through a bit of the garden first.'

She returned breathless, still holding the key. There were sounds from the hen run. Together, they walked underneath the archway into the vineyard, where Patricia had never been before.

'It's quite a big place. I can hear your fowls. You have turkeys!'

Gregory pointed the way down the worn steps and when they were in front of the peeling door, she gave him the key. The sunken area still smelled strongly of disinfectant, but the whole place was totally dry, as if yesterday's mishap had never happened.

'Let's see now,' he said.

Sunday church bells rang in the distance. The silence was broken by yapping from a neighbouring dog and one stray bang from the parish of Luqa.

Gregory would remember the time just before he opened the cellar door later, and recall Patricia's eager face, just like a child's. The key entered the hole easily, turned after a while when Gregory wrested with it. Leaving it in the hole to serve as a handle, he pushed. But nothing happened.

'It's jammed. It's totally jammed,' he said, disappointed. 'The wood is waterlogged.' But he would not be defeated. Together they pushed, sensing a slight yielding after a while. Gregory put his shoulder against the wood as low down as he could. Patricia leaned close to him, her hair tangled, the effort bringing them as close together as they were the previous night. Their combined weight served the purpose. The door gave way with a loud screech, when splintered wood at the bottom gave away suddenly.

Patricia yelled when they were both thrown forward into dank darkness. Both managed to stay on their feet.

'Dark! Dark and large – look at all the space!' She walked slowly forward.

Gregory held her back. He wanted to absorb the sight of the newly opened cellar, to observe exactly how they found it. His mind sped along, 'writing'. The room was unlit except from the door they just opened. When their eyes adjusted to the darkness, they could see a long stone trough along the left wall, over which several metal rings in a line were attached to the wall. From where they stood, the trough seemed full of rubbish, of the debris and accumulations of years of neglect. On the right, the wall was blank except for a large semicircular window; a fanlight whose apex touched the ceiling. It was fitted with a wrought iron grating sectioned into ornate segments. It had at some time been boarded up on the outside.

Gregory knew he had not seen boards on the outside. They were buried, no doubt, by earth building up over the years in the section of the garden Gregory weeded recently. His eyes swept the walls, searching. Against the far wall, in the right hand corner, was a large stone swelling on the wall, corniced with a lip and topped by a large stone slab.

'There's the well!' he exclaimed, moving inwards toward the middle of the room. It was damp and slippery underfoot, smelling unpleasantly of drainage water and disinfectant. The earth floor had not yet absorbed all of what passed underneath the door from yesterday's flood. Gregory held Patricia's hand until they both stepped onto a dry portion of the floor. They could see the well clearly now, the remains of a wooden pulley resting on the stone lid, hanging from a frayed rope looped through a ring in the ceiling.

It was a large room, but totally empty. Gregory tried to temper his disappointment at its emptiness by talking about the rings over the trough. 'They obviously kept livestock in here at some stage,' he said, his voice hushed as if he spoke in church.

'If that window were cleared,' said Patricia, pointing at the large fanlight, 'it would be quite bright in here.'

Moving toward the end wall, they both came to a halt, turning and looking back at the half-open door that stood drunkenly on one hinge. The lower hinge had given way in the rotten wood when they pushed together.

'It will have to be repaired, I suppose,' said the writer.

'Gregory, there's another door.' Patricia's voice cracked on the last word and he hardly understood her, but she was pointing at the wall behind them, almost invisible in the shadows.

'Another door!' he exclaimed. It had a small iron handle to one side, with a keyhole underneath it. 'Perhaps ...' Gregory said quickly, and hurried over to the garden door, almost slipping in the muddy floor as he did so. He grabbed the key from the first door.

It fitted. The two locks had been obviously fitted together, for the same key.

'There would be no reason to have separate ones,' she said, quickly and breathlessly, excitement making her voice husky as they pushed the door together. But it did not budge.

'Outwards!' he breathed. They pulled on the metal handle and the door creaked dryly open. There was some quick furtive rustling from the interior, which told of vermin of some sort.

'Yuk. Mice?' Patricia took a step backwards.

'They won't hurt us.'

'They can hardly see us!' She was enjoying herself, but she wished she could see more.

He pushed the door back, leaving the key in the hole. 'Shall we go up for a torch? I have one in the kitchen but it's not very powerful.'

'It will do. Matches too,' she said.

'Candles. I have candles for the blackouts that never came.'

'They will in winter,' she giggled as they crossed the slippery part of the room and out again into the harsh sunlight that blinded them momentarily and sent them groggily up the stone steps.

'Another room! Imagine that. So the cellar does go quite a long way underneath the house.'

'It had to. I told you, from the sound our steps made in the loggia.' Her voice was excited and broke, making him remember her hoarse laughter when they paced out the corridor.

'Of course we've found the well, and I'm satisfied now,' he said. 'But there could be more. I'm sure there's more.'

Back in the first room of the cellar, armed with a small torch and pockets stuffed with candles and matches, they once more pulled back the second door. Again, furtive rustling and pattering made them look at each other with wry grimaces. Gregory shone the torch inside and gasped. He did not talk for a long time.

Then, with a new reluctance in his voice, he said, 'Have a look at this.' His excitement was not gone, but it was flattened by something else.

Patricia sensed nothing. She moved round the open door and looked where his torch shone. The room was much smaller than the first. It was divided into two sections by a thick wall about a metre and a half high. The two parts appeared to serve as stalls of some sort. A fanlight window identical to the one before was on the right wall, boarded up in a similar way. This one was festooned with a large cobweb.

Patricia gave a small whine. 'Phew. Yuk. I'm glad I'm not alone.' She fumbled for matches, touching the side of Gregory's leg in the dark. 'Where's your pocket?'

He did not answer right away. 'Look! Look in that stall.' The words came out as if he did not really want to say them.

In the left stall, which was quite wide and almost totally dark, the large rounded shape of a clay jar appeared in the wobbling torch light.

'A bomblu!' she exclaimed. 'More than one.'

They moved together to the left. Something small scampered past their feet and ran out to the large room behind them.

'Seven,' said the writer. 'Wait. I'll count again. Yes, seven. All empty I think. Just a minute ...' He went absolutely quiet. He drew as close to the clay jars as he could and shone the torch into the mouth of each one. In the rank air, breathless and excited, he could feel Patricia's anxiety to get out of there. 'Wait, wait ...' He fell into a dull silence, shaken out of any desire to speak more while they were down there.

'What?'

'Let's go,' he said.

In the kitchen, in the bright clean atmosphere of home, among the happy crumbs and remains of their shared breakfast, Gregory's cramped feeling dissipated slightly, but he was still silent.

'What is it, Gregory?' Patricia finally sensed a change in the writer's demeanour.

He fiddled with the kettle, wanting to keep his hands busy, his mind occupied with little tasks to distract him from what he had found, trying to decipher his own feelings. Strangely, he wished he had made the discovery alone. The desire to keep the discovery of the jars to himself was strong, almost fierce. A slight depression entered his day, a slight feeling of despondency.

What had he really found? He did not know yet, but he wanted to be alone, to sort out his surprise, his total shock at the find.

'You're very quiet!' She injected her words with a jocular tone, just failing on the last word, when her voice descended into a whisper.

'New places ... dark places. They sometimes have an effect on me,' he lied. It was half a lie, an excuse, not a real lie, he thought. Why would he start lying to this woman, this soft and accepting person who had folded so intimately, so trustingly, into his arms? 'It's nothing. Let's have another coffee. It's really nothing, come here.' He spoke quickly, trying to change his own mood.

Patricia moved to him and he pulled her into his arms, resting his head against hers so she could not see his eyes. He was caught in his thoughts, unable to escape them, but discussion was out of the question.

'I felt you were a bit upset out there, but don't worry. It will pass,' she said, looking up into his face, edging him away slightly.

He did not resist.

'Perhaps I should go home.'

'No. Stay,' he said, shifting uncomfortably from one foot to the other. Then he took hold of himself mentally and looked straight at her. 'Really – stay. We'll do something else this afternoon. Will you shower first?'

She nodded. For the whole time she was in the bathroom, and the ensuing time when he himself stood under the shower, Gregory's thoughts, the gloomy image of seven large jars standing in the cellar, froze in his mind like a static picture. He could not believe the moment he saw the first jar. How was it possible?

Not a week ago – not five days ago – he wrote about exactly such a jar. He created it. Not from nothing, it was true, but he created it, from images put into his mind by Patricia herself and others. He created a *bomblu*, a clay jar. He even placed the body of a lost child in it. Sealed it with cork. With molten wax. It was incredible he should find such a jar, such jars, in the cellar of the very house in which he wrote it all.

He wrote it. *Wrote* it. And it was there under the house the whole time. Water spurted from the faulty shower-head, spat and fell about him, on him. He saturated himself in the shower, staying for much longer than was necessary, knowing Patricia was out somewhere in the house, waiting. He would not tell her of this. This was something he could not tell her.

Why? Why not? His hands rose to cover his face under the falling water. His amazement was natural. Hers would probably be equal to his if she knew what he had written. But he could not possibly tell her. Not something he could share. Vigorous drying with a rough towel brought back some of the balance, the equanimity, which had been his before the discovery.

'Let's have lunch in Mellieha!' he called as he bounded into the lounge. Patricia was sitting there, listening to music, waiting for him to appear. But his bright sentence fell a bit flat, felt artificial.

'Yes! Let's.' Patricia seemed willing to allow him his mood. 'We can be there in half an hour,' she said mildly.

❏

3

The darkness is complete. It enfolds him entirely. Censinu knows the darkness is there although he does not raise his head from the crook of his elbow, cannot open his eyes to its blackness, its terror.

She did it. She carried out her threat. He is locked in the dark cellar in inky darkness that so chills his heart. And what did he do to deserve it? He did not tease his young brother. He had not stayed out much longer than the last time he played in the fields. He even helped his father carry the sheets of cork home from the shop.

Why? Why is he locked in the cellar? Censinu does not dare raise his head. He lies on the rammed earth floor of the first room, just where he fell when Terezina pushed him in and pulled the door shut with a mighty slam. He could hear her wails as she went up the stone steps, until they grew fainter and more far away. She went into the house. She left him there.

'Ma! Ma! Ma! Don't leave me in here. Ma!' his shouts are muffled by his arm, his head tucked into his elbow. She will never hear him like that, but he does not dare raise his head, open his eyes and mouth to the dark.

He knows the space around him well enough. How many times has he helped his father fill and cork bottles and jars down there? How many times has he pulled sacks of vegetables out for his mother? Some time ago she made Nikol board up the windows. When did that happen? Long ago. Longer ago than when his brother was born.

Soon he will have another brother or sister. That's what they tell him. Soon. When he gets out of there. If he ever gets out. It is too dark in there. Too dark to think, to move or even to stand. How can he stand if he is blinded by the dark and by terror? It is worse than any fear he knows. Worse than listening to shrieks in the night. Worse than being beaten with the broom. Worse than having ladles and that sharp knife thrown at him. Worse than conjuring up ghosts in the corridor. Worse than anything.

'Ma! Ma! Ma – don't leave me in here.' Sobs begin to shake the young boy's body, making him cry more. Immobile where he lies on the cellar floor, he cries his loudest, his most desperate cries.

After a long time, he grows quiet, listening to small rustlings in the back room where the stalls are, where the sack of lime stands and where his father will rest the wine, bottle by bottle, bomblu by bomblu, when it is ready.

He hopes the dividing door is closed. He hopes it is shut. But he cannot raise his head to see. He remembers the well. At least, he is not afraid of that, like everyone else.

He knows all the talk about the belliha is meant to keep him away from its rim. But he is not scared. Not as scared as he is of the dark. He is not a scaredy-cat. Hasn't he even invented a ghost? Created one? The story of the belliha is nothing compared to what he tells the children at school.

He knows how to make up scary stories. But not about the dark. It is too dark. Too dark. When light used to pour through the fanlights, he spent hours in the cellar, playing with tins and stones. He even threw a few into the well, listening for the plopping sound seconds after he let the stone fall through his fingers. Is the water deep? Is it cold? His curiosity nearly makes him forget the darkness. He uncovers his eyes a fraction. Small sobs sound once more in the cellar – too far from the house for Terezina to hear. Nikol is out on an errand, despairing of his truant son. He has no idea his wife threw the boy in the cellar and marched screaming into the house with the toddler. When he returns to the house, it is quiet. Terezina says nothing, and Censinu has still not come home. It is a long time before the sobs in the cellar stop and Censinu falls asleep.

❑

4

Lieni's face appeared behind the thick brown door. 'Ah, it's you, sinjur. You are here to see the doctor?'

Gregory was surprised to see Katie's mother at Dr Micallef's house. She was obviously his housekeeper. Her prim mouth and thin face gave her smile a taut formality. Lines, etched by what he knew now to be sciatica pain, surrounded her eyes and divided her forehead into a fan.

He was left standing in the cool hallway, hat in hand. He noted for the first time that Dr Micallef's house had two front doors. A thick wooden brown one that could be locked and barred, and on the inside, a more ornate door; with many coloured glass panels, to be used by day, when the thick door was folded back. Other dissimilarities from the house he himself lived in gave Gregory the impression of definition of class and profession by style of residence.

His hallway was a mere opening, a casual space without style or decoration. It existed merely because it was useful to have a space in which to stand when sheltering from the sun, or where to place sacks and tools immediately on entering the house. This hallway was imposing in comparison. Limestone wainscoting and ornate half-pillars showed fluting made by a stonemason, a craftsman more than a mere builder. An archway of graceful proportions divided the hall, with a blue-glassed lantern swinging gently from the draught caused by his arrival. He was curious about Maltese houses. There were so many different types. This one was certainly worth a second look.

The previous occasion, when he had attended Dr Micallef's 'soirée' gave him little opportunity to note architectural details. He wondered about the Monsinjur's house, or the house in which the president of the band club lived. He wondered also about the kind of house Patricia lived in. She said they moved from Sliema to Ta' Xbiex, but he had never been to Ta' Xbiex. He could see the yacht marina there from the bus on the way to Valletta, but never found an occasion to stop there. Her parents were old friends of Phineas Micallef's. Did they have an ornate inner front door like this one? Or did they live in one of those modern architectural achievements called villas he had seen lining the coast, equipped with every known convenience, including a swimming pool?

He wondered about houses, trying to temper thoughts of Patricia, and how she had gone off on Sunday night. Lunch in Mellieha had been reasonably successful, after their quick departure from the farmhouse the day of the discovery of the jars. Gregory's determined efforts to contain his inexplicable dejection were effective, and they chatted and talked about other subjects; subjects that did not include either his writing or what they found that morning. It was a bit artificial. Normally, thought Gregory, they might have chattered on excitedly about the jars and what they could contain. It was his hesitancy and his anxiety that made things different. What could those jars contain?

Gregory gritted his teeth and shifted physically. He should be able to distract himself with other thoughts. He recalled how they wanted to walk down to the sand at Mellieha Bay, which was swarming with bathers. The beach was too crowded for solitude or conversation, so they walked close to the road along the escarpment. The terracing of fields, the flow of land, which seemed to pour its greyness into the sea, seemed to portray to Gregory the age, the venerability of the rock of these islands. He had looked at Patricia often, watching her talk, watching her features change with the altering sunlight; listening to her hoarse voice, its cadences that lost tone and fell into whispers which were so attractive, so sweet, in spite of what she thought of it herself.

Gradually, with the passing of the day, he managed to bring their level of affection back to that which had sprung between them in the night. But not without her help. He found her supremely tactful, sensing his reluctance to speak about his writing, his troubled mind about what he found in the cellar. So she prattled on about other things. She did it physically, too, touching him gently at first, on the arm or on his knee as she drove along at her usual speed. She sat close to him as they ate chips and drank beer at a seaside resort, picking up where she left off when the conversation was interrupted by a dialogue with the vendor at the kiosk.

By evening, they reached a plane from which they could very well resume, from which he could call her very easily or invite her back once more.

'I'll call you during the week,' he said calmly before she left, 'and we can have another weekend like this.'

'Yes, I'd like to.' Her response was just as level, but her eyes were warm and affectionate. Their kiss was a mere peck, but it sufficed. She drove off happily, with much to hold her to him.

When her car was out of sight in the lane, Gregory ran in to the word processor.

'Ah! My friend. You have come to visit me. Welcome, welcome.' Dr Micallef strode into the hallway, a magnanimous gesture throwing his arms wide. He was genuinely pleased to see the writer.

Perhaps the wait was caused by the hurry to change his shirt and make an effort to look presentable. The old man's hair was freshly moistened and combed back. Creases and hems on the shirt were sharp, evident of vigorous ironing.

'You are just in time,' said the doctor, a touch out of breath from his quick descent of the stairs. 'Lieni has prepared a salad and –'

'Oh, no. Thank you.' Gregory was taken aback by the prompt invitation. 'I did not intend to disrupt your lunch.'

'Disruption? What disruption? It is not every day I am graced by company at my table, especially when the sun is still shining!' The doctor laughed, making it impossible for Gregory to refuse the hospitality, as he was already being ushered to a small table away from the large formal dining room he had seen at the cocktail party. It was already laid for two. A tantalising salad full of black olives and capers in a wide glass bowl was being put on a cane mat by Lieni.

The men sat and served themselves. The noise of the cork being pulled from a beading bottle of white wine punctuated the incessant clicking of crickets coming from the windows to the yard. A round loaf of bread, whole and still uncut, was placed on a board next to a long knife.

The doctor was loquacious. 'I must explain the absence of butter. I do not have butter in the house in summer, despite owning a perfectly efficient fridge. That's how it used to be in my mother's house. I suppose I am a traditionalist.' He raised his glass. 'To tradition!'

'To tradition,' repeated Gregory. He had come here on a mission, with questions urgently pushing to be asked. He would wait until the meal was over. The doctor had not asked the reason for the unannounced visit to his house, but he seemed cordial and welcoming to the extreme. In spite of his pressing curiosity and need to ask questions, Gregory held back, respecting his host's regard for etiquette and decorum.

The wine was sharp and fresh, a fine accompaniment to the crusty bread, ripe tomatoes and wonderful olive oil with which the salad was dressed.

'These are my own capers, you know.' The doctor held up a fork on which were speared two plump capers, green-grey and redolent of the fragrant vinegar they had been pickled in. 'Lieni's children – she has four – go out walking the lanes, the fields and the rocky ridges on which no crops can be grown. They graze a few goats and pick wild capers – their generosity brings much of what they pick to my kitchen!' The doctor laughed, the loneliness in his voice tempered with humour.

He continued. 'To fill my days, in season, I marinate them in brine after trimming them. After the requisite period I drain them and put them under vinegar. Not just any vinegar, you know, Mr Worthing-'

'Please, my name is Gregory.'

'I know, I know, Gregory. As I say – not just any vinegar. I have a man bring me wine vinegar from a vineyard in Rabat. Excellent stuff – can almost be decanted and drunk from crystal!' The old man broke into a laugh.

It was then Gregory knew the delay in greeting him an hour ago was because the doctor was probably lying down, nursing a hangover. His eyes were too bright now, after just one glass of wine, to be natural. Of course: the old man was out on one of his infamous binges the night before.

The writer was astounded at the man's ability to conduct a social conversation and be so correct in his table manners after one of his nights.

'And this fish,' he was saying. 'For you, it has an unpronounceable name – *Spnotta!* – unforgettable texture and taste, though.'

'Indeed,' agreed the writer. 'After lunch, Fin,' he said, anxious to get on with his quest, 'there are some questions I'd like to ask you.'

'Lieni will bring us coffee on the terrace,' the doctor beamed, 'and for the space of two or three cigars, we can discuss anything you like!'

It was a veiled directive not to bring inquisitive conversation to the table, and Gregory understood immediately. He sat back with a slight nod and sipped from his wineglass. The bottle was already empty. To his surprise, he saw the maid bring out a silver tray laden with a whisky bottle, water jug and two small glasses to the terrace when they moved there, after she served them coffee. She placed the tray on a side table and left discreetly.

Gregory could not help noticing the beautiful setting in which they sat. The broad terrace, bounded by a balustrade of ornate wrought iron, was on the second floor of the house, reached by climbing the curving staircase from the hall. Double glass doors led out onto the balcony where comfortably cushioned wicker chairs were placed in the shade of a thick grapevine that curled and leaved over a trellis. Bunches of purple grapes hung all around them; spirals from the ends of each climbing bough touching the tiled floor of the terrace. Through the leaves, Gregory had a view across flat rooftops, past church domes and spires to an undulating panorama. Although the scene was crowded with limestone habitations, grouped or scattered among fields, it had its solitary beauty. In spite of the lack of deep green, the golden spread of land with its pink sheen of limestone had something he would never forget.

'The view is magnificent,' he remarked.

'I think so myself,' replied the doctor expansively. 'It is one of the compensations one has, I suppose, when living in the country. The landscape and the people, too. They are so genuine here, don't you find?'

'I find the honesty to be disarming, sometimes,' admitted the Australian, smiling at a recent memory. 'At first, I did not know what to make of it.'

'I felt almost as much a foreigner as you do, when I came. I found I had to lose a few decades' worth of superficiality and materialism.' The doctor said nothing of his reasons for leaving Sliema.

The men sat in silence for a while, drinking thick coffee laced with orange blossom water. 'Again, I have stuck to tradition,' said the old man. 'Orange blossom water scents and flavours coffee in quite a magical way.'

Gregory agreed. He had already found himself buying a bottle of it. Drops in his morning coffee were now a daily requirement. He looked into the small black puddle at the bottom of his cup.

The doctor was quick to offer more, with his fist clenched tightly around the handle of the heavy silver coffee pot. It shook.

Starting at the wrist, hand and pot together shook slightly, stopping when a tilt was achieved which made a dark stream pour into the cup. Gregory looked quickly for sugar, just too late to save the doctor from embarrassment.

Both men looked away at the panorama, eyes hooded against the glare. Gregory raised a hand to cap his eyes, shielding his gaze from his host's. There was silence until they both drained their second cups. It was not altogether an awkward pause. Gregory was enjoying the afternoon relaxation in the company of the genial old man. But his mind raced with what he had come to say; with what he came to reveal to the only person he felt he could.

Why not Patricia? She seemed the most obvious. Clasping his forehead with the hand he used to shade his eyes, the writer made a quick mental resolve to start talking. The doctor had just lit up, sending small puffs of cigar smoke, which dissipated slowly in the warm stillness above their heads.

'Fin,' said Gregory finally. 'I am writing something I think is quite good. I have written what I think is the basis for a new novel.'

'Really?' The doctor said nothing more. Perhaps he sensed that Gregory had not come to his house for lunch or light conversation.

'I am tentatively setting down the beginnings of a book. I am writing of a murder. Perhaps with a local setting.' The words seemed awkward to Gregory. He had rehearsed what he would say the whole of the previous evening. Now, he could hardly put sentences together. The older man's silence seemed to mean he could talk on.

'I think I will use the time frame of Malta immediately prior to becoming a republic. Perhaps ...' Words failed the writer once more.

'It was a very interesting time,' said the doctor quietly. 'The whole population – all of us – spoke of little else for the entire year. It had only been a few years since Malta became independent from Britain – the islands were changing. Changing rapidly. Party politics were intense. There was much debating and argument! I lived in Sliema in those days.' His face closed, regret clouding the shaded eyes.

Gregory sat forward. He had to speak now if he wanted to stop the doctor going into a reminiscent spin. 'What I am writing is not political, though. It is not a political murder, of course. I have done some research and I see the whole procedure – the whole constitutional change – was achieved without incident. Or at least, without bloodshed.' When was he going to say what he had come here to talk about? Gregory felt the quick pulse of his own impatience with his hesitancy.

'More or less. More or less.' The doctor smiled and nodded.

'It's incredible, really. I am writing about the death of a small child, and –'

Phineas Micallef cleared his throat nervously and choked. 'What? I'm sorry. I beg your pardon?' He bridled again, turned his head away and back. 'I did not hear you properly.' He shifted in his chair, leaning back and visibly calming himself by folding his arms. His politeness was intact in spite of what Gregory saw to be extreme agitation taking hold of the old man's entire body.

Carefully, extremely carefully, the doctor placed both his hands on the wicker arms of his chair. They were shaking convulsively. Placing all his weight on the palms, he levered himself slowly up and walked silently to the side table where the whisky bottle and glasses stood. His gait shambled, as if he were already drunk.

'I'm sorry ...' started Gregory, confused at his friend's reaction. 'I really did not –'

The doctor stooped and poured a stiff drink into one of the small glasses, completely forgetting his decorum and leaving the other empty. He stood to his full height shakily and drained the glass, stooping again to pour, but stopped himself abruptly.

'I'm so sorry,' repeated Gregory, totally overcome now with embarrassment and regret. Was what he had said so terrible?

The death of a child?

'The death of a child,' mumbled the doctor. 'Interesting. Now whatever put that theme in your head, my friend?' He had not recovered from his state, but rather was putting a formal face on it, turning to the writer and squinting in the sharp light. 'I surmised you would be writing about the village – the farmhouse itself, perhaps. Ah – some historic connection. What gave you ah – the other idea?'

It was impossible for Gregory to back out then. And in any case, he still felt his need to divulge what he had written and what he had found. 'I started writing about the disappearance of Censinu Mifsud,' he said in one breath.

The doctor's eyes closed, then opened slowly, like those of some reptile in the sun.

The writer paused. Then he watched the doctor pour two drinks and hand him one. 'Thank you.' He did not particularly want to drink spirits that hot afternoon, but he took the glass and looked at his host's face. Mention of the local boy had filled the doctor's features with panic.

'I have started writing about the boy and his family,' the writer persisted. 'I did the research at the Times like you suggested. I found very little. But I constructed a story around the house. Around the vineyard, perhaps. I have started to entertain the notion it could have been murder.'

The doctor looked away. The hand holding the glass had a slight tremor, but the face revealed no more of the initial startling pallor Gregory's words brought on. The man had succeeded in calming himself. 'It is a strange topic, my friend,' he said gravely.

'It was you who gave me the initial suggestion.'

The doctor spluttered. 'Me! I would be the last person on earth ...'

Gregory continued. 'I've told you – my genre is suspense and mystery. Sometimes verging on horror. I had some success with my first book and I continued in that vein –'

'I have read some good suspense novels myself,' said the doctor dreamily. He was not really concentrating on what Gregory said. His eyes had a vacant stare, as if he was lost in a sad memory.

'Well, this one expands on the theme of a child's disappearance,' the Australian continued. 'I heard child murders are not altogether absent from the island's recent history.' Again, Gregory had to regret his words.

The doctor squeezed his eyes shut and opened them again suddenly. A slight hiss left his lips. They stretched across clenched teeth in a deathly grimace.

Gregory had seen that contortion on his face before, when he met the man reeling in the square, struggling in the gait of the very drunk. His parody of a smile in salutation as they passed each other in the darkened village was now there again on the lined face.

He spoke through gritted teeth, the careful words coming out one by one, in an exaggerated monotone. 'No. Not – altogether – unknown. Not – altogether – absent.' The sound of grinding teeth was audible for a moment.

The discomfort he was causing gave Gregory equal anguish. How was he going to get out of this? Should he suddenly rise and depart? Should he persist? He took a small sip of neat whisky.

'Um – I think I need some ice or water in this.' The words broke the spell. He rose and poured water from the little glass jug on the tray. It was protected from flies by a beaded doily.

'But what is most exciting,' he continued, carried away by his own eagerness, 'is what has been happening while I have been writing, Fin. I have come upon a discovery which ... But I'd better tell you first what I wrote.'

The doctor whirled round. 'A discovery?'

Gregory saw his eyes were dewy and the cheeks red. If he spoke long enough about his writing, perhaps the doctor's emotion would subside.

'I wrote that the child had been killed, his body shoved into a *bomblu* and sealed.'

'Inside a *bomblu*?' There was disbelief in the doctor's tone.

'One of those large clay jars. I did some research about them. I even visited a potter in Ta' Qali.'

'I know. The Craft Village.' The doctor said, absentmindedly.

'You know? Anyway – that's not what is most surprising about all this. I wrote about the body in the jar …' Gregory saw a slight shiver travel through his host's body. '… and about the family, how they lived and so on – after I planned it all in my head, took notes, wrote long tracts on the computer – it is all there. I have re-read it many times in an effort to believe what I wrote.'

The older man looked at the writer with a lop-sided querulous expression. 'You have trouble believing what you wrote?' There was a slur between trouble and believing.

'You see, the most extraordinary thing happened.' Gregory leaned forward. 'I opened the cellar of the house and discovered seven of those jars. And three are still sealed. It is quite –'

Gregory's excitement was tempered by a sharp look from the doctor. 'Look, Fin. I seem to have upset you. Perhaps I should go.'

The crickets stopped their racket abruptly. Buzzing of flies was now more audible, and traffic and muted shouts from the village announced the afternoon rest was over.

Gregory rose from his chair and straightened the front of his shirt. Carefully he placed his glass on the side table.

'Sit down.' Only the first sibilant word was slurred. The other conveyed a request rather than an order. A request the writer found impossible to ignore without seeming impolite.

'There are a few things I am about to tell you that you might already know,' said Dr Micallef. 'In that case, please forgive me.' His formality was not unfriendly, but the words sounded like those of a somnambulist's, monotonic and flat. 'First of all, the house is not yours, and neither are its original contents.'

Gregory sat up. He shifted nervously in the chair.

'Then,' the old man, continued and started to sound more like an inebriated lawyer than a doctor, 'you must consider the sensitivities of the village population. There is of course the matter of libel.'

'*Libel*?'

Dr Micallef held up a finger. 'No matter how much you disguise the village, even if you change the names of your characters ... ah – Malta is a small place, Gregory.'

'But I am sure –'

'It would be wise, perhaps, to leave this sensitive topic alone.'

'Alone? I was just starting to –'

The doctor squeezed his eyes shut, as if searching for the right words. 'You have obviously not thought of one thing,' he growled at last, his voice now low and full of implicit meaning.

'What is that?' Gregory did not like mysteries. He needed clarity – it was his readers who demanded mysteries. He needed quick, clear information.

The doctor's pause was intentional. In spite of the spirits he had drunk, he was conscious of the importance of what he was about to say, and he was enjoying the suspense he created. 'That Nikol and Terezina Mifsud might still be alive. As a matter of fact, I know they are.'

The realisation made Gregory turn away in confusion. How stupid he was. Discovery of the jars had taken away all his reason and all his usual sense of judgement. The doctor must think he was a blundering insensitive clod bent only on the creation of his own stories.

'I'm sorry,' he said for the third time that afternoon. He felt ineffectual and stupid. He also felt dizzy, although he had not drunk more than half his whisky and water. He wanted to find reassuring words. Words that would convey he was not insensitive or inept, but only questions leapt to his lips. 'Do you have any idea who the owners of the house are? If it's the Mifsuds ... were they renting? Do you have any idea?'

'I was not here when it all happened.' Dr Micallef sounded smug, as if he was washing his hands of responsibility. 'I could not have been here. I was in Sliema. It's a long time ago. It's not wise to rake up such stories.' He was rambling.

'I know who might know, apart from the agent, that is,' said the writer under his breath.

'Who?'

'Miss Dimech – and her brother, the Monsinjur.'

'That man!' said the doctor.

Gregory looked at him. The same venom that had cloaked the priest's face suddenly appeared on Phineas Micallef's. The two village elders apparently harboured little respect or liking for each other. But why were they both so fierce about it?

'He is rather informative about village life,' said Gregory.

'Smoke screens, smoke screens.' Dr Micallef waved a hand in dismissal. 'He will talk about anything and everything to hide his leanings.' The words rumbled out before the doctor could stop them, but his eyes would brook no further inquiry.

Gregory saw the conversation was over. The doctor half-stumbled twice as he saw him out, but grimly retained a hard brightness, slitting his words carefully through his teeth and clenching both fists as if to will himself to walk straight.

The glass front door filled the hallway with light the colour of gemstones, but the old man was so used to his own home, or so controlled by some inner force, he noticed nothing of his surroundings. Neither did he notice his guest's confusion, the embarrassment caused by the slurred words, the shambling gait brought on by consumption of nearly a quarter of the bottle of whisky as they spoke.

The conversation was mainly about the vintner and his family, the parish priest and his sister, but Gregory thought constantly of a dead child, curled in a foetal position inside a clay jar. Was that, he supposed, the image the doctor himself was battling with, fear and dismay aroused by the notion of child death? But why? In spite of himself, in spite of it having nothing to do with his present line of inquiry, the writer was intrigued.

He was curious about the doctor's past, the reasons for his present loneliness: the cause of his self-enforced exile. He left after a brief cordial exchange full of the formality he was now used to, but holding the impression of warmth extended in spite of the sense of hopelessness brought on by the doctor's intoxication.

The latest letter from Emma was short and uninformative. He received letters like it from her before. The sentences were still erratic and strung together in a curious fashion, but they said little and disclosed nothing of his daughter's feelings.

Greg put the two green pages down on the kitchen table and rested his forehead in his hands. Rather than mull over what happened at Dr Micallef's that afternoon, he thought he would hurry to the computer and tap out a quick response to his daughter's letter.

It had come together with a notice announcing the connection of his telephone line the following Wednesday. Good old Mrs Friggieri. The assertive agent's initiative seemed to be working.

In the writing room, the window was closed, darkening panes reflecting Gregory's light shirt and trousers as he approached and sat on the new swivel chair. It was not exactly the chair he wanted, but was more comfortable and served better than the hard chair and pillow. He twisted round in the seat, but did not turn the computer on.

Emma was not writing her usual letters for a reason. It happened before when she had a crush on a basketball player at a neighbouring high school. What could it be this time? Maggie. It was Maggie looking over her daughter's shoulder at the cheap green paper as she read the print. It was her mother's breath on the side of her face, dangling earrings moving in the claustrophobic air of the girl's room, making her self-conscious about a simple thing. A simple thing like writing to her father.

Claustrophobic? How did he know? He had never been in the Melbourne flat; never saw Emma's room or any of the others. Writing. He was writing a rogue role for Maggie in all this.

In the morning, he would telephone Patricia. He would spend some time with her and dispel once and for all what he had been conjuring in his head, both about the writing and about his daughter. In the morning, that afternoon's visit to the doctor would be thrust further back and he would no longer be shaken by the old man's reaction to what he said. But the writer continued to wonder, curiosity holding him captive. What could possibly have caused Phineas Micallef to react so badly to the mention of a child's murder?

It was absurd to think he had anything at all to do with what happened in the village over twenty years ago. The doctor said he was not even there. It was absurd to think of any connection. But there was panic – he saw the physical response to his words in the doctor's body.

He knew the doctor had a drinking problem. He knew some typical alcoholic idiosyncrasies. The gait, the words slitted through gritted teeth, the jangled nerves and the tremors. But it was more than that. It had to be connected in some way to the reason Phineas Micallef left Sliema. It had to.

Gregory shook his head. He was not concerned with that. It was idle curiosity on his part to pay heed to the doctor's reasons for exile in this village. Never mind the doctor. Never mind his reasons. The jars, the boy – that was what he needed to concentrate on. That was what he was there to do. He rose to make sure the window was shut. As his hand touched the frame, he was blinded by a sudden flash of headlights from the lane. They shone and disappeared over the rubble wall. Bright lights, from a large car. Who was driving down narrow country lanes at that time of night?

❏

5

The coffee was good. Drops of orange blossom water, *ilma zaghar*, added an exotic scent and flavour to it. It steamed in Gregory's cup as he stirred and pottered around his huge kitchen. The little clay jar in the alcove had acquired a tracery of fungal growth on its side from exposure to the air after being buried for so long.

Buried. The little boy could also be buried, he supposed. Looking out of the glass door towards the vineyard, he also supposed the search after Censinu's disappearance would have entailed such a comprehensive probe into the village and surrounds someone must have thought of digging up the gardens. He had to ask someone. He had to go out to the village shops, but avoid the doctor. Ask the barman at *Il-Hanut* perhaps. But first, he had to read Emma's letter.

Usual green paper, usual light-hearted language and strange phrasing. But this time, Gregory looked down at the letter in disbelief. His daughter had the same mental capacity to create powerful images as he did. Her imagery and rebuttals were lively and vivid, and very close to reality. Of course he had described his surroundings to her, had enumerated idiosyncrasies, provided descriptions of each villager, but this was very creative of Emma. Her words brought back exactly what had happened that evening at the little Dimech house. It was as if he had written the words himself. They made him remember his second visit to the parish priest's sister.

'To Floriana,' the retired teacher had said. 'They moved away to Floriana after a tiny daughter was born. The woman was becoming more erratic in her behaviour and the poor vintner packed the family away to relatives in Birkirkara. When her condition deteriorated, she was hospitalised. The man then rented a small flat in a cheap tenement block in Floriana, where he could look after the two young children and visit her from time to time.'

He had made a hasty departure, excited once more by the prospect of being able to trace the owner of those jars.

'I must find Nikol Mifsud, Emma,' he said aloud to his daughter, as if she were not several thousand kilometres away in another hemisphere, but there in that Maltese kitchen with him.

'I don't know why at the moment, because I have enough material in notes to support my writing for more than a few weeks. But I want to see him – I want to listen to his own account of the boy's disappearance. I could even ask him about winemaking – and about those jars. Those jars still belong to him.'

Miss Dimech had said something about being careful not to upset Nikol, but Gregory was sure he could find a way to communicate with him without doing that.

He looked down at the green paper in his hand once more, shaking his head at his daughter's clear-headedness and her ability to sense his mood from the distance of miles and years. He read it all once more.

Patricia's office number was the first Gregory dialled on his new telephone. The installation had taken a couple of days. First the instrument was brought in and wired up, then the line came in a day and a half later.

To his surprise, Mrs Friggieri was there to see it was all done correctly. The agent's eagle eye and disconcerting authority seemed not be restricted to what the technician was doing, but spread to the contents of his house and his own demeanour and dress.

'I see you are comfortable in shorts,' she said, nodding. 'And you certainly have a few appliances in the kitchen now.' She was looking at the percolator.

'Oh – um ... would you like some coffee?' The writer was once more made to feel uncomfortable in her presence.

'No, no, thank you. But a cold glass of water would be nice.'

Gregory poured two cold glasses of Kinnie over ice cubes.

'I see you are learning local tastes,' laughed the agent. She swept a hand about, taking in the working technician and the new white telephone. 'Isn't this wonderful? It is no mean thing, you know, to obtain a telephone in such a short period. There was a time when one had to wait four years before anything happened after applying for a telephone!' She nudged the tall writer and winked.

Gregory knew what she intended. He had taken in enough of island party politics to understand the woman's suggestions, but he avoided the discussion. What was the use of getting entangled in some partisan debate with a woman whose company was unnerving? She seemed at ease and in charge of the situation, stating in a clear way to the technician where the instrument was to be placed.

'This gentleman is a writer.' She spoke loudly and importantly. 'He will be making many overseas calls to printers and proof readers and so on.' Her eyes widened as she stared at him, as if to say: see, I know all your jargon.

Gregory nodded, unsure whether to say his publishers handled all of that, but decided not to elaborate on what was more or less close to the truth. He could see the technician was firmly put in a pecking order by the agent, when he saw the woman move determinedly out of the room and into the kitchen as soon as Gregory handed the man a similar glass of soft drink. She did not drink in any sort of company, then.

A smile came to Gregory's face, which he concealed from Mrs Friggieri. In her efficient effort to see everything was done to her satisfaction, she missed his amusement.

'I must satisfy the owners, you see, that it was all done properly,' she stated primly.

'Ah.' Gregory raised an eyebrow. Then he adopted the secretive manner he felt the agent would relate to, circling her shoulders with an arm and leading her further out of the technician's earshot. 'And who might they be, the owners of this farmhouse? Have they changed at all since …?'

The woman looked around her. Her parody of secrecy, the way she nudged and winked in the direction of the telephone man was totally comical.

The writer stifled a laugh when he saw she was not joking. They moved out into the yard.

'I am not supposed to divulge details of that nature,' she said softly, self-importance ruffling her for just an instant, 'but I suppose there is no harm in telling you that the house still belongs to its original owner.'

'You mean …'

'Yes. The father of the lost boy. You must have heard the story by now from the locals. I hope this does not distress you, Mr Worthington. The house belongs to Nikol Mifsud.'

Gregory could hardly contain his excitement. 'So he is still alive.'

'Of course.'

'And where is he? Is his wife –'

'I cannot tell you more. As an agent, I have to respect their privacy, since they live a secluded life. What happened to them is not …' she stopped on a low note, intending diplomacy and tact. Her eyebrows exaggerated her style.

Gregory almost laughed. 'Um – humph. Quite. I understand, Mrs Friggieri.' Then it occurred to him. This woman constituted a source he could exploit. He had to discover more about a suspicion that kept recurring in his head.

'Mrs Friggieri – you are a fount of information. Your firm must find you a real asset.'

The woman preened, smiled and looked at him querulously. She was not too stupid to see he had a question. 'Yes, Mr Worthington?' It was as if she had said, 'What nice little titbit do you want now?'

But Gregory dismissed his uneasy feeling. 'The parish priest, Father Dimech – do you know him?'

A grimace fluttered across her face for an instant, then dissolved into a smile. 'A great bastion of the faith,' she said, uncompromisingly. Her face was like a tightly shut purse.

'Come, I'm sure you can help me with this,' said Gregory, wheedling now. He drew an arm around her shoulders and led her even further out of the technician's earshot.

'Well,' said the agent, her voice dropping to a whisper, 'it is no secret he is not well liked. He once had a parish in the three cities, you know. But then he was sort of – how do you say? – he was demoted to this village after the war.'

'Why?'

'Well – I don't know the real reason,' she said, in a way that suggested she was about to divulge it, 'but people said he had certain tendencies.'

'Tendencies?'

'What's the word? Leanings.'

'Yes! That's what I heard as well. Now, what was his vice?' Gregory expected any of a number of transgressions. Did the priest stray from his celibacy vows? Did he eye altar boys? Was he prone to indulgences like drinking, or gluttony, or gambling? No – it would have to be something more radical than that to stir the heckles of Phineas Micallef, the old doctor.

'In the war,' continued Mrs Friggieri, 'he was of the other colour – you know.'

'What other colour?' Gregory felt frustrated. The woman was going to have to explain.

'In plain words, Mr Worthington, your parish priest is a Fascist. In the war, he sympathised with the others – against the Allies. And we were all suffering so much, too. Shame on him.'

'And this was terrible, of course?' Gregory tried to draw a more illustrative reply. 'What did he actually do?'

'Well, he had a radio, for a start – you know, the kind that sent as well as received. And he would stand on his rooftop and wave encouragement at Italian planes.'

'Really!' The image she conjured seemed farcical rather than damning.

'Oh – and his *attitude*. He would lace his sermons with sayings such as *Mussolini is always right*. Now that was not nice.'

'No – not nice.' Gregory turned to hide his smile. Then he started to tap his foot in impatience. How long would the connection take?

Patricia's voice on the phone had its customary effect of calming him.

'I think I'll come down to your end of the island this time,' he suggested in a cheerful tone, coming straight to the point without dwelling on the tension of their previous meeting.

'That would be lovely,' she replied, her husky voice on the end of his line taking on a particularly intimate tone. 'There are some very nice places to show you around here.'

'Any good restaurants?'

'You know the answer to that one, Gregory. Sliema and St Julians are chock-a-block with good places to eat. But none of them is a ... a BYO!'

Gregory smiled. She was in good spirits, and raised his own. 'There are a few things I'd like to tell you about my writing. But there's plenty of time for that.' He put in those words intentionally. A decision not to exclude Patricia formed as he lay awake in the night.

He wrote words to his daughter about the discovery of the jars, and felt relieved as a result. He told Dr Micallef. Could he not also confide in Patricia? He should be able to tell her what the book was about; tell her how he visualised the small boy's body curled up inside one of the clay jars after he was killed. How he imagined someone had topped up the jar with wine and sealed it exactly like the others. How the *bomblu* was stored in the cellar among the rest and locked in the dark behind a wooden door whose key was firmly turned in the lock then hidden. But Gregory was careful not to tell her about the book on the phone.

Not really knowing why, he avoided its mention, perhaps because Maggie had shown such disgust at his writing. It was likely, though, that Patricia would not dismiss it all as rubbish. What did she think of the book he had handed her so casually that day? There had not been a word from her about The Altruist.

The bus to Ta' Xbiex was one he had to catch from the terminus in Valletta. It was after sunset by the time Gregory got off close to the yacht marina, as Patricia instructed. She told him to walk through the public gardens and she would be waiting near the promenade by Msida Creek.

'There you are!' he called as he glimpsed her slight frame standing under an ornate light post.

'You haven't worn your hat,' she noted.

'It seems to attract some attention. Anyway, it will be dark soon.'

She pointed out towards the opening of Marsamxett Harbour and to a promontory crowded with yacht masts to their right. 'That is Manoel Island. It is reached by the bridge we just passed. In a minute we'll get in the car and drive along the coast to Spinola Bay and St Julians. That's where we can have a little walk and find a good restaurant.'

Gregory could see that the entire length of the promenade, from where he alighted from the bus to the bay she mentioned, was crowded with people strolling up and down. It was almost dark now, and lights from shops and ornate street lamps lit up the whole paved stretch along the sea.

'Is Floriana like this too? It's near the sea, isn't it?'

'It goes down to the port. Its shore is lined with wharves that go all the way to Marsa. A very busy place during the day, but terribly quiet after dark. No promenading in the evening there!' She paused. 'Why do you ask about Floriana?'

'Before I tell you, there are a couple of things I must explain. At dinner perhaps.' More to soothe himself than her, Gregory needed the surroundings to be calm, the occasion to be right.

They arrived at Spinola Bay and Patricia squeezed the Volvo into an impossibly small gap between two other cars. It seemed she always managed to find a parking space somewhere, which was no small thing with the amount of traffic on the island. Crowds milled on the pavements and outside restaurants, voices and colourful clothing making the scene carnivalesque.

'Is it always like this or is there some festa on?' he asked, liking what he saw. It reminded him of the cappuccino strip in Fremantle.

'Always – all summer long!'

They sat at a table underneath a canvas umbrella at a terrace restaurant overlooking the bay.

Patricia leaned forward. 'The book is really interesting. I am enjoying it, Gregory.'

The writer studied her expression to find out whether she was just being polite. Her gaze was artless and seemed honest. He let her continue.

'Compared to some other thrillers I have read, it is really much more terrifying.'

'Really?'

'Yes, because what you write about is not impossible. It's feasible for readers to think it could all happen to them!' She made it sound entertaining, as if it was an exciting film she had just seen. 'I'd like to read all your other books. And the one you are working on now – when it is published,' she added quickly. 'I think you said you don't like anyone to read what you're working on.'

'When I allowed it in the past, it proved to be uncomfortable.' He waved a hand, trying to dismiss the past physically. 'But it was different then. Even a hardened cynical novelist like me must learn to be flexible.'

'You're not that cynical.'

'Little do you know,' he said, with a wry chuckle. 'I believe nothing of what I hear and half of what I see.' As he said the words, he knew them to be untrue, but they served as a light-hearted self-deprecation.

She took the joke in her stride, but he could see she was genuinely interested in him as a person. With a smile, Gregory tried to bring the conversation to the point where he could tell her why his discovery in the cellar was more extraordinary than it seemed to her.

'Perhaps if I told you a bit about what I am writing,' he said, 'you can help with some information. I need the Maltese parts – you know, the spelling of occasional words, places and so on – to be authentic. I – um, I could also need an interpreter soon. But first I must get your real impression.'

There was a small pause, then he asked, 'Don't you think my choice of subjects is macabre? The product of a sick mind?' Using words Maggie had thrown at him seemed to Gregory to be cheating in a way. He did not really want to put notions into Patricia's mind like that. It was only his sense of urgency that warranted it.

'A sick mind? No – I think you are rather clever. You do create ghastly images, and you did make me rather scared. I didn't like to read the book at night when I was all alone upstairs!' She put down the menu and smiled when she saw Gregory's relief. She went on, anxious to put him at ease. 'But they are just impressions, after all. I don't think you are a disturbed person, just because you are capable of creating clear images in a reader's mind. On the contrary, I think you must have a clear mind – one that knows how other people think, knows what scares them and what makes them feel reassured.'

They ate grilled swordfish with a bottle of local white wine. Chatter from other tables and the constant hum of traffic from the coast road prevented conversation of a truly intimate nature, so they spoke mainly of his books, how he worked when he was on a novel, and about life in Australia.

'What I am trying to write now is another suspense novel, which of course is no news. What is really surprising in all this is its connection to what we found in the cellar the other week.'

'In the back room? The jars?'

'Yes. You must have noticed my reluctance to speak about it that day.' Gregory fidgeted with his napkin. 'The reason is that I was in mild shock.' He regretted the word, but saw Patricia was intent on looking for her car keys in her bag. They were going to drive back to his place and she had planned a route they had never taken before.

'Patricia –' he started, wanting her full attention. 'I started writing tracts for a novel based around the disappearance of Censinu, a little boy who lived in my farmhouse about twenty years ago. You might have heard of it yourself.'

The young woman shook her head. 'No – perhaps my parents know about it, but I can't say I remember. Twenty years ago I was just a child. Ten or so!'

'It's just occurred to me that if he'd lived, the little boy would now be about your age.' The writer made a mental note, but determined to stay with the subject and disclose to her the cause of his disquiet at the time. 'I made up a story around the disappearance and wrote that the child had been killed.' He looked at Patricia, who seemed interested rather than shocked, which relieved Gregory that she was not having a similar reaction to Phineas Micallef's.

'Well – I continued to write that his body was pushed into a *bomblu*, sealed up like the others and hidden away.'

'And then you found sealed jars in your own cellar!' she exclaimed.

'Yes. Do you see how such a strange coincidence can shake you if you have just written it down?'

'No wonder you were distraught. You hid it quite well,' her hoarse voice was compassionate rather than admonitory.

Gregory was not used to such capacity for understanding. 'No – I thought I had managed to spoil what we ...'

'I don't think so. After all, Gregory,' she said, opening her arms dramatically and laughing, 'here we are!'

'Yes,' he said. Yes, he thought. There they were. She was warm and open and understanding. She was just as hard to get used to, with her sympathy and endearing ways, her enthusiasm and warmth, as a closed hard woman would be.

Gregory was startled, berating himself inwardly. He should be more trusting of such a person, not closing her off in fear and self-preserving isolation.

'Now – who else do you think would know about those jars?'

She shrugged. 'Impossible to tell, after twenty years. Why?'

'I may be imagining things, but someone's watching the house. Driving past at night, that sort of thing.'

She smiled. 'How exciting. Are you sure?'

'No,' he admitted. He rose after leaving some notes on the table. They reached the car, where he pulled her towards him and embraced her quickly. The street was still milling with people. A crowd of young men was getting into the car next to the Volvo.

'Let's go,' he said. 'What I am wondering now is what could really be in those three sealed jars we found!'

Patricia seemed very excited, happily reversing out of the tight spot and continuing the conversation. 'Wouldn't it be strange?' She stopped suddenly, her hand on the gear stick, and looked directly at Gregory. 'Oh, my goodness! No – the coincidence would be too great. There couldn't be anything else but wine in those jars. Could there?' Her voice fell into a hoarse half whisper.

'Of course not.' Gregory did not know what he thought. 'Well – no. I don't think so. But I cannot touch them or damage them in any way, you see, because they belong to the owners of the house.'

'Oh – of course. I thought we were going to have some more fun piercing the seals ... but no, of course not.' She drove quickly away from the popular bay side suburb and sped along a wider road, shaking her head in a gesture that seemed to say they had to be more reasonable, rather than get carried away by the curious find.

'This way takes us along the coast to the North. Do you want to drive?'

Gregory had not thought of doing any driving, but her invitation stimulated his desire to steer the car along the strange dark roads. Driving was on the left, like in Australia. It was only the scant observance of road rules that never failed to amuse and alarm him. 'What could happen?' he laughed as he took the wheel.

The following day, he sat in the waiting room at the little pharmacy to see the local doctor, and Gregory thought back to the previous evening with Patricia. He remembered her slim tanned body lit by the dim light in his room, after they made love. They entered the house laughing, tumbling into the bedroom with the big white bed in the corner, hurrying out of their clothes and falling into a passionate embrace.

More comfortable this time, less explorative but infinitely more giving and confirming, their caresses moved him in a strange way. Gregory felt he had discovered more than just a new lover in this young vibrant woman whose husky voice and lively conversation were so pleasant. He discovered sympathy and a kind of encouragement to be whoever he was, to act without consciously examining each reaction for fear it would cause disapproval or censure.

'You are very unusual,' she whispered sweetly.

But he felt her favour, her delight, so his singularity in her eyes must have been a good thing.

'You are almost hesitant, compared to some men,' she continued, flattery the furthest thing from her mind. She was being candid.

Gregory smiled in the dark. He could become used to this. If she had only known his strife and unease in dealing with some women, perhaps Patricia would not be surprised at his hesitation.

'But when you relax,' she went on, her hoarse whisper eager in the dark, 'I can feel how you really are.' Her voice seemed to come from inside the tangle of white sheets where she was buried. They lay together breathlessly, recovering from the urgency of their lovemaking. Her tanned limbs were warm, snaking around his under the sheets. He slid his hands over her, making her sigh.

'Are your eyes closed? I can't see,' he whispered.

She took his hand in reply and gently led his fingers to her face, over closed eyelids, over nose, parted lips. She led his fingertips down her neck, between her breasts, down her stretched abdomen and finally along her thighs until they rested above her knees.

He made the journey softly upward again, pleasuring her gently as he stroked his hands on her warm skin. Her hands were then clasped behind his back, and began a fingertip journey over his body, feeling the contours of muscles on his buttocks, back and finally his neck.

'I can't stay all night,' she said, after the union that left them embracing ardently, their quick breath fusing in the small space between them. 'I haven't made an arrangement for my sister to cover for me.' She giggled. 'It sounds like a serious alibi, but I suppose I must protect my parents' sensibilities from my errant ways!'

'What do you tell them?'

'Babysitting for my sister. It's not worth the drive home so late, so I spend the night. All that.'

'Ingenious,' he declared. But he sensed a twinge of jealousy behind his own humorous word. How many similar alibis had she planned before she met him? Gregory looked into the middle of the dark room. It was foolish to expect no other involvements in her life until he came along. After all, she had spoken of an engagement.

She touched his neck again, curling her fingers and joining both hands behind his neck. He sighed and breathed the scent of her skin.

Then he retracted sharply. 'It hurts when you do that. Ouch.'

'Here?'

'And here,' he winced. 'When I move from side to side like this.'

'The drive!' they exclaimed together. They both dissolved into laughter again, remembering the close encounter with disaster they had on the way home.

Gregory had driven at similar speed to hers, managing admirably on the dark coast road and coping with the traffic that, even at that hour, proved to be quite heavy. It was on the narrow country roads, the ones bounded by rubble walls and prickly pear hedges that he met his near-accident.

'Oh no!' he yelled, as the headlights of another car blinded them. He braked suddenly, hearing the screech of tyres from both cars and waiting with a cringe for the ensuing crash. But there was no impact and no resounding bang. The cars came to a standstill a few centimetres from each other. Patricia's hands were up in front of her face.

'Are you all right?'

They asked the question at once. Laughter immediately doubled them both up.

'Are you all right?' The driver from the other car walked up to Gregory's open window to find them in paroxysms of laughter.

'It is not funny at all,' the man said gruffly in perfect English, accented heavily by his undisguised anger. 'We could all have been hurt. Tourists!'

They listened to him mutter as he walked back to his car, then drove away chastened by the man's frustration and the realisation they could have wrecked Patricia's expensive car, if nothing more serious. As he reversed to allow the other car through, Gregory glimpsed a reflected flash in his mirror. Was there another car out there in the dark? He peered closer, took a long look over his shoulder.

'What is it?' asked Patricia.

'I thought there was another car out there. A large one.'

'I can't see anything. Come on, don't get nervous now! You've got the hang of this crazy island driving!'

Laughing together, they made it to the farmhouse with no further incident.

Now, with the pharmacist eyeing him curiously and the doctor's waiting queue shortening to his turn, Gregory twisted his head this way and that and wondered if it was a severe case of whiplash and whether he could stand to stay up at night to write without making it worse.

'These pills will prevent any muscular inflammation,' the young GP said gravely, 'but you must do gentle exercises of the neck muscles like I showed you, and by no means put unnecessary strain on your back.'

Gregory nodded and winced. The pain seemed to be getting worse.

But the doctor had not finished speaking. 'It is very nice to meet you, Mr Worthington. Perhaps, though, it is not a very fortunate occasion. Anyway, I hear you are writing a novel. Will it have a Maltese setting? Our village, perhaps?'

So word had got this far. In spite of his apprehension, Dr Micallef must still be proud enough of their acquaintance to discuss his writing in the village.

'Probably,' he answered, not prepared to divulge much. 'Do you read much, Dr Borg?'

The doctor sighed. 'I have no time, but my wife loves novels. Romances, that sort of thing. Nothing highbrow.'

'When one comes to the Mediterranean, Doctor, one takes an entirely different view of romance. I don't know what it is, but Maltese women are certainly unusual.'

The statement made the medical practitioner raise an eyebrow, but the writer could not make out whether there was disapproval in his look. He handed Gregory the prescription and formally saw him out of the room.

Gregory smiled. Perhaps the doctor heard of Patricia's visits to his house. The social and moral codes of the island were inconsistent. Had he shocked the young GP? Surely it was nobody's business but his and Patricia's what they did. Still, what he said to Dr Borg was true. He would never have thought until he met her that he would ever regard relationships in any other way than he had all his life. Now, he seemed converted to a classic almost old-fashioned reverence for romance and tenderness. He was sure it had everything to do with Patricia's own responsiveness and compassion. She said he was unusual; but she was similarly out of the ordinary compared to his previous partners.

'I think we were both expecting different reactions from each other,' he almost said to her on the telephone when he returned to the farmhouse.

Instead, he exclaimed, 'It's whiplash!' And asked when he was going to see her again.

❏

6

Nikol Mifsud opens the door to the cellar and calls out his son's name. Eyes wide in darkness after the bright sunlight of the vineyard, he walks a few paces blindly into the large room where the pungent smell of fermenting grapes reminds him of the many tasks still awaiting him down there.

'Censinu, where are you?'

'Here.' The voice comes from the darkness. A small voice, relief filling it with a tremor. 'Is she with you?'

'No. I am alone.' The father is reassuring.

'She threw me in the darkness. She l-l-locked the door.'

'I know. I know. I thought you were away in the fields. Your mother only just told me you were naughty and she locked you down here. If I had known ... but where are you? I can't see.'

'Here.' Censinu climbs down from the trough where he slept in a small mess of hay. 'First I fell asleep on the floor. Then I climbed in the trough.'

'Come here. Your mother is all right now. She kept you some soup and some chicken. Come up into the house.'

The small boy goes out into the bright twilight, his arm up against the glare. He wonders why his father boarded up those fanlights, and why it was so dark in there. He will never go in there again. Not at night. Not alone in the dark. He can still play with the door thrown open, on the floor in the shaft of sunlight, with sticks and trucks.

Once, when he was very little, his father lifted him to see over the rim of the well.

'See? Black. Black and dark. Full of water. Now you know what is in there. No more curiosity, see? Don't come near the well again.'

'Will the belliha get me?'

'Yes! Even I am scared of the monster,' the man said, quite truthfully.

The boy smiled. He was not afraid. Mention of the monster made his father uneasy, but he was not afraid.

Nikol lifted his son down, nudged him away from the stone belly of the well, slid the stone lid back firmly in place and exhaled loudly.

Now, back in the kitchen, his mother ladles soup while humming loudly, as if she had never raised her hand to him, as if she never took him bodily and threw him in the cellar. It is bright in the kitchen – easy for the boy to forget the hours spent in the dark.

'She's forgotten all about it,' he thinks.

It is true. The dishevelled woman probably recalls little of the bout of anger that made her throw him so viciously into the dark space and pull the door to with a violent thump.

'Go to bed and sleep after this,' she says vaguely. 'Tomorrow we must all help your father to strain the wine.'

Straining is hard work. Censinu remembers the previous year, when he was smaller and got tired more easily. His brother was a tiny baby then. And his mother? Was she calmer and softer then or was she always like this? Censinu cannot remember a time when he was secure in her presence. Even his father is no shield against her. He is too docile and ineffectual a man to be of any protection. When she starts her daily diatribe against him, he will be off again. He will give her no opportunity again to throw things at him, to grab his arms forcefully and pin them to his sides, to grab him and drag him to the cellar door as he protests and babbles all the way. He will not utter his fear of the dark any more. He will be faster next time. When she starts shouting, when she brandishes the broomstick, he will be off as fast as he can.

The next day, Censinu leaves his room sheepishly, keeping to one side of the hallway, scared that if he nears the door of his parents' room, he would receive the brunt of his mother's explosive anger.

'Where have you been?' She is waiting in the kitchen. Her eyes fly to his elbow, which is bound up with a scrap of cloth. 'Let me see that. What have you done to yourself? Have you hurt yourself?'

Has she forgotten that she threw a knife at him herself only a day or two ago? Her hands are hot and dry on his arm. She seems intent on finding out to what extent he is hurt. 'Be a good boy, Censinu. Why can't you behave like other children? Why are you such trouble to me?' She is almost in tears, sniffing and curling her head into her elbow like a child. She wipes her eyes on her sleeves.

Censinu does not trust these moods. They as often as not blow up into angry scenes, finishing with the whole family in a hysterical muddle, with the mother wailing her demented words at them all.

Nikol does his best to smoothen the storms in his house, but his ineffectual efforts only make the woman worse. His children always seem to be crying, his wife always tearing away at their eldest, his heart always wrung with his plight.

Censinu slips silently away from the kitchen when his mother binds up his cut elbow with a small bandage found in a drawer, and with unaccustomed gentleness holds him close to her while she winds it round his arm.

Later, he is hungry and tired after a day hiding out in the fields, but he will not return to the kitchen until after she has gone to bed. When the house is dark, he creeps back, to prise the tin lid off the bread box and break off a large hunk.

With his ears pricked up for noises from the bedroom, he lifts the corner of the net that covers the cheese bowl and takes gbejniet, two tiny circular cheeses made from sheep's milk that his father rolls in coarse pepper and lays out to dry. With his supper wrapped in the tail of his shirt, the boy goes out to sit on the steps leading to the roof, eyes accustomed to the dark by now, and listens to rustlings from night creatures in the vineyard. He eats slowly, feeling the night air brush his skin, which makes him shiver.

❑

7

It was crowded in the little hardware shop. As usual, the Monsinjur was there, ordering a large quantity of screws and hooks. Dr Micallef too was there, standing in the middle of the shop, his broad frame steady, feet planted wide apart under him. He apparently was purchasing mats. The two village elders were aware of each other, but embarked on no conversation. There was no overt animosity, but Gregory sensed their distance.

Franz the ironmonger was trying to do the impossible: serve two customers of equal status simultaneously, in order to offend neither. When Gregory entered the shop, he was followed immediately by Rigoletto, the plumber, this time without his bunch of canes and plungers.

Franz raised his eyebrows and addressed the Australian, eager to please. 'I'll see to yew, mate. In a minute.'

His friendly approach made both the doctor and the parish priest look at the Australian to see if he approved of such informality.

Gregory smiled at them all, nodding at Franz in order to return the salutation. 'When you're ready, Franz. All I want is some pliers.'

'Doing work on the house, then?' the doctor asked. He seemed alert, but his eyes were glazed and wary, as if he were still conscious of their conversation of a few days ago. Do not say anything here, he seemed to be pleading. Please do not intimate anything to these village souls.

'Yes,' added the priest querulously. The presence of the doctor had him on tenterhooks. What was it between these two men? Then the reason of their distance occurred to him. Had not Mrs Friggieri told him about the parish priest's Fascist leanings? And the old doctor was a pure colonial, an Anglophile if ever he met one. They were on opposite sides of a historical European fence, with personalities to match.

Gregory nodded to the priest, which got him to continue.

'We thought you might be so busy writing you would have little time for anything else. But if one were to look over the rubble wall, one would probably see the fruits of your labour!' He laughed at his own pun. Everyone knew the vineyard was now heavy with grapes.

Gregory was more than certain the priest did have a peep over the wall himself, and more than just once. His curiosity was etched all over his face, screening another, heavier, expression.

'It improves the place, to have a bit of a clean-up,' he replied, and rotated his head a bit painfully. He over-played the casualness in his own voice and movements in order to reassure the doctor, who was still staring at him with wide eyes. 'I'm sure the owners won't mind if I make it more comfortable. And no, it doesn't keep me from writing – I generally write after dark.'

At the mention of the owners, Phineas Micallef's mouth moved. He was not agitated, but Gregory recognised anxiety, even on his apparently sober face whose creases seemed this morning to be elegant and mature rather than dissolute, and whose only sign of evening drinking was the bright eyes.

'You do not intend to contact them, then?' the doctor asked. He turned to Franz, who raised an eyebrow.

'*Ghidli, Tabib,*' said the ironmonger. 'Tell me, Doctor, are you here for those mats for the Jaguar?'

Jaguar. Gregory thought of the deep rumble of a powerful car, the bright lights of headlights in the middle of the night.

The doctor did not answer immediately. 'Will you advise the owners of your digging and clearing?' he asked the writer, appearing anxious to know what he was doing at the house.

'Well, all I am doing is removing some boards from the cellar windows. It will be nice down there when it's clean and light.'

'Did my sister tell you what she remembers about the owners?' the parish priest asked, knowing very well that she had.

'They moved to Floriana, but she doesn't know where,' answered Gregory.

'Huh. Tal-Kaptan, most probably,' said the ironmonger. His face was screwed up into a humorous grimace, which indicated his disgust.

Rigoletto, who hitherto had stood silently in the back of the shop waiting with the patience of ages for his turn to be served, muttered. 'It's not so bad these days.'

'No,' said the parish priest, holding out a hand as if to still gossip, to encourage a bit of charity with his speech. After all, it was his position to instruct parishioners. 'Perhaps they cannot afford better.'

Phineas Micallef squinted at the priest. He was silently cynical, the writer was sure, of this obvious attempt to stifle gossip.

Outside the shop, new pliers in hand, and the doctor by his side, Gregory felt another piece of information had been gleaned and was feeling extravagant. Tal-Kaptan. He would easily find out where that tenement block was in Floriana.

'Patricia is coming round tomorrow evening, Fin,' he said, turning to the doctor and again injecting his voice with casual friendliness. 'Why not join us for dinner? After all, it was you who introduced us.'

'Mm, I have heard you have become friends.' The doctor was neither expansive nor reticent. There seemed to be no outward show of gratitude that the writer had not broached the subject of their previous conversation to the company in the shop. The raised eyebrow and warm smile confirmed to Gregory the older man did not harbour resentment over their exchange about the missing boy.

'I shall bring two bottles of some good red wine,' said the doctor good-humouredly, 'if you promise not to try and imitate Zija Roza anymore, and cook something Australian! And you must tell me what it is – if anything – that you have discovered.'

It was said brightly, but Gregory noticed a slight hesitation in the man's left leg as he started to walk off. The hesitation of a fumbler in the dark, who places a foot out with such care that it becomes an awful parody of precision.

The writer turned towards the steep street when he remembered what he had meant to ask the plumber. The small bent man was just leaving Franz's shop, with a tightly wrapped newspaper parcel under his arm.

'Um – Rig...' Gregory was not sure how to address the mousy little man, so stopped mid-sentence and gestured with his hand to catch his attention. It seemed to do the trick. The plumber stopped in his tracks, shifted his parcel to the other arm and seemed to raise the right hand in a kind of old-fashioned salute, tugging his forelock.

It made Gregory uneasy.

'Joe, sir,' said the small man. 'My name is Joe. More easy to say for you, I think. De drains all okay?'

Gregory found himself once again filled with gratitude that came from others making words to reassure him. He used his hands in a smoothing gesture to indicate there was nothing to panic about. 'Yes, Joe. I wanted to ask you about my rainwater pipes. You know, the ones from the roof to the well. I would like you to check my well, to see if it has been filling or not.'

The small man made a grimace. '*Mela x'naghmel*!' he muttered. Then he pulled himself together after erasing with comical swiftness the look of horror that flashed across his face. 'Sorry, sir. No, sir. Not job for me. I keep away from wells, you know. Anyone with sense ... keep away from wells. The pipes, yes. I check pipes. But down into well – not many will risk that! You check. Throw a pebble in – if you hear a splash ...'

'But surely you don't believe –' Gregory's disbelief had him stifle a guffaw.

'Empty wells, full wells. All the same. The full ones have water – to drown. Empty ones have bad gases – to suffocate!' And with that, the plumber shifted his parcel once more, nodded his head cursorily to the writer and hurried away.

The telephone was ringing as Gregory opened his thick wooden front door. It was an unusual, high-toned ring that at once pleased and disappointed him. His total isolation was broken, but it was good to be connected to the world he knew.

'It's great, mate,' he heard immediately on picking up the light plastic receiver. It was Paul De Souza's voice, loud and booming as if the man were there with him within the thick stone walls of the Maltese farmhouse and not hours and thousands of miles away in Melbourne.

'How much more of it have you got down?'

'Hallo, Paul! What time is it there? You couldn't still be at the office?' The writer looked at his watch.

'Look – it's two in the morning, if you really want to know, but I'm just back from a book launch that went on for a bit longer than usual. I thought I may as well try to catch you!'

'So – what do you really think of the story?'

'Great, great.' Paul sounded just as he always did after indulging in the champagne of a successful launch. 'You haven't lost it, mate. Just put in the requisite amount of terror and suspense and I think we have another bestseller!' The euphoria seemed distant, attached only to the brightly lit distant city from where it came.

Gregory could not somehow feel similarly optimistic, so said nothing.

'So, Greg, mate – there's a cheque in the mail,' the disembodied voice went on, euphoric and rambling. 'We thought twelve as an advance against royalties. Or do you want to negotiate that with Colin?'

'No. No – it's fine, Paul,' said Gregory. 'You know I leave these things to you.' The thought of a twelve thousand dollar cheque, although nowhere near what he had once drawn as an advance, was a relief. Gregory listened to the publisher in Melbourne wind down the conversation, thinking he could now manage to stay in Malta for almost as long as he wanted.

There was a loud rapping at the door as he placed the receiver in its cradle. Katie stood on his threshold with a kind of proprietary look.

'Good God – is it Friday?' he exclaimed.

'Yes, Mr Worthington, as you say – *thank God*.' The maid's tiny reprimand was said slowly, as Gregory stood back to let her in, her beautiful eyes downcast as usual. He would remember in the future not to take the Lord's name when in the presence of these earnest people. For them, religion and church were personal concepts whose slighting went hard against the grain.

He smiled and noted his own respect for her subtle observation.

'Today,' she said carefully, 'I polish furniture and dust properly. And the windows, you know. Where are the clothes for washing?'

'On my bedroom chair,' he answered, chastened by her businesslike approach.

'Perhaps we need a basket,' was her prim suggestion.

'Um – perhaps we do. I'll get one next week.'

She looked at him with a tight smile, seeming to wonder tacitly whether a man bent on spending his time writing would be capable of purchasing a washing basket.

'Give me two pounds and my mother will buy a good one in Mosta when she goes on Tuesday. That is where we buy mats and cloth and other things for the house.' It was said softly, but her information sounded like some self-evident truth she was imparting, to put him on the right track.

Katie's zealous cleaning of the house sent Gregory to his writing room, if only to keep out of her way. He heard the distinct squeaking of moist newspaper, balled up and rubbed against windowpanes until they glittered clearly without a smudge or streak in sight.

Was it worth turning on the computer to go over what he had written the two previous nights? Did he have enough material to warrant a print-out he could edit while sitting at his kitchen table? He thought of the cheque.

He thought of the tomatoes and cos lettuce with which he was going to make a salad. There was also a large slice of swordfish in his fridge, bought a few hours ago.

A man had stopped his van in the steep street, yelling out about the freshness of his wares with such shrill urgency that Gregory looked out of his front door and up the lane. He saw the man, in shorts and gaudy T-shirt, standing near an old Morris van and shouting. The writer ambled up the lane, hands in pockets, wondering what this vendor could have inside the wide-open back doors of his vehicle. There had been similar vendors at markets.

When he looked inside the blue metal doors, Gregory saw the almost complete carcass of a large fish lying on a slab of nylon board. A long sharp knife and cleaver hung from one of the van door hinges, and a pair of old-fashioned scales with highly polished brass pans stood next to the fish.

'Real swordfish, sir,' said the hawker. 'Narrow or broad?'

Gregory was nonplussed by the question. 'I'm sorry, I don't understand.'

'I can cut a nice slice from here …' the fishmonger indicated the broad end of the fish, which exposed the abdominal cavity, clean and empty of entrails. 'Or here.' The man's strong hands moved the carcass and showed the narrow end of the fish, pink and circular, with thick black skin on the circumference and a perfectly white bone in the centre. The diameter of that end was almost as wide as one of the writer's dinner plates. The fishmonger held a knife against the fish's skin, indicating the thickness he was about to slice. 'Like this? Thinner? Thicker? More? Very cheap, sir. Two pounds a rotolo.'

'A rotolo?' The writer had never heard the word before. The man laughed, throwing back his head and showing two rows of gold teeth. 'In the old days, before the kilo, we used the *ratal*, or rotolo, here in Malta. A pity, sir, that we lost some of those old things.'

'What was a ratal, then?' Gregory was intrigued not only by the strange musical word, but by this man's sense of history.

'About a pound and three quarters,' said the man, proud of his accuracy, '– or one and a quarter kilos,' he held out a hand and waved it sideways and back, '... more or less.'

'Well, I'll have a ratal, then!' said Gregory, feeling around in his pocket for the money.

The man laughed raucously, touching the writer tentatively at the elbow, in a friendly way. 'I guarantee, sir, it's real swordfish, and it's fresh.' He indicated with the point of the knife something at the back of the van. It was a fresh swordfish snout, complete with notched blade. The severed end dripped blood.

'Oh dear.' Gregory caught himself just in time. He had written about blood, about murders and mayhem. Blood and guts, Maggie called it. But this was different. This was real, and full of a kind of simple gruesomeness he could hardly stomach. He watched the man wrap the large slice of swordfish in a piece of greaseproof paper, and then in newspaper.

As he received the money, the man grinned again. 'Straight in the fridge, eh, sir? And when you cook it, plenty of salt, lemon juice, and black pepper straight in the frying pan!'

Gregory stood by the printer while it churned out its sheets, one after the other. There were not many. He slit them apart easily at the perforations, clipping them at the top with a small bulldog spring. In his hand, the negligible weight of paper made him think again about the twelve thousand dollars they had earned him. It was a small advance compared with what his second book had provided in its first months, but it reassured him about the publishers. Their faith in him was restored, and he knew all about the fickleness of some Australian publishers. Paul De Souza would not have scruples about dropping him for someone else; some younger and more promising author, someone offering a stream of horror and suspense perhaps more easily than he had lately.

He looked out over the curling vines that greened the area outside the window. Looking forward to an evening at his kitchen table, eating fish and salad and finishing a bottle of white wine into whose neck he had re-jammed the cork last night, Gregory flipped the corner of the thirty or so pages in his hand. He would give them a quick read and mark in the margins, as he usually did, what needed to be researched more fully; which passages could be elaborated and which dropped.

Two yellow pencils were quickly taken from the mug and sharpened. He tried the sharp new points on his thumb. He had to find Nikol Mifsud in Floriana. He had to open those jars. It was not a new decision, but the thought of opening the jars, of the possibility ...

There was a small noise behind him.

'Um –' he mumbled, startled by the maid's appearance behind him. 'You don't have to clean in here, Katie.'

She pointed into the room. 'But the floor – full of papers. There is dust on the desk – and what about the windows?'

'You can leave it. It's all right to leave it.' He saw the look in her eyes. 'I – um ... I actually do not like anyone in here but myself, you see.'

The girl cocked her head.

'Do you see? I'd prefer you not to do this room, please.' He wished he would not have to go into a lengthy awkward explanation.

Straightening her pretty head, Katie looked him directly in the eye. He was surprised by the sweet piercing look, surprised by the depth of colour in her eyes, which she lowered again quickly. She was captivating, he decided. Captivating and utterly beautiful. Her hands were folded straight down in front of her, tanned skin golden in the light from the vineyard.

'*Kif trid,*' she said softly. She seemed to be looking at her own feet in their small white sandals. 'As you say, then.' Her very short skirt showed knees roughened by the washing of many floors. 'I will feed the chickens.'

After she had stepped back into the corridor, with light from the coloured glass loggia glimmering in her straight dark hair, Gregory exhaled firmly. He had seen her cheeks colour slightly as she withdrew. If he were younger, quite a few years younger, and if he had less sense, if he were not so taken by Patricia's vitality and intelligence, her sensuality and her warmth. If he had started things differently since he came here, he would have been in trouble encountering this dark shy girl in his own house every Friday. He shook his head at his own crazy thoughts, his sore neck emitting an audible crick.

'Gregory Worthington, you old goat, pull yourself together and don't get side-tracked by beauty!' He growled to himself and laughed aloud walking into the kitchen, counting out the maid's pay and calling to her that she could help herself to a cold drink when she liked.

He did not hear her answer because the telephone was ringing and it was still an unusual enough noise in the house to startle him into taking quick notice, as if it had jangled as loudly as one of the old black sets he had seen in some shops.

'Dad?' The voice on the other end was faint, but perhaps it was from shyness rather than distance.

'Emma! Emma!' He shouted. 'Is that you? How lovely to hear your voice!' How long was it since he spoke to her on the telephone? It felt like years.

'I couldn't resist,' she admitted, her voice clearer now. 'I've been looking at your Malta number for such a long time and finally banged it in. How are you?'

He told her excitedly about the acceptance of the synopsis by the publishers, about the advance. 'Now I can stay here as long as I like, really. I'm not writing as fast as I used to, though. But how are you?'

Emma spoke clearly, her sentences erratic and complicated like the ones she wrote to him. They were both avoiding mention of Maggie. They spoke around her, as if his daughter's life was as free of her mother as his had become. 'I'm trying to find a university course I like. I want to take a writing major,' she said.

Gregory wrinkled his forehead without saying anything. Maggie would certainly object to that. Could her daughter be as foolish as to do anything so similar to her father's ill-begotten career? 'I'm sure you'll find something,' he said at last. Then, hesitantly, 'What does your mother think?'

'Oh, she'll be right,' Emma answered boldly. 'I haven't really told her yet. I told her it would be English, you know ...' Her voice tailed off.

'All is not lost, Emma!' he said, at a loss for words. She laughed and repeated the words.

'All is not lost! Do you remember, Dad?'

'Remember?'

'My sandals, my teddy ... I must have been about four?'

He smiled, knowing she was grinning at the other end as well. Of course he remembered. She was a tiny thing, bright and intelligent. *If you know where something is*, she had asked him, *is it lost?* He smiled again as he remembered her tiny upturned face. No, he had replied, full of wonder that this sweet girl was part of him. So different, so small, so bright – and yet part of him.

No, he had said; if you know where something is, it is not lost.

Then my sandals aren't lost, and neither is Teddy. And she proceeded to describe how she had hidden her treasures at the bottom of her paddling pool. Everything was ruined, of course, but at least they were not 'lost'.

'Send me photos,' she said, raising her voice too much now, and bringing him to the present, as if she were on a ship that was rapidly gaining distance from the shore. She was going to end the conversation there.

'Yes!' Gregory found himself shouting too. 'I will. Keep well, darling!' He cradled the phone and turned to find Katie's eyes on him. 'That was my daughter,' he said needlessly, rubbing the back of his neck, suddenly awkward in the company of the little maid, who herself now seemed not much older than Emma.

'In Australia?'

'Melbourne, yes.' And again he wished Emma were in Perth, that the phone call had been from Perth, so that he could have been momentarily linked with his home.

He thought of the coast in winter, the flat beaches promenaded by people and dogs. The gulls in their thousands. He thought of thick grey posts in the river near Fremantle, mooring posts bearing pelicans flapping enormous wings in the sun. Sailing boats streaming slowly under the bridges, their masts tilted downward, heading for a twilight sail in Cockburn Sound. He wished to be connected, even if only briefly and tenuously, to the lovely drives, the roads along the river, the grassy reserves where he used to roam when searching for inspiration.

This island was beautiful, the climate almost identical to Perth's and he liked it, but somehow, he missed home. He had driven with Patricia along the north Maltese coast road, and then back again through the suburbs. Walking along the top of the ramparts in Valletta, they stopped at the Upper Barrakka Gardens. The sun was going down, lights in Grand Harbour were coming on. Dock structures and cranes took him immediately back to Fremantle, a place at once different yet so similar.

'That reminds me of home,' he said to Patricia, pointing to a crane silhouetted against the darkening sky. 'When the sunset is red after a very hot day like we had today, the river is still ... and the sea is still. The port at Fremantle lights up gradually, against the red sky, and you can see people coming down to the beach to cool themselves with a swim.'

'In the evening?' She seemed to like the strange idea.

'Yes. They swim and walk along the sand until darkness sends them home again. Some spend the entire night on the beach. I have sat at Port Beach many times myself, all on my own, waiting for the red sky to turn black, waiting for Venus to rise. The cranes, the dock structures, ships coming in and going out. The rail yards at Leighton Beach, the freight yards full of containers. Of course it is different here, but it reminds me a bit of Fremantle. The white beaches speckled here and there with bathers stretch away from the port. When it is dark, lights from beachside restaurants light up the sand and sea gulls fly low over the waves. It is rather beautiful. In the distance, you can see the low profile of Rottnest Island and the flashing of its lighthouse. On the mole, anglers start to cast lines out into the dark water. I have fished from South Mole, Rous Head, Cottesloe Mole … a million times.'

'It sounds wonderful.' She was enjoying his nostalgic words and sentiment.

'There is nothing there of history as great as these ramparts and bastions, of course,' he gestured out to take in the scene before them. The three walled cities opposite Valletta rose from the grey port waters, their perimeter lights reflecting and twinkling.

'What are those cities called again?'

'Senglea, Vittoriosa and Cospicua,' she recited. To her they were ordinary names. To him, they rang with music and history.

'I suppose you'd remember this view in the same way, if you were away from here,' he suggested.

'I've never been away long enough to become sentimental or homesick. I don't think I've really thought of it that way.' She turned away from the scene and into his arms. He knew she was wondering whether she would ever see Australia, but would not say so, in case it seemed inopportune.

He did not mention it either.

❏

8

Gregory spread the new tablecloth over his kitchen table with a small flap in the air. Its pastel colours and thick cotton weave gave a distinct Maltese country feel to the whole room. He set down plates and cutlery, looking at his wristwatch. His guests were both slightly late, but it would give a few more minutes to the lamb roast in the oven. Finding a leg of lamb was much easier than he had supposed.

'Australian, sir,' the butcher had said expansively, indicating a red circular stamp on the meat. 'Just like at home!'

He was told of the large quantities of Australian meat imported to the islands, and of the enormous appetite the Maltese had for lamb and beef. 'Containers full, sir! Huge refrigerated containers full of your meat.'

He was glad to hear the cargo was of the frozen kind. He had a marked repugnance for the notion of exporting livestock on the hoof. But the image of large livestock ships berthed in Fremantle, their tangent rankness settling over the port town before the ocean breezes swept it inland, the sadness they brought to those who watched from afar, was strangely nostalgic.

At home, he hated those ships, their smell and the cruelty they stood for. Here, their memory seemed a benign one. He thought of his evening walks past the boatsheds on the wharves at Fremantle, looking at the ships' sides, the ropes that were now loose, now taut, looping toward the bollards. Touching one of those loops of rope on the bollard was for him a kind of gesture, as if he had touched something that had seen many ports, many seas, and the contact of his hand meant participation in those presences.

Patricia and Fin arrived together, one on foot down the lane, clasping to his chest two bottles of local red wine, looking like some character out of a play, and the other hopping out of the parked Volvo near a rubble wall.

'You're not slaving over a hot stove in the kitchen, then!' Patricia's voice in the dim lane seemed unusually high.

Gregory, waiting out on his own threshold in the balmy night air, felt the rise in her voice came from excitement, from a kind of celebratory mood. Their romance was being aired socially, even if only in a small way. The company of the doctor was welcome to her.

She smiled up at Gregory.

'It's all taking care of itself in the oven,' he said, sounding like an amateur chef.

'The oven – a summer roast?' The doctor seemed enthusiastic about a feast with which to enjoy the wine.

At table, the conversation wavered slowly between a kind of formality Gregory knew now to be an island social requisite, and the joviality brought on by the combination of their individual liveliness.

Patricia was in fine form, chattering in her rasping voice about work and her parents, the antics of her sister's baby.

Phineas Micallef sat heavily on one of the kitchen chairs, making a spirited ceremony of the uncorking of one of his bottles.

'So you own a Jaguar, Fin.'

The doctor looked up, his eyes slitted and cautious. 'That old thing. It's always garaged. I hardly ever leave the village. On my infrequent trips to Valletta, I take the bus. Have you ever tried parking outside Valletta? It's practically impossible.'

Talk turned to traffic and parking which, as popular as politics, generally found a mention in most conversations before long. At the stove, stirring gravy and checking the potatoes, the writer wondered how long he would wait before leading in with his questions about the boy Censinu, his parents, and how they were going to attempt to open the jars. He decided earlier, in spite of the reception the subject had at the doctor's house the previous week, to bring the older man in, to include him in the investigation. Why the doctor's blessing seemed so necessary was not yet fully clear to him.

He looked at Patricia, resting her chin in her hands at the table, listening with a sweet smile on her face to what the doctor was saying about the wine and its provenance.

'The Rabat area is blessed with a host of clever wine makers,' he said. 'I receive gifts from their presses from time to time. Still, I am not averse at all to indulging in the produce of the Coleiro, Dacoutros or Delicata wineries at all!'

The bottle he was uncorking with such ritual had a plain well-designed label from one of the three commercial vintners. Gregory had sampled it before, and knew it to be quite delectable.

Conversation during the meal turned more and more friendly and jovial. Gregory was loath to spoil the atmosphere with what had obviously upset Fin before, but he was anxious to introduce the subject. 'Well,' he said, when everyone seemed satisfied with what they had eaten, 'this week, I have to go to Floriana to continue my investigation.' There was a brief lull. Then Patricia and the doctor looked up together.

The writer continued without giving either a chance to interject. 'I have found out the Mifsuds are probably living in a tenement there. Tal-Kaptan.'

Patricia pursed her lips. The doctor tilted his head as if he made an instant decision to treat the subject as a neutral one. He had only drunk two glasses of wine, Gregory noted, and his demeanour was that of the daytime Dr Micallef; correct and sociable, for Patricia's benefit.

'I am going to look for the winemaker,' continued the tall Australian, 'to ask him whether I can open the jars. The cellar is now well lit, because I cleared the fanlight windows. I've cleaned out the debris. It is quite pleasant down there.'

'Have you moved the jars?' The question came from the doctor, who cleared his plate with a satisfied nod. He looked down at his fork and knife on the plate.

'Would you like some more, Fin?' Gregory played the

hospitable cook. 'There is plenty here.'

'I couldn't possibly, my good friend. You have treated us royally with this excellent Australian meal!'

Patricia reached for the bottle and poured herself a small measure of wine. 'Have you moved the jars?' Repetition of the doctor's question in her hoarse voice hung in the kitchen, under the bright light, between their three heads triangled above the cluttered table.

Gregory had a sudden image of himself down in the cellar, 'walking' the large jars out of the back stalls and ranging them in a line, in the centre of the large space, which was now bathed in shafts of light from the garden through half-monocles of wrought-iron. He saw himself take great pains to ensure each *bomblu* was exactly in line with the other six. The empty ones were to the left, sealed ones to the right. The vision flashed through his mind and was written in the mental way he had of taking notes. They were not words exactly, these notes, but ideas that would later germinate and find themselves on paper as he wrote.

For the moment, they were gone, melted away, fading into the present time and the present circumstance. 'No,' he answered after a while, 'I have swept around them, but left them just as we found them.' He did not mention he had taken several photographs of the jars. He looked carefully at the doctor's face to see how he was being affected by the conversation.

The older man poured and drank, thirstily, draining the red wine as if it were a light beverage, as if it were not the full-bodied, heavy wine that left a purple stain and a trace of sediment at the bottom of his glass.

'We are very curious about their contents,' he said slowly. His words had not slurred, but the eyes in his face seemed to have sunk, to have shrunk and brightened. His lips stretched over his clenched teeth. 'Although ... I am intrigued, Gregory. Although I too have developed an avid preoccupation with the contents of your jars, I see no wisdom in opening what could be a

... what could be a ...' He did not seem to know how to end the sentence.

The writer looked at him intently. The doctor had obviously given much thought to his discovery. What was so engaging and yet so upsetting about the story that could so occupy the old man's mind?

'I'm absolutely mad with curiosity myself!' The way Patricia interjected lightened the atmosphere in the kitchen. She laughed and stood up, clearing away plates and making herself busy near the sink.

'Please leave those,' said Gregory, taking utensils from her hands. 'Let's move to the lounge. Coffee and brandy? There's also some local nougat – I'm afraid there is no Australian dessert I can make!' He moved away from the kitchen, leading both his guests before him.

'I am going to ask Nikol Mifsud whether I can open those jars,' he said, finally, when they sat down and he set the window shutters ajar as he usually did.

'And perhaps we can do it together.' Phineas Micallef's eyes widened, his head loosened on his neck. 'You are going to involve me in your investigations?'

'If you'd be so kind,' the writer said formally. It seemed to please the doctor.

'I suppose I may as well join in. If any discovery is made, I may as well be one of the first to know, I suppose.'

Gregory felt the question surge to his lips. Why, he wanted to ask. What could the jars possibly mean to him? But he kept silent as he watched the older man place a stealthy, careful hand on the door jamb as he passed into the sitting room, steadying himself and avoiding a shuffle or small stumble.

He enunciated his sentences slowly, avoiding slurs by precisely spacing his breathing. 'I should be – very glad – to assist you. Perhaps – I can help – you to move them, my – friend.'

Gregory was surprised. He had asked for help in the search for Nikol Mifsud and his interview with him: the doctor could have provided the comfort and interpretative skills such an awkward conference would certainly require. That he offered to be present when the jars were actually opened was totally unexpected.

'I am certainly not going to miss that!' exclaimed Patricia, her voice failing on the last word and making a small squeak. They all laughed.

Gregory was trying to draw the shutters to an angle that would hopefully exclude mosquitoes from the room. With his back to his guests, the conversation continued in such an animated way he could hardly believe it. He anticipated reticence, reluctance and even dread. What could the doctor be doing? Was it some kind of self-negation? A determined effort to dispel some personal restraint? He could, of course, be intrigued because of some personal connection.

'I rather needed help in finding the winemaker and interviewing him,' he said hopefully, turning into the room from the deep window recess. He walked over to a tray on which he had prepared a bottle of cognac and three glasses, feeling Fin's eyes on him as he undid the stopper of the new bottle. This time, of course, the interest was in the spirits, of which he poured a golden stream into each glass.

'A very small one for me, Gregory,' said Patricia. 'I'll help myself to some nougat – I don't want to have to drive home in a daze!'

He looked at her, masking his disappointment she would not be staying with him all night. He took in the short blue dress and her tanned legs stretching out as she relaxed in the armchair. Her hair was tied back in the attempt at a chignon he had seen her wearing first, at the doctor's house. Her face was smooth and calm, lips together, pursed after a small sip of brandy.

Then he saw the huge wink.

She stifled a giggle and he made an effort not to laugh. So it was for the doctor's benefit she was pretending.

Gregory turned once more towards the window after

handing the brandy glass to the doctor's already outstretched hand. Dim light seen through the shutter slats, indistinct drones from a couple of mosquitoes which had managed to enter the room, and the reports from some distant village's fireworks, were welcome precursors to the night. He felt a pleasurable shiver and thought of the night with her, then turned and pursued the question of the winemaker once again.

◼

9

Nikol Mifsud was not at all what Gregory Worthington had expected. In his writer's mind, he projected him as a thickset bent old man whose years of lifting heavy jars, bending over pans of grapes to be pressed or strained, and handling large quantities of empty bottles and baskets of fruit left him hunched and drawn, but still powerful.

The man they found in the Floriana tenement was wispy and lean. He sat at a small table, a young man to one side and a bespectacled girl on the other.

'He'll understand everything you say,' Patricia had said in the car, 'but don't be surprised if he decides not to talk at all.'

They came to Floriana before midday, parking the car in a quiet street parallel to the concourse and walking through several others before approaching the large tenement block known as Tal-Kaptan.

'Is that it?' asked the writer.

A large building stood at the end of the long street leading to the medieval granaries. It looked adequately well kept on the outside; wooden balconies painted bottle green lined up on every storey of the six or seven that rose from the street. Most of the windows were shuttered, but a few sported matchstick cane blinds that clattered lightly against windowsills in the breeze that blew through straight narrow streets, most of which were bounded by tall tenement blocks.

'It doesn't look so bad.' Gregory had to remove the mental image of what he was expecting – walls of flat windows and square external staircases, such as blocks of flats were in Australia – and replace it with this scene. A narrow street lined with cars parked bumper to bumper. The neatness and good condition of the houses impressed him. But it was not the repair of the building they faced that brought on a kind of melancholia.

It was the feeling of the place: children playing in groups on street steps, teasing dogs or smaller siblings. The slinking of occasional thin adults with tight grim mouths. All were sufficiently well shod and dressed, but they filled the air with despondency, a kind of suspicion or distrust Gregory did his best to shrug off.

Patricia looked up at him, trying to gauge his attitude. She seemed glad Fin had not accompanied them to look for the winemaker. Her driving was as erratic as ever, and she was cheerful and informative about each place they passed.

'Not exactly the height of luxury,' she said with a grim smile. 'They will wonder why we came to this slum. A lot of this area here, and that leading down to the wharves on the other side, were what was known as the Floriana Gut in the days of the Fleet.'

Gregory had heard of the district and the original Gut in Valletta where the honky tonk bars frequented by seamen from all over the world used to be. 'Like Strait Street?'

'Mm.' She shook her head. 'It is nothing spectacular these days, I'm told, but there was a time, especially when Malta was still the main British naval base in the Mediterranean, when these alleys were rowdy, bawdy and quite notorious.'

He looked around, trying to imagine the scene then. The mental vision of a drunken sailor, teetering from one seedy doorway to another, regrettably brought up the memory of Fin the night they had all eaten together in his kitchen.

It was late, and following a couple of glasses of brandy, Gregory was anxious to wind up the evening and spend some time in intimate solitude with Patricia.

'I'll see you home,' she had said brightly to the doctor. 'It's on my way.'

'Nonsense.' Phineas Micallef was starting to slur his sibilants. He placed undue stress on his words and spoke too carefully through slitted lips. 'I have – always made – my own – my own way – home at night.'

'I insist!' She took him gently by the elbow, as she would an elderly grandparent, and guided him quickly down Gregory's hallway. The old man placed each foot precisely in front of the other, enunciating a meticulous verbal appreciation to his host, whose slight embarrassment was hidden by keeping back in the shadow of the doorway. She helped the doctor into the passenger seat with solicitous efficiency, something Gregory admired and saluted with a smile she must have seen only briefly in the dim lane.

'Well, thank you, Gregory,' she said formally. 'We must do this again some time!' And with another of her winks, she got in and the Volvo sped away, only to zoom back the other way in under ten minutes and park in exactly the same spot.

The writer was still standing on his front step. He took Patricia into his arms the instant they pushed the thick wooden door shut behind them. There were few words between them after that, save for sweet mumbling she made in her husky voice, in her sheet-tangled fervour. It seemed to Gregory the more she got used to him, the more the novelty wore out of their relationship, the more she seemed to melt, to thrill with ecstasy when he touched her.

'I have never felt like this,' she said breathlessly, when they lay back afterwards, warm and enfolded in an affectionate clasp. He thought she said it in spite of herself, as he felt a kind of reticence about her, an unwillingness to totally reveal her feelings.

'I know,' was all he could think to say. 'I don't want to push you into saying anything.'

Patricia seemed confused. 'I don't want promises.'

The writer laughed, trying to untangle his ankle from the knot of sheets. 'We won't make any, then.' He stroked her dishevelled hair, smoothing it away from her forehead and trying in the dark to look into her eyes. He knew his tone implied something other than what he said. He wanted to say more, taken as he was by the closeness of the moment. But was that all it was, a moment?

Her eyes in the dark were almost invisible. No light came through the shuttered window. He lowered his head to her neck and kissed a necklace around the hollow there.

Now, Patricia was marching ahead of him in the Floriana street, looking determinedly around her for someone to ask questions to. 'I'll do the talking,' she said, enthusiastic about the whole thing. 'I'll speak Maltese and introduce you gradually, if things are going well.'

They approached a woman standing at the steps of a small shop whose plastic multi-coloured fly-curtain was clacking in the breeze. She wore a stained apron and suspicious hooded eyes.

'*Xi tridu?*' The question was strident. She wanted to know what they wanted, instantly letting them know they were conspicuous and certainly not there on a touristy jaunt.

'Do you know Nikol Mifsud? Does he live in that building?' asked Patricia in Maltese.

Gregory noticed she adopted a stance similar to the fat woman's, holding one arm akimbo on her left hip. The effect Patricia hoped for was not immediately forthcoming.

He understood little of the exchange, not wanting to interject in English and spoil any progress. When they finally left the shop entrance, Patricia told him what the woman said, concealing a smile until they were far enough away.

'She wouldn't say so directly,' she said softly, 'but I'm sure she knows he's around here. The undertaker, she said, knows exactly where he is. You see, they first want to know if what you are bearing is good news. If it isn't, they don't want to be the one to direct a messenger of doom to the victim!'

Gregory noted the folklore. It would be useful for the book.

'So where is this undertaker?' he asked.

'In Valletta, but I don't think we have to go that far. Look –' She pointed to the top of the street where a small café sign hung over the last door on a continuous wall of houses.

Gregory wondered what she meant at first. But he knew enough about cafés and wine-bars now to know that information could very well be forthcoming in such a place. Like a traveller at a well, a nomad at a waterhole, one was able to pick kernels of information from a jumble of neutral small talk.

A small knot of men in dark blue singlets sat at a marble-topped table inside. Patricia immediately sat at a table and asked for two Kinnies in a carefully modulated voice to the young man behind the bar.

He was strikingly good looking, light brown eyes never leaving the writer and the young woman as he uncapped two cold bottles and poured their contents into thick tumblers. The men too kept vigilant eyes on the couple, returning ostensibly to their beers but not saying anything, in order to eavesdrop on the conversation of the newcomers.

They looked to Gregory like stevedores, like the universal dockside worker whose brawn and energy transported the crated goods of the world, whose tattoos spoke a common language, and whose appearance was ubiquitous on wharves and docks everywhere.

For a few minutes, there was complete silence in the café. After the stolid interval, during which Patricia and Gregory kept their silence, the men drained their glasses and filed silently out of the door, each looking pointedly at them as they passed. Perhaps they were disappointed at the lack of entertainment.

'*Tafu lil Nikol Mifsud?*' Patricia asked the barkeeper. She kept to her seat, but the way she used her eyes and her body suggested a kind of new intimacy after the stevedores' departure.

The barman cocked his head. From his expression and the way he gabbled on, Gregory guessed Patricia was being more successful this time. She drank her soft drink as she listened to the young man's directions, nodding many times and interjecting in monosyllables.

'He said he knows his son and daughter,' she said, as they emerged into the street. 'But he is not known here as a winemaker. For a while, he was a bus conductor. Now, the barman said he is known as a *deffien*. A gravedigger.'

Traffic resumed after the afternoon hiatus, and radios blared to the left and right of them.

'He does live in the *kerrejja*,' she added, 'but not in the one we thought.'

'Not in Tal-Kaptan?'

'No. The one on the next corner,' she said victoriously. 'Flat sixty-six!' She sounded elated.

They walked to the main door of the block and started their ascent up a wide shallow staircase bounded by a simple balustrade. Looking up into the stairwell above them, Gregory saw a host of washing lines strung between flights, as far up as he could see, pegged with a wild variety of garments and linen.

He had expected something like slums he often created himself in writing; full of the detritus and garbage of poverty. Here, there was litter; there was the threadbare feel of destitution and misfortune, but it reeked of a smell other than that of grime and squalor. It smelt of disinfectant and cheap whitewash. It smelled of wholesome cooking and something he could not quite place.

Baby powder. Strident cries of children and women discoursing at the tops of their voices were all around them. Adolescent girls, with hair tight in curlers, sat on the stairs and painted each other's faces and nails.

About half way up, a broad-backed woman with a cigarette firmly clamped to her lower lip accosted them. '*Xi tridu?*'

Again the aggressive question about what they wanted indicated they were unusual visitors to the block, conspicuous creatures most noticeable for their silence. The woman swept a small heap of dust from the front of her broom onto the step where they stood.

'Oh dear,' Gregory muttered, in spite of himself. He looked down at his dusty shoes.

'Oh! Sorry! Sorry. Didn't know you're English.' The woman's apologetic regret filled the landing around them. She swept the tops of Gregory's shoes with the broom. 'Sorry!' she kept exclaiming, smiling brightly and standing aside to let them past.

'What you want? What you lookin' for?'

'Nikol Mifsud,' said Gregory, amused once more by the ardent hospitality that immediately overcame the barriers he encountered. He never ceased to be surprised by the candidly xenophilic qualities of some of the people on the island.

'Sixty-six!' The woman exclaimed. 'Up there, look. See? His daughter.' She raised her head and in a shrill voice, addressed a girl higher up. '*Aw - ejja*, Rosie, come - *ghandkhom in-nies* - people to see you!' she shrieked.

A bespectacled face peered over the balustrade one storey above them. Front teeth that overlapped each other were what distinguished her from other adolescents milling on the stairs. The hair was in a set of identical pink rollers; the lips were painted mauve.

'Pa! Pa!' She shouted into a doorway that there was someone to see him.

Gregory and Patricia were ushered inside quickly and made to sit at a cheap laminated table. The wispy man who was Nikol Mifsud slipped his arms quickly into a threadbare shirt that had seen abundant washing. His eyes were hooded and suspicious, tired lines of anxiety and pain etched deeply onto either side of his mouth and in vertical lines on his tanned forehead. He seemed neither out of place nor uncomfortable, in the spotlessly clean modest surroundings.

But Gregory pictured him in his farmhouse, among his vines. 'Tell him I am his tenant, first,' said the writer.

What Patricia told him in the car proved true. The man understood every word but kept his silence. Patricia held a quick exchange with the daughter, Rosie, smiling frequently and talking softly. The girl in curlers nodded often, smiled too, and looked at her father from time to time. For now, it seemed, the conversation was limited to polite platitudes.

Rosie bustled around after a while, bringing out some cold bottles of lemonade. Gregory noticed there were five glasses.

'Charlie! Charlie!' The girl shouted shrilly. She pronounced it Chully, the shrillness totally unnecessary in the tiny confines of the flat. Although it was tidy enough, the hint of penury was strong, though combated and kept at bay by a fierce kind of energetic pride.

A curtain moved and Chully put his head round to look at the visitors. The girl at last closed the front door, where a host of bright-eyed children had gathered to watch them. The instant Chully sat around the table with them, it was abundantly clear who was in charge of the situation.

The young man questioned Patricia in civil tones, but the suspicion was unmistakable. Still, she held her own, Gregory almost ignored except to be smiled at hospitably by one and all.

Sitting back in his chair and trying to disappear in order that the conversation could flow freely, Gregory hoped he would ultimately get what he wanted: permission to open the jars. He looked at them, scrutinising them all in order to set it all accurately in his head. So these were the children he heard about in the village: this was the toddler brother of Censinu Mifsud, who had played around the vineyard.

And this short-sighted naïve young girl in garish make-up and curlers: this was the child born to Terezina after the boy's disappearance. Gregory looked at them closely and imagined their faces as small children. He summed up their common features and composed for himself another face. The eyes and mouth that were rapidly impressing themselves into his mind, that were so obviously present yet absent from that room. He was creating the face of the missing boy.

Conversation rippled around him, sometimes guttural and forceful, sometimes jocular and smooth. There were intervals and pauses during which no one said anything, and Nikol Mifsud looked only at the table in front of him. There were long spates of question and answer, and times when the son Chully seemed determined to do all the talking himself.

Gregory recognised swiftly interjected words in English, in Italian. When he thought he understood, he looked at Patricia who nodded quickly. She would tell him everything later. She should be asking about the winemaking, about the process. He needed to know about timing, about storage, but most of all, about the sealing of the jars. As he looked around him, a sudden feeling assailed him. There was a heavy feeling in the room, a sense of dread. Or was it just sadness and futility?

Perhaps. But something told him there was more to the story than the disappearance of the boy. Nikol Mifsud's face looked as if a whole lifetime of trouble was once more placed before him, demanding to be sorted out, resolved.

It was a long time later, having descended the stairs to the street, followed by a knot of urchins and about six dogs, that Gregory and Patricia made their way to the car in silence.

'What?' he asked eagerly. 'What did he say? Is it okay? Can I open the jars?'

Patricia started the car and manoeuvred her way out of the narrow street. 'They were very upset, Gregory – especially the father. You could see that,' she said dully. She drove with her eyes on the road.

Gregory was repentant. He sighed and slapped his thigh. All he thought about was his quest. His inquiry, his writing, his book. Sensitivity was not his strongest point. He hoped Patricia did not think he had no compassion for these simple people who attended to them so solicitously in their tiny home.

The girl in curlers, Rosie, had presented a small plate of almond biscuits and smiled sweetly at the couple. The young man was cocky and arrogant, but never out of step in his regard of them. It was his anger, Gregory thought, which made him talk in the guttural assertive way that made the writer think he was not going to get the permission he requested. At the end of the visit, Patricia had risen and Gregory did the same, totally in the dark as to how the whole colloquium had gone.

'*Aghmel li trid,*' the small man said. He said the words directly to Gregory, who did not understand but nodded, thinking it was some kind of salutation. The small man's face was filled with a sad futility, a kind of resignation Gregory could not identify with anything he knew.

'*Ghamlu li tridu, sinjur,*' Nikol repeated. Gregory thought the man's words were a courtesy addressed to him out of politeness.

He nodded and looked again at the sad trio of faces. The father, whose tanned forearms contrasted strongly with pale skin on his biceps partially visible underneath the short shirtsleeves, obviously had the sharpest memories of their time at the farmhouse.

The son Chully, whose belligerent looks softened somewhat to a cordial assertion, was traditionally hospitable but harboured a kind of fierce loyalty and protection for his family. And the girl Rosie, who could not have been more than about nineteen, in her curlers and bright lipstick, bustled around the room trying to entertain the visitors whose purpose in being there she could not have fully understood.

In the car, he thought differently about the old man's last words. 'What was the last thing Nikol said, Patricia?' he asked. 'What did he mean?'

'He said *Aghmel li trid.*'

'Yes, I know. I remember.'

She looked away.

'What does it mean?' Impatience welled up in Gregory's head. He rolled down the window and saw they were speeding down the concourse towards Marsa and the bypass, which would take them out towards the village.

'Do what you like, he said. He said you can do as you please with the jars, Gregory.'

❏

10

Censinu pulls the bandage his mother wound round his elbow away from the skin. The cut has not healed. It is swollen, fiery and red, and throbs continually, filling his arm with a beat of fever.

He helps his father stack the corks, all roughly circular, all blackened on one side. There are more than thirty, and soon they will be placed in the neck of each jar.

Then his father will start to melt the greasy wax, its smell pungent on the courtyard, its deceptive smoothness and clarity clouding after the heat leaves it. The wax clouds over and sets after someone pours it, leaves dribbles and drops on the lip of each jar.

Censinu knows he should not touch the wax when it is hot, when it is clear and molten in the battered pot his father stirs on top of the spirit stove in the corner. Nikol pumps the stove. The fire spits and hisses, just before the man lowers it to a blue flame. He stands the pot of wax on the circular trivet on top of the flame. This morning, the pouring of the wine is done. A man from the village comes in to help Censinu's mother and father with the job. The whole house smells of red wine, of the heady fermented grapes grown in their own garden.

Terezina is having a calm morning, sweeping the yard, making a meal for the men and her children, and hanging out clothes on the roof, swaying up the rail-less stone steps effortlessly and without fear.

Censinu watches her go, holding on to his little brother so that the toddler does not attempt to follow his mother up the steep steps. 'Keep him there,' she calls from the height of the roof. 'Distract him. He will soon forget I am up here.'

Censinu plays with his little brother. He puts a smudge of soot from the corks on each of his own cheeks and performs a brief pantomime, jabbering nonsense and making the toddler shriek with delight. The little plump face creases and reddens with laughter. Censinu too is lost in the brief moment of hilarity he himself created. He dances a wild caper, shaking his head and grimacing at the baby, laughing as he goes.

Nikol looks at his children, smiling vaguely and counting something in his head. Usually vague and distracted, he tries to be accurate at bottling time. It is the income from this wine that will improve the way they cope for another year. His wife is invisible to him, curtained by a shaft of glare from the high sun. He should get a girl from the village to help her. It is not wise to raise the arms so high in pregnancy, he hears womenfolk say. It tangles the umbilical cord round the infant's neck. He should run up the steps and hang out the washing himself.

'Leave it, Terez!' *he shouts from the yard.* 'Let me hang out those clothes!'

Terez is disdainful, mocking. 'Hah! What do you think will happen? How much more tired can I get than this?'

He does not always understand her. Is she joking? 'Come down, Terez,' *he says.*

The children stop playing, and all look up to the roof where the glare hides the mother, whose abdomen has in recent days become more stretched and swollen under the blue apron.

Censinu looks up. His mother's face is visible for a moment, placed exactly in the centre of the sun's rays, the bright halo making her appear formidable, a vengeful angel, like the frightening pictures he sees in church and at catechism classes.

'Look!' *she screams.* 'Look what you have done now! Look!'

Neither father nor son realise immediately at whom she is shouting. Both look around them guiltily. It is the effect of Terezina's choler; they all feel it stings them individually. 'Look!'

The last scream makes them look to the last two stone steps, where the toddler has climbed. Nikol's words to his wife bring the baby's attention to where his mother has gone, so he tries to follow.

Father and son leap forward together, arms outstretched to catch the small body, which loses its balance immediately they look – and falls, just out of their reach, to the tiled floor of the yard. Screams and cries fill the farmyard. From her elevated position, Terezina shrieks an accompaniment. It is a demented scene, one that will remain in Censinu's mind for a long time.

His mother, lit from the back by the fiery sun, screaming her reproaches from where she stands. His father, face fallen, comforting the baby whose tumble produces nothing more than a small red bump on the temple. The toddler himself – a damp and wailing small bundle that laughed so sweetly an instant before.

Censinu turns tail and flees, fearing his mother's ire. If his brother is really hurt, he will be beaten. If he is not, he will be beaten anyway, for angering his mother.

He runs. Past the gate, through the house, out of the front door and along the rubble laneway out to the fields and quarries. There, in the bright sunlight that seems somehow more diluted than in his own backyard, he encounters a cart. It is a wooden donkey cart, heavily laden with a crop of turnips, prickly artichokes, and carrots, wending its way slowly towards him, blocking the lane. The farmer who leads the beast is well known to him by sight. He peddles vegetables from that cart, door to door, all the year round. How often has he stood with his mother as the pedlar weighs potatoes for them? How often has he peeped inside differently shaped baskets to see blackberries, prickly pears, figs and loquats?

The old man sometimes slits open a prickly pear for him, and Censinu picks the fruit from the barbed skin held in the farmer's gnarled hand, to pop it in his mouth and let the seedy pulp run down his throat in one swallow.

But now, the cart is a hindrance. He does not care what is in the baskets today. Again, he turns in his tracks and flees the other way, running effortlessly up the steep street and into the village square, running into the path of a bus that sways into tentative motion just at that moment. He lurches aside, running past the church and the band club into one of the streets leading out and away through the fields to one of the neighbouring villages.

He runs. He runs in terror, wide- eyed, lest his mother follows him with a broom, a ladle, a knife, to punish him for injuring his brother. Lest she catches him and throws him in the cellar again. Past the terraces of houses and the terraces of fields, past rubble walls and cactus fences, past fig and carob trees, he runs, his feet beating a dusty rhythm of escape, keeping time with the feverish throb from his infected elbow. He wipes sweat from his brow, from the straight nose and the eyes set close together. He wipes sweat that drips from his firm jaw and pointed chin.

❑

11

'They were so upset,' Patricia said quietly, once they were back at the farmhouse. They had talked very little on the drive home. Now, as she placed her bag on a kitchen chair, moved to take the glass Gregory offered and sat at the table, she appeared concerned, perturbed by the meeting they had with Nikol Mifsud's family in Floriana. She related, in short hoarse sentences interspersed with sips from the glass and short silences, what Nikol Mifsud and his son and daughter told her of their situation. 'They use your rent from this place to keep Terezina in a nursing convent. It was very difficult before you took the lease.'

Gregory looked down. He had wondered before why the family lived in the tenement block. The stories and gossip he listened to at *Il-Hanut* momentarily seeped away. He had forgotten about the wife, the unbalanced woman who had to be institutionalised soon after the boy disappeared. Again, his repentance appeared plainly on his face. Lack of sensitivity plagued him. He was obsessed with obtaining material. He thought only of his book, of his so-called research for writing. Patricia's eyes, though, were sympathetic.

He looked at her despondently. 'You must think I'm a heartless mercenary writer with no other thought except for his book.'

'On the contrary,' she said. 'I know you were touched by their situation. I noticed your eyes, taking in their faces and expressions. Although you did not understand the words, I think you understood how they think and live. You're very taken up, though, by the jars and the story of the boy.'

'I am. Sometimes I think of nothing else. I have only written a few tracts, but the whole story is taking form in my head. All I will have to do is put it down in words. It is practically written in my head.'

'I've often wondered how writers think,' she said, half to herself.

'But you see, this is not usually the way with me!' Gregory rose and paced in his large kitchen, bright light from the naked light bulb placing his features alternately in shadow or glow as he turned, back and forth. 'I scribble. I make profuse notes. I spend a lot of time looking things up and getting my facts right. I rip up newspapers, write in the margins of books, and photocopy an enormous amount of information before I even start to write a single word of actual text.' He ran a hand through his hair, drained his glass and looked at her. 'This time, I've broken all my own rules. I'm not even sure I understand the real processes I am trying to write about. Wine making for example – I haven't even started to take in what it really entails. I can only guess at how they sealed those jars.' Again, he paced on the tiled floor, the sound of his steps dulled by the thick limestone walls. 'I wish you could see what I've written so far.'

'But I thought –'

'Yes, yes,' he said impatiently. 'I know what I said. I don't know.' He raked his hair again. 'Perhaps in a couple of weeks, when I have enough down. Or I might feel different then. I don't know.'

Patricia saw his confusion. 'Let's go through exactly what Nikol Mifsud has told me about winemaking.'

Gregory looked at her in surprise. He was not used to being comforted or helped in this way, this soothing, matter-of-fact way that indicated such understanding. Was this what women used to be like? Was this what all women were like on this island?

Patricia looked at him pointedly. He nodded and strode quickly to the writing room for a pad and the mug of pencils. For the next hour, he scribbled notes about grape harvests, squeezing and pressing of fruit, straining, fermentation, and felt he was slipping once more into the comforting routine, into the practised habit that had ruled the creation of his previous novels.

'He said they put the bulk of liquid produce in glass bottles and demijohns,' said Patricia. Her thick hair came loose from the slide she used to keep it away from her face. She looked eager, tousled and mildly excited by what they found out that day. 'The rest goes into clay jars, mainly for home use – for village use.'

Gregory leaned across the corner of his kitchen table and kissed her. Her eyes were soft and dark, saying, without uttering one word, that her presence and her eagerness were meant for him, only for him. 'Won't your parents wonder where you are?'

'Come on, Gregory. These are not the middle ages, you know,' she laughed. 'I am quite a free spirit. I may live at home, but my parents are liberal and they know I can look out for myself.'

'Yes, but I heard about customs ... um – strict Catholic upbringing and all that.' He gave a lop-sided cynical smile.

But her reply was level and serious. 'Mm. It's difficult to explain the subtle balance that's possible, even in a country like this, where religious and social mores are so important. In my family, we manage a fine line between broadmindedness and propriety.' She lapsed into a jocular mood to match his. 'Mostly, it is done by not talking about it very much in any direct way! My mother is an expert at discussing other 'anonymous' families and their behaviour. She and my father believe we are quite perfect compared to some!' Her husky laugh filled the kitchen.

'I think you're perfect.' Gregory pulled her close. 'So it's all under control?'

'As long as I am not blatantly wanton or conspicuously uninhibited, everything is!' She leaned back in his arms. 'This is – in spite of all appearances – a fiery passionate country,' she said, laughing, 'where we have managed to combine the affection and warmth of the Mediterranean with almost Anglo-Saxon calm and phlegm and Christian temperance and moderation!' She gave another low-keyed giggle. 'Or so my parents would like to believe, anyway.'

They returned to the notes. Gregory was mystified by the mention of glass bottles. 'Hundreds of bottles, he said?'

'Yes. He told me they only filled a *bomblu* or two with wine. The clay jars are generally used for water. Sometimes, for olive oil or vinegar.'

'I must remember to get that right.' He scribbled a few lines, crossing out many words and adding others.

'Is it important to be absolutely accurate?'

'It depends. In a work of fiction, it depends on what you want your reader to believe. You said so yourself – you liked my writing because it seemed real enough to be frightening. If the facts presented are accurate, then the story becomes plausible.'

They continued, and the writer listened to Patricia's translation of what had gone between her and the Mifsud family.

'They believe Censinu fell into some quarry, you know,' she said in a sad voice. 'They talked about it so briefly – so hesitantly, of course. They seem to have no notion of rumours that circulated in the surrounding villages that –'

'– that Terezina had done harm to her own son.' Gregory nodded.

'Or at least, they were not willing to show they did.'

Gregory nodded again. He heard the grim story many times at *Il-Hanut*. No matter who the narrator was, whether dusty quarryman or cocky bus driver, the gist of the tale was always the same. They laughed grimly about a madwoman wielding a kitchen knife, running after her son, wailing like a banshee. They made up episodes and sometimes competed, coming up with grislier and grislier descriptions of how she had hidden her son's body somewhere in the farmhouse.

'Yes. The Mifsuds are still affected by the whole thing. They still have the mother to look after. They still feel there is gossip going about, but they do not know the details of what is said about them. It was upsetting for them to even mention it. Nikol said that after they gave up the search for Censinu, the mother had to be restrained. She was incoherent and even violent.'

'It could have been grief,' said the writer, scribbling on a fresh page. 'Apparently many thought it was remorse, or fear, or insanity.'

'One village man said she had harmed the boy before,' Gregory told her, 'with a kitchen knife.'

Patricia said nothing. Her eyes dulled and she lowered them.

'What did he say about the jars? Tell me again what he said about the jars.' Gregory put down his pencil.

'Well – when I mentioned them he just nodded. He did not seem surprised we managed to get in the cellar. He even seemed pleased you cleaned it out and un-boarded the half-windows. When I said the word *bomblu*, he appeared a bit distressed. I told him you were interested in the contents and the historical significance. That was when he looked at you strangely. What possible significance could be contained in such an everyday vessel, he seemed to think. But then, village people are used now to being regarded curiously by foreigners and tourists.'

'But has he heard nothing of the gossip at all?'

'Not that I could see plainly on his face. He might know what people think – that Terezina actually ...' she stopped short of the word killed and let him talk.

Gregory nodded. 'That Terezina murdered the boy and pushed his small body into a bomblu,' he said.

That was the original premise that sparked off his idea for the book, and now he could not remember clearly which had come first; the gossip he listened to, or the first line that came into his head, the first line he tapped so easily into the keyboard because it had resided in his mind for so many hours.

The first line that appeared on the monitor when he had finally sat down to write was what germinated the whole thing.

'I must open those jars,' he said. He rose from the table and stood at the yard door. The sun had gone down, leaving a warm orange aura in the sky above the vineyard. The archway and metal gate he had thrown wide himself were silhouetted against the warm background.

'I think so too,' said Patricia.

He heard her voice break on the last word, the sound dull and un-echoing in the confines of the kitchen behind him. 'Fin has some sort of fear or reluctance about the whole business,' he said.

'He seemed eager enough to help you.'

He turned to look at her, his eyes earnest. 'You weren't there when I first mentioned the jars and the possibility of the body being down there somewhere. He was shocked, aghast. Something I said threw him entirely, but I can't think exactly what it was. He was incoherent, paralytic.' There he went, writing in his head again. 'Could it be something to do with why he left Sliema and came out here? Do you have any idea?'

'Oh – it might have had something to do with his family. My parents might know the story, I think, but they are much too prudent and diplomatic to turn it into gossip. I don't think they'll even discuss it with me. He's been a family friend for ages. I think a lot of people in Sliema turned completely against him in the early years. It might have been impossible for him to continue to practise there.'

'He stopped altogether.'

'He could probably afford to, anyway,' she shrugged.

Gregory knew Phineas Micallef had never practised medicine in the village. Why? Did it have to do with the disappearance of Censinu Mifsud?

'First he wanted to stop me going into the story. Now he wants to be involved. Has he got a stake in all this?'

'I don't think he'd tell you if you asked,' she answered.

'What would happen if we found something in the jars?'

She shrugged. 'You could be confusing his interest with the way he is – you know, his drinking.'

But there was more to it than that. 'I'll tell you what we will do, Patricia,' he said. 'This weekend you, Fin and I will go down to the cellar and open the jars. It should be exciting. It could prove quite spooky, but I think we're all very curious about the contents.'

'What if we find ...' She stopped and looked at him, her eyes wide and candid.

'We'll see,' answered the writer. He took her hand and for a moment, they were both silent. There were sounds of chickens scraping from the yard, traffic in the distance.

'I don't know what to think sometimes,' she said. 'What do you think we'll find?'

Gregory held her close. 'I don't know – we'll see,' he said again.

❑

12

The doctor sat in a corner of the wine bar, deep in thought. Gregory walked up to him, but had to clear his throat and move to attract the old man's attention. He was deep in some reverie; or deep in the grip of an alcoholic haze.

'Ah – Worthington.' There was no slur in his speech. 'The village still holds you in thrall.'

'It's a great place to write,' said Gregory, signalling for permission to sit with the hand that held his glass, and settling himself opposite the doctor. The light in the bar was not kind to the doctor. His sleeked back hair still held the marks of comb teeth, harshly raked back and exposing the pink scalp underneath thinning hair. Lines etched around his eyes and mouth by years and care seemed deeper here than they did out in the sunlight.

'And the people are hospitable and very nice,' Gregory said, anxious to keep the conversation on a neutral keel.

'And informative, Gregory? Do they tell you all you need to know?' The sarcasm was hard to miss.

'Not quite enough, I'm afraid,' he said reassuringly. 'There are still some large holes in my story. Someone harmed that boy, but I still have no clear-cut motives, I still do not know enough about the mother, for instance.'

Phineas Micallef pulled himself upright on the wooden chair. His eyes took on a pinkish tinge, and he sighed. A neatly ironed handkerchief was pulled slowly, deliberately, from his pocket.

Gregory knew he was about to divulge some other important aspect to the story of the boy, so waited in silence. Phineas Micallef might have been absent from the village when the boy disappeared, but his demeanour seemed to suggest he knew much more than he was willing to tell.

'The mother, you say.'

'Terezina Mifsud.'

At the mention of the woman's name, the doctor lowered his eyes. 'Her name was Thérèse – only the villagers called her Terezina. She was lovely, you know – quite captivating.'

'That's not what I hear from ...'

The doctor's eyes flashed. 'They know nothing! How could they possibly know?' He spat in anger, his mouth slack and then slitted across his teeth. Regretting his outburst, he wiped the handkerchief across his mouth and shook his head. 'She was not originally from the village, Gregory, my friend. In a sense, she was like you and me – an outsider. In a sense, she was never accepted here. Of course you are bound to hear ambiguous things about her.'

'But the things I've heard. Screams, quarrels.'

'Do not persist with this, please.' The doctor was now seriously distraught. His shaking hand sought the glass, and brought it uncertainly to his lips. In an instant it was drained of the last drops of wine. 'I knew her at one time. Not here – not here, of course. I am only here now because ... Never mind why I am here. There is no literary need for all this, is there? You need no revelations from me.' The sarcasm was once again heavy between them.

'Look, Fin – I'm very sorry. This is distressing you. Let's forget it.'

'Worthington, I like you. I admire your efforts to research a book well. I like the way you look for instances in life then restructure them into a novel. If that's what you do. Is that what you do?' The doctor's dewy eyes seemed to indicate there was so much to tell he was bursting with the need to disburden himself of it all, to tell all, even if it were to end up in some pulp novel.

'More or less, Fin. Yes, more or less it's what I do.'

'Thérèse was from St Julians, you see. She fell in love with Nikol Mifsud – a match deemed entirely inappropriate by her family, who fought her every step of the way. When they married, there was little else they could do. No good self-respecting St Julians family is going to oppose an upright Catholic marriage, are they?'

Gregory could not detect whether it was irony or bitterness, or some recognition of involvement that tainted the doctor's tone. It could have been mere drunkenness. 'Did you know her? Did you know her well?' This was a new angle to the story.

The doctor was now leaning precariously to his left, and seemed to be in danger of falling off his chair. But he righted himself. 'How well can anyone really claim to know anyone else? Do you know me well, Gregory Worthington? Does anyone really know you?' The doctor lurched out, setting the bead curtain swinging and clattering. He left without warning or salutation, and Gregory was left to muse on his own.

So there was another side to Terezina Mifsud. It was useful to get a different side to a story. But he knew very well Phineas Micallef's outburst was not merely the other side of a story. There was personal involvement there, grief, a feeling of frustration and sadness of which he could only see the surface. Perhaps the man would tell him more, one day.

One day when he felt he could confide in a writer who, after all, created works of fiction, created aggregates of words to make an entertainment, rather than narrating a strict truth.

❑

13

'What do you think we will need?' Gregory looked at his meagre collection of tools, the newest of which was the small pair of pliers bought just recently at Franz's hardware store. He laid out all his tools and a few promising-looking utensils from the kitchen on a small piece of canvas in the newly cleaned out trough.

'Definitely a sharp knife, my friend, and you won't need that mallet!' said Phineas Micallef. He came to peer over the writer's shoulder and saw the lined up implements.

Gregory heard a small intake of nervous breath sucked quickly into the doctor's throat. What did he see? Gregory looked before him. The tools were ranked like a surgeon's instruments in a hospital theatre.

The moment passed swiftly, and the doctor looked steadily at the canvas with a grave look. 'You don't seem to have a long enough knife there,' said the old man. His face was pale, but his demeanour calm again.

'How are we ever going to empty one of those things?' asked Patricia. She came early that day, and ate a light lunch of fruit salad and yoghurt with Gregory before the doctor joined them in the early afternoon.

'Into something else? How?' She asked a thousand questions as she stood near the far wall, looking at each *bomblu* in turn, noting similarities and differences.

'They must be glazed on the inside,' she had said earlier. Gregory could not be sure whether she made the observations for him to take mental notes, or out of natural curiosity. He was still not used to the supportive nature of her ways, the gentle suggestions she made that sometimes sent him scribbling on his notepad. He had spent a great deal of time at his old customary scribbling and screwing up of scrap paper, taking notes and circling things he read, making photocopies of pages at the library and sticking them on the wall in the writing room. It was now in a peak state of disarray, worrying Katie the maid into a similarly peak state of concern about dust and litter.

'We'll not disturb that room, I think,' he had to say each Friday. And each Friday, the pretty dark girl would take special pains with other rooms, to prove it was not laziness on her part that prevented her from doing a thorough job on the whole house.

'Are we going to empty them?' the doctor asked, cocking his head and sliding one hand into a trouser pocket thoughtfully. His hair was faultlessly slicked back, greying sides neatly trimmed only that morning, it seemed, by the local barber. His eyes were bright, attesting to yet another night of severe intemperance, first probably at the band club, then at the more forgiving *Il-Hanut*, where regulars were used to his slow decline into rambling drunkenness and disjointed babblings.

Gregory could imagine him making his way to his own front door in a stupor, the road so well-known and well-travelled it became a matter of letting go, of letting himself ride on his own irregular gait until a final tired step raised him onto the threshold of the house with two front doors. How did he manage the key and the keyhole? How shakily did he lurch past the delicate etched glass door without setting it rattling in the silence of the night? And how weakly did he finally lower himself onto his empty bed, giving in to the overpowering torpor that thankfully numbed his thoughts? Were the thoughts shoved away to where they would not constantly hammer at his body, replaced by emptiness, a void composed of whirling giddiness?

It had been about a week since his last exchange at the bar with the doctor. Since then, he concentrated on filling in his research. Paying visits to locations in the country, taking the dusty crowded buses and musing at their efficiency, which was at the same time comical and impractical. During some of the time, especially when walking down crowded streets in places like Mosta, St Paul's Bay, or Hamrun, he would feel the inexplicable sensation that someone was following him. Stopping and turning suddenly, he would gaze into the crowd behind him, scanning faces to find one he would recognise. He would turn in a bus and look at the faces of passengers, each one in turn, seeing dark and light skin, freckles, bald pates, the sheen of swinging ponytails on schoolgirls, waiting to see the one face he would surely know. But he was wrong. There was no one there he knew. Was he waiting to discover the face of Fin among those of strangers? Was he somehow sure the doctor was so uncertain about his role in all this that he had started following him? And why? What could his motive be?

He could not be trying to stop him anymore. The doctor would surely have seen by now that his invitation to help with the jars had been accepted and there was no going back. Or was it Chully he was expecting to see riding the bus behind him? Trailing him in a crowd? Chully the sullen brother of the missing boy; the disgruntled relative who resented intrusion by a foreign stranger into his family's grief? Perhaps he expected the black dusty robes of the parish priest, Monsinjur Dimech, to be swinging silently in his pursuit. It was unclear whether the priest had anything at all to do with the lost boy, but he was certainly vituperative towards the doctor, certainly had opinions hidden behind the façade of piety and charitable grace. The parish priest, unlike the old doctor, was not well liked in the village. Respected, certainly, and because of his station and mission regarded as an elder, one to whom one must defer; but not a figure on which much love or admiration was lost.

'You are treading on shaky ground, Mr Worthington,' the priest had said to him once. His cliché resounded around them as they stood on the forecourt of the church. 'There are many other stories you could choose. Malta is full of history, of colour and of life. Our heritage is contained in thousands of oral anecdotes. It would be fascinating for you to listen to some village people, their stories, their tales.'

'That's exactly what I am doing, Father,' said Gregory calmly, saying the words slowly and with gleeful intent. He wanted to see the expression in the priest's face when he showed him he was not going to succeed in deflecting him from his path of discovery.

The cleric was taken aback. He was not used to such casual insults. His eyebrows spoke his surprise, then they lowered, as if to say it was no wonder he did not get any respect from a foreigner who knew nothing of simple courtesy and Christian prudence.

Gregory recalled the exact expression as it shifted from surprise to condescension; each little wrinkle, each dusty hair on each side of the corrugated forehead, each little red lump on the badly shaven chin. He pulled himself up. He caught himself writing again, mentally composing a personality as if it were to be a character in his fiction. It would be better to address the more immediate matter of the jars.

The problem of decanting the liquid they contained was considerable one. The three grappled with it for some time, standing in the cool wide space and moving around each individual *bomblu*.

'We don't have to keep whatever's inside them,' decided Gregory. Since the interview in Floriana, he had taken mental and physical possession of the jars, and all thought of Nikol Mifsud was temporarily dispelled. Neither the old winemaker's approval nor his ownership was any more a matter for discussion or consideration. It was decided, and for Gregory it was now filed safely away like so much material that had been researched.

The doctor had cordially confirmed acceptance of the invitation to be present, and had even demonstrated alacrity and eagerness on the phone. Patricia was her bright and optimistic self. All that was ahead of them now was a period of discovery, of physical exertion, of fun, if possible.

'Let's see how we are going to remove the seal and corks, first.' He ran up to the kitchen for his bread knife, returning quickly with it in his hand.

The doctor regarded it with a raised eyebrow. 'Good,' he said, 'slide that in between the clay and wax and cork, and lever it upward.'

'You could work it in all the way around first,' offered Patricia, gesticulating a cutting movement that showed Gregory what she meant.

'But we haven't looked inside the lighter ones yet – the ones that look empty,' said Gregory. Once again, he desired solitude. It would have been better, perhaps, to have done this on his own.

'Well – they are unsealed and obviously empty,' Phineas Micallef held out his hands palms upward. The delay made him impatient. 'What do you hope to find?'

'You know,' said Patricia with a grimace, 'there could be remains or –'

The word *remains* worried the older man. Gregory watched him turn away slowly and back again, cupping his chin in one hand while a clenched fist was plainly visible inside his trouser pocket.

'We shall see,' said the old man. 'Mm – I don't think so. Maybe not ... we shall see,' he mumbled to himself. 'Remains? Years and years. Hardly – well. Indeed ...' He turned to the writer and the young woman, who approached two of the empty jars and were attempting to look inside.

Gregory shone a torch into the wide mouth, but was unable to see because of Patricia's head.

'This one's empty,' she said. She took the torch from his hand and wielded it herself, directing the beam so she could be sure there was nothing at the bottom of the *bomblu*.

Gregory looked into another one. 'So's this one.'

The third jar had a wider neck, but was badly damaged. Gregory invited the doctor to have a look.

'Empty as well,' the older man said. He craned his neck to get a good look inside. Gregory had a close look at the back of the doctor's head, his lined pinkish neck. 'Except for dust and a few fragments of broken cork and clay.'

He took the torch from Patricia and aimed it inside the neck of the fourth jar without a seal. Gregory watched his carefully groomed head tilt first to one side and then to another, eyes squinted as they searched for something at the bottom of the jar.

'Aha!' exclaimed the doctor, his words trumpeting into the mouth of the jar. They were both at his side immediately. 'Rags. Rags and ...' The doctor looked up, paled by the effort of inspection at an awkward angle.

Gregory realised he had almost said bones, then saw the portent of the expression.

'I mean,' said Phineas Micallef, drawing himself to an erect stance and correcting himself, smiling uncomfortably. 'I mean – just rags.'

They all laughed together, prompted by a small smile from the doctor, at the unfinished phrase that had nevertheless unnerved them momentarily.

Quickly, the two men rolled the large jar onto its side on the floor. Gregory lay down and reached an arm into the mouth, pulling out a dusty knot of fabric he unravelled immediately, as he sat on the floor in front of the bomblu, which the doctor wedged with a foot to prevent it from rolling.

Patricia stood on the other side and held a hand against the wide belly of the upturned jar. They all looked down at the flattened bundle of old cloth the writer had withdrawn. It was nothing: a length of threadbare mattress ticking rolled up inside what looked like the remains of an old blue apron, full of holes and saturated with dust.

'Nothing.' Phineas Micallef's voice was full of latent relief.

The old man is on a similar mission to mine, thought Gregory. He is as eager as I am to have the contents of each bomblu exposed, with the motive of eliminating once and for all any possibility of ghoulish remains.

'Now – the main operation!' Gregory leapt to his feet and reached for the bread knife. He turned and looked with some surprise at the doctor's face, regretting his casual use of the last word.

A look of horror appeared on the older man's face as the word operation left the writer's lips.

'Or shall we have a drink first?' Gregory added quickly. This time, the delay was prompted by the doctor himself. The pallor of his face and the slight tremor in one hand.

'A drink!' exclaimed Patricia. 'What a capital idea.'

In the kitchen, Phineas Micallef drained his glass of beer without pausing to breathe, wiping his mouth on a folded handkerchief extracted from his pocket in a careful motion.

They all stood around the kitchen table, none of them willing to sit or rest, to let any more time pass before they set to and opened at least one of the sealed jars before nightfall. The beer was cold and refreshing, sending the three of them back down to the cellar steps invigorated.

Now slanted with shadow, the courtyard was full of the noise of chickens, voices from the alley and the drone of jets from the distant airport. Gregory thought of his daughter's last letter. But they ignored everything and hurried to resume their task.

As he wielded the breadknife, trying to slide it between the layer of wax and the side of the jar, Gregory had a sudden vision of the first words he had written, the first line of the first tract of the novel. *They say that when Censinu Mifsud died, his small body was ...*

He looked up at Patricia, who was scanning the line of tools for something to prise the cork with, once it was free of the layer of wax. He wondered what her impression would be when she read what he wrote. His hand slipped slightly. It was going to be impossible to separate the wax from the cork. 'The whole seal – cork and wax – is going to have to come out together,' he said.

As he spoke, a sally of bangs shook the whole house, startling them and making conversation impossible. 'Hey! The festa.'

Dr Micallef's face lit up. 'Coming up soon. *Id-Duluri*. You must not miss it, my friend. The celebrations will be spectacular.'

'We'll have time for that,' said Patricia. Her husky voice showed her impatience. 'Besides, Gregory and I are going to Gozo for Santa Marija.'

Another spate of bangs cut off the end of her sentence. The doctor said something about a celebratory dinner at his house, then the three proceeded to try to wrest the cork from the jar. The heavy bomblu was firmly held in place by its own weight, the liquid inside acting as ballast.

'We'll break off a section of the seal, then prise the whole lot off together,' said the writer. He managed to slide the knife in edgeways and was attempting to work it back and forth. Particles of old wax flaked away. After some time, he managed to sever a chunk of cork seal off. A pungent vinegary smell assailed them.

'Phew!' The doctor cupped his chin in a hand again, and then approached, bending his head over the mouth of the jar. 'I'm afraid this one has long lost its bloom! Totally unpalatable.' He shook his head solemnly.

Patricia looked at the older man, cocking her head, trying to decide whether he was joking. 'It's not vinegar, then?'

'It may be that now – but it was not always intended to be so!' Phineas Micallef appeared jocular. Was that his mission then, to acquire some perfectly preserved wine? To sample the vintage produce of some twenty years ago from a clay vessel that would have retained its bouquet? It could be simple lust for vintage wine that shone so avidly in his face. But the doctor's eyes betrayed something more than just an inveterate craving for alcohol. Gregory could not think what it was.

'How are we going to get the stuff out?' Patricia's impatience was contagious.

'This one has a tap,' said Gregory. 'But we can't just let it all gush out around our feet!'

Together, the two men half walked, half dragged the jar, its contents slopping messily over the brim. Past the cellar door, they brought the *bomblu* to the grating the plumber had recently uncovered. Gregory set the spigot directly over the iron grille and wrested it with his new pliers.

It worked. Slowly, the pungent contents gurgled down the drain, filling the garden air with the acetic fragrance none of them would easily forget.

Patricia huffed. 'This will take ages.'

Phineas Micallef paced the small sunken area outside the cellar. 'It will be dark soon. Perhaps we'll do the others some other time.'

Patricia held up her arms, a comical picture of intolerable impatience. 'Tomorrow, of course!'

'Yes, tomorrow,' said the writer. 'But we'll check the bottom of this one before we go back inside tonight.' Finally, the tap stopped running, and dripped the last dark brown drops over the grille. The men turned the jar on its side as they had the other. This time, Gregory's arm and shirt sleeve became saturated with wine vinegar as he groped inside.

The torch light, aimed into the cavity, showed a gaping earthenware void. 'Nothing,' he said, lumbering breathlessly to his feet. He was tired, grimy and a bit vexed with the messy job.

Patricia seemed satisfied enough with the day's work. The doctor too seemed pacified and agreeable about proceeding with the rest of the jars the following day. They both ascended the steps outside the cellar door ahead of the writer. He pulled the lop-sided door to, wondering about the contents of the other jars, realising suddenly it was totally dark outside. Over his head, fireworks erupted in frenzied volleys.

In the distance, the staccato rhythm of a brass band playing a Souza march lent a mad festive flavour to the night air. Gregory imagined Rigoletto the plumber, who was the amateur percussionist in the village band, wielding drumsticks with as much vigour and rhythm as he did his plungers and canes.

❏

Part Three

1

Why was Gregory Worthington always reminded of the fact it was Friday by the arrival of Katie at his front door? She marked the passing of the weeks, her presence a calming influence. She was hardly needed so often. The house was clean except for a faint dusting of white limestone powder from the quarries.

Gregory let her in with a nod, looking at the carefully ironed and folded pile of his own clothes in her basket. She had given his front door her usual strenuous knock, belying any forthrightness immediately he opened, by lowering her eyes and stepping past him lightly as he held the door open.

'Today I wash the floors of the front rooms,' she said. 'And I take all rugs and mats onto the roof for a good shake.'

He nodded again: she knew best what needed doing. The tiny figure, with straight dark hair knotted sensibly at the nape of the neck, strode purposefully to the kitchen where the ritual assembly of cleaning materials, brooms, brushes and cleaning rags began.

Gregory would leave her to it and ensconce himself in the writing room, knowing they were safely out of each other's way. She knew now not to disturb him or to offer to clean the wild incomprehensible mess that worsened with each day of writing. Balled up paper, perforated edges torn off computer pages, pencil sharpenings, and torn envelopes bearing unmistakable red and blue airmail edging littered the floor. The cardboard box Katie provided for his rubbish lay in a corner conspicuously empty, surrounded by badly-aimed paper balls.

He had hardly scribbled one line when the telephone started to ring, followed immediately by sharp rapping from the knocker on the front door. He knew Katie would not attend to either, so stood up reluctantly and picked up the phone first.

'Thank you, thank you. I'll come in on Monday,' he said

quickly into the receiver. A bookshop in Sliema had unearthed the book on architecture he was seeking. 'Thank you, but there's someone at my door.'

He put down the phone, regretting having to be so short with the obliging man on the other end, who had embarked on a lengthy explanation of how the book was found.

The insistent rapping was so like Katie's mother's he prepared himself mentally for a conversation during which he would be informed in no uncertain terms of certain procedures of housework or the organisation of clothes.

When he opened the door to the blinding sunlight in the lane, he saw the figure of a small female stranger, whose face was hidden by the brim of a large straw hat. She stood with her back to him, looking towards the top of the steep street, so he had to attract her attention, giving him the immediate feeling of being at a disadvantage.

'Um – hallo? I mean ... Good morning.'

The woman turned as if startled; as if it had not been her persistent rapping that brought him to his door. Large sunglasses obscured the small face, framed by perfectly cut shoulder-length red hair.

'Good morning, Greg.' She removed the glasses and looked bemusedly into his face.

'Maggie!' It was Maggie. Maggie, his wife. His ex-wife, who he had not seen for over seven years. Where were the earrings, the cropped urchin haircut?

Gregory stood transfixed on his doorstep, looking at the stranger he had not set eyes on for so long. She looked different – older. Younger. Standing in the bright lane, with rubble walls and a crowd of village children around her, she looked out of place, sophisticated and conspicuous.

Gregory managed to find words. 'What are you doing here?'

'I tell you – you're not easy to find! Aren't you going to ask me in?'

Still mortified by his surprise and her advantage in the

situation, Gregory stood back and let his estranged wife past into his hallway.

'What are you doing in Malta?' he repeated. 'And where is Emma? I received a letter from her only two days ago.' He listened to his own words as if they emerged from a third person's lips. 'Oh – come in,' he mumbled, too late.

Maggie strode into the lounge, looking to the left and to the right of her, as if inspecting the property for faults and omissions.

The writer was distraught by his lack of recognition of her. Her hair was different. Her clothes were strange. When she took off the large hat and shook her straight red hair, the tiny sparkle of small gold studs shone in her ears. This was so unlike the Maggie of years ago. Had the changes occurred suddenly? All at once? Or gradually, during the years they were separated after her sudden and final flight to Melbourne?

'Emma is safe at home,' she said calmly, a private half-smile showing she was relishing the attention, 'plotting her escape from me. You do know she is going to university in Perth, don't you?'

'Perth? No. No – she wrote something about applying. But –' Gregory's confusion was complete. He felt foolish for not knowing what he could not possibly know. Facts about his own family he was not told about. His ineptitude was magnified by this woman, whose poise and advantage was managed with such ease.

'I thought it was your encouragement,' she said, accusingly, 'and your constant talk of Perth that set her off.'

'Talk of Perth?'

'In your letters – all about the past. Her childhood.' It sounded like an accusation, an indictment, but she was smiling.

'So what are you doing *here*?' Gregory stood in the middle of his lounge, feeling an interloper in his own life. The old familiar feelings came rushing back. This was how she always made him feel.

Maggie sat in an armchair. Her short skirt showed winter legs reddened by holiday sun. She was about to talk again, but her head turned sharply to a noise in the small hallway.

She muttered a small breath of exclamation. 'I see!' Who she saw was Katie, who stood there, dark ponytail sleek in the light, her petite frame and floor-hardened knees almost plaintive.

'I see,' said Maggie again, under her breath. She took in every detail of the maid's appearance, the dark modest eyes, the small feet and pretty shoulders.

Gregory's confusion increased. Then he took control. Why should he attempt to explain Katie's presence? He would not succumb to Maggie's old ways and crumble under her accusatory suggestions, which had always sent him tumbling in the past.

'Have you finished?' he asked the girl, his tone unusually proprietary and in charge.

'I put all rugs and mats on the roof. I cannot find the small brush and dustpan.' Her words rose at the end in a kind of question. She did not look at the visitor.

'Um – this is my ... Mrs Worthington, from Australia, Katie. This is Katie,' he said needlessly, trying not to tumble over his own words. 'The dustpan is in the cellar, I'm afraid. I will –'

'No trouble. I find everything,' said the girl, who darted away almost as soon as she said the words, giving a small nod to Maggie to acknowledge the introduction.

Gregory almost said he knew what Maggie was thinking, but steeled himself and held in the words. A feeling of unusual strength, the strength of indifference, came to him.

'I haven't used Worthington for years,' said Maggie. 'I went back to Bates, remember? I've been Maggie Bates for seven years now.' Her voice was frigid.

'I must get you a drink.' Gregory's sidestep was adroit. He was not about to enter discussions of that sort. 'Why don't you come into the kitchen?'

'I'm here to visit the Spiteris, with Alice, my cousin,' said Maggie, talking as she looked inquisitively right and left.

'Remember Alice?' She answered his question of some minutes ago with the same smooth assuredness she had not lost for an instant. She walked ahead of him and inspected the kitchen, turning her head this way and that, looking around her, through the glass doors, out across the yard. 'This is quite a nice place. You always had a knack for finding places.'

Gregory had to find something to say. 'The Spiteris ... I had no luck there – the phone book is full of them.'

'Of course. Like all Maltese surnames. You probably forgot he is an architect, and lives in Birkirkara. It would have made things so much easier for you.'

'Of course.' Gregory gestured ineffectually and busied himself pouring Kinnies over glasses of ice cubes.

'I see you have acquired local taste.' She said it ambiguously, so Gregory did not know whether she referred to the drink or to the young maid, who crossed the yard and climbed the steps to the roof.

Gregory decided to ignore the implication. 'Yes. It's surprisingly thirst quenching. Maggie –' he decided to be firm, assertive, '– you could have visited Malta any time you liked. Why when I'm here? Why now?'

The woman shook her head and shrugged. Her hair swung and shone in the light from the glass doors. She sipped her drink pensively.

Gregory knew there would be no straight answer, but the way she smiled took him back to the days they were together in Perth, the days when they had tempestuous alternating bouts of fighting and reconciliation, of making up in unnerving wrenching ways after conflicts that nearly always turned out to be his fault. He was constantly being forgiven for transgressions he hardly knew he had committed.

This smile from Maggie was a forgiving smile.

My God, he thought: she is in a conciliatory mood. Even after seven years, it was recognisable. But Gregory had changed. He felt different. There was no dread in his mind, no tremor in his heart as he waited for her to speak again. He looked at her from the physical distance of the width of the kitchen as he stood with his back against his large new fridge.

I have nothing to confess, he almost said aloud. Indeed, he had nothing to be contrite about.

'Look,' she said. 'It was about time. I needed a holiday. Emma's grown up. Seventeen – I can hardly believe it. My responsibilities have lightened.' She said it in a formal way, shrugged her shoulders and turned, her eyes piercing, searching his own. 'Well – lightened a bit, but not vanished altogether.' Her eyes seemed to stress she was still required to care and provide for Emma.

Still reeling from the surprise of seeing her after all those years, Gregory took strength from the physical distance of the room width. He had banished the feeling of being trapped, like some small quarry in the face of a mean predator. He knew her well. He knew she was after something. Whatever it was, she was going to prove an obstacle. He thought of the jars. He thought of Patricia.

'You were always a schemer, Gregory,' Maggie said suddenly. She made it sound like a joke. Her small peal of laughter rang false in the bright kitchen. There she was, accusing him of her own fault, he thought, fixing her own behaviours squarely onto him. Well, it would not work very well now, after all these years. He could hardly be accused of doing anything at all with her in mind after all this time.

But she said the words because she caught a glimpse of the young maid coming down the roof steps, burdened by a pile of small mats.

'Where are you staying?' he said, to distract her. He was not going to have her here. How was he going to state his refusal strongly enough?

'Oh – Alice and I have been received quite royally,' she said, with a hint of something he could not be sure was sarcasm. 'Peter Spiteri and his family treat us like long lost cousins. Which is what we are, I suppose!' She laughed again, forgetting about the maid and inspecting her surroundings again. 'Show me the rest of the house,' she ordered. 'I had a terrible time finding this place. You've buried yourself in a tiny village they hardly know about in Sliema.'

'I didn't come here to enjoy society – I came here to write.'

'Oh yes, I haven't forgotten your sordid little stories. So – what lurid little horror have you dreamt up this time?'

Gregory ignored the dig. He led her through the small back rooms, giving her only a glimpse of the writing room and deciding to omit the cellar entirely. He led her out into the brilliant glare of the vineyard.

Maggie placed the large hat back on her head. She looked a total anomaly in the country garden.

Gregory looked at her. She was not interested in what he wrote, but her question was intoned with a pecuniary concern. So she was looking over Emma's shoulder as their daughter read his letters. He should have known he could not keep much hidden from Maggie Bates.

'Anyway, never mind that,' she was saying. 'I'm only here for just over a week, and the Spiteris have a long itinerary of *amazing* historical sights they want us to look at.' She tilted the hat brim so she could look at him better. 'But let's not be strangers. I hope to take advantage of this and see you as much as possible, Greg.'

'Of course.' His naturally cordial nature leapt ahead of what he would really have liked to say. He shaded his eyes from the sun, standing bareheaded in his vineyard, speaking all the words he would normally have avoided with a woman like Maggie.

Maltese hospitality and awe of strangers was contagious, he thought. He was extending an invitation to share his company in spite of himself. But what about Patricia? Mentioning her to Maggie would be a capital mistake. Derision and rebuke would stream forth if she discovered his relationship with the Maltese woman. No – he would keep Patricia to himself. But he had to warn her of Maggie's arrival.

He thought back to the weekend, when they opened the jars with Fin, savouring again the excitement, the fun they had in spite of the mess, the pungent smell of wine turned vinegar, the scattering shreds of wax and cork.

The second sealed *bomblu* proved a much harder exercise on the Sunday. Once more, they stood in the cellar, all three feeling slightly more at ease after the experience of draining the first jar. They brought the heavy vessel into the open space outside the cellar door, working in the sunlight of the afternoon.

Wresting the cork and wax out of the neck was complicated and messy, Gregory almost cutting his hand with the long sharp knife. Its blade sparked in the sun as he wielded it, reminding him of lines out of his own writing; of Terezina grabbing a similar knife from the kitchen table and throwing it after the young boy as he escaped from the house. He thought of the doctor's words about the woman – how his depiction of her was so different, contrasted so acutely, with the prevalent opinion of her in the village. The writer could not really see her in his mind's eye. He would have to get a description from Fin somehow. But how, without plunging the doctor back into what seemed to be infinite sadness, real grief? What did Fin know?

There was a ream of words he would write contained in the eyes of the old man, if only he would let them out. But this was no time for that. They had to attend to the task at hand.

This particular jar had no tap at the base. Its mouth emitted no vinegar smell like the other one. Instead, the unmistakable smell of olives rose in an aura, like a belch.

'Oil!' someone exclaimed.

'Olive oil. But it's …' the doctor wrinkled his nose and peered into the bomblu. He could see little, but his nose twitched. 'It's rancid,' he declared.

'Oh, what a shame.' Gregory knew the doctor's was a nose he

could trust. 'We couldn't possibly throw away all that oil.'

Patricia shrugged. 'What could you do with it? It's off. No use to anyone, really.'

'But to pour it down the drain – I don't know. What if it runs out to sea?' He looked at the jar and thought of the slick the oil would create wherever it surfaced. A slick of rancid oil forming a stain in some sheltered pebbly bay. Like the one he had seen in Mistra, where there were boathouses carved into the rock face of a limestone cliff.

'As a matter of fact, my friend,' the doctor said after a pause, 'I don't think it would be that harmful. Organic waste, you see.' The doctor nodded, his sleeked-back hair glimmering as if it too had been anointed with oil. 'The fish would gobble it up in no time.'

The writer was unsure of the truth in the statement. But he wanted to empty the jar much more than he wanted to preserve the limpid Mediterranean waters. The twinge of guilt that assailed him did not last.

He and the doctor lowered the jar gingerly onto its side in stages, aiming the flow of oil more or less over the drain's metal grille. They poured the entire contents gradually, lifting the bottom of the jar higher in slow degrees, until it was completely drained. The liquid made thick heavy glugging noises, and the rancid olive smell was overpowering.

Anything at the bottom of the jar, Gregory thought, would surely slide down and be caught on the grating, preventing it from washing away in the green stream of slick gurgling liquid.

They heard a clatter and looked down. A small object was caught in the grid, so they up-ended the jar quickly. What they heard landed with a ringing rattle onto the metal.

Eagerly, Patricia rushed forward and picked the thing up. It was a glass jar. An empty glass jam jar without a lid, which had lain at the bottom of all that oil for twenty years. Brown and green stains ringed its edge, the glass screw edge was ingrained with sediment. She held it up for the men to see; a normal household object that held no mystery and no meaning.

'That's all!' Her comical smile of disappointment made Gregory laugh, and lent a note of respite to the moment. Relief was not apparent in the doctor's face, but it was there in his body, his movements. He looked up from where he knelt on one knee, craning his neck and giving a half smile.

'That leaves only one,' he said, placing a hand in the small of his back as he brought himself to stand upright after the effort of holding the large jar at an angle.

'Yes,' Gregory said. 'Next week sometime, perhaps.'

That night, at Zija Roza's, across a red checked tablecloth stretched between them, Gregory looked at Patricia's face and hair, her dark eyes that held the capacity to instil such humour into a situation, yet inspire such warmth and affection when they were alone together. They looked at each other over a table crowded with the remnants of a hearty meal of spaghetti and rabbit sauce. There stood a small bowl of grated cheese, an almost empty bottle of wine, and an earthenware water carafe, whose texture was almost identical to the jars in his cellar.

'Shall we go to Gozo for Santa Marija around the fifteenth of August? The festa is celebrated in several parishes around the islands, but the Gozo one is quite special,' she said.

'Of course.' He was enthusiastic. 'By then, we'll have opened the last jar and settled the whole question. I'll have a substantial part of the book on paper, and I can perhaps send a sizeable portion to Paul De Souza in Australia.'

'I have a feeling about that last jar.'

Gregory looked at her, surprised she shared his absorption and feelings. But they did not discuss it much longer. Their drive back to the farmhouse with the windows of the Volvo down was intimate and mostly silent. The balmy still night seemed close around them even as they entered the darkened house and finally the bedroom, where the white mosquito net looped over the white bed. The draped net and tangled sheets lustred in the almost total darkness, relieved by a dull shaft of light through the shutters from the yellow street lamps in the lane.

Patricia disappeared, tanned skin fusing with the darkness. It was only when she lay down on the bed that he could see her shape, her slim body dark against the sheets. Her hair was a thick cloud around her head and shoulders, in which he buried his face. She was warm, smelling lightly of scent, of sea spray, of crushed herbs and flower petals.

They made love with a languor evolved from a cognisance of each other, from an acknowledgment at once tacit yet expressed; in her touch, in his caresses, in their coming together with such sweetness and such force.

Later, Gregory remembered drifting off to sleep with his head cradled between her arm and her breast, his hand tangled in her hair. The length of his thigh against hers and her tiny movements and nuzzling sounds roused him once more to desire. He stirred, feeling his body tense as he stroked her awake again, lowering his head to her bosom slowly as she became aware of his intentions. She took his face in her hands in the dark, kissing him deeply while rotating herself slowly in the bed so her body welcomed his. Gradually, their legs slid against each other until her kiss melted away, lips travelling down his neck with a small bite of pleasure and acceptance when she felt him entering her.

Without a word, they conversed in a kind of breathing, a kind of inhaling at the same time, letting captured air escape slowly, finding the next breath on the following swell of elation.

In the quiet, distant explosions split the heavy night. Gregory listened to the bangs until they ceased, waiting for the first stirrings from the hen coop. He could not remember falling asleep after that.

He woke to a sharp warm slant of sunlight moving imperceptibly over his body in the early morning.

Patricia had already risen. 'It's very early,' she whispered.

'Go back to sleep. I must drive home and dress for the office.'

But he quickly pulled on some clothes and stood at his wooden front door with her, holding her close and sensing an unwillingness to let her go emerge into his behaviour and his words.

'Come back soon.' His voice was as hoarse as hers in the morning. 'Phone me from the office.'

She drove away in a cloud of dust whipped up by a gust of wind in the lane.

In the same lane, in almost the same light, only a few days later, Gregory watched Maggie get into a small rented Ford, twisting her body to get into the seat; throwing the large hat onto the back seat. Thankfully, he had no need for a formal leave-taking, because she drove away without a hindward glance, and he heard his telephone ringing in the house behind him.

❑

2

'Listen, Patricia. Something unexpected has come up.' He regretted the silly words the minute they left his lips. 'I mean – we'll probably have to put off opening the last bomblu.'

'What? What happened?' Her husky tone suggested complicity. She thought it was something to do with the house or the Mifsuds.

'Um – Don't ask me why, it's a mystery to me too, but – look, my ex-wife is here from Australia. Maggie – she came here this morning.'

There was silence on the line. Not even the crackle of static or the feeling of distance or depth. The complete silence made Gregory look down into the mouthpiece. 'Patricia? Are you there?'

'I'm here. Is she ...? How long is she staying?'

Gregory put her right immediately. 'Oh – she's not staying here at the house. Of course not. She has relatives in Bikik ... Bir ... somewhere.'

'Birkirkara.' Her voice was flat. She seemed to be thinking, thinking slowly about what she should say next.

'Patricia – it doesn't change anything. I really don't know... But look, she is not very pleasant. I haven't told her about us because she'd be sure to irritate me with some snide comment. Still, I wouldn't have liked you to come here and meet her unprepared.'

'I don't think I should meet her at all.'

'No. Yes. Of course not.' Gregory was irritated by his own confusion. 'I wasn't thinking. No, you're right.' Gregory swept a lock of hair off his forehead. He felt uncertainty, hesitancy, in the woman at the other end, a reticence he wished he could ease away. 'Listen, Patricia, I know this will hold up opening the jar, and maybe even delay my writing a bit, but there's no reason you and I cannot continue as usual. It's not like –'

Patricia interrupted him again. 'It only makes sense that I should not come to the farmhouse. At least for now.' There was another silent pause. Then, 'Gregory. Gregory? I'd like to see you. I hate talking over the phone like this. Come to Valletta, please.' Her hoarse voice sounded entreating, but she had made a quick decision, and she was not about to divulge it on the phone.

'Yes, yes. Of course I will.' He was willing to do anything to maintain what they had, what he had discovered with her. 'I'll catch a bus in about twenty minutes. I'll be at Cordina's at about three-thirty, all right?'

When he got off the bus at the Triton fountain, Patricia was walking towards him, weaving through the crowd and waving, her smile a bit solemn, a bit formal.

'Are you all right?' Gregory took off his hat, feeling young, foolish and inexperienced in spite of the difference in their ages. He stood in a strange place, a country in which he had only vague understanding of social mores. He had no right to confuse and upset this woman, who had so openly and enthusiastically become part of his life. He should understand if she withdrew slightly at this rude interruption of what they had started together. He should understand even if she shut him out completely.

They were nudged and jostled by people boarding and alighting from the green buses. Some stared at them accusingly, as if standing in the way was in some way unacceptable, just as his thoughtlessness was unacceptable. But how was he to know Maggie would suddenly re-enter his life after such a long interlude?

'Are you all right?' he repeated.

'Yes.' She nodded vigorously. 'Of course I am. Still, I'm a bit annoyed that this happened right now. It all seemed so perfect.'

He could not see her expression, but she was right. It was so perfect. Too perfect. And this was an obstacle, the interruption he had almost expected. What he had not expected at all was that it would come in the shape and form of Maggie.

'It was all going so well, Gregory. Oh – am I sounding adolescent?' She looked up at him sideways as they walked over the drawbridge into the city. In Republic Street, which was closed to traffic and teeming with tourists, businessmen and gaggles of young people, they made slow progress towards the café where they had planned to meet.

'I couldn't stand waiting at Cordina's. It's packed, and everyone seems to be getting in my way today. I was half an hour early, anyway,' she said.

Her small pout of anxiety made Gregory laugh. 'Look,' he said in despair. He would never forgive Maggie for creating such confusion. 'Look – this is no major disaster, you know. Maggie has little or nothing to do with my life now.'

'Then why are you worried about it? Is it that she could delay things with the book? With opening the jar?'

'Yes,' he said without hesitation. 'And with you. I don't want anything to ...' He was interrupted. A crowd of people threatened to sweep them along the street against their will. To avoid walking among a troupe of loud German tourists, they stepped off the pavement outside the museum. The rest of the walk to the café was made in comparative silence, as they negotiated the crowded street.

Inside, shimmering counter and small tables, smells of coffee and confectionery reminded Gregory of frantic coffee drinking on a trip to Rome as a young man. People sipped hot coffee standing up, on the run as it were, bolting it down between one appointment and the next as they worked in the commercial centre. Here, sophisticated ladies and fashionably dressed young people jostled each other, talking at the tops of their voices in an anglicised vernacular he was almost beginning to understand.

'Yes,' he kept saying. He wanted to keep a positive outlook. 'Yes. What I am worried about is that she will create obstacles for me as she has in the past, and that she might prevent me seeing you as often as I'd like just by being on the island, by being here. Whatever brought her here in the first place I simply don't know. It's seven years since I'd set eyes on her. Seven years.' He looked at her. Was he trying too hard to impress upon Patricia the distance that had formed between him and Maggie?

He could see she was thinking, as she had during their telephone conversation. This time, he could see the small crease in her brow and the fidget she made in her lap before reaching for her coffee cup. 'I've been thinking, Gregory.'

His face fell. 'I can see you have. Please don't ... Don't think that –'

'Legally, she is still your wife, I suppose. I think I should keep out of the way until – until the coast is clear. I have finally succumbed to threats and offers my sister and her husband keep making. I don't spend enough time with them. I think I'll go shopping in Sicily with them for a week.'

Gregory was startled by her announcement. 'Sicily?'

'It's barely two hundred kilometres away, Gregory.' She smiled, but it was only a small pause in her grave look. 'And it's only a week. It'll give me time to think, and it will give you time to be with your wife.'

Be with his wife! He did not want to be with his wife. She was not his wife at all. He did not know what to say without going into a long diatribe about separation, papers, divorce. It would make it all sound so sordid. 'But I –'

'I didn't think I'd feel this way,' she was saying. 'But I do. I feel I should step back and let you have your time with her. I really cannot – in all fairness and conscience – get in the way.'

'What do you mean, fairness and conscience?' Gregory could not believe what he heard. Perhaps he had not explained his situation clearly enough. 'I told you, we are really not married any more. It's just that we have not finalised a divorce. There was never a real reason to, is probably why.' But he suddenly saw her line of reasoning.

Her dark eyes, a sad little crease on the bridge of her nose and the elegant knot of hair which was beginning to release unruly tendrils, were all too familiar to him now, he knew her. He understood her.

He also understood something of the moral tenor of the island. Patricia probably believed she could not ethically stand in the way of a man and his wife if there were the slightest chance they could be reconciled. Since they had never divorced, she thought the chance existed.

He looked away to where a woman with a complicated coiffeur was fidgeting with a teaspoon, making irritating noises in her saucer, tapping brightly painted nails against the lacquered surface of the table. She looked at them frankly, a raised eyebrow and pursed lips making the stare a caricature of what Patricia was trying to appease.

Still, he understood. 'Only a week? Promise? Are you sure?' He made it sound as if he would be willing to put up with a parting as long as it were not too long.

'That's all. It will kill a lot of birds with one stone.' She looked determined and in charge of the situation.

'Perhaps. And I'll be at the airport to meet you when you come back!'

'No.' She laughed, genuinely pleased to see his eagerness.

'The ferry then?'

'No, Gregory. I'll come up to the farmhouse to see you on the twenty-second.' She put out a hand and stroked the back of his with one finger. 'We'll talk again then.' She seemed to have worked it all out. The way she said twenty-second with such certainty meant she had planned it all mentally beforehand. Were these rehearsed words he was listening to from her?

'This means we'll miss the festa in Gozo,' he protested. He had been looking forward to a full weekend on the smaller island. It would have felt like a holiday. It would have felt like an interlude nothing could have spoiled. Now it was all ruined, changed, and he could not believe it had been Maggie who had broken the spell. It was too much.

Patricia made a wry grimace and gave a small shrug. She said little else after that, and Gregory did not want to spoil things further by lengthening the discussion, bringing Maggie up all the time. They simply had to do what Patricia suggested. What she planned for them.

When they said goodbye in the comparative peace of the courtyard of the Governor's Palace, their conversation was witnessed only by the statue of Neptune, whose shadow fell among the leaves and buds of a flowerbed.

Gregory held her tightly, feeling her sadness, feeling the resolution to handle the situation in what she thought was the right way, in spite of the anguish she was obviously fighting. Her eyes were bright and clear, but her voice broke often, and her fists were tightly balled round the strap of her handbag.

'Only a week?'

She nodded. When he watched her walk away, leaving through a stone arch, going back to the bustle of Republic Street, he realised how well he had got to know her sentiments and her moods; how well he knew her movements, her body, and her unspoken thoughts. He knew she would not look back.

❏

3

In the yard, Nikol Mifsud finally fills all the jars and prepares to seal them. The disks of cork have been blackened, the wax stirred. Something moves on top of the rubble wall and catches his eye. He climbs two steps from the space in front of the cellar and watches his son climb into the garden.

'Where have you been?' His voice is sterner than he intends. 'I've done nearly everything without you. Your mother is complaining again. She really should rest inside, in the shade.' He looks at the dusty state of his son's shorts and shirt. 'You've been at the quarries again. How many times have I warned you, Censinu? Those places are dangerous. Go – wash. Have something to eat. And please don't let your mother see that dust on your clothes.'

Inside, the Rediffusion set is playing softly. Censinu hears the voice of an announcer say the lotto numbers, first in Maltese, then in English. His mother always has a lotto ticket, bought for a few pennies and stuck into the frame of the holy picture on the loggia wall. The blue numbers, written by the lotto clerk the previous day, are separated by little dashes. He stops to read them. None of them are announced by the voice on the radio set.

He tiptoes to the kitchen sink and drinks a quick glass of water. The pipes shudder as he closes the tap.

'I made you a plate of fish and potato, but it's cold now.' His mother's voice is behind him. She pushes a small plate towards him on the table. Her eyes are bright, feverish. 'Sit down and eat it – here.' She slides the plate until it rests against a crease in the tablecloth.

Censinu pulls back a chair silently and sits in front of the plate, taking up a fork and piercing a slice of baked potato in the middle. He is ravenous, yet he eats slowly, mindful of his mother's eyes watching him pierce morsel after morsel and carrying it to his mouth without looking up.

'What do you wish for most in the world, Cens?' she finally asks. She sweeps hair from her forehead, resting an elbow on the table and holding her head in her palm, looking like a bedraggled schoolgirl. Her eyes are hooded, but there are no traces of the dark rings that marked her eyes that morning. Her skin seems bloated and stretched, but it must be the light in which her son looks at her.

Surreptitiously, from time to time, he snatches a look between mouthfuls, now that his plate is almost empty. 'Ma. Ma – are you sleepy?'

'No, not sleepy. Dead tired.'

'Go and rest,' he offers. 'I will play with the boy.'

The mother shifts, uneasy. 'He has a bump the size of a penny on his head. He cried for a long time.'

Censinu urges again. 'I will play with him. I'll keep him quiet.'

'What do you wish for most in the whole world, Censinu?' she asks again, turning her head in her hand and looking at him as he rises and places the plate and fork in the sink. It is as if she is asking him because it has just occurred to her what she herself wishes for above all else.

Without answering, the boy leaves the kitchen and joins his father in the yard. In a corner, playing with scraps of cork, his toddler brother squats, bare feet touched by the sun slanting past the wall of the house. A livid purple bruise, large as a beer bottle cap, stains his forehead.

'What happened to you, eh?' Censinu jests, using the voice adults reserve for small children. 'What happened? What's this on your head?'

He makes a funny face and dances a few grotesque steps, waving curled fingers and uttering small grunts. The baby chortles and grins, scattering the pieces of cork in front of him.

'She was all right,' Censinu says to his father without looking at him, as he sits down to play with his baby brother. 'She is calm, resting.' They look at each other like two grown men sharing secret empathy.

Nikol nods at his son. He has grown up too soon.

◻

4

It was a hot week, temperatures escalating each day until dryness and bright light made Gregory long for a break, for a thunderstorm to break the monotony and lethargy that dulled his thinking. He longed for a downpour, a flood.

'We do not get breaks here,' said Phineas Micallef. 'No respite, no cool breezes or rain. You sometimes hear thunder at night, but it is over the sea, over the hills in Sicily, perhaps. We never get rain here until the middle of September. Sometimes not even then.' The doctor turned, addressing Maggie politely.

She sat primly on the edge of one of Gregory's unmatched kitchen chairs, listening to the doctor with her head tilted, red hair forming a curtain and hiding the side of her face closer to her estranged husband.

The writer took the bottle of imported red wine the older man had brought and topped up the three glasses on the table. Soon, he saw, he was going to have to open one of his own less expensive bottles. The doctor had nervously downed several glasses in quick succession.

Gregory watched him closely. Was he nervous because of shyness caused by introduction to Maggie? Or was he still unused to sitting in the very house where the missing boy had lived?

Still, Fin was gracious and sociable, turning to Maggie. Including her in friendly conversation. 'But you have Maltese blood, Maltese relatives,' he said to the Australian woman. 'They would have told you of our summers – of the overpowering humidity we get towards the end of each season – and then the floods in Msida when the rains finally come down!' He made a joke of the last sentence, raising an eyebrow at Gregory, who had heard ample discussion of the reconstruction of the Msida Creek to prevent future flooding of the valley.

Maggie gave the doctor a bemused smile. 'We heard different things from our parents when we were growing up in Melbourne,' she said archly.

Gregory detected more than a hint of annoyance in her voice.

'We listened to how better off we kids were, in comparison to their childhood. And the difficulties of being migrants – they went on and on about that,' she sighed.

'Ah – integration, assimilation and synthesis,' said the doctor philosophically. 'They are the bane of every exile's life.' Was he speaking wistfully of his own banishment from the smarter suburbs?

'And the impossibility of raising Maltese Catholic children in the Victorian suburbs,' continued Maggie, but she stopped when she realised she was not speaking to someone she could condescend or talk down to. Suddenly, her sense of superiority was dimmed by someone who could carry a vigorous conversation on any subject she might bring up, in spite of his inebriation, in spite of her feminine power, which he seemed to either ignore or not notice.

'I have my own ideas about raising children,' she said suddenly, looking at Gregory pointedly. Without saying anything further about their daughter, the writer and his estranged wife looked at each other. The look did not go unnoticed by the older man.

Maggie started to say something. Then, changing her mind, came out with a platitude. 'Tell me about living in this village, Dr Micallef,' she said, turning the conversation away from her own family.

'It is vastly easier to bring up a Maltese Catholic family here!' exclaimed the old man.

The doctor and Gregory laughed together, for different reasons.

'Take this house, for instance,' she insisted.

The doctor looked confounded. 'This house? What about it?' He gulped, looked around him and stood, moving to the garden door and looking out, although all that he could see was his own reflection. 'This house ... now let me see.'

Gregory saw he was staving off some sort of emotion, some personal feeling, and filling the space with platitudes. 'Here,' started Phineas Micallef, 'Here, a solid family of hard workers must have lived. Or really, generations of them, one after the other. They grew their small crops, attended to their chores and animal husbandry. They brought up their children frugally, piously, and sincerely hoped the little ones would grow to benefit from their work. Grow to occupy a better station and lot in life.' He turned towards Maggie, but his eyes were on Gregory. 'Your ... ah – Gregory here probably knows much more about this house than I do, now. Don't you, my friend?' His eyes were full of sadness, a sadness Gregory could not explain.

Why was this man so torn up, so apparently heartbroken? What was his real connection in this village, where people treated him well enough, but who would always make him feel like a stranger, an interloper in their midst? There had to be a connection, something to do with his past.

Something, Gregory felt, that was inexplicably linked to the disappearance of the boy. It had to. And here was Maggie, making light of it, treating this venerable old man as if he were a chance encounter, an unimportant acquaintance, to be forgotten as soon as he made his exit. The writer looked at the woman sitting in his kitchen, feeling for the first time he was at an advantage. In spite of her origins, or those of her mother, he sensed a deeper affinity with the island and its people than hers. It was not a mistake to invite Fin to meet her: Gregory steeled himself for what he knew he had to say to her, and the doctor's amiable presence, fine wit and composure were putting him into a comfortable mood.

Comfortable but separate. Suddenly, she was placed alone,

with Gregory and the doctor firmly facing her across an almost tangible line that ran across the deal table.

'But surely there's more to life than ...' Maggie persisted, regardless of the doctor's expression.

He does not like her at all, thought the writer, looking at his inebriated friend shake a sleek well-groomed head at Maggie, treating her almost like an intractable child.

'It is not very sensible for people – on either side of the globe or either side of the same country, even – to try to tell each other how to live.' He kept his language neutral, but Gregory realised he was telling her off.

When the evening drew to a close, the doctor rose to his feet from the settee, where he had slumped after two or three after-dinner brandies. He staggered slightly, slurring a slow sentence of thanks only slightly. 'De-lighted to – have met ... to have met you, I'm – sure,' he said carefully to Maggie, slitting his lips tightly over his teeth.

'My God,' she exclaimed, after the doctor disappeared up the gloomy lane, staggering, his long shadow angular in the gloom. 'That man was blind drunk!'

'Fin will be fine in the morning,' said Gregory, displeased with her judgement of his friend. But he had more on his mind than her objection to the doctor's drinking, and wanted to get on with what he had to say.

When they were back inside, he stood firmly in his own hallway, drenched by the bright light that fell from the naked globe hanging over them. The light gave him assurance, made what he had to say easier to enunciate, as if he were on a stage.

'What I have to say to you won't take long, Maggie,' he said clearly. 'Then you can leave Malta on the weekend, feeling you have achieved what you set out to achieve when you came to look for me here.'

'Whatever do you mean?'

Gregory ignored her stagy question and continued. 'I feel I am in a position to offer you a compromise.'

'I came here full of hope,' she said, pouting. Her red hair tossed in the bright light. 'After all, it's not out of the ordinary to feel we could mend some bridges, is it? I thought – after all these years – we would find a level we could relate on ...' She stopped when she saw Gregory's look of disbelief.

Did she actually think he would be at all open to the idea of reconciliation? Now? In this way? Perhaps it was not only Fin who was affected by the drinks that night.

'Cross & Ormondsey have sent a cheque to my bank in Perth,' Gregory went on, saying the words he prepared mentally some hours before. 'I'm going to instruct them to send you eight thousand dollars. It should be ample to cover Emma's extras for the next two years or so. She'll be nineteen then, and I'll be able to help her directly.'

Maggie's mouth fell open. 'I really don't understand how you –'

'Not much to understand.' He held up a hand to interrupt her physically, with a sign that was forceful in the bright light. 'Take the money and go. And when you get to Melbourne, please draw up divorce papers.' He held the thick wooden door open and let her through.

In the gloom of the lane, she looked at once angry and dejected, but said nothing else.

Gregory had guessed correctly. Maggie was in Malta on a quest, rather than a mission. All he needed to do was fulfil her search. The sound of the rented car leaving the lane was muffled when Gregory closed the wooden door. He breathed a sigh of relief, letting the air out slowly between his lips. He had not served himself much to drink that evening, keeping his wits about him, not willing to relinquish the strength he discovered; the strength with which he could address Maggie and send her off with what she could consider a kind of victory.

'All she needed to do was win,' he said to himself.

The last he heard of her was by telephone. 'I hope you haven't changed your mind about the eight thousand dollars,' she said clearly over the line.

Gregory smiled to himself and was almost tempted to give her a small scare. But it was hardly worth it. He had no time or desire for games. 'I haven't changed my mind about anything at all,' he said distinctly, imagining the tilt of her head.

In spite of the absence of dangling earrings and the stark statement of urchin-cut hair, Maggie presented the same intimidation, the same feelings, until he had felt steady and forceful enough to redress the balance between them.

He thought of Patricia. He never stopped thinking of Patricia, of her soft appeal and the definite sympathy she demonstrated ever since he met her. He thought of her face and her body, and the way she spoke. He grew distracted, then remembered he was on the phone.

The voice on the other end said something and then he heard a click.

'Today is the twenty-first,' Gregory Worthington said to Katie on the following Friday.

The date meant nothing to the small dark maid. Perhaps she thought it was meaningful for Australians, Gregory thought to himself as he listened to what work she would be doing that day. She arrived carrying a large wicker basket, bought with money he had given her two weeks ago. In it, his laundered and ironed clothes were in a tidy pile.

'And tomorrow,' he said with a light-hearted lilt in his voice, 'is the twenty-second!'

The maid looked at him strangely then nodded and smiled dutifully, as if satisfied it was permissible to be eccentric if you were foreign and a writer, and to utter obvious things even children could calculate. It was permissible, if one were a foreigner and strange, to live with a room so full of dust, paper and pencil sharpenings it was impossible to sit in. She watched him with a bemused expression as he took the camera and leapt out into the yard, under the archway and down the hollowed stone steps to the cellar. The wooden door had been repaired, and stood open to show the inside space, well lit by the two half windows.

The six empty jars had been moved away into the back room. Gregory looked at the single remaining bomblu. It stood in the middle of the earth floor, throwing a slight shadow towards the wall with the trough and the metal hoops in the stone. He raised the camera to his eye and looked through the viewfinder.

Detached visually from its surroundings, the clay jar's shape and texture came through, closer to his eye and his mind. He took several shots. When Patricia came back, they would open it. Tomorrow, Saturday, she would drive to the farmhouse after her week in Sicily. On Sunday, with Fin there as before, they would open the jar.

Was it becoming a game? Did he need to find anything – or nothing – there, to feel he accomplished something? Gregory wondered whether his story needed another discovery, or whether it was the doctor's intrigue that spurred him on to turn this into a mystery. What, after all, was so special about this jar? He removed his eye from the tiny hole without pressing the button again and looked at the brightly lit vessel.

It needed to be empty – empty of anything else but the liquid it held. At the same time, it needed to contain something – something to confirm what he had conceived in his head, what he had written.

A small rustle outside made him look behind him. In the doorway stood Rigoletto, the plumber.

'Katie let me in. You said to check the pipes?' The small man wore a cloth cap, which he doffed casually, smiling cautiously and looking about the large room.

Gregory saw he was looking with trepidation for the mouth of the well. 'Here's the well, Joe!' he pointed, walking over to the stone rim and slapping a palm down on the heavy lid.

The plumber stayed in the doorway. 'The pipes,' he

repeated.

Gregory saw there was no way the man would approach the well. 'Okay – the pipes,' he said reassuringly.

The two men ascended the steps. Rigoletto set about tapping and listening, pushing lengths of cane up and down the red earthenware pipes which were belted by metal rings to the outside of the farm building. From the roof and from the yard floor, the funny bent man grunted and mumbled, wiping his forehead often on a checked handkerchief. Finally, he stood in the middle of the yard and uttered two words that sounded most ominous. 'Like before!'

Gregory understood. He was starting to like his dealings with the village folk. 'Like before?' he repeated, smiling broadly.

'Everything wrong,' said the plumber. 'Roof drain hole blocked. Middle junction blocked. Soak well blocked.'

'How long do you think the whole thing's been like that, Joe?'

The plumber scratched his head under the cap. 'Very long time, sir.'

'Twenty years?' Gregory prodded, probed.

The plumber made an earnest expression, as if to say, how on earth was he to gauge the time the rainwater pipes from the roof to the well became blocked? '*Kif tridni naf?*'

The two men smiled at once.

In spite of the impenetrability of the language, Rigoletto had made himself clear.

'Let's have a beer in the kitchen. Your time ends now, right?' Gregory laughed.

The village man smiled and shook his hand, as if he were thinking the writer was learning village ways rather quickly.

5

'Then, while drinking his beer, he told me there were rags pushed into some of the pipes, to deliberately stop water from going down into the well!' Gregory looked at Patricia.

His narration of what had gone on the day before made her smile, especially Gregory's descriptions of the plumber and his picturesque way of detailing the trouble with the pipes.

Patricia was tanned, refreshed, and animated by their reunion. She sat at the kitchen table with her chin in her palm, listening wide-eyed to everything Gregory said. Her light blue dress and hair in a knot emphasised her relaxed demeanour. She had a pleasant rest in Taormina.

'But I'm overjoyed to be back!' she exclaimed, touching Gregory on the arm and lowering her head for a moment.

He put a hand under her chin and raised her face to be kissed. 'I missed you.' It was all he needed to say.

Since her arrival at his door that afternoon, he was filled with the realisation of how desperately he looked forward to seeing her again. He swept her into his arms in the lane, embracing her tightly as they both laughed with excitement and relief. Relief at finding what they imagined for the last week was still there, still vigorous and waiting to be enjoyed.

Drinking Kinnie in a tumbler jangling with ice cubes, Gregory felt it was almost as if Patricia had never gone, never left his side. Except for the memory of Maggie. It was not a dream, not a nightmare. His ex-wife had really been there, surprised him at his doorstep, sat in his kitchen with new shoulder-length hair and old determination. But she was gone, and perhaps her coming had served some good.

'She promised to start divorce proceedings,' he said, without fuss. 'Since we have been apart well over seven years, and Emma is well over sixteen, it should only take a matter of weeks.'

Although she said nothing, there was a kind of repose in Patricia's eyes, a kind of comfort that settled upon her gradually.

'So,' Gregory slapped his thighs and leapt to his feet. 'Everything is now back to normal!'

'What were you saying about the pipes?' Patricia's voice caught on the last word, making it sound secretive and mysterious. Her smile was infectious. 'Are you having them unblocked?'

'There might be no real need,' he replied. 'I'll try to decide before the rains come.'

In Gregory's arms, she mumbled and sighed, obviously delighted to be back in his embrace. That night, they would celebrate her return.

'And tomorrow, we'll open the last bomblu.' Gregory drained his glass. Then he went on to finish what Rigoletto had told him. 'The plumber said the pipes between the roof and the well have been stopped in places by rags, wedged in as if deliberately by someone. But he could be wrong.'

Patricia nodded. 'You'll find that in a lot of old country houses, most gaps have been stopped up in some way. Room air vents are boarded over or crammed with rags. They were suspicious of fresh air – thinking it chilled the bones, or brought sickness.'

'Did they? Well – yes. As a matter of fact,' said Gregory, nodding and pointing to the square ventilators close to the ceiling, 'those were full of balled-up newspaper!'

'They did it to stop draughts,' she said. 'And some people feared germs coming into the house. The caution probably dates from the time of the Great Plague. So you're not having the pipes unblocked?'

'Joe said he has a lot to do this month. The man is actually afraid of the well – I can't believe it. Like I said, perhaps I can engage him just before the rains start.'

'September. That's only a couple of months away. Sometimes we don't get rain until the first week in October. It's the first rain that fill the wells,' she said. Then she laughed at the aphorism. 'I'm beginning to sound like my mother.'

'I would love to be able to have my own water store. Just think, next spring, when the vines start to bud.'

She looked at him wistfully. 'Will you still be here next spring?'

Gregory sat back for a moment, looking away through the flung-open double doors of the kitchen. He thought of the remaining four thousand dollars in his account. It was useless trying to calculate how long he would survive on it until Cross & Ormondsey started to pay royalties. The book had to be released first, in any case, and start to sell. To hope it would sell well was not what he did these days. It was pointless to count chickens. It was also pointless explaining to Patricia he gave Maggie a lot of money to ease her out of the way and into the past, where she belonged.

'If I can afford it.' He made it sound like a joke, but realised it filled her with relief and hope. 'I'll be here if I can afford it. If not, I shall have to use the return portion of the three-month ticket I came on.'

Patricia made a mock grimace. It was too much of a happy afternoon to shadow with what could happen in several weeks.

As if by agreement, they sustained the mood, embracing intimately and passing to the more urgent question of whether to eat at Zija Roza's and how long it would be before they were back at the farmhouse to spend the night together.

❏

6

Fin was late. Gregory spoke to him on the telephone the previous evening, agreeing they would all go down to the cellar at about eleven. By noon, Gregory and Patricia were putting together a salad using ingredients the writer had in the fridge.

'You have some *gbejniet*!' she said, taking out a small dish of little peppered cheeses.

'They are wonderful on hot toast,' said Gregory. He had become used to asking for *gbejniet* at the little local shop, and would watch the woman take the cork off a glass jar, scoop two or three cheeses onto a slotted ladle and place them in the middle of a piece of greaseproof paper she dented first, fist in palm, to form into a hollow for the cheese. She then screwed the paper into a semi-circular shape, making it as secure as a paper bag.

Gregory poured a bottle of beer into two glasses, when there was a knock at the front door.

Phineas Micallef was out of breath from hurrying down the steep street, and then down Melon Spring Lane. 'I got involved in a long discussion,' he puffed. 'Humph – with Monsinjur Dimech, after Mass!' He made a comical lovable figure as he wiped his forehead on a folded handkerchief and sat at the table, accepting with alacrity the glass of beer Gregory held toward him with a deep *Ahh*.

The writer had no idea that the doctor attended church, but let the statement go without taking it up. Perhaps then, it was a matter of conscience that was keeping the doctor an exile from Sliema. Did it have anything to do with his private life or relationships? He would ask Patricia later about the doctor's marriage and how he became a widower.

'About morals and mores at the turn of the next century?'

joked Patricia, whimsically asking the older man about his debate with the parish priest.

'About water polo!' exploded the doctor, his hands extended dramatically as if there were no other subject worthy of mention. 'He actually believes the Sirens will win this year! He sides with Sirens – I can't believe it – a grown man! It may be because his family took holidays in St Paul's Bay when he was a child. I don't know.' He shook his head in disbelief, comically taking the subject quite seriously.

'Who do you think will win, Fin? I didn't know you took water polo so seriously!' Gregory tried to stifle a laugh.

'What a question! Who else could win the water polo league this year apart from Neptunes?' It was not a rhetorical question. The doctor looked up at the writer and waited for an answer.

Gregory valiantly tried to keep a straight face. 'I really don't know. I, er – I'm not into sport.'

'All Australians are into sport,' said the doctor. From his tone, he might as well have said, you ought to be ashamed of yourself.

Gregory laughed, deciding to end it there and then. 'After lunch, we'll go down to the cellar.' After that, talk was restricted to how they would open the last jar. It was animated and friendly. They were all absorbed in the task ahead. But Gregory watched Patricia eat. She nibbled at a bread roll and speared small pieces of cheese and tomato onto a fork. He remembered similar delicate movements she made when they were alone together, enfolded in their intimacy.

The previous evening, they had returned from a restaurant in Mdina well after dark; a strangely silent drive during which they looked often at each other in the moving light of street lamps over the travelling car. The car radio played softly.

Gregory held her close the instant they were in the house, with the bedroom lit up only momentarily as they prepared for the night. She stood with her back to him, undoing her hair and brushing it slowly. He turned off the light and she turned, to see he had lit one of his blackout candles in a saucer and stood it on a chair by the bed. By the light of the candle, they undressed, whispering as if there were someone within earshot who could hear their excitement.

'It's been a long week,' she said, taking the words from his mind and saying them as she moved to the bed.

The mosquito net was hastily pushed to one side as they lowered slowly onto the smooth cool sheets. Patricia's body was warm, as if she had only just entered from taking a sunbath.

Gregory ran his hands lightly over her body, feeling silky skin, touching her for his own pleasure, giving her hers. He lay over her, making her gasp slightly with his weight, feeling her limbs encircle his body; now tightly, now loosely. He sensed her mounting pleasure from her movements and the small noises she made, nuzzled as she was against him. It was not like the first time, when he had seen her young body and discovered the shape of her, the scent of her skin, the sensual pleasure of getting to know her intimately.

He now knew the contours of her, how her breasts rose and how they felt when he kissed her there, his cheeks and lips encountering hardened nipples in the dark. She would guide him, hands tangled in his hair, her head thrown against one of his pillows. Inside her, he moved slowly, inching himself towards a peak only gradually, enjoying her bidding to more urgency. She moved her hips persuasively, her low voice uttering incomprehensible breathy syllables in the dark.

She relaxed into a slower pace, then increased her tempo, turning slowly until they lay side by side. Gregory paced himself, feeling pleasure in holding back, using small pauses to hold her fast against him, to listen to their breathing together, to feel her squirm with delight against him, the movement edging him on.

And then she was astride him, over him in the darkness, the candle throwing only a small diminishing glow on her body as

Gregory looked up at her.

She raised her arms to sweep hair away from her face, without breaking the tempo in their movement. With her head thrown back, she uttered a long explosive cry, then fell forward over him, clasping his body with hers, breathless. He held her there, loosely, moving underneath her until she met him in synchrony, sensing his arrival. It was more than a physical apex; it was a release of satisfaction, a flood of bodily sensations heightened by his newly found feeling of power and freedom from the past.

His body tingled, and a small spasm shook his legs involuntarily. It was a harkening back to his youthful days, prompted by a physical reflex he had not felt for years.

'You're here.' Words left his lips in spite of himself.

'Mm,' she whispered hoarsely. 'Yes, I'm back.'

When she fell asleep, he noticed the complete darkness. The candle must have gone out a while before.

❑

7

In the cellar, it was bright and still. Noises from the chicken run filled the afternoon outside. Someone had thrown scraps over the wall and the gobbling of turkeys, the soft flutter of feathers as hens scrambled and fought for food, and the warm smell of dust gave the garden and vineyard a sunny domestic feeling.

Gregory put aside his lazy wish to simply lie in the sun listening to his birds and concentrated on the task to hand. He had the old doctor at his heels, and could hear a slight wheezing coming from the man's chest.

He looked sprightly this morning, with hair well slicked back as usual and sharp creases in his trousers. Patricia was calm, and almost purred like a cat in the sun. Her eyes were bright and she anticipated the work in the cellar with cheery eagerness. The three entered the large room, intent on getting the bomblu open.

'We still have all our tools laid out here,' said the writer, indicating the sheet of canvas with its odd assortment of knives and utensils.

Patricia handed the knife to Fin. 'This is the knife we used before. I wonder whether this clay jar is full of oil or wine.'

'Or water,' answered the old doctor. He turned a bit pale, and the heat madeg his top lip glisten slightly only seconds after he replaced the handkerchief in his pocket.

'Now,' started Gregory, 'If we –'

'Like this –' the doctor interrupted. 'Like we did the first time.' He was already wresting the knife back and forth forcibly, trying to edge it underneath the wax seal and cork together. The effort gave no result. The wax seemed to have hardened, fused into the porous clay surface of the jar neck. 'Like this!' the older man repeated, words coming out in a grunt through clenched teeth.

Gregory gently took the knife from his hand when he looked up with sweat standing out in beads on his forehead. Fin's skin looked blanched and pale. Gregory tried himself, levering the blade at a different angle, cautiously forcing it with both hands. He did not want to risk a cut.

'Shall I try the other side, opposite to you, with another knife?' asked Patricia. She sensed the doctor's impatience, and was now full of it herself. She hopped from one foot to the other like a child.

'Here, here ...' The doctor reached nervously for the knife she handed him, then dropped it suddenly. The clatter was muted on the rammed earth floor. He was muttering under his breath.

Gregory had managed to insert the point of his knife under the wax rim. He needed something to hold the handle with. It was going to require precise movements. Patricia looked as if she was thinking of some other method to remove the wax plug from the jar mouth.

The writer had already thought of melting the wax by some means. He looked at her as she gripped the earthenware rim thoughtfully. The silence in the cellar was broken only by rustles from the garden and the audible breathing of the doctor. Out of the corner of his eye, a sudden movement made the writer straighten up from where he was bent over the tools.

It was the doctor. He brushed past him to grab the mallet abruptly, very abruptly, his arm flashing. His audible breathing filled the cellar. His arm waved, gesturing with the mallet. The movement nudged the writer, who moved quickly out of the way.

'What the ...?' But he was too slow.

Patricia stood where she was, watching in disbelief as the doctor strode quickly with the mallet up to the clay jar. Almost immediately, she and Gregory were by the doctor's side, but it was already too late. With one massive lunge, Fin swung the mallet round sideways at waist level, bringing its impact to the broadest curve on the bomblu's side.

The jar smashed.

A cry from Patricia accompanyied the crashing sound made by the fragments of earthenware and the sudden copious flow of vinegar that splashed out, soaking the three of them from the knees down.

'Good grief!' Gregory was too startled to say anything else. He looked at his friend, expecting an explanation, or an exclamation at least. He did not get one.

As if in slow motion, Phineas Micallef wheeled around on his heels, raising hands to head. The mallet fell with hardly a sound to the ground. His face was ashen, his teeth gritted underneath stretched lips. For a moment, it seemed as if only the whites of his eyes were visible, rolling in their sockets.

Patricia stood immobile, the expression on her face frozen. 'What on earth did you do that for?'

Gregory watched the doctor squeeze his head between his hands, then lengthen the movement, sweeping and scraping his hair back. There was no sound from the old man's lips. His eyes seemed to glaze over when he turned, as if looking for something or someone. He looked at the broken pieces of clay at his feet, appeared startled to see them and the vinegar that pooled on the ground and drenched his trouser legs and shoes.

'Is it blood?' he asked dully. 'It's blood.' He seemed unaware of anyone else around him. Then he lurched, lumbered two steps and suddenly took off in a lop-sided run, out of the cellar door, up the stone steps and away from where the writer and the young woman stood.

'Blood?' Patricia looked at Gregory. 'Why did he say that? Why did he smash the jar?' Her face was a picture of incredulity.

'I don't know. What a mess.' Gregory felt blank. 'He seemed dazed. It was as if he couldn't bear to wait any longer.'

'We all waited a week for this –' Patricia gestured, indicating the wreckage about their feet. 'He seemed to check there was nothing there, on the floor, before he left,' she continued, baffled. 'He said blood. Why did he say that?'

'Oh – I don't know.' Gregory was resigned to the mystery about the doctor's confusion. 'All our eyes were on the jar. We all looked to see if there was anything there. Well – there isn't. All there is, is vinegar. Just vinegar.'

Patricia started to flick ineffectually at her jeans.

Gregory could not tell whether she was disappointed or glad they had not discovered anything more gruesome than several litres of acetic wine. He realised he did not initially register surprise at finding nothing in the liquid. But he was surprised. He fully expected to see a sodden bundle of clothes and flesh, a little parcel; the remnants of a life, virtually pickled in rancid wine.

He had lain awake at night when Patricia was in Sicily, picturing what they would see if they peered inside the emptied *bomblu*. Grey fabric in colourless tatters preserved by the wine, gruesome and troubling visions of grey skin angled over bone; the skull rounded and turned forward, over a small caved-in chest. He was surprised it was not there.

'You imagined it –' Patricia did not finish. She looked at the writer's eyes.

Gregory raised a hand and shielded his eyes from her. She knew him too well, too soon. His feet had still not moved from the puddle of dark vinegar. 'I – yes,' he said finally, accepting the scrutiny. 'I imagined more than just the words, you see.'

She came round to him and touched his arm. 'I know.'

How could she possibly know? He turned to her, perplexed, a touch annoyed. He was still not completely accustomed to the way she would never chastise him for having feelings or imaginings, for pre-empting things, for having a totally separate world in his head. He was silent for a long time, allowing her the closeness.

'But there's nothing there,' he said finally.
'Nothing there,' she repeated.

❏

8

Censinu is once more surrounded by darkness. This time, it is not the cellar, but his own room, the room he shares with his baby brother. Why is it so dark?

'Ma!' he cries. 'Pa! It's too dark! Please – put on the light.' But no one hears him. He is alone. No: he can hear sniffles in the dark. His brother is stirring. But where is he? He cannot see a thing. It's dark.

Usually, he can see outlines of things, the folds of the mosquito net. The lump his brother makes under the covers, the shape of the half-open door. The door: it is shut. Someone shut the door. Someone turned out the light in the loggia, and there is not even a strip of light under the door ... under where he thinks the door might be. Every night, his father leaves the light on in the loggia, and sets the door of the boys' room ajar, so they are comforted by the glow. So they can hear the rumble and whisper of their parents down the corridor, and be comforted by their presence. Where are they? Tonight, he cannot hear their voices.

'Pa! Fejn int?' He stops to breathe, and hears his heartbeat in the dark. 'Where are you?' But he cries in vain. Soon, he is sobbing. He wishes it would soon be day. He wishes for sunlight. He wishes, for once, that his mother would come in and try to arrange his covers. But she does not come. He is alone. His brother, tucked away somewhere he cannot see, is sleeping. The whole world is silent. The whole world is dark.

❑

9

The sun drummed down on Gregory's head as he handled the spade. Mounds of red earth piled up around him. He had no real reason to be digging in the noon sun, but it was a kind of penance, a kind of repentance. He had never been so mortified – no, that was not the word.

He was struck, staggered by what had happened two days before. On Monday, the words rained from his fingertips in a torrent. On Tuesday and Wednesday, he hardly wrote a word, and regret filled his eyes when he read what he had written. He could not take the lives of these people and turn them into mere words. Someone said what he was doing was wrong. Who was it? They could have been right.

On Monday, he was taken by a rush of inspiration. On Tuesday and Wednesday, the doctor was foremost on his mind. Today, he had been digging since dawn, with frustration, impotence, and a feeling of guilt making him try to expunge what he had unearthed by working in the garden. It was as if he could bury what he had found, inter his discovery once more: let it lie where it was. But he knew he could not. Had it helped for him to go looking for the doctor? Did he manage to soothe and pacify the man?

No. The answer was no. As usual, he was driven by curiosity and the desire to find more grist for his mill, to find more words and motives, and actions and reasons and … All he wanted was to find out why Fin had smashed that jar. That was why he followed him. There were no other reasons. Or perhaps there were. Perhaps he did really want to help the doctor, placate him and make him talk himself out of the struggle he was obviously going through.

He had left Patricia at the village square, where he asked her to drop him. He told her he was going to look for Fin, and she knew, somehow, that he had to do it alone. He found him far from the village, in a place that seemed at once familiar, because he had already been there, and strange, because of his quest. It was not the first place he looked. The wine bar was deserted when he thrust his head past the bead curtain and tried to make out faces in the contrasting gloom inside. The doctor was not at the band club either – there was a clutch of men at the ancient wooden bar that spanned one end of a long room, each with glass in hand and each, it seemed, babbling at once at the top of his voice in a garbled guttural rush of jolly words.

Fin was not at Franz's store. Neither was he at the haberdasher's, where he was often to be seen reading a page out of a newspaper before he bought it. There was no sign of him at the butcher's or the green grocer's, where little knots of women parted for the writer to pass. They showed no sign of alarm or curiosity as he passed, as if they expected foreigners to behave in unusual silent haste.

At the chemist's, it was deserted but for the pharmacist. There was the usual medicated smell and the old-fashioned bottles of brown glass, now used only as ornament, or to attest to the length of time the shop had stood in the village, creating an atmosphere ripe for description in a writer's florid words.

But Gregory was not in a writing mood. He was bent on finding the doctor and getting him to explain his behaviour. He was not about to wring an explanation from him, but perhaps it was time the air was cleared. Time Phineas Micallef unleashed whatever it was that kept him in that village, an exile. Whatever it was that blanched his skin every time a dead child was mentioned. Whatever it was that had him follow Gregory around the island.

Gregory was now quite sure it was Fin he sensed on his heels whenever he ventured out of the village. He could not be absolutely certain, but he had seen what looked like his form on two occasions as he prowled around the narrow Floriana streets, marvelling at the architecture, trying to establish locations he could write about. He also thought he glimpsed the old man when he was walking along the bastions near Fort St Angelo, standing back to admire the fine portico, the colour of the limestone walls, the way the fort pitched forward on a promontory away from the ancient city behind it.

Was it Phineas Micallef who drove by in a horse-drawn *karrozzin*, partially hidden by the checked curtain? Gregory was almost sure. He was almost positive the large black car he kept seeing was the doctor's Jaguar. But this was all before the day in the cellar when the doctor had smashed the jar. There was no sign of him now. It was as if he was spirited away from the village by the same mysterious force that had taken his hand with the mallet and brought it up against the side of the bomblu with such impact.

'Looking for something?' The female chemist was all smiles. She had helped Gregory before and was today calm and friendly in an empty shop.

'I'm looking for F... I'm looking for Dr Micallef,' said Gregory. 'Have you seen him? I must really speak to him today.'

'It's Wednesday, Mr Worthington. On Wednesdays he goes to Mdina. But he's usually back by dinnertime.'

Gregory turned and rushed out of the shop. The bus. He would have to catch the bus. 'Thank you!' he shouted as an afterthought to the chemist. He did not know if she heard.

In any other country, thought Gregory, it would have been ridiculous to pursue anyone given the mere name of a city. But Mdina was a different city. It was tiny, labyrinthine, and it would be hard not to find someone known to be there at any given time, if one looked hard enough. The ancient walled citadel was termed the Silent City, but it was not always so, despite it being closed to traffic. Crowds of tourists were like a perpetual river creeping through the curved streets, which were like canyons of limestone walls bearing tiny windows, most protected by curved wrought iron bars.

He found Phineas Micallef five minutes after he descended from the bus outside the city gates at Saqqajja. Once more, he found himself walking through the ornate portal, passing the infinitely ancient tower watchhouse to his left and marching down the narrow street past the convent. His footsteps echoed around him until he emerged in the square opposite the grand cathedral.

And there, walking purposefully towards the cathedral museum, was the form of the old doctor. Rather than hail him and make a spectacle of himself among two throngs of tourists that emerged simultaneously from the alley next to the cathedral and the street leading to the Norman House, Gregory marched on, following the doctor until he watched him disappear between the thick green doors of the museum. He was only a few steps behind.

'You!' Dr Micallef turned to the sound of someone entering immediately after him. But he did not stop moving. Intent on his destination, he did not stop walking until he stood in front of an exquisite Dürer.

For a long moment, both men stood in front of the monochromatic pen and ink drawing, as if mesmerised by its beauty.

'I had no idea there were Dürers in Malta,' breathed the writer, his voice hushed as if they were in church.

'I do not mean to be unkind, Mr Worthington – *Gregory*. But there are many things you have no idea about.' The man's voice was hoarse, as if he had spent the night shouting, or crying. His pink-tinged eyes were clouded, as if drugged, and he had to clear his throat harshly when he finished speaking. In spite of the meaning of the words, his tone was not unkind, just as he said. He looked as if he knew exactly why Gregory was there and how the conversation would unfold.

'Fin – look, I had to catch up with you. I want to say sorry for what …'

'There is no need to apologise. But I suppose you now want some explanation from me. After all, I broke your jar.'

'It's Nikol Mifsud's jar – the boy's father.'

'The boy's father!' The words were followed by a whine, a cry, which filled the large hall in which they stood. A small group of tourists turned and looked.

'You are very distressed by this. Perhaps it would help to talk about it.'

'It would not help,' said the doctor, 'but we shall talk about it anyway, my friend.' He held out a hand as if to guide Gregory, and together, they left the museum and made their way past the cathedral into a small alley that led upwards to a gated tearoom.

Inside, underneath a set of wooden coats of arms hanging on ancient uneven walls, they drank coffee.

'This story, Gregory – the story you are attempting to write, is not about Censinu, but about Therèse.'

'His mother?'

The doctor nodded. 'You know she is now in an asylum?' His speech faltered on the word. The man was in real distress. 'I have not seen her for over a decade.'

'You …'

'Yes, of course I knew her. She was my … I was … Ah – this is not easy, you know. Have you ever felt in your life as if you were pulled inexorably in two directions at once?'

Gregory looked down into his coffee. His cup and the doctor's were almost touching on the tiny table. He saw the old man's hand grip the tiny handle, and shake with a tremor he knew was induced by something other than anxiety.

'You and I, Fin,' he said, 'could both do with a real drink.'

Once more, they were walking together, leaving Mdina through another archway, and ascending on foot through a passage in the old moat towards Rabat. At a driver's café, Gregory knew they could get any kind of drink they asked for.

His was a lager. The doctor ordered a double whisky.

The cold marble top and the tinkle of a bead curtain were so similar to the ones at *Il-Hanut* that it had them settled almost immediately. Phineas Micallef soon dispensed with his drink. The barman brought another without having to be told.

'When that boy disappeared, it was just another blow,' started the doctor. 'Another blow that came after a series of others. The story is a long one, and before I tell you anything else, I beg you to consider one thing.'

'I know what you're going to say, Fin – I always respect people's privacy. The sanctity of people's lives is dear to me.'

'But the drive to discover the facts of a story is strong, as I have seen.'

'So it was you who was following me.'

The doctor shook his head and shrugged.

'Never mind. What were you going to say about the boy's parents?'

'The boy's mother, you mean.' The old man paused, shook his head again and continued. 'Well – a long time ago, she was a different person to what you might have heard in the village. She was young and vibrant, beautiful, the middle daughter of a respected St Julians family – and newly married to Nikol, who was sweet, good-natured, and very well meaning. But a peasant nevertheless. And she had left the modern suburbs, the seafront where she grew up. She came of an educated family, you see, which was very disappointed to see her bury herself in village life when she had shown so much potential as a child. Her father was a civil servant, he …' he stopped to drink.

'But what is your connection to these people?'

'Ah, Gregory – perhaps you hardly understand the emotions of island people, of small communities.' Was he going to start to ramble? 'You have been so curious about my exile from Sliema! Why did I come to this tiny dusty village to drink myself to death?' His angry voice rose in the bar, but there was nobody there to notice. 'I came after the child disappeared, because I knew how she would feel. I knew it would be the final thing to tear her apart. Poor Therèse.'

'Why? What else was there?'

'You cannot guess? What else was there? It was the final thing to tear her apart after her anguish about Censinu. Who he was. Where he came from. He came as a burden, the result of a great dishonour. And he disappeared into a haze of guilt – an enormity of guilt and hopelessness.' The words seemed overly dramatic.

'But tell me why,' pleaded Gregory.

'I'll tell you why I smashed your jar.'

'Yes.' The sound of a bus backfiring interrupted the doctor's speech. 'I had to find out whether the boy's body was in that jar. The boy was mine, Gregory. He was the son I had never seen.'

Gregory gasped. He had no idea. For a minute, there seemed to be no words to say.

But the doctor had no need for prompts. 'Therèse and I met in St Julians once, when she was visiting friends. She would get away from the village from time to time to escape boredom. She loved Nikol, but somehow her new life lacked something. She was intelligent, she needed more than what village life could give her.'

'So she was disappointed with what she'd done?'

'In a way. You don't seem shocked.' For the first time that afternoon, the doctor looked straight into Gregory's eyes.

'I'm surprised more than shocked. Surprised at myself for not guessing.'

The doctor went into a long explanation, but there was no sign of relief in his voice. Perhaps there was no truth in the belief that confession cleared the soul. 'And after a while we became lovers. It was not ugly, you understand. It was more of a refuge than an infidelity. She was seeking mental stimulation. I was seeking ... I do not know what I was seeking. I was torn in half by what I sought. Because you see, I felt the gravity of what I was doing and I loved my wife. But still I sought something. And what I found was altogether a greater punishment than we ever deserved. I had no idea our liaison was to be fruitful, because my own marriage was childless. When I heard, from her own lips, that her first child was mine, I was seized by all sorts of doubts, fears and insecurities. I had no idea what to do. Thérèse said there was nothing to do. She would say nothing. The child would pass as offspring of her marriage. She was, even as she said the words, filled with shame. That was when she started to have problems. Mental. I don't know – emotional. Psychological. I don't know. I never saw her again.'

'But you heard stories.'

'Of course I heard stories. But by then, in my own emotional upheaval, I had made other mistakes. My practice started to suffer. Eventually I found myself in the middle of a malpractice suit and friends started to turn hostile.'

'And then?'

'Then nothing, for a long time. The court case took years, my wife died. I was alone and helpless. The boy was growing up, unseen by me. I did not dare approach the village for fear of putting her into an untenable position. I kept away and … turned to other things for comfort. I heard all kinds of gossip about Thérèse. I was going crazy. I drank like a fish.'

Of all admissions, it seemed this was the most shameful. Phineas Micallef dropped his head into his cupped hands. 'Is this something you can write about, Mr Writer?' he asked sarcastically. His confusion was complete.

Gregory had nothing to say. How could he write about this man's pain?

'Then there was the disappearance. It was in the papers. Only a couple of paragraphs, mind – there was too much going on in politics – but it was not easy to take or understand. Then the verdict on my lawsuit came out. Not against me – but against me in a way. It was the last straw. I could no longer show my face in Sliema, it seemed. Except for a few loyal friends, everyone shut me out. And I had no idea what had happened in the village.

Therèse was taken away, they told me. So I moved – took the house you have seen, renovated it. Tried to find out what happened, as discreetly as I could.'

'And did you?'

'Don't you think I turned every stone I could? No one knows what happened to that boy. I could not get my hands on the property – would *you* have faced Nikol? That child could be buried in your vineyard for all I know.'

The doctor's last sentence closed the conversation. For a long while, the two men sat at the marble table in silence, not allowing their eyes to meet. Gregory wished he could reach for some appropriate words of sympathy, but they would have sounded hollow. So much time had passed, people had changed and moved. But the doctor still seemed freshly affected by the boy's disappearance and Terezina's decline into instability. He must have moved to the village in an effort to discover more, and in a way to watch over the place where she had lived. Where she had borne her children, where she had helped Nikol with his peasant chores. Where she had hidden her secret burden of guilt, which had unbalanced her.

What must have riled Phineas Micallef most was his inability to determine whether Terezina herself had hurt their child. What must have pained him most was the powerlessness to find out what she felt when Censinu disappeared. Whether she had anything to do with it.

The doctor's last sentence drove Gregory into a frenzy. Whether it was out of contrition for causing pain, out of guilt for having opened up the doctor's old dilemma, he did not know, but he could not confide this to Patricia.

Nor could he tell anyone else. He could not write it – in the present form it occupied in his mind – into his novel. That would be tantamount to disloyalty, to betrayal. His sympathy and liking for Phineas Micallef had not diminished. Rather, he felt more affection for the troubled man, now that he knew his story.

He hoped the telling would somehow lift Fin's despondency,

make him somewhat lighter for having disburdened to someone not involved directly in the village's past.

Yes. Gregory was sure Fin would be better, but it was not with that thought in mind that he left him in that drivers' café that day in Rabat. The doctor had nodded, as if to dismiss him, as if to say he had spoken enough and wanted to be left now, to his abject sorrow and to his drinking. They were private, these things, and too humiliating to address in the company of another. So Gregory made a discreet departure, almost a silent one, and made his way by creaking bus to the village, his thoughts a buzz of questions. Some had been answered, and many others posed.

The doctor's sentence: *He could be buried in your vineyard for all I know*, sent him scurrying to the cellar, looking for a shovel. In the morning, blinded by the sun and by something indefinable nagging at his head and chest, he started to dig. If he were to find a small body, if he were to find bones, who could he suspect? Who was the person most likely to have buried little Censinu Mifsud in the garden of the house where he lived? Why had those very words sprung to the doctor's mouth? Were they just an off-hand remark, or did he know something he was not prepared to tell?

Gregory dug, picking random spots among the vines, shovelling rich red soil up into heaps and creating a series of rough holes he did not bother to fill in once he had tired. Sweat poured from him and he rubbed his forehead on the back of his hand frequently, in spite of the fact it was not his forehead that perspired, but his entire body. He was drenched, exhausted, and was yet to realise the futility of his task. Many a time, he would stop to listen. From the house came the sound of his telephone.

Once or twice, he would throw down the spade before pausing and taking it up again without moving his legs. Other times, he ignored the ringing as he worked, not stopping for a second. A pile of rubbish grew against the trunk of an ancient olive tree in a corner. Bottles, tins, pieces of spark plug and large pieces of sawn bone – the remains of some dog's feast.

He flung everything away to hit the olive tree, and angrily resumed digging, pausing only when once more, his spade struck something solid and he stooped to pick up a bent bird cage, a large root, part of an old hoe, another bottle.

One object made him pause as he sweltered in the sun. It weighed heavily in his hand, and made him smirk with irony. It was a large key, a *muftieh* – the very key he had searched for and finally replaced. The key that would have got him into the cellar. He threw it towards the tree, where it came to rest among the other rubbish.

❏

10

Sunlight streaked obscenely over the large crowd. Gregory, hatted and sombre, felt out of place physically and socially. Taller than anyone in the crowd, he stood out, his fairness and the hat he wore making him more conspicuous than in the village.

The Addolorata Cemetery was a formidable place, and he saw it in its appropriate mood, in the throes of grief brought on by a funeral. It was a funeral attended, it seemed to the writer, by a large proportion of the island's population, although he knew this exaggerated calculation was brought on by his surprise, shock and dismay. Headstones, granite monuments and imposing white marble mausoleums glittered in the sunlight. It would have been more appropriate to have had a storm, a sombre thunderstorm to mark the day and the ceremony. It was at once familiar and totally strange, this ceremony, and it went on, interminably, in Maltese; monotonous guttural mumbling reaching his ears over the heads of the close crowd in front of him.

'*Mulej isma t-talba tieghi.*' Monsinjur Dimech droned to the end of his prayer. A buzz of mumbling and whispering rose from the crowd, which started to move bodily, as one organism, like a black swarm of bees, away from the grave. 'Amen,' they kept repeating. 'Amen.'

It went on and on. Gregory had the inordinate feeling he ought to look around for Nikol Mifsud. After all, was he not a *deffien,* a gravedigger? Was this not the main cemetery of the island, where thousands of graves were arranged along a series of lanes wending round a slight undulation in the land, under a spindly Gothic church that was visible for miles? It was where most Maltese families were to find their final resting places, in plots paved with lime flagstones, girded by black railings, decorated in the main by some symbolic statue. Graves were prepared by men such as Nikol. Was this not where the slight wiry man was most likely to be: attending a funeral, waiting on the sideline until it was his turn to shovel earth back into the ground?

The writer's hundred questions were harsh, self-punishing, causing his lips to move, making him look around self-consciously, to see if they thought he was deep in prayer, like they were themselves. He acknowledged guiltily he was also working, writing in his head as he looked at the cavity. Four great slabs of stone lay to one side. No shovelling to be done here – the stones would be placed back on top of the hollow cavity when the crowd moved away, leaving a dark rectangular space under the slabs.

A mass of flowers, many in funereal wreaths, some in large cane baskets, stood close by. The scent hit Gregory and tilted his senses with displeasure. It would be a long time before he could smell flowers and not think of the funeral of Phineas Micallef.

The news was carried to him wave upon wave, four days before, as he strode up the steep street to the village square, on the way to the grocery shop. He felt he understood the Maltese words as ashen faces said them.

'*Miet it-tabib!*'

'The doctor is dead!'

'*Miet it-tabib!*'

The doctor? Dr Micallef? His friend ... Gregory Worthington looked around him helplessly. It was Lieni, distraught and helpless with grief, who grasped his elbow. Her face was wracked with more than the usual lines of arthritic pain and there was a nervous spasmodic tic in her neck. Her eyes were rimmed with tears. 'He is gone ...' she started to say, before being borne away by a crowd of village women.

They were anxious to get her into her house as quickly as

possible. Among them was her daughter Katie, pale and withdrawn. She hardly noticed the writer.

Gregory hurried on across the square, faces around him all bearing a uniform pallor. The mumbling, the exclamations and cries of grief were full of disbelief. He could not believe it himself. Fin dead? Impossible. His friend was at his farmhouse as recently as Sunday, when he had impatiently smashed the last clay jar. He had later spent time with him in Rabat.

'What happened?' He asked no one in particular, speaking his words out loud over the heads of the women, who all seemed small and hunched over. He hoped someone would tell him what was going on.

At his elbow, a low modulated female voice bade him step aside. 'One word with you, if you please, Mr Worthington.' It was Miss Dimech, the retired schoolteacher. Her enormous bulk was already in black. She had just come out of the church door, a large veil still covering her head. She crossed herself, her hand corded with a string of silver rosary beads.

Gregory drew with her to one side of the church forecourt, removing his hat although the sun beat down on the square, the glare making them both squint at each other.

'Yes, quietly now,' she said talking in a very low voice, as if the square were teeming with eavesdroppers, speaking to him as if he were a child in a classroom. 'Quietly now.'

The place had emptied suddenly, leaving only two dusty dogs and the incessant clicking of crickets. A bus arrived and halted at the terminus.

'Listen – Dr Micallef has passed away. His maid discovered his body this morning.'

Gregory could not reach for words to say. He half closed his eyes against the glare and lowered his head, both out of confusion and in an effort to hear what the fat woman was saying.

'Although I would not ordinarily say so, Mr Worthington, I think there is something you should know. No, no, no ...' She bridled, turned away and back. 'No – on second thoughts, my brother will talk to you himself. Ah – look – he is arriving from the doctor's house just now.' Her voice was still hushed.

In spite of the sunlight, the whole village felt like the inside of a church. Gregory looked to where the priest was approaching, cassock covered by a white lace surplice and swinging with his stride, and dust swirled on the ground around him. The writer decided to allow him enough time to enter the sacristy. It would satisfy the priest's sense of decorum and allow himself time to find suitable words. He was still bathed in confusion.

'I'll wait here for a while,' he said to the priest's sister. 'And then I'll go in by the side door.' But looking around quickly, he discovered the fat woman had disappeared, and he was speaking to himself.

Inside, it was cool and sombre. The sacristy was deserted except for the priest and a small altar boy folding vestments in a corner. The coolness, the carved mahogany and smell of incense served to reinstall Gregory's balance. 'I don't know what to say, Father,' he started to say, hat in hand, feeling like a penitent.

'Indeed.' The frosty tone of the man in the black cassock suggested the writer should say nothing.

But Gregory continued, momentarily unaware of any reason the priest should be so undemonstrative, apart from grief and surprise. 'Miss Dimech said there is something I had to know. Was it to do with the doctor's habits? His health? His drinking?' The minute the word left his lips Gregory regretted its uttering. There was a cool silence that confirmed his mistake. The priest looked sideways and upward at him, a flat grimace holding his mouth just short of a reprimanding scowl. The eyes were bland and unfriendly, but held enough calm to avoid plain animosity. Even in anger, Monsinjur Dimech piously refrained from blame or castigation. 'Doctor Micallef took his own life, Mr Worthington.'

Gregory gasped.

'I think that is what my sister meant me to tell you,' said the priest. 'I must say I find it a difficult sentence to say. The church has a view on ...' the priest's face reddened, and he shook his head as if to discount this as an occasion he could offer Christian lessons. 'But I must not go into that with you now,' he said at last.

Gregory heard little of the priest's last words. Took his own life? Fin? He was at a total loss for words, standing in the sepulchral sacristy, smelling the faint scents of candle wax and incense he would from then always associate with death and shock. 'I can't believe it! Fin – um, Dr Micallef – was with me on Sunday.'

'Indeed,' said the priest for the second time, just as frostily. 'So I understand – I heard his confession on Monday,' he said then, as if divulging a fact of monumental significance. He turned his back to Gregory, opened a cupboard door and placed inside it the thick missal he was carrying. 'Lieni found him this morning. I administered the last rites in spite of the fact he had been dead for some hours.'

It took Gregory a few moments to register the reason Father Dimech was telling him all this. Then he saw the priest wanted to indicate he had acted charitably. Suicide, last rites – what was the difference? Would Fin have appreciated it? He remembered the doctor's ways, his exile, the sorrow he nursed about gossip and people's opinions of him. What was the difference – rite or no rite? Charity or no charity?

The writer pictured the doctor, the way he had of sweeping his hair back, of balling his fists in his pockets. He remembered his discomfort and anxiety the day they tried to open the last clay jar: how the doctor rushed from his cellar, the smell of vinegar in the air, its stains on his trousers, and the man's mention of blood recurring in his head. He remembered their last conversation, the doctor's desire to be left alone, and his own feeling he had benefited from talking to him. Still, he was uneasy.

'Why?' he asked. 'Why did he do it?' He reached with one hand, as if to wrest some sort of explanation from the priest.

Monsinjur Dimech stepped back, wordless, turning his back to the Australian.

'I am totally astonished,' Gregory insisted. 'That he would do something like that, I mean.' He wished the priest would turn and face him. He addressed the broad black back, noting the way the priest concentrated on folding a stole meticulously, matching the fringed corners and breathing audibly in the gloomy mahogany-panelled room.

'You would like a reason for something inexplicable, sir.' The parish priest's formal words boomed in the space. He turned slowly. 'Surely you appreciate my position. Surely you understand I cannot speak on the subject without the danger –'

'*Danger?*'

'My position and mission in life put me into a situation that is very clear in the eyes of the Church,' he said pompously. 'The danger is betrayal, Mr Worthington. Betrayal of knowledge held in confidence, knowledge not mine to divulge. My lips are sealed. That which is placed in my confidence – the confidentiality of everything I hear in the confessional ...' Monsinjur Dimech joined his hands. Not in a gesture of prayer, but in a domed motion, finger against finger, forming a pyramid, demonstrating the power he sensed in his unique position. His condescension was complete.

Gregory was offended. 'I really don't expect you to betray any confidence! And I hope you are not suggesting I would do anything of the sort! All I want to find out is why. Why?' He looked again to find the priest's piercing eyes studying him.

'The funeral is on Friday afternoon, Mr Worthington,' the priest intoned, formally. 'There will be a Mass here in Church, and the cortège will proceed to the Addolorata.'

With that, the conversation was closed and Gregory realised he had been summarily dismissed from the sacristy.

The crowd of mourners included Patricia and her parents. He saw her in the distance, in the middle of a small crowd of elegant people dressed in grey and black. She acknowledged his small wave with a nod.

She had been almost silent on the phone when Gregory called her after speaking to Monsinjur Dimech. He was not surprised to find she already knew about Fin's suicide. Her parents had been informed by some incomprehensible telegraph; faster than the telephone, faster than anything electronic; the bad news telegraph that linked city to town to village on that small island.

Her voice was hoarse on the phone. 'I can't believe it,' she said softly.

Gregory felt she had been crying. He wondered whether she understood better than he did. 'What could have been the reason, Patricia? Why now? Why just after what happened on Sunday?'

'I don't know.' She was more mystified than he was. 'My parents won't discuss it at all. By the way – they will be at the funeral. It is not the right occasion for an introduction. I don't know if ... Do you understand?'

'Of course. We'll leave it for another time. I'll be there of course. I suppose his family is totally distraught.'

'He has few relatives,' she said. 'He was a widower, with no children. I think I told you.'

Gregory put down the phone after the desultory conversation with a slow hand and a heavy feeling in his chest. Striding out purposefully into the garden, he sprinted down the cellar steps and stood in the middle of the wide space. He had cleared away the splinters and shards of clay from the broken bomblu, but the smell of vinegar still lingered. He wondered about Fin, pictured him taking the mallet and smashing the jar with such impatience and such force. The man was lovable, sweet in spite of his drinking habit, harmless. He had intelligence and wit, and had offered good advice even when aghast with shock. It was a severe loss.

Gregory stood still, thinking. Yes, he was a friend. An unlikely one, but a friend. He had placed his confidence in the writer, had offered something of his past and what troubled him. But there had been no hint he would go to such an extreme.

Patricia's parents nodded in his direction as well, as if acknowledging his presence. Gregory felt an overbearing formality descend on the whole place, the entire occasion. They consigned Phineas Micallef to his Maker, and they would not break out of the formality until they left the cemetery gates. The writer watched elegant mourners get into their cars. Their black apparel filled the bright afternoon. He wondered about their numbers. They shunned the doctor in life, yet turned up to mourn his death. Their cars formed a jam at the bottleneck leading to the main roads to Pawla, Tarxien and Marsa.

His own black Mercedes taxi followed the cortège as far as the Marsa bypass, then turned abruptly at a roundabout and took the road towards the village. The two or three miles seemed today to be interminable. It set him down at last in the square, almost simultaneously as another black car, which disgorged Monsinjur Dimech, a tiny altar boy in a white surplice and the voluminous black mass of the parish priest's sister.

'It was very nice of you to attend,' she said primly, and before Gregory had time to answer, she waddled away towards her house, her broad back a definite statement.

The priest could not avoid him as easily. Gregory made sure the cleric heard what he had to say. Short of holding his arm, he barred his way.

'I still can't understand, Father,' he stated in a voice that could not go ignored. 'I have gone over the events of the last weeks – he always seemed so jovial, so resigned to retirement in this village. He got on well with everybody. I mean – from the plumber to the grocer, they all liked him. The local GP, the chemist, the bandmaster – myself! What could have driven such a well-loved man to do such a thing?' Gregory was mystified how nobody seemed to question the doctor's action.

The priest was silent, waiting politely for Gregory to finish so that he could withdraw without being rude.

'Father? Monsinjur, do you understand?'

'It is plain, Mr Worthington,' the priest said cuttingly, 'that you would do well to emulate your namesake's example.'

'My namesake?' Gregory was becoming increasingly irritated, apart from being confused. It was no wonder this priest was not well liked. His attitude was contemptible. This sanctimonious treatment, this cool and distant stance that suddenly shut him out was in strong contrast with the way the village folk had welcomed him only weeks ago.

'Yes, your namesake – St Gregory the Great. He was patient, temperate and ...'

Gregory made a monumental effort not to explode with rage. Only a small hiss left his lips. How dare this village priest instruct him in patience and tolerance when he was being treated so tepidly? He held his counsel only because he knew he would not get any information at all if he had a tantrum in the village square, in plain sight of goodness knew how many pairs of eyes behind closed shutters.

The priest continued, infuriatingly calm and sedate in the secure knowledge the foreign writer was at a disadvantage. 'There are some things in life, Mr Worthington,' he said softly, 'that were never meant to be understood. We do things that produce results and repercussions we never expect.' He lifted an eyebrow meaningfully, then lowered his head and continued after pausing slightly, as if making a decision to say something and then leave.

His voice grated. 'We must learn to be circumspect in life,

sir. We learn, especially after something as dramatic as this happens, that we cannot always be sure of what the ramifications are – what the repercussions could be – to the things we do.'

'What do you mean ... the things we do?' Gregory felt an uncomfortable implication in the priest's words. What did the priest think happened at his home on Sunday? The writer saw the priest was implying it was something he had done.

Perhaps he knew Fin had confided in him. But what had he done? He could never have guessed Fin's reaction, or that there would be any reaction at all. He could not even be sure it was anything to do with the jar in his cellar, or their last conversation. He would put the cleric right. He had no right to make assumptions.

'Hey, listen,' he said angrily, starting to lose his control and respect of this sanctimonious man. 'There was a lot about Dr Micallef I knew nothing about, Father. I was not privy to everything he thought and did. There are things I simply do not know.' Gregory shook his head.

The priest raised a finger, then saw the anger in the Australian's eyes and lowered it quickly. 'And you want to know, don't you? Well, life is not a novel, Mr Worthington, in which everything is resolved by the last twenty pages. There are some things we were never meant to know and never will know.' The final rebuke was the last straw.

Gregory resented the priest's condescension and dismissal rather pointedly. Without another word, he turned his back on the priest and left him without salutation. The walk down the steep street and into Melon Spring Lane was fatiguing, taking the breath out of him in the dry heat. The day had taken its toll.

Shock, grief and dejection assailed his body until he was physically exhausted. His head rang with words. The priest's words. Ramifications. *Repercussions.*

Franz's shop had the usual gaggle of men at its entrance. Rigoletto, Franz himself, and two or three others whose faces were familiar from evenings of friendly company, drinking at *Il-Hanut*. They were all wearing unaccustomed dark suits and black ties, having just returned from the funeral. A couple of cloth caps bobbed in the sun.

The writer felt a sigh of relief leave his chest as he approached the group, his hand already moving to the brim of his hat in a small salute, gratefully expecting the respite of a convivial sharing of experience, consolation and warm conversation. 'Hello there,' he said.

There was no mumble of response. Gregory looked around at their lowered faces. This cold reception was even more baffling than the parish priest's condescending diatribe. There was a long embarrassing interval when not a word was said.

The sound of a motor scooter buzzing in some distant lane emphasised their silence. Gregory raised his head. For a minute, he thought he heard the high-pitched scream of an angry woman. He waited, hoping the men's silence was custom, hoping a couple of hands would fluttered in response, a couple of heads nod in sympathy. But nothing came.

In renewed shock and confusion, faced by the sombre grey of the back of Rigoletto's suit, Gregory stumbled on down the lane.

When he had gone a few yards, he heard their rumbling voices and guttural words. And knew he was the subject of their conversation.

❏

Part Four

1

Gregory stopped reading. The letter from Emma was sympathetic and sweet, but it brought back all his doubts and confusion about Fin's death. He had tried, in his own letter, to organise his thoughts. The act of writing always gave him a sense of equilibrium, of being able to find a way through problems by some sort of literal system. But this time, words brought little comfort.

He thought back to what Katie had told him on Friday morning. He had written long sentences to Emma, then realised it was not such a good idea to describe to a seventeen year-old what Lieni had found. His finger had gone to the delete button and he watched the cursor move in reverse, taking back the words.

He was surprised at the speed with which his daughter had replied, and even more alarmed at the way her words affected him all over again. The village folk were still ignoring him, and it was worse than if they had all scolded him verbally, assaulted him with a guttural onslaught of invective. As it was, he was bruised and confused. Their passion led them to silence, and it seared him. Trying to write in all this made matters worse, after all. Adding tracts to the novel felt especially callous now.

Gregory sensed he was trying to fictionalise the very reason he was there, the very creation of his situation. It was consolation and sympathy he needed now – not a constant reminder of what he felt the villagers thought he had done. How could he write when they treated him like this? It was as if they had conspired to treat him in the same way – to ignore him, cut him off.

All except Katie, who carried on with her cleaning as if nothing had happened. He had been surprised, in fact, at Katie's cool narration of what her mother told her. Her beautiful eyes had not glimmered, and she had not faltered in her speech. 'Dr Micallef was a clever doctor,' Katie said. 'He gave himself injection. You know, sir – *labra*, a needle.'

Gregory nodded. He wanted her to go on.

'My mother went upstairs to clean. Usually, the doctor would be up – awake. But there was ... how do you say, quiet – silence, in the house. Then she found him.'

'It must have been a terrible shock. What then?' Gregory prompted, and thought suddenly and inexplicably of Maggie. His ex-wife would have accused him immediately of having an insensitive mind, wanting to know only the grim and gruesome details.

The maid continued. 'My mother called and knocked on the bedroom door. She thought he was sick – you know, heart attack, something like that. She pushed the door and saw bedside light still on, curtains still drawn, but the doctor not in bed. *Tabib*, she called. Tabib! Doctor!'

'Not in bed?' he asked.

'Not in the room,' she said. 'No – not in bed. In the bathroom, she found him. Sir – I don't know if –'

'Go on, Katie. I want to know.'

'My mother said he fell over the side of the bath.'

Gregory winced. He imagined the scene, the terrified housekeeper taking it in as she pushed open the bathroom door.

Katie continued. 'On the bathroom floor was the flat blue box that was always on the bedside table. The one he told her never, never touch.'

'What blue box?' These were the details he was after. There might be a clue to his state of mind.

'Flat, wide – like a jewel case. My mother never saw inside it until then. You know – not nice to be curious. But she said it was always on Dr Micallef's table, you know. Always there, ready.

272

Inside was one remaining small bottle of ... of *medicine*, and on the floor of the bathroom another, but empty. In the doctor's hand, they found the thing ... for the injection.'

The syringe. Gregory stood transfixed in the middle of his kitchen. There was silence for a moment, a small pause in which scratching from the chicken run and the interminable song of crickets filled the air. He looked at the girl, who shifted in her sandals as if she wanted to go.

'I must start the housework,' she said uncomfortably.

'No – finish first. What else?'

'Nothing else,' she said, displeased with his insistence. But she was trained to be obedient. 'My mother was crying. Screaming. She ran into the street for help. You know, for doctor and police. For the priest. But of course he was dead a long time. But Monsinjur gave him – what you call it? Last rites. He said something about heaven and being good. No, not good, *just*. My mother said, just. The priest said he gives the benefit of the doubt ... I don't know what it means.'

Gregory was only vaguely interested in how Father Dimech decided about the fine line between accident and suicide. He imagined the priest's eyes as he deliberated whether it would be permissible in the eyes of the Church to allow the doctor could have died by accidental overdose rather than a fatal self-administration.

'Tell me again about the blue box,' he said. The writer saw the maid's eyes, drawn momentarily into melancholy ovals. But she told him again; how she saw the case on several occasions herself, when helping her mother to spring-clean the doctor's house.

'It was always there, always to be ready, he told my mother.'

'Ready?'

'My mother thought it was medicine ... in case of heart attack, but the policeman read the label aloud. Afterwards, the whole village knew it was not medicine. Not good medicine, I mean.' She lowered her eyes and raised them again quickly, waiting for him to say she could go. 'Some kind of –' She stopped, not willing to utter the word.

'Drug,' he said.

She pursed her lips. 'It's terrible.'

Gregory nodded. Then nodded again to dismiss her.

'You going to write in that room again, sinjur?'

That was it. He caught the hint of accusation in her voice. That was what the villagers must be thinking. His coming here, his writing: it was the reason it had all happened.

'How can I write now?' he found himself mumbling. He nodded again to let her go.

Katie gratefully moved away, pulling a cupboard open quickly to distract herself, looking for cleaning materials. But there was something unfinished, something left to say. He would have to look at the last few pages. Just one more reading of the words he had put down before he learnt about Fin's death.

❏

2

The afternoon is quiet, incessant droning from crickets and the occasional rustle and cackle from the hen run are the only disturbances. The background noise is hardly noticeable to Censinu. His mother, father and baby brother are all asleep.

Earlier, Nikol threw himself down on what they call the kannapé, a day bed with an upholstered seat that stands under the great window in the loggia. A cloth cap covers his face and his chest rises and falls rhythmically. Terezina and the baby lie in the half-lit big bedroom, whose yellow tiled floor keeps it cool, where the slow buzz of a dying fly tells Censinu his mother pumped the spray can vigorously before lying down. The red spray can, its long piston handle supporting it at an angle, lies on a newspaper on the floor just outside the bedroom. The boy nudges it with one toe, half wishing everyone would wake up – sit up and bring the house alive again. It is too quiet, too lonely in the house when everyone is asleep. When they are all awake it is distracting and lively, there is chatter and noise, even if it is his mother's laments and shrieks most of the time.

Censinu brushes a fine beading of sweat from his upper lip. It is peaceful. His mother is not screaming at him. She is not throwing things in the kitchen as she did that morning. A white enamel plate with a blue rim and two black bruises on its side was hurled at him and it spun so close to his ear its wind whistled and stirred his hair.

'Ej! Ma!' he protested. What did he do now? Terezina's hand flew to her mouth at the same speed that the plate hit the wall behind him and clattered, spinning, to the floor. Like a noisy top, it jangled; the only sound in the bright kitchen, catching them all as they stood, waiting for it to stop.

'Hallieh. Leave the boy alone,' Nikol said mildly, sighing aloud and nudging his chin at his son, bidding him to leave the kitchen, the kindly

eyes explaining tacitly it would be better for Censinu to disappear for a while.

The boy turned and ran, as he is preparing to do now, recalling what happened after his return to the house. Terezina had shuffled towards him across the kitchen, her mouth twisted unusually. She reached out a hand and the boy flinched. The hand was soft though, rested on his head for an instant, a brief caress. Censinu drew away, avoiding the unwanted gesture.

Now, out of habit, with the soft breathing sounds of his sleeping family in his ears, he leaves the house at speed, banging the big front door behind him and running up the lane to the steep street and the square. Can it be the very same bus driver as before, yelling at him, leaning nearly to the waist out of the driver's window of the light green bus?

Censinu skilfully avoids all vehicles, dogs, and the donkey-drawn cart surrounded by a small crowd of women. The vegetable vendor stands immobile, a pair of scales hanging from an out-stretched arm. Everyone watches the boy as he scurries across the square.

'Ara taqa!' someone yells, bidding him to be careful, not to fall.

But Censinu runs, more out of habit than from anything that happened that day in his house. At the edge of the village, he turns suddenly and runs down a side street, circuiting the back of the church and the band club. In minutes, he is back at the farmhouse, over the rubble wall, down the cellar steps and in the cool space where the jars and bottles stand, newly filled. It is quiet. But not as quiet as the house, where the sound of slow breathing makes him nervous. Here the garden noises, the rustle of a slight breeze through the grapevines, the squawk and scrabble of the hens and occasional distant bangs of fireworks from another village are companionable.

Censinu can play alone until the family wakes and the summer evening unfolds as usual. In a corner, a hessian sack full of toys, empty boxes, balls and other bits and pieces he and his toddler brother play with is leaning against the wall, across from the well. Censinu shakes the sack open and looks inside. A tin top, a red rubber ball, a cloth puppet, some empty biscuit tins and a dozen or so small cars clatter against each other. He is looking for a big wheeled toy, a truck in which he can load small stones from the garden.

Where is that cart his father knocked together from bits of wood and some old plastic wheels? Where is the wooden train someone gave him one birthday?

In the distance, more fireworks explode and nearer, a sudden peal of church bells announces the hour.

Censinu sits on the floor near the sack, picking the bandage on his arm that suddenly starts to itch.

❏

3

The telephone was ringing when Gregory came back to the farmhouse from Valletta. He threw his white hat onto the sofa and sat back before lifting the receiver. He knew who it was on the other end before she spoke. He hoped she would be different, but he could not be sure. He hoped she would not hold the same mysterious grudge everyone else seemed to be holding against him.

The image of the villagers' faces was still vivid in his mind. He had been snubbed at the newsagency, receiving no answer to his salutations, no response to his half smiles. He had been almost rebuked in the street, as he was made to sidestep and descend from the footpath as a woman went rapidly past, pushing a pram.

'Hello, Patricia.' He spoke slowly at first, then formed a resolution and went on. He would only find out her mood by being as normal as possible himself. 'I thought I'd come down to Sliema today and we could take that ride you talked about.'

The young woman's voice was hoarse but light and jovial, almost making an extra effort to avoid talking about the death of Phineas Micallef.

'We'll go anywhere you like! What ride?'

Gregory leaned back on his sofa, relieved he did not have to tread lightly, or confront resistance. 'You know – the horse cab.'

'Ah – a *karrozzin*. Of course, I remember. Why don't I meet you at the Valletta terminus? It will mean one bus less for you to take.' She paused, as if trying to find something else to say, then, 'I've been trying to get you all day, Gregory. Have you been out?'

'I can't hear the phone from the garden.' It was not strictly speaking a lie – it was true that when he was immersed in a chore out at the back, the ringing phone went unnoticed. It happened many times. He had often run into the house, only to hear the ringing stop just as he entered.

But why was he lying to Patricia now? First, he had avoided the phone. He worked like a navvy in the garden, trying to exhume a reason. Trying to bury another. But yesterday was different. He implied he was at home when all the morning he had been in Valletta, waiting in offices, making small purchases, running errands and going through motions prompted by a decision made after four days' agonising.

He was not going to tell Patricia he had already been to Valletta that day. At least, not on the phone. Not like that.

'At seven thirty, then,' he said steadily, affecting a tone as light-hearted as hers. 'We'll have dinner at St Julians, if we can find a table.'

'Great!'

After putting the phone in its cradle gently, without noise, as if there were someone in the house he did not want to wake, Gregory rose and paced the length of the house. Through the hallway, into the large kitchen, through the corridor past the loggia and into the yellow tiled room that was his writing place, he went. Bright rays of sun came through the door and reflected on the computer screen. Paper and balls of dusty fluff lay everywhere on the floor.

Pencil sharpenings filled a stationery paper bag, spilling onto the desk and chair underneath. The writer brushed the yellow edged shavings away and sat, pressing a button and waiting for a prompt to appear on the screen. The computer hummed, competing in his ears with the drone of crickets, the rustle of leaves from the vines. The leaves seemed drier, even though the weather had turned slightly more humid. He sensed the mellow warmth of the vineyard from where he sat, the musky smell of vine leaves, the absorbent scent of quarry dust, the latent heat in the flagstones of the area outside the cellar, the stone steps that would radiate the afternoon's sun long after sunset. But he did not want to be drawn out there again.

Not after the hours he spent there these last days, digging, digging, brooding and trying to decipher the changing attitude of the villagers. He dug until he hit rock – the very limestone of which the island was made. He dug to dispel his mood with physical work, extending his chores until it became a frenzy of activity; raking out the hen run, moving the potted plants once more, staking top-heavy sunflowers and harvesting prickly pears. But his heart was heavy, and his head could not be shaken free of the annoying words the Monsinjur said to him the day of the funeral.

He needed reassurance like a child. He tried to talk himself into a better mood, like a child. But the way the villagers snubbed him could not be erased, nor dismissed as some cultural difference over which he had no power. He felt somehow to blame, as if he were the reason for his own exile. Yes, like dear old Fin.

He had entered *Il-Hanut* a few days before, removing his hat as soon as he entered the cool interior, moving towards the bar with the comfortable knowledge the barman would pour him his usual afternoon Hopleaf. But the young man stood silently, heels of both hands resting on the bar edge and head tilted querulously, as if he were a stranger, someone he had never seen before, asking him what it was he wanted. The gaze was not antagonistic, not unfriendly, but the neutrality, the indifference, negated everything the writer felt in that bar as long as he lived in the village.

'So!' he said, making an effort to affect a cheerful tone, 'Are you going to pour me a Hopleaf, then, Mike?'

'If you like, sir. Fifteen cents please.' And he poured the icy golden liquid into a tall glass. Pulling coins out of his pocket, Gregory was upset by the man's abruptness and the atmosphere in the bar. A group of men – all familiar faces – sat at a marble table. None of them turned to look at him. No voice addressed him.

Chastened and embarrassed, Gregory quickly downed the beer, replaced his hat with an awkward gesture and parted the bead curtain that let him out into the bright street again. He had hardly been in there five minutes. No one acknowledged his departure. Descending the steep street at a trot, not looking to either side of him, the writer threw open the front door of the farmhouse and drew into the shelter of his home. It was cool, dark and still smelled slightly of mildew, and it was home. He was scalded by the reception at the bar. It was not just a temporary thing, he decided. The Monsinjur was definitely frosty, his sister quite short with him. They were all in mourning, he decided.

Tomorrow, after the passage of another full day, everyone would return to the same old jovial hospitality and friendliness that had overwhelmed him at first. But it was no better the following day. Meeting Lieni and her daughter on the street elicited two prim formal nods in his direction rather than the animated conversation about household cleanliness he was expecting. In the grocery shop, conversation did not cease suddenly as he entered, but wound down gradually, until his requests for cheese, anchovies and olives had to be given to the woman behind the counter under the scrutiny of a silent band of women.

He felt self-conscious; annoyed at himself for caring that the friendliness had disappeared. 'Do you have any more of those delicious small cheeses – the ones rolled in pepper?'

'We always have *gbejniet*, sir,' came the curt answer, and the cheeses were placed on a square of greaseproof paper for him, weighed and wrapped in small precise gestures.

Gregory handed out coins with the identical feeling that overcame him in *Il-Hanut*. A quick departure from the shop spared him any more frustrating embarrassment.

Where was the warmth he had experienced during those first weeks? Why had everyone turned so hostile?

'It's all changed, Patricia. Nothing is the same in the village since Fin died.' Gregory looked at her and shrugged. 'I don't understand any of it.' The sheer disappointment in his voice surprised even him. It was a shock that came on in stages, which persuaded with its gradual force.

He missed the old doctor. The feeling descended on him as he looked out of the passenger side window, trying to remember the doctor's face, the way his hair was always combed sharply back from his forehead, the way he raised his finger when he lost his train of thought, the way he slitted his lips when he was under the influence.

They were driving at some speed along the Pietà seafront, catching up with a snarl of traffic he knew would not abate until they reached their St Julians destination. Patricia had picked him up at the Triton fountain outside Valletta, a light grey linen dress making her look clothed in silver in the evening light. He thought he knew exactly what he would say to her, until he saw her moving towards him.

She said quickly in a husky voice that by some small miracle, she had found a parking spot by the Phoenicia Hotel, so they walked slowly to the car, Gregory silenced by a new inability to tell her about his decisions, and Patricia apparently quiet in expectation. Her tact and deference was still very unusual, when he compared it with the behaviour of other women he had known. He looked sideways at her and saw, from the broad smile, from the clear look in her eyes, that everything was fine; it was all exactly the same with them.

The death and funeral of Phineas Micallef were a regretful episode, a sad and troublesome interlude, but because of what had developed between them, that was all it was. They could somehow overcome such troubles.

'Oh, Patricia,' he said, totally dejected. 'I'm so glad you haven't cut me flat, like everyone else. I can't understand why they have all turned so cold.'

'I can't understand it either,' she said. 'They are usually so forthcoming – so eager. It must be something going around in the village. Do you know what they are saying? Have you heard anything?'

'If I hear anything, I don't understand it,' said Gregory. 'They would bend over backwards before, to say everything in English – just for my benefit. It was great and made me feel special, grateful and welcome. Now it's almost complete silence, or soft mumbling in Maltese. No one addresses me directly, they whisper behind my back. I get terrible looks from the women whenever I venture anywhere in the village.'

'You're really upset,' she said comfortingly.

'I liked it there, Patricia.' He shifted in his seat, concentrating on the truth of what he had just said. 'I like it here. It is unusual and – and disorganised and mad and bureaucratic and strangely peaceful, in a noisy way!' He held his hands out, fingers spread in frustration. 'Malta is a great place for a writer. The people are wonderful. But this! I never expected this change. It's as if they are a whole different set of villagers. They changed suddenly – in one day. I cannot write like this.'

She placed a hand on his knee and drove with her right, not looking away from the road but nodding her head slowly. Progress was slow up Tower Road in Sliema, where the pavements were jammed with pedestrians and the road impassable for cars. 'I'll try and get us through this as quickly as I can. Perhaps St Julians is too busy for us tonight. I'll drive on to Bahar ic-Caghaq.'

Gregory nodded. What he had to say to Patricia needed a quiet place. Did she sense already what he wanted to talk about that night? He looked at her driving, smiling at the way she puffed in frustration and gripped the steering wheel at the intransigence of other motorists. No one gave way. At any other time it would have seemed funny to Gregory, who was now used to the absurd, irrational yet strangely practical way the Maltese drove.

That evening, he became as impatient as she was to head for a quieter part of the coast. At the small restaurant they found after freeing themselves from the clamorous traffic, there was a small silence before Patricia started to attempt an explanation of what happened at the village. 'They must think it was something about your friendship with the doctor that provoked his suicide.' She twirled a drinking straw and looked at Gregory. Her hair was loose, crowding her shoulders thickly, the grey fabric of her dress making it seem darker than ever. Still, her skin was almost fair and translucent.

Gregory could make out the almost indistinct blemish of a childhood scar under carefully applied make up. He reached out a finger and touched it lightly, the place on her cheek where a tiny dent gave the hint of a permanent dimple. 'How did you get this?'

'On the corner of the kitchen table – my sister and I were playing one day and she pushed me. We were both this high.' She smiled and held a hand about waist high. 'Months later, when the floor was slippery from washing, she slipped and got herself an almost identical cut. So my parents bought a round table!'

They laughed together, comfortable once more. Gregory decided not to broach discussion of the village atmosphere again. This evening was important. His rehearsed words would not come to him, but somehow he had to tell Patricia about his errands in Valletta that day.

She seemed unperturbed by his silence, and chatted about her family, then paused, looking at his knotted hands on the table. 'Look,' she said, appearing to realise he was still thinking about the previous conversation, 'perhaps it will all be better soon. Village people are keen to maintain a kind of balance. They love the odd bit of drama, but soon revert to normal.' She did not sound very convincing.

'I keep looking for a reason. I keep going over what happened,' said Gregory. 'The Monsinjur hinted it to me. The day of the funeral. He stood in the square, still in his surplice, with the altar boy holding the silver cross aloft, just behind him. He said something about consequences. Repercussions. Words like that only mean one thing. They do think I had something to do with what Fin did.'

'How could you have?'

Was he going to confide in her? Somehow, it did not seem right to rationalise Fin's suicide by divulging what he had spent a lifetime trying to hide. Gregory looked about him. It was all like that, he supposed. A choice between personal comfort and betrayal. A choice between honesty and deceit.

'There's something you don't know. Something the doctor never spoke about. But he had ...'

'That last day –' Patricia interjected.

But he went on. 'No, no. It was something he had lived with for a long time. Something he surely had come to accept in a way. It was why he left Sliema. Why he was disturbed enough about the jar to smash it to bits. You saw his face that day – you saw how he acted as if we weren't there.'

Gregory lowered his head onto both clenched fists. 'But I will never know for sure. Fin had things he didn't talk about. We all have things we're not very proud of. Things that would upset the smooth running of our normal life if we decided to expose them. Could Fin's have driven him to suicide?'

Patricia placed a hand on his knee again. She did not talk.

'Father Dimech told me as much. I will never know,' he repeated. He raised his head with a final gesture and drained his beer glass. 'I will never know why he chose this very moment in his life,' he said again. But suddenly, it dawned on him. Of course he knew.

He knew, but did not want to admit it either to himself or to Patricia. He looked away from her again, knowing it was his fault in a way. He had come here, a complete stranger, and raked up a whole village's past. And Fin was forced to confront it once more.

Not only that, but to participate in an episode he could have done without. It must have proved to be too much for the old man. Gregory swallowed. He realised what it was now – perhaps he had avoided looking at his own role in the whole thing. Maggie was right: he thought only of his own motives, his writing: his book. He swallowed again and looked at Patricia. Could she guess his part in Fin's death and hold it against him?

'I feel guilty now,' he admitted. 'There's a lot I should have realised. I'll never feel entirely comfortable about the way Fin went.'

'Oh, in time perhaps, Gregory.'

'There isn't time.' There: now he would have to tell her, come out with what he had done in Valletta that day, what he was planning to tell her in such precise words.

'What do you mean, there isn't time?' Patricia sat up. Her eyes were bright and a glimmer of trepidation started to dawn.

'There just isn't time.' The writer turned and looked at her, eyes searching to find understanding, calm.

Her direct gaze was all he needed. Perhaps she would understand, after all. 'I was in Valletta today. In the morning – almost all day.'

'But you said –' There was a slight hint of disappointment in her tone.

'I know what I said. I'm sorry. I wasn't in the garden at all. I went from shop to office, from office to shop in Valletta. Filling forms and things. I finally managed to get a seat on a Singapore Airlines flight.' This was not going as he had rehearsed at all.

Patricia inhaled, gasped slightly, but did not interrupt.

Gregory looked at her, noting her patience. Even now, she would not break into arguments or protestations, but gave him space to make his explanations. 'I'm going to make use of my return ticket, Patricia. I'm going back.' He said it in one breath, looking down and away just before he finished and back again at her quickly.

She did not make a sound. Her eyes were wide. Disbelief took her unawares. Perhaps she thought they would have discussed his return at some length. Perhaps it was unreasonable and unkind to spring the decision on her that way.

'You've already done it,' she muttered.

'Yes.'

'Without –'

'Yes,' he said again quickly. He felt his own apologetic tone in the single word. He should have told her. 'We should have talked about it,' he added.

'Yes.' It was her turn to utter one syllable. She stopped, thought and nodded, as if acceptance had already taken over. 'This is awful. When?'

'There is more I want to say about all this, Patricia,' he said, before continuing. 'I don't want to leave you. Not now. Not like this.'

'But you are.' She said it flatly, rationally.

He could not deny it. 'I am,' he accepted.

'When?'

'Before I say when, will you promise me something?'

'Yes,' she said. She did not ask *what*, or *why*. Without any hesitation, she said yes.

A long time afterwards, Gregory was to remember that word. She said yes, not what. She was ready to promise whatever he asked, and that was the difference between her and other women.

She trusted him, and it was like nothing he had ever known. She trusted him, and made him feel that they somehow wanted the same things.

Now, in the silence of the all but deserted room, in the gloomy restaurant that belied the strong sunshine and shimmering heat outside, he said the words quickly. 'Will you promise me you'll come to Perth?'

'To Perth!' Her eyes lit up and she laughed aloud, making another couple at a table across the room look up and smile too.

There was a long silence, in which she seemed to be thinking. A waiter came to the table, wiped it down and took away the empty glasses. Gregory gave him another order in a voice he found strange, disembodied, as if it were not his own.

When he was gone, the writer sat back in his seat, disallowing any thought from entering his head, making space, as it were, for her response, just as she had done.

'Not immediately,' she said after a pause, 'but yes, I will.' She paused again and turned to look at the couple across the room. She seemed still to be thinking, deciding. 'I will come, but later. Later in the year. Next year.'

He knew what she meant. It was unusual, but he knew exactly what she was thinking. Without any doubt, Gregory sensed her mood, her rationale. He had never been this close to anyone; so close he could work out what thoughts were at that moment coursing through her mind, what feelings were coursing through her body. He knew what she wanted. She wanted time for things in his life to become organised: that was what she wanted. It was Maggie and the divorce. Patricia wanted it all to be tidied away and consigned to the past, where it belonged, before she could enter his life fully.

He sighed slowly, not knowing whether it was relief or apprehension. 'So you'll come? I – look, I thought up all these lines to say to you and now I can't find the words.' He smiled in spite of himself. There was no real reason he should feel so apprehensive. There she was, accepting, willing. All he had to do was be himself. It was good enough for her.

'I want us to be together, Patricia,' he said simply.

She raised a finger to her lips to silence him. 'Sshh. I know. I do too. It will be fine.' Suddenly, her eyes filled with tears and she put her face in her hands.

This was another surprise. Gregory put out a tentative hand. What was going on? But then, that was how she was. Patricia was strong and determined, and at the same time, soft and romantic. The combination was attractive. So seductive it created mystery, a feminine kind of mystique he had never really proved existed.

'Hey, come on. Now – now,' Gregory muttered. He only

barely understood her sudden show of emotion after such an apparent rational acceptance of his departure.

She cried audibly, grabbing the handkerchief he offered from between their half joined hands. 'I'm sorry.' She made a valiant effort, not in the least tainted with artifice, to compose herself. 'When are you going?' It was the third time she asked.

Gregory could circumvent it no longer. 'Tomorrow night. It's the only available seat for some time.'

'Tomorrow!' Her eyes clouded once more.

He knew she would protest at the short notice.

'What about your fridge?'

'My *fridge*?' It was the last consideration he expected her to raise. He spread his hands out in resignation. 'It's yours. It doesn't belong with the house. Neither do the other appliances.' For a minute, Gregory was taken by a kind of hilarity, looking into her eyes and laughing softly. He had never felt so elated, yet so dejected, in his life.

Patricia saw the absurdity of her mundane question, and burst into a peal of giggles. The sound of their laughter attracted the attention of the couple across the room again. The waiter hurried up to their table, to be skilfully dismissed by Patricia, who was still grinning widely.

'Don't worry,' she said to Gregory in a hoarse voice she tried to compose into a businesslike tone. 'I'll look after it all for you. All the appliances, and your computer. Don't worry about a thing.'

Gregory looked at her, half in disbelief, half in wonder. Perhaps this is what it all should have been like to start with: this sympathy, this comfortable acceptance of all that he was and did. Don't ever let me take advantage of you, he thought without saying a word. Don't ever let me take all this for granted.

He was filled with crushing disappointment at the way things had gone in the village, full of grief at the loss of his friend, but a wave of happiness engulfed him. He looked at her, and their gaze was fixed for a long time. There was no need for words.

'But tomorrow night ...!' Patricia's eyes grew sad again, filling with tears.

Gregory took a small package from his pocket and opened it. 'I found this in Valletta this morning. I couldn't resist getting it for you.' From the tiny box, he took a tiny gold filigree ring with a small red stone. 'But please, don't cry.'

At that, Patricia burst into a fresh spate of tears, crying into his bunched up handkerchief.

He slipped the ring onto a finger of her right hand, clumsily, trying not to feel young and utterly foolish, realising after he did it was her middle finger.

She looked at it, wiping her eyes. 'I'll be all right now. It's lovely.' She looked at the ring and back at Gregory. 'I didn't expect this – it is lovely. Oh – I had planned for you to meet my parents. They asked so many questions.'

He smiled, lost for words.

Patricia shrugged comically. 'But we still have time for a ride in a *karrozzin*.'

The little cab was drawn by one chestnut horse, whose mane was neatly plaited. A single feather decorated the brow strap.

'Take us to Tigne and back.' Patricia spoke to the man in his own language.

He was old and wrinkled, with tanned skin like the harness leather of his rig. They had driven to Balluta and parked the car, finding a single horse-drawn cab exactly where Patricia said they would. The *karrozzin* swayed.

Gregory sat on a narrow leather seat across from Patricia, feeling the gait of the horse through the wooden wheels. 'No shock absorbers on this thing,' he laughed, but was surprised at the pleasant rumble of the large wheels with turned spokes.

The clopping of hooves on bitumen punctuated traffic noise.

They moved on the sea front along the coast road, a route now familiar to Gregory. He looked out in the darkness across the

bay, seeing lights from boats and the curve of the road behind and ahead of them. He saw rocks leading down to the sea, boathouses fringing the creek, a cloudless sky turning deep blue. There were dozens of restaurants and blocks of flats along the way, and the promenade was crowded with people strolling in the evening breeze.

Patricia did not give her usual running commentary. Silent but apparently content, she sat in the corner of the seat facing away from the direction they were taking. 'I think ...' she said, then stopped, shaking her head as if to say she would not continue.

The *karrozzin* kept up its regular sway, the horse walking at a moderate pace. Cars whizzed by close to its right side, overtaking impatiently on the narrow road. The occasional flick of a small whip high above the animal's back was just audible above the traffic.

'I know,' Gregory could read her thoughts, sensing all she tried to convey to him, even without words. 'When we return to Balluta after our little ride,' he said, 'I shall take a taxi back to the village.'

She looked up at him gratefully. One side of her face was momentarily lit up by the red taillights of a car that just overtook them. They swayed together in the cab. 'Yes. I'd like to go home. I don't know why – I think you understand, don't you? I'll be at the airport to see you off tomorrow, though,' she promised.

Softly, a bit sadly, they discussed how he should leave the keys of the farmhouse with her, so she could make final arrangements with Mrs Friggieri, the house agent, and see to the storage of the appliances.

'Thank you,' he said.

She stayed in the *karrozzin* when they reached Balluta again after the long ride into Tigne, where they drove past the old colonial barracks that someone said were to be converted into

some sort of tourist facility.

'This is where Dragut, the leader of the Turks, was hanged,' she said, indicating a promontory. The sea glimmered past where she pointed.

Gregory looked, not sure he wanted to hear any more history, thinking Patricia was saying something distracting, to diffuse the tension of the moment. He was simultaneously grateful and impatient, but listened in silence.

'During the Great Siege. He was killed in the assault on Fort Saint Elmo. They say his corpse was put on display to reassure the people he was really dead.'

To reassure the people he was really dead. Gregory looked away. He fidgeted in the silence and thought of a corpse. Thought of a family who could not be reassured a lost boy was really dead; who would never know the whereabouts of his body.

'I've read a bit about the Siege,' he said, but his mind was on the Mifsud family, on his book, on his reason for coming to the island in the first place. He thought of the phrase, memorising it, then felt ashamed for taking mental notes at such a moment.

Patricia smiled and said little more for the rest of the ride. Gregory knew now she understood. She knew him and accepted the way he was, the way he thought. She was supportive and subtle. He could not believe such a find at his stage of life, and could hardly dismiss the reluctance he felt to put it all in jeopardy.

He jumped from the cab when they finally drew to a standstill, using the quaint single metal step, only wide enough for one foot.

Patricia stayed in her seat. 'I'll see you at the airport tomorrow,' she said. But suddenly, she rose, held out her arms to be lifted down from the cab. They embraced silently in the half-light of Balluta Bay, the cab driver looking discreetly away at the water with a mild smile.

Without another word, Gregory hailed a taxi and was giving instructions to the driver before he looked around to see Patricia running in the dark to her car.

❏

4

The flight stewardess poured a gin and tonic, smiling automatically with the requisite flight attendants' smile. The Australian writer avoided her starched, made-up gaze and looked out of the small window. They were circling the islands at some height. Malta and Gozo looked like two small wedges of grey and gold rock, with a sprinkling of other little islands around them.

The sun set the sea a-shimmer, and as they gained height, he looked towards where the wedge sloped to the water, where Sliema and Valletta were. The crowded buildings were a fused mass of limestone, bristling with television aerials. Streets formed canyons in the stone, black serpentine lines in the limestone that glowed, golden and solid, in the strong sunset. Even from this height, the drone of traffic and the dusty crowded streets could be sensed, a tangible presence he would take away with him.

The aeroplane banked and he lost sight of the islands, a stretch of illuminated sea filling the window in their place. Gregory equalised the pressure in his ears, gulped uncomfortably and closed his eyes. It was ridiculous to become so emotional about leaving the place: he had only been there a couple of months. But he had grown to love it. He thought of the villagers, and their initial welcome, the strange poky shops. Once again, he tasted the wine and the lemons, the grapes and the swordfish. He thought of rabbit stew and the funny little cheeses he would miss so much. But it was the thought of Patricia, still standing at the airport, he knew, that made his throat swell.

She was probably still looking up at the departing plane. It was as if she too had shared his fascination with the dusty little village and its people, the funny flat roofed houses, the churches and their bells, the ancient rubble walls and medieval farmhouses. And now he was leaving her and everything else behind, heading for a difficult re-entry into normal life, trying to accept what had happened, to place everything in perspective.

Her upturned face, her unshed tears, were still with him, and her sweet farewell kiss that followed repetition of her promise to join him soon, very soon. He had spent a difficult last week. The loneliness of making decisions and the difficulty in telling Patricia about his departure were behind him now, but he could not suppress the feeling of loss and guilt.

Guilt: he felt guilt, in spite of what Maggie might say about his cynicism and his so-called heartlessness, his penchant for delving into the grisly and the unsavoury. The villagers viewed his writing with suspicion. Viewed his investigations as the cause of Phineas Micallef's death. It was his activity that had caused the resurrection of the missing boy, that had caused their strife and their loss. The faces of Nikol Mifsud and his grown up children revisited him as he sat in his aircraft seat, trying to ignore the ministrations of the stewardess.

He closed his eyes. Should he have visited Nikol Mifsud again, told of his opening of the jars, of the death of the doctor? Should he have disclosed his final discovery? No: he had caused enough disruption. His inquisitiveness had already cost the life of someone he knew and liked. Phineas Micallef might not have died if he had not insisted on the whole thing with the jar. And what Patricia told him at the airport confirmed it.

They sat, with untouched coffees before them, the airport lounge behind them milling with people loudly voicing pre-departure conversations. Conversations that reminded the writer of the passion and hyperactivity of these Mediterranean islanders. It intruded into their privacy and gave him a parting impression – almost a gift, wanted or not, of phrases to remember and write – of warmth and vivacity.

'Papa told me, Gregory,' Patricia said gravely.

'Told you?' He did not know whether to expect some sort of parental admonition or warning, or some change in her decision to join him in Perth.

'Yes – he told me about Dr Micallef's past.'

The writer started. 'Your father knew! What did he say? Was he sure it was why he drank – the reason he left Sliema?' He took a gulp of coffee, which was stone cold and rasped at this throat. He was reluctant to say anything more. He wanted her to continue.

'Phineas Micallef was a general practitioner, but people tended to take children to him, even though he was not a specialist paediatrician. He loved children.'

'Yes?' He willed her to go on, so that he would not have time to think for himself, to jump to telling her what he knew. What the doctor had confided.

'You do want to know, don't you?' Patricia seemed hesitant.

'Yes, yes – of course I do,' he said. 'It's all I've thought about day and night.' He could not help thinking of the old man, the creases in his shirtsleeves, the wrinkled skin on trembling hands.

'He loved working with children, because he and his wife could not have any of their own. But there were two reasons the club set in Sliema cut him off.'

Gregory looked quizzical.

'The first reason is to do with his wife and is not really important. Apparently he married below him, which in those days was just not very acceptable socially. His family thought he would leave her everything when he died one day – which made them rather angry that family money would go to some family whose name and connections were lesser than theirs. The fact he outlived her did not make them any friendlier through the years. They hardly ever spoke again.'

'But all those people at the funeral!' Gregory remembered the well-dressed crowd, the masses of flowers.

'Funerals are different,' she said.

Gregory nodded, thinking he had grown to know Maltese custom enough to understand how misunderstandings and feuds would not be allowed to carry on after death.

'It's different, because he's now dead,' he said blankly, with only the slightest hint of irony in his tone. 'Is that it?'

'Yes,' she said, surprised he understood. Then she went on. 'Then there's the other, more relevant reason. One of his patients, a little girl, was very sick. This is years ago, you understand, not long before independence, I think. She contracted diphtheria. He was called to the home, and she was strangling to death, suffocating, so he performed a … you know, he cut into –'

'A tracheotomy – he cut into her throat.' Gregory swallowed hard. Fin loomed into his mind's eye. The doctor leaned over a sick child, wielding a scalpel. His hand shook. Blood. Blood – the last word he had heard him say.

Patricia swallowed too, her eyes taking on a sad look. The room around them hummed. 'The child died, Gregory.'

'And everyone thought it was his fault,' he whispered.

'In those days –'

'Whether it was his fault or not, they blamed him,' he said. He sat back, wondering whether he should be content to allow Patricia to keep thinking there was nothing else. He remembered the doctor's grey complexion as they sat in that Rabat bar and the words of his past came out of his lips. Those lips that were alternately livid and slack, or tight and slitted across his teeth. The doctor's past weighed heavily on him. The guilt of having a son somewhere in a remote village could not have been easy to live with. The fact he could never see the boy must have been untenable. The way he had disclosed it all to Gregory concealed the emotion, revealed little more than the facts. Phineas Micallef's hands on the marble table had not fidgeted, and his anguish had hardly shaken his body physically. But mentally, the man was at the end. He had taken enough, heard enough. And the smashing of the last jar must have expressed a lifetime of pent up frustration and sorrow.

'Yes,' Patricia answered, appearing satisfied that he understood. 'They blamed him, whether it was his action that actually caused her death or not.'

He could not help understanding Fin's situation. It was not unlike his own. He had not caused Fin's death, but he was being blamed for it anyway.

'And that's not all. From the way he reacted to what I said, the day I visited him and we sat on his terrace, I know he felt he was to blame.' Gregory looked down. Yes, it was enough for Patricia to take the malpractice case as sufficient motive for Fin's suicide.

She seemed convinced.

He continued. 'He never forgave himself. He withdrew from everything, believing – like everyone else – that he had caused the child's death. And there was a court case.'

'Yes,' she replied. 'It dragged on for years. He was not convicted of malpractice, or anything else. But the gossip, the social scourge, was his ruin. He could not practise again.'

'Especially not with children, I suppose,' the writer said.

They were quiet for an instant. The noise and clatter of the airport lounge entered between them, making them remember where they were. Gregory looked around him, then at his watch. He was leaving. His flight was in a few minutes. He would leave behind him a life, a way of being, on which he hardly left an impression. The space he occupied, the room he filled, would be erased the instant he vacated it, and the people he had known, especially the people in the village, would forget him easily.

He hoped it would not be the same with Patricia, with this woman he found so accepting, so willing to include him in her life. Perhaps that too was a presumption on his part.

He shook his head. How could he have presumed to enter these people's lives and insert more trying, more emotional, events? How could he have reopened old wounds, bring back the doctor's pain, the discomfort of a distraught family who barely understood, who did not even know where the body of Censinu lay?

We do things that produce results and repercussions we never expect. That was what Monsinjur Dimech said. He was right. How dared he? He had stirred up things it would have been better to leave unresolved. It would all have to rest. Rest with him. He decided this during an agonising hour after a last visit to his cellar the night before he left. An hour in which the face of Phineas Micallef revisited him, pleaded with him to preserve his confidence.

He looked up at Patricia. Would he tell her about his last visit to the cellar? She was looking at him in silence. Perhaps she thought her words about the doctor had moved him so he could not speak. No – he could not tell her, especially not after what happened to dear old Fin. His thoughtless actions so far had produced regrettable reactions. He could not jeopardise what he had with Patricia, not now. Their farewell had to be unsullied by any more of what went before. He had to put it all out of his mind.

He stood, patted his pocket for his ticket, and concentrated on his farewell. Then he looked at her again, trying to contain all of her in an image he would conjure later. Patricia in her beige trousers, white blouse and tied back hair, trying to be rational and controlled. Emotion surprised him. Leaving her upset him incalculably. She had become precious, special, to him. She and everything she stood for. It was not only leaving her that upset him, but her whole surroundings, the entire island.

He held her to him, fast in his arms, and she came close to crying again in spite of her promises not to. Tendrils of unruly hair escaped the slide and she looked rumpled and very young. Emotion made her voice even more husky, and the ends of her sentences disappeared almost completely. But she had no need to talk.

'You'll come,' he said, making it a statement, rather than a question.

She nodded.

'You'll come?' Suddenly, he needed reassurance.

She nodded again. 'Yes,' she said softly. 'We'll phone. We'll write. I'll make arrangements and try to come next year. Early next year.' Her eyes were earnest: she was telling the truth.

Gregory counted in his head. What was this – end of August? A matter of months. He hugged her again before turning away at the gate.

Airport police, mainly female, looked on as he turned and waved and turned and waved again, even when he lost sight of her round a corner, he waved.

The passenger in the next seat shifted and Gregory opened his eyes, closing them swiftly again when he saw a steward bearing down on them with a trolley of duty free items. Behind him, he heard a conversation going on in Maltese. All the way to Rome, it would go on, a modulated discussion between a man and a woman.

He listened for the occasional words in English he knew were inevitable, and remembered Nikol Mifsud talking and Patricia translating what he said about wine and winemaking. The lean man's face returned to his mind. He had lost a son. A small son of eight or nine who would never grow up. A son he never doubted was his. Perhaps it was for the best – for the best that the body was never found; would never be found. Perhaps learning to live with a mystery and having it remain a mystery was better than having the whole tragedy, the whole truth, revisited upon them.

Gregory did not know. What he was certain about was that his discoveries would leave him upset for a long time, perhaps affect his ability to write, or even to think, clearly. The writer moved restlessly, thinking of what Emma had said when she was little. 'If you know where something is, Daddy, is it lost?'

He had answered the child that no, a thing was not lost if you knew its whereabouts. If you knew where something lay, it was not lost. Was this something he could have said to Nikol Mifsud? It was certainly too late to say to Phineas Micallef. It was something he was going to have to keep to himself forever, thought the writer. Not to Patricia, not to anybody else could he say anything like that.

Censinu Mifsud was dead, and would stay a mystery forever. Phineas Micallef was dead, and the sadness of his reasons died with him. Who could he go to with what he knew? Emma – Emma was too young, too far away, too uninvolved in all this. There was nobody else. Gregory shifted in his seat, wondering about his decision to keep his secret, thinking back to the misery of the last four days, when he had roamed the farmhouse, thinking, looking and finally deciding.

❑

5

The long ladder was exactly where Franz said it would be: at the back of the shop, lying on its side along the angle of floor and wall in a storeroom full of sacks of lime and cement, bales of wire and box upon box of nails and screws. The smell in there was suffocating, dusty, his feet raising clouds of loose cement as he walked.

Asking to borrow the ladder had been awkward. Franz's face was impassable, neutral. No more declarations of mateship or efforts to impress with vernacular. The man was alone in the shop and quiet, apparently embarrassed that the Australian had ventured in there again.

'Yessir. Borrow if you must. But mind, I need it tomorrow.'

Gregory nodded, picked up the heavy telescopic ladder and carried it down the lane to his house. He had thought a long time about a ladder. What he was going to do would horrify some; fill others with uncertainty at best. He was going to brave the myth of the *belliha*.

Night had fallen. The whole farmhouse took on an eerie feeling. It was somehow changed. There were no rustlings from the chicken run, no farmhouse dogs barked in the distance. A large yellow moon rested on top of the rubble wall near the prickly pear hedge, filling the vineyard with black shadows. The stairs were bathed in yellow light, which slanted down through the fanlights into the cellar. Down there, he rested the ladder on its side again and straightened up before moving to the mouth of the well and sliding the stone lid away.

The noise of stone grinding against stone filled the large but confined space of the cellar, for he had closed the outer door behind him, as if wanting to make sure no one would see him descending where no sane person ought to go. He slid the stone slab out of the way, lifting it with some difficulty onto the floor.

He looked down into the mouth and saw nothing; a cylindrical chute of total darkness: a few feet of stone throat, a few vague threads of cobweb. Behind him on the floor, Gregory placed two torches; the small red one from the house, and a big yellow one bought with this very deed in mind. Reaching behind him, he changed into a pair of shorts, thinking he would descend into a body of water, or at least have to wade in it.

The hardest thing was to get the long unwieldy ladder into the throat of the well. After trying several different angles, Gregory managed to slide it in while still folded, letting the bottom section slide down through his hands, then coupling the staying hooks as the ladder reached its fullest extension. The top reached a few feet from the rim and rested against the inside of the throat. He shone the torch down its length before shinning down and finding the first rungs with his feet.

He could see nothing. With one torch in his pocket and the other in his teeth, he descended the ladder, fear of heights momentarily set aside in his mind. This was depth, not height, he told himself.

So it was true. Maltese wells were like big receptacles sunk into the ground, swelling out into a large cavern that would fill with rainwater from the roof after a storm. At any minute, Gregory expected his feet to sink into cold water. But they did not. He reached the third rung from the bottom and turned slightly, shining the torch around him. There was not a drop of water down there. The large grey cavern was totally empty except for some large cobwebs close to the throat that he had just brushed past, and some debris at the bottom.

Two large cracks in the rendered rock wall snaked upward from the ground, to as high as he could see, splitting and dividing in places. All the water that ever was in there had drained away into the surrounding earth through those crevices. He remembered someone had told him to drop a pebble into the well and listen for a splash. He had forgotten to do that, but there would have been no splash. The well was dry.

Gregory went down the last two rungs and stood in his bare feet at the bottom of the well. If only Rigoletto could see him now, he thought, thinking of the plumber with the morbid fear of the *belliha*. There was no monster that would swallow him alive, no *belliha* that ate humans, even grown men, if they as much as tried to look inside a well. There was only silence, and dust, and the smell of enclosed spaces.

The floor felt dusty to Gregory's feet, and the air musty, but the atmosphere, in the light of his torch, was churchlike. A catacomb. He cleared his throat: there was no echo. It was tomblike, as silent as the grave. The debris on the ground was mostly heaped together across from where he stood. Gregory approached it and suddenly realised what he was looking at.

The dawning of realisation made him talk to himself. He muttered under his breath, thankful he was alone, and simultaneously wishing there was someone there to see what he had found. It was clutter, a heap of dusty old clothes. And bones and a small skull. All that remained of the small body of a human being. A nine-year old boy. He had found Censinu Mifsud.

'Did you fall down the well?' He spoke softly in the yellow light of his torch. His voice rang dully around him. They were poor words, the only words the writer could find for the boy. They served as eulogy.

'You fell down the well, you poor child.' He thought of the words he could write, but could say no more than that. It had to serve as tribute, rite and ritual. His voice was flattened and solemn in the enclosed space, sounding like a prayer.

He felt foolish and sorrowful; grieving for a boy he never knew, who was never found. Phineas Micallef had never seen the boy, but had lost him too. It was a double loss, one the old doctor could never resolve. The boy was a child he could never have claimed, whom he could never even have tried openly to find. And who would never be found. No one would ever find him. No one would ever know the boy was there if he said nothing. Nobody would go near the well. But Censinu, poor Censinu, was not entirely lost, because someone knew where he was.

Someone far away, in Australia, knew where he lay. Someone in Australia knew. Someone had made sure the well would always be a resting place, by tidying the remains, and securing them the best way possible. The plumber had said the pipes were blocked. It was doubtful whether anyone would inhabit the farmhouse again. It was a peaceful safe resting place – tomblike, a catacomb – underneath the very place where he had grown up and played. A few feet from where the writer stood, only some inches from where the small jumble of bones and clothes lay, he found the probable cause of the accident. Lying at the bottom of the dry well, Gregory Worthington found the wreckage of a wooden toy train.

❑

More thrilling novels by Rosanne Dingli

According to Luke
Shattered by the breakdown of yet another romance, Jana Hayes becomes a recluse in her tiny Venice apartment, and buries herself in work, as an expert art conservator - until an ancient religious icon brings Roman Catholic priest Rob Anderson into her life. The secret they discover hidden in the mysterious artefact turns out to be not only devastating, but deadly. It has the star-crossed couple running for their lives across Europe and the Middle East, pursued by three ruthless opposing factions, each for its own reason determined to do anything to lay hands on the world-shaking evidence they uncovered. While Rob struggles with his priestly vows and Jana with an overbearing billionaire mother who holds the purse strings to an outrageous ransom demand, they discover, with the help of an ageing genius symbologist, more and more damning revelations about one of the New Testament's most sacred gospel writers – and as the evidence mounts, the stakes rise and the blood flows.
BeWrite Books ebook **ASIN:** B004U2T0CI

Camera Obscura
Photojournalist Bart Zacharin's camera doesn't lie ... but his mysterious new lover Minnie Cuff double-deals for a living. Love-struck Bart can't get that into focus, until he follows her from Australia on a flimsily trumped up trip to Europe, only to become embroiled in an obscure web of international organised crime, deception and death. Minnie's humdrum job as a computer programmer, her deceptively carefree style, and passionate affair with Bart merely provide an innocent front for a sinister role in a ring of ruthless museum raiders and smugglers. Bart attempts to reform her on a dash around some of Europe's most colourful port cities, which becomes a frantic race thwarted by misfortune. Fast moving yet poignant, Camera Obscura is one desperate man's struggle with obsessive love that competes with a million-dollar crime empire: a search for meaning and belonging, frustrated by happenstance and misadventure.
BeWrite Books ebook **ASIN:** B007MVB3G0

Printed in Poland
by Amazon Fulfillment
Poland Sp. z o.o., Wrocław